SEASIDE ROMANCE

THREE-IN-ONE COLLECTION

DARLENE FRANKLIN
TAMELA HANCOCK MURRAY
LYNETTE SOWELL

BARBOUR
PUBLISHING

Published by Barbour Publishing, Inc., P.O. Box 719, Uhrichsville, Ohio 44683,
www.barbourbooks.com

*Our mission is to publish and distribute inspirational products offering exceptional
value and biblical encouragement to the masses.*

Member of the
Evangelical Christian
Publishers Association

Printed in the United States of America.

BEACON OF LOVE

Darlene Franklin

Dedication

To my beloved daughter, Jolene Elizabeth Franklin, who has gone ahead of me to glory far too soon. I admired your generous spirit, your dogged determination, and your gift with words. I miss your ready smile and bear hugs. The world lost a treasure when you went home.

Note to Reader

In 1815, a hurricane (known as "The Great Gale of 1815") devastated Rhode Island, including an octagonal wooden lighthouse at Point Judith. The following year, the people of Galilee erected a stone lighthouse to replace the original, and an automated light continues to protect the entrance to Narragansett Bay today. A native New Englander, I love the romance of lighthouses. The Point Judith story inspired me to write about a lighthouse keeper's daughter determined to keep the lamps burning—no matter what.

Chapter 1

Waves taller than a man and blacker than midnight curled over Sam's head and foamed white at the crest like a mad dog's mouth, ready to devour anything in their path. One small wooden boat could not survive such a storm.

Papa knelt in the stern, holding his hand over his eyebrows as if to clear his vision of the rain that obliterated the shore near Capernaum.

Turn back. Sam wanted to shout the words, but no sound came out of his mouth.

"We've seen worse." Papa placed his hand on Sam's shoulder. "Join me on the oars."

Sam sat next to Papa on the seat, hundreds of dead cod soaking his shoes, his oil coat, and his very skin with their smell. Why had Papa ever given up his farm for the sea? Because fish were abundant and New England summers short, that was why.

"Pull, son." Sam strained at the oars. His puny, fourteen-year-old shoulders could not match Papa's. He wished he could drink an elixir of sea water that would grow him into a giant in an instant—a giant who could power the boat, walk through the ocean if need be to get them to safety.

But he remained his normal, gangly self, his body not yet accustomed to his newfound height, hands more acquainted with the quill of the schoolroom than a fishing boat's oars. Nevertheless, he pulled with all his might.

Sam shut out everything except cycling the oars, dipping them in and out of the water, riding up the waves before crashing back into the sea. He couldn't tell if they had rowed for ten minutes or an hour, if they were approaching the shore or riding out farther into the sea. The storm colored the sky a constant gray, whether twilight or deepest night. Lightning spun through the clouds, stirring up the wind. Thunder cracked across the pounding waves. At the top of the next wave, lightning gave him a glimpse of the shore.

The treacherous, rocky shore that every sailor must avoid lay only yards from their little boat.

"No, Papa, no!"

Sam thrashed, trying to scream the words that could save Papa. Lightning broke into his vision and startled him into awareness.

"Sam. Wake up, Sam."

Mama's gentle hand shook his shoulder; she held a candle in her other hand. The flickering outside the window told him the lightning was no dream.

Sam sat up in his bed, his damp bedclothes rumpled around him, feathers trailing from the pillow he had fought in his efforts to keep the boat afloat.

"You had the dream again." Mama poured a cup of water from his nightstand and handed it to him. "When you remember the night your father died."

The night I wasn't strong enough to save him, Sam thought. He didn't bother to answer. He hadn't had the dream for years, not since before he left for his medical training. Why now? The storm? The return to the island?

"Come downstairs, and I will warm some milk for you."

Sam smiled. Whenever he had the nightmare—a nightly occurrence for a year after Papa died—Mama fixed him a cup of hot milk with a drop of molasses. It helped him to sleep every time, although he suspected its effectiveness had as much to do with Mama's calming presence as it did with the warm liquid.

"Change into this." Mama handed him a dark blue robe, one he remembered Papa wearing.

"I can't . . . ," Sam protested.

"You can, and you must. It is time." Mama went to the door. "I'll be waiting for you in the kitchen."

Sam stared at the robe. Where had Mama found it? She had taken only a handful of things from their cottage when they moved to his grandparents' home in Connecticut after Papa's death. She brought even fewer things when they returned to the island. She must have left the robe at the cottage for all these years.

He sniffed the blue wool. It smelled of salt and sweat. He felt his father's personality, sharp and clear, as though his deep voice would ring through the years and speak wisdom into Sam's heart. He had not earned the right to wear the robe yet.

Don't be foolish, Sam scolded himself. He needed to change from his night shirt, soaked during his nightmare, or else run the risk of catching a chill. And his father's robe should fit him now. He removed the shirt and hung it on a peg, shrugging into the robe. As his hands reached down the arms, he wished he could take on the persona of the man who had worn it. If only it were that simple. He looked at himself in the looking glass: at one inch shy of six feet, dark hair tumbling over his eyes, he might fool a stranger into thinking he was his father returned to life. Only he knew the real truth.

"Sam?"

Mama's voice called up the stairs. Sam tightened the sash and plodded down the stairs, pausing on the third step. It still creaked.

"Look at you." Mama stood with hands to hips. "So like your father." Her eyes misted. Other widows might have remarried to another fisherman. He knew several men had asked. Not his mother. Instead, she examined her options and removed her only son to her family farm in Connecticut.

"You are meant for a different life," she told him. "You should go to Yale and study."

Mama had expected him to enter the ministry, but God had moved Sam in a different direction. He traveled among the sick of their parish and discovered his calling: to heal, to be the hands and feet of the Lord Jesus among the sick. He was contemplating where to set up practice when war broke out with Britain.

By the time the conflict ended, he had performed countless operations as an army surgeon. Somehow, in the cauldron of war, his decision had been made for him. In the depths of his being, he knew where God wanted him to serve. The skills he obtained in treating the war wounded had prepared him to care for men torn from the sea. He must return to the one place he had hoped never to see again—Capernaum Island.

He took a deep breath, salt air mixing with the familiar spices of Mama's kitchen. Home on Capernaum. He took the mug of milk she handed him.

"It feels like I never left." Mama cut him a piece of gingerbread. "Seeing you sitting there. We did the right thing in coming back."

Sam smiled at her use of *we*. "I pray the good Lord makes it so." He didn't trust himself at all, but he trusted God. " 'My grace is sufficient for thee: for my strength is made perfect in weakness.' I wonder if Paul ever visited Capernaum."

"We know he was shipwrecked three times," Mama reminded him. "And our Lord Himself spent many nights at sea. He understands."

Light gleamed through the window. He carried his mug to the window and looked at the tower on the point. "At least they built a lighthouse."

"Only a fool refuses to learn from his mistakes." Mama joined him and watched the light blink on, then snap off.

Sam counted to himself. *One, two, three, four, five.* The light came back on. "The smartest thing they did was hiring Eli Morrison as the keeper of the light." Eli had worked as the island wheelwright when Sam knew him.

"He never met a wagon he couldn't fix. He'll keep the lights burning whatever happens." Mama's smile turned pensive. "I wonder how Judith fared. I felt so sorely for her, so hungry for a woman's touch, so alone."

Judith. The name brought memories of a slender girl who loved to read and hated doing sums. Her mobcap never quite captured her brown hair. How many times had Mama told him to bring her home after school? She came to their house so often that she felt like his little sister. How old must she be now? Twenty?

Evening black gave way to predawn gray. Sam looked out in the direction of the lighthouse, wishing once again it could have been erected before the storm took his father's life. A dark figure emerged from the door at the base of the tower, strong, powerful. He wasn't the lighthouse keeper, too young and vigorous for that. Who could it be?

Judith's husband, off to spend the day at sea. That seemed like a logical explanation.

He thought of the girl with silky hair the color of a sugar maple, her serious blue eyes that livened when Mama told a funny story, and wondered why the thought of her married to someone else made him sad.

∽

Judith Morrison paused on the landing on the way to the lantern room where Father kept the lamps burning at Rocky Point Lighthouse. From this vantage point, she could see most of Capernaum Island. She felt a little bit like a tern watching the town from her nest at the top of the highest tree on the island.

This morning, a man had walked through the clearing between the lighthouse and the next closest house. Had someone taken up residence in the cottage, abandoned since the Widow Hathaway had moved away with her son, Sam, ten years ago? A breeze blew dark hair around the man's head; broad shoulders filled a fashionable black waistcoat, cut long to accommodate his height. So her new neighbor wasn't a fisherman, but a man of business. Something about his carriage, his profile seemed familiar. She willed him to turn around.

A seagull circled over the rocks, and the man lifted his head to watch.

Judith sucked in her breath. She knew that face, that straight nose and firm chin, only it had matured since the last time she had seen him. Her new neighbor was in fact her childhood friend, Sam Hathaway. The lad she had last seen ten years ago had grown into a fine-looking man. What was he doing back on Capernaum?

"Judith!" Her father's voice rang down the stairs. She turned her attention to the day ahead and climbed the remaining stairs. She counted them as she had since they first moved into the lighthouse, her own personal rhyme she had created to celebrate the importance of her father's job. *One, two, three, men at sea, four, five, six, boats of sticks, seven, eight, nine, light sublime.*

At the fourteenth step, she reached the lantern room, awash with the day's light bouncing off silver-plated reflectors. The brightness stung her eyes as if she were looking at the sun itself.

"Well, stop staring, gal, as if you're seeing it for the first time." Father sounded gruff, but Judith knew he didn't mean anything by it. "Did you bring up the whale oil?"

Judith gestured with the bucket. "Piers said he would deliver more tomorrow morning."

"Good man." Father *always* said that when Judith mentioned Piers, his hand-picked successor as keeper of the lighthouse and the man he hoped would win

Judith's heart. If only she could feel as warmly toward him as Father wished.

Judith set down the bucket of oil and took out her polishing cloth. When they had first moved into the lighthouse, Father had taught her to clean the glass chimneys with great care. Each day, she polished them to spotless brilliance, so that the light shone bright as midday even on the darkest nights. She started with the first lamp.

For half of those ten years, Piers had been Father's helper. Monday through Saturday, he went to sea to harvest fish, and on Saturday nights, he kept the light going in the lantern room. He came more often when Father ailed.

"So what did Piers have to say for himself this morning?" Father asked.

"He brought over fresh corn cake. I put the pan near the fireplace to keep warm while I clean the lamps." Judith spit on a stubborn smoke smudge on the third chimney.

"Ah." Father made quick work of the parabolic reflectors, bowl-shaped discs that made the lamps visible for sixteen miles at sea. A night's work on the lanterns always left him hungry.

Piers came by every morning before he went to sea. Often he brought a plate of muffins or a pot of beans, sent by his sister-in-law because they happened to have extra. Judith knew better. Her poor cooking skills were the talk of the town. Most people considered her a hoyden, too rowdy and high-spirited, not quite knowing her proper place as a woman in their sheltered society. On the days Sara Vanderkamp didn't send over breakfast, Father resigned himself to scorched porridge that even a generous amount of molasses couldn't rescue.

There was a time when she had felt feminine. Mary Hathaway, Sam's mother, had taken the lonely, motherless girl under her wing and showed her how to sew and how to turn a biscuit. When Mary left the island, Judith lost heart in learning and had stopped practicing. She still did neither with much skill.

"Do you think we'll ever get machinery to move the lamps?" Judith asked, changing to a topic Father had mentioned many times. She finished the last chimney and started on a reflector, polishing it until she could see her reflection: a thin face surrounded by brown hair the color of baked beans and pale blue eyes barely visible in the silver sheen.

A gleam entered Father's eye. He loved all things mechanical, and he longed to experiment. Then his face dimmed. "Not likely. The townsfolk built the Rocky Point Lighthouse to last for a hundred years, and they won't take kindly to my tinkering with it. And it's done its job, whatever the sea has thrown at us, since that last big storm."

The killing storm. The one that had chased the Hathaways away from the island. Judith considered telling Father about Sam's return. For some reason she couldn't identify, she wanted to keep that news to herself for a short time. The knowledge of Sam's presence nearby warmed her insides. Although a few years older than she, Sam had always treated her kindly. At school, he took the time to explain the numbers that squirmed around on the page like small children, and he did it in a way she could understand.

"The job's done for the day." Father poured fresh oil into each lamp in preparation for the evening ahead. "Let's go enjoy the corn cakes before they overheat."

Judith poured them each a mug of coffee and broke the steaming hot corn cake into pieces. Father prayed for a quarter of an hour before every meal, while the food cooled and fat congealed, making it more unappetizing than it already was. This morning, her stomach rumbled in response to the rich scent of the warm bread. Her mind wandered. She wished she had something to take to Sam as a welcome-back present.

"And O God, our heavenly Father, who commandeth and raiseth the stormy wind, which lifteth up the waves thereof, we thank Thee for this lighthouse which has protected the men of Capernaum for these past ten years, and for allowing me to serve Thee as its keeper."

Judith jerked her attention back to the present. Father was ending his prayer as he did every morning, by quoting from Psalm 107.

"Amen." Father lifted merry blue eyes to hers. "Eat, gal, before you announce your hunger to the village."

Judith felt heat rise in her cheeks. She added a small dollop of molasses to the corn cake. Ever since she had spotted Sam Hathaway in the meadow that morning, her insides had felt like they were falling apart. Maybe the sweet syrup would help stick them back together.

Father always ate breakfast with a hearty appetite. He spent his nights making sure the lanterns remained lit and clear to all sailors at sea. To his credit, he never complained about any of Judith's mistakes, even when she burned biscuits or added clabbered milk to eggs. Today, she had cut a slab of ham; they ate it cold, in silence.

Only one thing remained before Father would rest for a few hours, trusting Judith to see to the lamps if anything happened that required lighting them—the daily Bible reading. Every January, Father started with the first chapter of Genesis and read four chapters a day until they reached the twenty-second chapter of Revelation. In mid-May, they had reached 2 Chronicles; history made for interesting reading, much better than the endless begats that began 1 Chronicles. Judith wished Father would let her read. She would give meaning to the words, the feelings behind the stories. Father read them in a monotone that would make Shakespeare sound boring.

"What hymn do you wish to sing this morning, gal?" Father asked.

Gal. Sometimes Judith wondered if he remembered her name. Of course he did. She shared the name with her mother, and most days, he couldn't bring himself to say it. She reached for her copy of *Olney Hymns*, her most precious possession after her Bible. The book opened to her favorite hymn—her father's favorite, too, as well as that of nearly everyone in Capernaum. " 'Light Shining out of Darkness,' Father."

He allowed a smile to play around his lips, then started singing, his voice a pleasant baritone. " *'God moves in a mysterious way. . . .'* "

" *'His wonders to perform.'* " Judith sang with him, adding harmony to Father's melody. " *'He plants his footsteps in the sea and rides upon the storm.'* " As she always did when she mentioned the storm, she looked out the window at the oak tree that grew its roots into the foundation of the lighthouse. Yesterday its leaves had turned upside down, and sure enough, wind and rain had fallen before nightfall. Today, though, the leaves sparkled in the sunlight.

Perhaps the island itself rejoiced with her at Sam Hathaway's return.

Chapter 2

Sunday morning, Judith walked to the Capernaum Meeting House with Father on one side and Piers on the other. Poor Piers. He spent Saturday nights in the lantern room, then could not rest until after church. He often nodded off during one of Reverend Snodgrass's lengthy sermons.

They ate a quick breakfast and left early. The lighthouse sat at a distance from town, on the edge of the rocky point of the island. The walk to town took a good hour. Judith enjoyed Sundays, with the break in routines from the rest of the week. She changed her everyday dress for one made from linsey-woolsey. She also looked forward to visiting with other islanders. During her childhood, a different family had invited them to break bread after Sunday meeting every week. Over the years, practice had dwindled to the Vanderkamps and Morrisons sharing most special meals together.

Judith had spent many sociable hours with Piers. When had that enjoyment turned to a more uncomfortable feeling? Perhaps when he began work at the lighthouse. If only she could care for Piers the way Father hoped she would. Judith sighed.

"Is everything all right with you this fine morning?" Piers noticed her discomfiture, as he often did.

Judith forced herself to smile. "I am only looking forward to the service." She should, too. Think about God and not about her desire for a man she could love with all her heart.

They had just reached the cottage that had sat abandoned for ten years, the old Hathaway place. The aroma of fresh baked bread wafted through open windows. The front door opened.

All three of them stopped. Mary Hathaway stepped out. She appeared smaller than Judith remembered, although that was not surprising. Judith had grown up in the intervening years. Otherwise, nothing had changed on the kindly face.

A lanky form followed her out the door. He looked so tall, so like Samuel Hathaway, that Judith could have sworn the fisherman had returned to life. Her breath caught in her throat. How could this handsome man be the same person as young Sam, the boy who had taught her figures and tossed a ball with her at school recess? A cowlick still sprang from his head in the same place it always had, and the same gray green eyes, as changeable as the sea, smiled at her.

"Mistress Hathaway!" Father took the lead. "I heard that you had returned to

Capernaum." He nodded at Sam. "Sam. Or perhaps I should say Mr. Hathaway?"

"It's *Dr.* Hathaway." Mary beamed, the proudest mother on the island.

Doctor? So Sam had furthered his education, as his mother had always hoped.

"Call me Sam." He shook Father's hand but looked at Judith inquiringly. "And who is this charming lady?"

"Hello, Punch." She clasped her hand over her mouth. Surely she hadn't mentioned the puppet show aloud.

Sam's face froze for an instant, and then he laughed. "Punch and Judy. You used to call me that when you were mad at me." He bowed in her direction. "It is good to see you have kept your sense of humor."

Judith relaxed at Sam's easy acceptance of her gaffe.

Next he extended his hand toward Piers. "And you must be—" Sam's face scrunched with the effort of placing a name with the familiar face. "Piers Vanderkamp."

"Hathaway." They shook hands.

"We'd best not tarry," Father said. The five of them set out for the church at a brisk walk.

∽

Sam studied the two young people next to them. Piers and Judith seemed comfortable with each other, but they didn't show the degree of familiarity he would expect between a husband and wife. He didn't know how to find out if they were married or why it mattered to him.

"What has happened on the island during the past decade?" Sam looked back at the lighthouse. "I see you've built a lighthouse. A wise plan."

"It's a thing of beauty." Morrison's chest puffed a little bit. "Ten lamps and reflectors."

"Come by for a visit," Judith invited. "We'd love to show you around."

The young girl he remembered in pigtails had grown into a comely woman, her brown hair shining under her mobcap. Humor shot through her lively blue eyes.

They approached a white clapboard building, gleaming with a fresh coat of paint in honor of spring. Sam had spent many happy hours there as a child. The old teacher, now retired, had inspired a lifelong love of learning and books in him.

Townspeople rushed to greet them, and his mother made introductions. By the time they entered the doors, everyone present knew Sam was a doctor. He appreciated Mama's pride in him—what son didn't?—but it embarrassed him, nonetheless. A doctor was only a man, no different or better than any other.

"Miss Morrison!" Mrs. Wembly, their next closest neighbor, called out a greeting. Sam's ears prickled at the name, and he struggled to pay attention to the person Mama was introducing. "The new teacher and singing master, Horace Wilson."

13

Miss Morrison—not Vanderkamp. So Judith had not married Piers—at least not yet. Sam smiled with genuine pleasure at the schoolmaster. "And you will lead music during worship this morning?"

Wilson could have modeled for a newspaper caricature of a singing master, with his lanky form and ill-fitting clothes. Still, his voice resounded with a surprising bass. "Yes. You sound like you have a goodly tenor. I hope to hear you join in joyous song."

Or at least a joyful noise, Sam thought.

A few minutes later, Wilson stood to lead them in a hymn. He lost all awkwardness when he began to sing. Sam remembered "Light Shining Out of Darkness" from his childhood days on the island, and who didn't know the hymn starting "There is a fountain filled with blood"? The three-quarters hour they spent singing flew by.

Reverend Snodgrass approached the pulpit. "Next Sunday, please join us after meeting for an oyster shucking contest and picnic. It is time to see whether anyone can take the title from Mr. Lauder."

Laughter rippled across the room. Sam remembered Lauder, one of his father's fishing partners. A big, strong man, with quick hands, he would be hard to beat. Sam sat up straighter.

"Before I speak from God's Word today, I want to welcome back the Widow Hathaway and her son, Dr. Sam Hathaway. I have asked Sam to share a few words with us this morning."

Sam walked behind the pulpit and looked at the rows of people sitting on plain wooden benches. His fingers trembled, something that never happened during an operation. He bent his head for a word of silent prayer, then looked at the congregation. Judith smiled at him, and he gathered courage to speak.

"People of Capernaum, it is good to be back among you again. This town and its people have always held a special place in my heart." In more than one way, but he wouldn't mention his father this morning. "After all, God first showed me my need of a Savior in this very building. I remember that Sunday well. We sang the same hymn we sang this morning—'Praise to the Fountain Opened'—when I realized that I was one of those guilty sinners who needed to plunge beneath the flood. Reverend Snodgrass talked with me and my parents that very day, and I asked Jesus to be my Lord and Savior."

Several people nodded. Sam continued. "From that point on, I've tried to obey my Lord. He led me away from Capernaum for a time, and then to Yale, where I studied medicine. When I asked God where He wanted me to practice my trade, He answered me clearly: back on Capernaum. No one knows better than I the dangers that a life at sea can bring."

Heads nodded again, faces more solemn.

Sam allowed himself a moment to remember his internal struggle over God's clear call. He'd fought God's direction and sought another, any other, answer. In the end, like Jonah, he went where God led. He saw Judith smiling at him and wondered if *she* was part of the reason for his return.

"I am happy to be in the place God has brought me." He couldn't think of anything more to say and joined his mother on the bench.

"Be sure to say a word of welcome to the Hathaways after meeting," Reverend Snodgrass encouraged the congregation. "And the next time you need a physician, you can find him at the old cottage." He beamed. "Now turn in your Bibles to Mark 10."

∽

Father had retired to bed on Tuesday when a knock came at the door. Judith straightened her apron before answering. Who would visit at this hour?

Sam stood in the doorway with his mother.

"Come in." She invited them inside. "Father has only now laid down to rest, so he isn't here to greet you."

Mary's face wrinkled. "Shall we return at another time? We don't wish to disturb his rest."

Judith shook her head. "Once he falls asleep, only a storm awakens him. Something that threatens the lamps."

"I brought these for you." Mary handed Judith a plate of freshly baked cake. *Does she already know what a poor cook I am? No, a neighborly gesture, no more.* "Thank you. These will taste good with cold milk." She wrapped the sweets in a towel and set the plate aside. "The lantern room is this way."

Sam paused at the landing to look out the window. "You can see our cottage from here."

"I spy much of what is happening on the island," Judith confessed. "I saw that you had returned." She blushed. Would he consider her statement forward?

"Judy has to keep track of Punch." Sam's gray green eyes crinkled. "It is good to see you again."

At those words, Judith wanted to skip up the steps, but she climbed at a sedate pace. The stairs issued a familiar creak under Sam's weight; he was taller and more muscular than Father.

"Here it is." Judith gestured at the room, remembering the first time she had entered it. How shining and sturdy the lighthouse seemed, with the wood well-caulked against wind and waves, the lantern room thrusting thirty feet in the air.

"We have ten lamps, but the reflectors magnify the light." She placed her hand on the dinner-plate-sized objects. "The first time I saw them, I thought they might light all the way to Boston." She laughed. "They don't, of course. I have seen them from the ocean."

Sam winced. "I hate to think of you that far out on the ocean."

"The whole town celebrated when the lighthouse was completed. We sailed a flotilla out to sea to admire the results. On a clear night, the lights are visible for sixteen miles." She had seen the point where the light thinned, then vanished, extinguished by the blanket of the night sky and fog banks that rolled in from time to time. All these years later, she still loved their polish and shine and took pride in her father's work.

"You have done well." The look on Sam's face suggested he meant more than the lighthouse. Judith's heart danced.

∞

A week later, Sam noticed that the hymn singing lasted barely half an hour, and the pastor's sermon only stretched over forty-five minutes, not an hour. Even the preacher was anxious to get out to the rocks before the tide turned, so they could begin the festival.

"Hathaway!"

"Call me Sam," he said automatically. Piers Vanderkamp moved toward him, with Judith following.

"We were wondering, that is, my parents were wondering. . ." Piers hesitated.

"Will you eat with us at the festival?" Judith jumped in. "We have bread pudding and cold milk."

"Just make sure she didn't bake it herself," another young man called a warning. *What was that all about?* Sam wondered.

"My sister-in-law always bakes enough for a fleet." Piers spoke in a normal voice.

Mama questioned Sam with her eyes. He shrugged. "We can put our meals together, then."

At that point, Reverend Snodgrass called the people together. "Let me explain the rules of the shucking contest. The oysters have already been steamed. Every man will receive a bucket with twenty-five oysters in the shell. The first half to finish their buckets will advance to the second round, and will open thirty-five oysters. Three men from the second round will advance to the finals, and they face the challenge of fifty oysters."

Around Sam, men nodded and clasped their hands in anticipation. He scanned the crowd for John Lauder, the reigning champion. A little gray flecked the man's hair, but otherwise, he was the same stalwart figure from Sam's childhood. The fisherman touched the reverend's arm as if asking permission to speak.

"Good folks of Capernaum, as an added incentive, I promise to give half of my next catch to the man who can best me in the contest." He wiggled his eyebrows. "Catch me if you can."

Snodgrass called all participants to the table.

Sam waited a moment to see who would join. To his surprise, every man took a seat, even the scholarly Wilson with his soft hands, and the shopkeeper. Only the preacher, who would judge the event, and the infirm remained absent.

"I suppose you won't be taking part, now that you became a landlubber," Piers called to Sam from his place at the end of the table.

His taunt decided Sam. "You'd be surprised."

Mama handed Sam his apron, the one she had bleached and pressed into brilliant whiteness after each turn in the surgical wards. He had never worn it to shuck oysters before, but there was always a first time. He drew on his father's gloves, grasped a pair of pliers and a knife honed to a sharp edge, and headed over to the table.

If it took shucking oysters to prove his manhood, Sam didn't object. He was more than ready to perform an operation on the unsuspecting shellfish.

∞

Sam's arrival at the table surprised Judith. His hands—she couldn't help but notice them when he had grasped the edge of the pulpit at last week's meeting—were strong, for certain, but as white and uncalloused as Mr. Wilson's. She expected a surgeon to value his hands too highly to risk cuts from the sharp edges of an oyster shell. Father had joined the contest, of course. He never won, but he enjoyed the trial.

Next to her, Mary Hathaway drew in a breath. "I suppose he must." She spoke almost under her breath.

Thirty buckets with twenty-five oysters each were placed in front of the assembled competitors. "Shuckers, ready!" Reverend Snodgrass called. Each man grabbed an oyster firmly in one hand with their preferred tool in the other. Reverend Snodgrass lifted his hand into the air, then swept down. "Begin!"

Judith knew the process of shucking oysters. They were pretty things, dressed like a society man in evening attire, white shells with black stripes and trim. A shucker had to separate the top and bottom shells to get at the muscle. The few times she had tried it, the shell had cut her fingers in half a dozen places, and she mangled the muscle before prying the oyster open. She would need much practice to become expert.

The best of the shuckers made it look easy. Pinch the side with pliers, insert a knife into the hole made by the pliers and open the shell, continue to slide the blade to sever the muscle.

Judith wondered how Sam would handle this competition. After all, he had spent the last ten years away from the sea and oyster beds. To her surprise, his pile grew rapidly.

As expected, John Lauder finished first by a good three seconds. Cries of "done!" rose among the men, with the preacher keeping count. "Twelve, thirteen, fourteen, and. . .fifteen! The first round is completed!"

The men who didn't qualify shrugged good-naturedly and left the table. Among them, as expected, were the schoolteacher and Father. Once every few years, he made it to the second round, but a life as a wheelwright and then lighthouse keeper had not trained him in the fishermen's art.

Piers, of course, made it to the second round. The man she never expected to make it, the town's new doctor, remained at the table. He had finished his pile in tenth place. Judith felt a small warm spot grow inside her. What a good way for Sam to rejoin the community.

Around her, Judith heard murmurs begin. "What would you say to a wager . . ." Of course, they wagered about second place. No one was expected to beat Lauder.

Fresh buckets were placed in front of the remaining men. Once again, the pastor called "Ready!" waited for the competitors to grab an oyster, then cried, "Begin!" with a slice of his hand. No one spoke while the men worked steadily, the only sounds the cries of seagulls overhead, the pounding of waves on the rocks, the wail of an infant.

"Done!" Lauder again finished first.

The other shuckers didn't hesitate, continuing to wield pliers and knives, their hands a whir of motion.

A couple of seconds later, Piers called out. Judith smiled. He had dreamed of this honor for weeks.

She focused so much on Piers's accomplishment that it took a moment for the third finisher to register.

Dr. Sam Hathaway would compete with Piers and Lauder in the finals.

Chapter 3

A thrill raced through Sam when he realized he had made it to the finals. The man next to him, his neighbor Mr. Wembly, shook his hand. "Well done, lad. It seems the sea never left ye."

While the others moved away from the table, Piers leaned over the empty space between them. "Where did you learn to shuck oysters?" Amazement mixed with something else—consternation?—colored his voice.

"I have had practice here and there." Sam didn't care to mention all the things he had cut open as a doctor; he could not recall the numbers.

Reverend Snodgrass called for quiet. "We have reached our three finalists. John Lauder needs no introduction."

At this, people hooted and hollered their support.

"But joining him for the first time in the finals is Piers Vanderkamp."

More clapping followed.

"And our third finalist, proving just how able he is with his hands, is our newest resident, Sam Hathaway."

Enthusiastic applause greeted this announcement, along with shouts of "Well done!" and "Welcome back!"

Sam glanced at Judith. Her face beamed with delight at the results of the competition. He was determined to do his best.

Assistants brought three buckets filled with so many oysters that Sam wondered how they could eat them all. Fifty each, hadn't Reverend Snodgrass said?

The bracing briny scent filled Sam's nostrils, along with the flavor unique to Capernaum oysters, a taste sensation as different as sweet or sour, salty or bitter. His mouth watered.

"Ready!" Reverend Snodgrass called. Sam took the top oyster in his left hand and grabbed the pliers with his right. "Begin!"

Sam already had a hole in the first oyster before the preacher's arm reached the bottom of his swing. Hole, open, slice, hole, open, slice. Over and over he repeated the process. He didn't hear or see or smell anything except what was directly in front of him.

Maybe ten, maybe twelve, oysters remained in front of him when Lauder called "Done!"

Did you really expect to win? Sam thought, and continued to hole, open, slice. He felt Piers's eyes on him and glanced at his opponent's pile when he grabbed the next oyster from the bucket. They were close, so close. He shouldn't care, but he did. Hole, open, slice. One last—

"Done!" Piers jumped to his feet.

Sam sliced the muscle from the last shell, as drained of energy as if he had operated for hours.

"And the winner is. . .John Lauder!" Reverend Snodgrass called. "You won't have to share that catch after all."

Lauder beamed while the townspeople applauded. Sam walked to Piers and extended a hand. "Well done. You came close to winning."

"As did you. Congratulations, Doctor."

They said no more as people from the town crowded around them, eager to shake the hand of the man who had surprised them all. The welcome stirred something inside Sam, something he had not felt in all his years in Connecticut. He was home again, home in this place that simultaneously terrified him and enveloped him in its warm embrace.

"Well done, sir, well done." Wilson, the schoolteacher, wrung Sam's hand. "While the womenfolk prepare our meals, perhaps you would consent to join us for a game of rounders?"

Wilson didn't fit Sam's picture of a winning ball player. But Sam didn't care if he won or lost; he had already accomplished far more than he thought possible for the day. "Gladly." He joined Wilson's team.

"Mr. Morrison? Will you join us?" Wilson extended the invitation to Judith's father.

"No, thank you." He laughed. "I will leave all that hitting and running to you youngsters."

Sam looked at the rough area set aside for the game, and the tide that had turned and crept up on the rocks. What if someone hit a ball toward the ocean? How would he respond? He shoved the thought aside. No need to borrow trouble.

He took his place in the field.

∽

Judith joined Mary in laying out their lunch. She had helped steam the oysters. Laying the shells over the fire wasn't as hard as getting the ingredients right for a cake. Her stomach rumbled. Breakfast had long since passed. She liked the oysters, liked the way they made her think of the earth, their flavor of copper, iron, clay, and minerals as delicious as a well-plucked chicken. The women would eat after the men finished playing ball. She felt a hand on her arm.

"Let's watch the men play for a few moments," Mary Hathaway said. "The food is ready."

How did this woman she hadn't seen for ten years understand her yearning to enjoy the pleasant day rather than stand guard over the picnic basket?

"I would like that."

The men had set up the diamond on a clear patch of ground near the lighthouse. Any ball that passed the rocks would be considered an ace and would score a run. Judith sought out Piers, who bowled for his team. He could throw anything, from a slow dew drop to a breaking ball.

Sam was the next striker at the dish. Judith looked at the other players on his team and shook her head. They didn't stand a good chance. Piers's team would most likely win.

"Come on, muffin, show us what you're made of," the basetender at first called out.

Sam smiled and swung his bat in a practice swing. Piers released the ball, and Sam hit it into the outfield. He took second.

Mary cheered. "He always loved playing rounders," she told Judith. "He often played at Yale, when he needed a break from his studies."

Unfortunately, the three strikers after Sam failed to make contact, and the teams traded places.

"I am so glad you returned," Judith said during a break in the action. "I never expected to see you again."

Mary turned her deep brown eyes in Judith's direction, eyes as dark as Sam's own. "While Sam served in the army, God was working in my heart as well. After my father died, I remembered all the people I loved on Capernaum. I thought of the families struggling to make it after their husbands or fathers died."

Sam caught a skyball, and Judith cheered with Mary, who then continued her story. "When Sam told me that he wanted to return to Capernaum, I knew God wanted me to come back with him. I can help. I understand, because I, too, have experienced loss."

Judith wanted to hug the older woman, the closest person she had known to a mother.

The next striker hit a ball in Sam's direction. It skied toward the boundary of rocks. He ran toward it and stopped. Instead of bouncing onto the rocks, an automatic ace, it fell onto the ground. Sam caught up with it and threw it toward the dish, but it was too late. The striker tallied a run.

"Muffin!"

Judith recognized Piers's voice.

Sam stared out over the rocks and shook his head, clearly embarrassed by his performance.

What is wrong? He seemed almost afraid to walk onto the rocks to retrieve the ball. Could it be. . ."Is Sam afraid of the sea?" The words came out without thought. Judith asked the question of herself, but Mary must have heard.

"Please don't repeat that." Mary spoke in a low voice that only Judith could hear. "He never got over his father's death, and a part of him. . ."

"Is afraid it will happen to him."

"Sam Hathaway's afraid of the ocean?" Father's deep voice boomed behind them. Judith had not noticed his approach. "What kind of a man is afraid of the water?"

∽

Sam froze when he heard Eli's voice. All eighteen players stared, on the bench and in the field. He knew his face gave away the truth, without his speaking a word. Heat rose up his throat, turning his ears the color of red earmuffs before spreading across his face.

Reverend Snodgrass rescued him by calling everyone to eat. He hung back behind the other players, waiting until they cleared the field before he moved on.

"Judith?" Ignoring Sam, Piers paused by the place where the young woman sat with Sam's mother.

Judith looked at Mary, and at Sam, then shook her head at Piers. The fisherman stiffened, then walked toward the gathering crowd.

Judith. She was the one single bright spot on this awkward day. Her hair shone to a coppery brightness, and the afternoon sun had pinked her cheeks. While others didn't know how to react to his appalling weakness, she appeared willing to talk with him.

"Oh, Sam." Her face turned a brighter shade. "It's my fault. I saw you hesitate when the ball headed to the rocks, and I asked Mary. . . . I had no idea that Father was standing there or that he would hear."

"The truth isn't your fault." He kept his voice flat. Her obvious distress touched him. Here was someone more concerned about his embarrassment than about the appalling lack it revealed. "Are you sure you're not ashamed to join us for dinner, now that the truth is out?"

"Oh, Sam. Of course not." She composed herself. "You made quite an impression today. A finalist in oyster shucking. No one expected it."

"Of a lily-livered doctor, you mean?" Sam grinned. "I am handy with a surgeon's knife, and the oyster was not much different. And before you ask, I enjoy a good match of rounders as well."

"Don't worry about what Father said," Judith implored. "The people of Capernaum are good-hearted. They will look past my gaffe and accept the good you can do for our community."

They arrived at the oyster kettles. Sam carried platters for the three of them. As they walked down the long table, most people greeted him warmly. They didn't mention Eli's embarrassing outburst and question him. Others whispered after he passed by.

Only Reverend Snodgrass mentioned the incident openly. "Don't worry about Eli. He has a loud mouth, but an even bigger heart. He will come around."

He clapped Sam on the shoulder. "You will show your true mettle in the days ahead."

Sam took a spoonful of every dish, following the time-honored tradition to not offend any of the cooks. Soon cornbread and ginger cakes, wax beans and oysters filled their plates. He reached a platter of biscuits that was almost untouched.

"You may not want to eat them," Judith warned him. "They're mine."

"In that case. . ." Sam took three of them.

He heard her groan beside him. "Don't say I didn't warn you."

He noticed that she took two of the biscuits, however. The plate no longer looked quite so ignored.

Sam took a bite of the biscuit and grimaced.

"What's the problem with them this time?" She sounded resigned to failure.

Sam forced himself to swallow the bite. No way would he admit that the biscuit had too much salt. "Nothing that butter and honey can't cure." He hoped.

Judith smiled at him. "Don't feel you must." She paused. "There is Father. Do you still wish to sit with us?"

Sam pursed his lips. He couldn't avoid the man forever. Besides, if sitting with Eli was the price he must pay to spend the remainder of the afternoon with Judith, so be it.

He knew he wanted to spend as much time as possible with Judith Morrison—whatever her father had to say.

Chapter 4

Judith had to suppress a giggle when Sam slathered her biscuits with enough butter and honey for a loaf of bread. He caught her gazing at him. With a smile, he bit into the piece and swallowed.

She followed suit and nearly gagged. The rounds were as salty as sea water. She grabbed her drink and swallowed it down. By the time she finished, Sam had polished off all his biscuits.

"You didn't need to do that." Now Judith felt embarrassed.

"Do what?" His smile involved his whole face, turning the corners of his mouth and creating wrinkles around those eyes the same color as the sea.

Father choked on a biscuit at that precise moment, and the table erupted in laughter.

To escape, Judith carried her remaining biscuit away from the table. She broke it into crumbs and tossed it in the direction of seagulls strutting along the rocks. Two birds dived for it at the same time.

"Don't worry. There's plenty for all of you." At least the food wouldn't go to waste. As she tossed the remaining crumbs to the waiting birds, she fought the embarrassment of such a poor job of baking.

"You didn't finish your lunch." She heard Sam behind her. He offered her an apple.

"I'm not hungry."

"They weren't so bad. Truly. I've eaten much worse in my time." A gentle smile lit Sam's face.

"Thank you for trying to make me feel better."

They waited in comfortable silence, staring out at the sea. The soft lapping of the waves against the shore soothed Judith's fractured spirit.

"Shall we return?" Sam offered Judith his arm.

Father watched them rejoin the group at the table with a curious expression on his face.

∞

"What are your plans for the day, gal?" Father closed the Bible after reading from Ezra.

Judith paused. "Mistress Hathaway invited me back today, to teach me more cooking skills." She had spent the previous day with Mary. She gestured at the underdone biscuits sitting on the table. "You would surely appreciate an improved breakfast."

Father grunted. "At least these are an improvement over those salt cakes you served at the oyster festival." He pondered for a moment. "You have my permission. But stay away from that son of hers if you can."

"I will not be rude."

"I only ask that you not seek him out."

"I would never be so forward." Judith didn't add that she had enjoyed yesterday's noon meal. Sam read from the Bible, yes, but then they discussed the passage. He welcomed her questions and her opinions.

"She's showing me how to make hasty pudding today. We should have a tasty supper." She kissed the top of her father's head. "I should return before dark. Rest well."

Yesterday, Mary had asked Judith to bring the ingredients for hasty pudding so she could judge how much Judith already knew about common recipes. She looked past the stone bench to the shelves of supplies. She needed cornmeal, that much she was sure of. She tucked two eggs into a basket and added a jar of fresh cream with a small sack of cornmeal. Did she need molasses for sweetening during cooking or would they add it afterward? After, she thought. She covered the basket with a napkin and walked down the road to the Hathaways' cottage.

"Good morning!" Sam stood in the open doorway to his surgery. Had anyone taken advantage of his services yet? Little sickness ailed the community at present. Whatever the situation, he remained in good spirits.

She lifted her basket. "Your mother is teaching me how to make hasty pudding this morning."

"Judith!" Mary greeted her with a warm hug. "Welcome. Let's see what you brought." She peeked in the basket and chuckled. "We could make Connecticut Dabs with what you brought. All we need for hasty pudding is cornmeal, water, and a pinch of salt. We have time before we begin cooking. You may help me with my mending or"—Mary looked at the two of them with a twinkle in her eye—"or you may wish to take a tour of Sam's surgery. I know you have been curious."

Judith couldn't prevent heat from creeping into her face.

"You can be my first patient of the day." Sam acted as if he didn't notice. "One of my first patients at all."

Judith hesitated at the open door. When had Sam learned carpentry? He had added a small room to the original cottage for his medical practice. She spotted two entrances to the office, one from the side and one from the living quarters. Everything gleamed with new oil, and a pleasant scent teased her nostrils.

Curiosity overcame her hesitation, and she stepped in. She had never seen a doctor's office before. She had never gone to a doctor. None had been available. Forced by circumstances, people had learned simple medical care.

A curtain hung in one corner of the room. A spot for disrobing, perhaps, if needed? A raised cot stood next to a counter where Sam's medical bag sat. Numerous vials—maybe a hundred?—filled the shelves. Behind the desk and chair stood a number of books—medical volumes, surely. One book lay open on his desk. She took a peek and smiled. The Bible.

Sam noticed her attention. "I am nothing without the Great Healer. I pray with my patients, if they allow me."

"Do you have many patients yet?"

Sam shrugged. "Reverend Snodgrass came in about his rheumatics. Nothing wrong with him that summer's warmth won't cure, but I believe he wanted to set an example. One young man came in with his wife. She has lost three pregnancies. . . ." He paused, unwilling to mention her delicate condition.

Judith knew the woman in question. Sally McNeil had yet to bring a child to birth. She knew how her husband, Matthew, worried.

"Perhaps things will go better this time, with a doctor in attendance. They are blessed that you are here. I am glad they sought you out." She ran her hand over his medical bag. Rather than the new leather she expected, dirt had ground into its creases. "This bag looks as though it could tell some stories."

Sam nodded. "Nothing I care to share, though, after two years in the army."

"You served in the army?"

"War with Britain broke out after I completed my training. I offered my services."

Sam fought in the war? The thought closed Judith's throat. She might never have seen him again. He might not have survived and returned to Capernaum. *Don't be a ninny*. He had survived and returned, and she was glad for it.

She thought of how Father and Piers had scorned Sam for his fear of the sea. No man who served in any war could be considered a coward. She wanted to offer her support, to let him know she admired him. At last she said, "Piers is a fool."

Sam shook his head. "It is true that I wish the people of Capernaum didn't know of my. . .aversion to the sea, but I trust that will change in time."

What would change? The attitude of men who made their living at sea, or Sam's own fears? "All in God's time."

"I do not like to talk of the war. It was ugly. Suffice it to say that my trials inspired me to return here. My experience treating those wounded in battle will benefit those injured by the sea."

Sam expressed the same sense of calling he had mentioned at church. Judith wished she felt the same compulsion for anything in her life. Father would say her calling would come when she found the man she was to marry. Somehow, the thought of making a home with someone like Sam appealed to her a lot more than Piers.

∞

"Sam? Dinner is ready," a pink-faced Judith called.

Her voice jerked Sam out of his reverie. He had spent the last forty-five minutes rearranging his few tools and looking at his office through Judith's eyes. With her, he felt acceptance, not condemnation. Now if only he could return the favor with her offering of food. He hoped his mother's tutoring improved her skills.

Mama had put out every sweetening they had available on the table: maple syrup, honey, molasses, as well as rich cream and fresh-churned butter. If the hasty pudding needed that much help. . .

Judith bore in a platter with a perfect round of hasty pudding. She beamed. "I wish someone had told me about the double boiler before. I never could get the knack of stirring."

Mama poured cold water and placed a bowl of greens on the table. "Will you return thanks, son?"

Sam spoke standard words of thanks, but in his heart, he was praying, "Lord, let me enjoy the pudding." He cut himself a small slice and took a hearty helping of the greens.

"Now, if any of the pudding is left, you can slice it in the morning, dust it with flour, and brown it in butter." Mama instructed Judith. "But I know Sam. I doubt there will be any left."

Sam reached for the cream and syrup. He had missed the maple sweetening during the war; now he ate it at every opportunity. He added a liberal amount to the cornmeal mush and cut a corner with his fork,

Judith watched. He smiled and lifted it to his mouth. Sweet maple, thick cream . . .perfectly cooked pudding, with a pinch of salt. He grinned. "Truly good."

Her shoulders relaxed. Only then did she take a bite of her own dinner. She had poured molasses on her serving.

Mama was right. He didn't leave enough of the pudding for the morrow's breakfast. Sam readied to read from the Bible when a loud knock came at the door.

"Doctor! There's been an accident!"

Chapter 5

S am took in the scene at a glance. One man lay unconscious on a stretcher. Others, the walking wounded, presented a variety of injuries: blood pouring from a gash to the head, an arm dangling at the side, all of them shivering. His mind prioritized the wounds, determining who should be helped first. "Take them into the surgery," he instructed.

John Lauder led the way. Sam was thankful the community leader sought him out when the need arose.

"That fool son of mine loaded the equipment wrong," Lauder explained. "Our boat capsized. Then we bumped into another boat, and it capsized as well."

Sam saw the face of the unconscious man on the stretcher—Lauder's son. From the kitchen, Sam heard the sounds of the water pump. Mama knew what was needed.

"How can I help?" Judith approached Sam.

He studied her. Her face appeared calm, her hands steady. If the injuries unnerved her, she didn't show it. "Gather blankets." As she headed away, he added, "Get a strong fire going."

Mama joined him a moment later, carrying a pail of water. "I set a bucket to heat over the fire," she told him.

Sam nodded. He worked without thought of time. He sewed wounds and set broken arms. Lauder's son, Johnny, had received a blow to the back of his head. Sam could do little but keep him warm, wait, and pray. Judith helped his mother bundle the men in blankets and led them to the fire. Exposure to the frigid waters of the ocean could do more harm than the small cuts and bruises most had received. Lauder stacked more wood near the hearth.

The entire time Sam worked, he prayed. Nehemiah prayers, he called them, like the king's cupbearer who prayed to God and spoke to the king in the same breath. *God, help these men. God, heal them. Let young Lauder wake up in sound mind.*

By suppertime, everyone had left except for Lauder, who kept vigil by his son's bed. Judith knocked on the door and entered. A strong scent of cod rose from a pot she carried wrapped in a towel. "Your mother gave me some of the kedgeree she's fixed for your supper. I must get home before Father worries about me." She looked at the man on the cot. "I will pray for your son, Mr. Lauder."

"Excuse me a moment, John." Sam walked Judith to the door. "You didn't expect to tarry so long today. Thank you for all your help."

Judith looked uncomfortable with his praise. "It was the least I could do."

Sam thought of the women he had met in Hartford, women who would have fainted—or pretended to faint—at the broken bones and blood spatter of the day. "It took courage. Don't belittle yourself."

She sucked in a deep breath and looked directly at him. "Nor you, sir. We are blessed to have such a fine physician among us." She adjusted the pot in her arms and prepared to leave. "The next time I come for a cooking lesson, pray God we do not have a repetition of today's excitement."

Sam looked into the depths of her eyes, eyes that stirred him every time he looked at Judith. No matter what she prayed, he would not escape excitement when next they saw each other.

∽

Judith hummed as she made her way to the lighthouse. How could she feel so light at heart when young Johnny lay unconscious in Sam's surgery? *Forgive me, heavenly Father.* She prayed for Johnny's return to health, then considered the reason for her good humor. *Sam.* From the open way he shared his dreams for his practice in Capernaum, to his obvious reluctance to try her cooking again, to his relieved delight when he tasted the perfect pudding, to his masterful treatment of the men involved in the accident—she found much to admire. She had promised Father to return before nightfall, and already she could see the moon rising over the ocean.

"Where have you been, gal?" Father called as soon as she crested the rise to the lighthouse. "I expected you home before I arose."

"John Lauder had an accident with his boat today. I stayed to help with the injured men." Judith walked past Father and arranged the still-steaming kedgeree on the table. "Mary shared her meal with us."

Father looked in the direction of the Hathaway cottage and grunted. "Who was hurt? How are they doing?"

"Johnny Lauder remains unconscious. We do not know if he will recover. Everyone else has gone home. We are fortunate that Sam was here to help."

"We've always managed without a doctor before," Father said. "Let's eat before the food cools."

Judith wanted to protest the slight on Sam's skills, but she kept quiet. Father would see Sam's worth in time.

Judith didn't return to the Hathaways' the following day. Mary would have welcomed her company at any time, but Johnny needed their full attention. When Sam knocked on the door on Friday morning during the middle of family devotions, Judith invited him in.

"Good morning." Sam held out a plate of muffins. "My mother made more than we can possibly eat."

Sam had taken care with his appearance. He had tied his hair with a ribbon to tame his dark curls. He had dressed as if for Sunday morning, his black coat straining across his broad shoulders, yet he looked at ease with a plate in his hands.

"Come in, Doctor," Father called out. "Join us as we read the Bible, then state your business."

"But Father, Sam needs to return to his surgery. He can't stay away from his patient for long."

"That's what I came to tell you. Johnny regained consciousness yesterday morning, and he went home last night! I will see him again later today."

"Praise be to the Lord."

Father read from Nehemiah.

"Nehemiah is one of my favorite people in the Bible," Sam said. "I love the way he prayed and then acted boldly." He commented on the scheme of building the walls. "Much like the town's decision to build the lighthouse. It was a wise choice."

Later, when Judith cleaned away the breakfast dishes, Sam headed up to the lantern room with Father. Father shot her a warning look that kept her at the bottom of the stairs. She allowed herself to daydream. Had Sam possibly come a-courting? Such thoughts were wishful thinking. Why would a man as well mannered and educated as Dr. Sam Hathaway want someone like her, a woman who couldn't even cook? He could have a sweetheart back in Connecticut, waiting for him to send for her. Perhaps Father wanted to ask him about the cankers that erupted on his tongue—thanks to her hit-and-miss approach to salt. Then again—he had dressed as a man wanting to impress a woman, or her father. She argued the matter in her mind as she washed the dishes.

"Judith!"

Judith stopped to listen when she heard her name. Father was shouting. She couldn't help but hear.

"Judith will never. . .last man. . .no coward—"

Footfalls sped down the stairs. She knew she should move, but she remained rooted to the spot. Sam paused in his headlong descent and stared at her.

"Judith, I had hoped. . ." His eyes conveyed what his words didn't.

"Be gone with ye!" Father bellowed down the stairs, and Sam took the remaining steps.

Judith followed him to the door, wringing her damp hands on her apron. "Things may yet be well. Give Father time."

"Is there hope for me then?" Sam asked in a rushed breath.

"There is." Judith wondered at her own boldness. "Now go, before Father finds you still in the place."

Sam flashed a smile and left. Buoyed by thoughts of him, Judith floated through the day. He *had* come courting. Father had thrown him out on his ear. The one man besides Piers who had expressed interest in her. The one man who made her heart race every time she saw him or heard his voice.

Father didn't mention the confrontation until they finished supper. "Dr. Hathaway asked permission to keep company with you." Father added a spoonful of honey to his mush and took a bite. "I know you well enough to believe you didn't do anything to encourage his foolishness."

Judith shook her head. She didn't trust herself to speak.

"I told him no coward who was afraid of the sea would ever be good enough for my daughter, not even if he was the last man on earth."

Judith sat still, refusing to nod in agreement.

"Do you hear me, gal? Find yourself a good, solid, seagoing lad, like our Piers. The doctor is probably a fine man in his own right, but he belongs back ashore." Father's face softened. "You're island-born and raised. Your heart would break if you left the sea."

Is it true? Judith wondered. *Would Sam give up on Capernaum and return to Connecticut?* She respected her father's opinion. So why did she feel like her heart would break, whether Sam stayed or went?

Father didn't speak of the matter again. Mary—dear, kind Mary—had knocked on the door the afternoon following Sam's visit. She brought a pan of poached cod with egg sauce. "I've missed you these past few days for our cooking lessons. I brought you something you can heat for tonight, and perhaps we can meet again next week." She winked. "There is no need to let the differences between our menfolk interfere with our friendship, now, is there?"

Judith pushed the memory aside. She added biscuits—only slightly overdone tonight—and leftover hasty pudding fried to perfect crispness.

Piers arrived as usual for dinner before his Saturday night shift in the lantern room. He had bathed and donned fresh clothes. He even smelled different. The odor of salt and fish as strong as clam chowder normally permeated his clothing. But tonight, Piers smelled of. . .flowers. He had not come empty-handed; he brought a small ceramic flower pot that held nosegays growing on the island, jack-in-the-pulpits, columbine, triphyllum. All her favorite colors.

"For you." He bowed.

Judith took the flowers and breathed the scent deeply. "I will put them on the table."

Piers made sure to praise her cooking.

"Mrs. Hathaway provided the cod," Judith felt impelled to reveal. "I hope she will teach me how to make the egg sauce next week."

She expected her father to object to her plan, but he only grunted. "If she can teach you how to make anything as good as this hasty pudding, we'll be blessed."

After the meal, Piers invited her to join him in a game of chess. He often won, seeing patterns that escaped her eyes. At the end of the game, Father nodded at the two of them.

"I will get the lamps going. Why don't the two of you take a walk?"

Judith looked at Father, then at Piers.

She knew what the clean suit, flowers, and compliments meant.

Piers had asked permission to court her.

And Father had agreed.

Chapter 6

Let me get my shawl." Judith needed a moment to gather her thoughts. She didn't wish to offend Piers, who had been a stalwart friend, but neither did she want to encourage him. She turned to the One who could help. *God, if You can spare time from ruling the wind and the waves, I need Your wisdom.*

I will direct your ways. The Bible verse came into her mind and gave her peace. She draped her shawl around her shoulders and left the lighthouse with Piers.

They walked along the path worn down between the lighthouse and the Vanderkamps' home near the docks. Piers's freshly washed hair gleamed gold in the moonlight, and she could see the sun creases around his eyes. He was attractive, kind, a good provider—everything a woman might want in a man.

Piers stopped about midway. The last rays of sunlight illuminated fishing boats bobbing at anchor. The sight, as familiar to her as the contours of the lighthouse, always made her think of Jesus and all the hours He spent at sea with the disciples.

"That was a mighty fine dinner you prepared this evening," Piers said at last.

"Mistress Hathaway has been tutoring me." Something Piers's mother had never offered to do before her death from a fever a few years ago.

"You must be an apt pupil." Piers took his hat off and stared at the ground as if it contained the answers to his questions.

Don't say it. Judith willed Piers to stay quiet. *Let us remain good friends as we have always been.*

Piers drew a deep breath. "I spoke with your father this week. He has given me permission to court you." He looked at her with great hope, baring his soul with an uncertainty he rarely allowed to show. "You must know how I feel about you."

Now came Judith's turn to look at the ground. Without looking at him, she said, "Piers, I fear I do not return your feelings." Lightning streaked across the sky, and she jumped. Was God agreeing with her or chiding her for her foolishness? She raised her eyes to the man who had shown his love in a hundred different ways.

His face pulled into a scowl, teeth clenched together. "Do you hold any regard for me at all?"

"I care for you deeply, Piers—as I might for a brother." Judith hated to inflict more pain.

"In time, that regard could deepen into something more." Piers chose to take her words as encouragement. "Will you walk with me again Monday evening?"

How could he expect her to develop feelings in the next few weeks that had not grown in the past five years? Still, Father would expect her to give Piers a hearing. She had been honest.

"Gladly—as long as there are no further expectations on your part."

"That is all I ask."

A second flash of lightning raced across the sky, and the couple turned back to the lighthouse.

∞

Sam stood in the doorway, gauging the weather. A single boom promised a thunderstorm. Rain splattered the ground. Would the storm increase, or weaken? He looked to the point where the lighthouse stood. Two figures dashed for the edifice—Judith and Piers.

Eli Morrison would welcome Piers as a son-in-law. He proved his courage every day by going to sea, and he also knew all the workings of the lighthouse.

But what did Judith think of Piers? She had promised there was hope for Sam. He clung to that when he felt the cold wall of Eli's disapproval that kept him away from Judith. Even the lighthouse keeper would not force his daughter to marry against her will.

Sam remained outside and watched as the lamps came on. One, two, three, all the way to nine and ten. Would such a warning have made a difference on the night his father died? He shook his head. Only God knew the answer to that question.

Rain pelted the ground as hard as new pennies against stone. Lightning screamed through the clouds; thunder struck his ear. Rather than ducking into the safety of the parlor, Sam took another step into the open air and bellowed.

"I'm not frightened of you! I trust the Lord, the Maker of heaven and earth! He carries the lightning in His fists!" Sam repeated words from Job, begging God to make them true in his heart. The wind whipped waves into a frenzy, pounding the rocks near the lighthouse with a furor as loud as a canon's roar.

He sensed his mother's presence and felt her hand press against his elbow. "Come inside, son. You will not prove anything by catching cold."

Only then did Sam realize rain had soaked him through to the skin. Warm breezes carried the rain, although sickness never plagued him through nights of sleet and snow during the war. He followed her inside and took a seat by the fireplace.

She disappeared into the kitchen, only to return with a mug of warm milk and a piece of gingerbread. He smiled his thanks. Neither spoke while Sam ate the sweet one morsel at a time, relaxing in the childhood ritual. While he ate, the fire dried his clothes. Wind moaned through cracks, the boards creaking as rain found weak spots. It almost had a musical sound, God Himself directing the orchestra of thundering trumpets, rain drums, and wind instruments. Sam stared out the window at the lighthouse. Flashing lamps punctuated the rhythm of the storm, highlighting first a rock, then a wave, then the sky. It gave him an odd sort of comfort.

Comfort, that is, until one of the lamps went black, then a second. Sam stood to his feet. "I must go." He dashed out the door and across the open field to the lighthouse. A few minutes later, he pounded on the door.

An eternity passed before Judith came to the door. "Sam? What is it?"

"The lamps. Did you see. . . ?"

"Father." Judith sucked in her breath and opened the door wide for him to enter. She moved to the stairs. Sam followed behind.

If the storm sounded like a symphony in his cottage, it became a thousand blaring trumpets in the lighthouse. Every board creaked, and the very tower swayed in the wind. His nightmares would multiply if he lived in a building like this one.

Sam raced up the steps two at a time, only slightly winded. Eli was relighting a lamp as Sam entered the lantern room.

"What are you doing here?"

"He—" Breathless, Judith spoke from behind Sam. She inhaled and continued. "He noticed that the lamps went out and came to check on us."

"Hmph." The older man studied Sam. He must look a sight, with his sodden clothes and wind-blown hair.

"I wondered if I could help, sir."

A smile tugged at the corner's of Eli's lips. "I appreciate your concern, lad, but it's not the first time the lamps have gone out during a storm, and it won't be the last."

In fact, all tens lights beamed as if nothing had happened. Rain lashed against the windows. Lightning flashed so much closer than at ground level. Sam took an involuntary step back. A single lightning strike could burn this brave outpost to the ground. Why had they ever made it of wood?

"As you can see, I am fine. You can leave me in good conscience." Eli placed a hand on Sam's back. Sam thought he saw a hint of approval in his eyes. "Thank you for your concern. It's been a long time since we had neighbors."

Judith accompanied him downstairs. "Thank you for coming." Her voice was low, a soft woodwind instrument added to the storm's orchestra.

"I would never let anything happen to you." He paused, searching for words to say. "Call on me if you ever need anything."

"I will." A small smile lifted her lips. "Tomorrow, in fact. Your mother promised to teach me how to bake bread."

Sam smiled widely. "Until then."

The musical note of Judith's voice drowned out the wind and waves as he returned to his home.

∞

"I prepared the sponge last evening, since it has to rise overnight. I'll show you how to make that another time." Mary took down the mixture. "This morning, we will add flour and knead the dough."

Judith stared at the enormous sponge, enough for five loaves. Her mouth watered at the thought of fresh-baked bread. Her few previous attempts had failed; she bought bread from the town baker.

Mary placed a crock of flour next to the bowl and dusted the table with flour. "Add flour to the dough. Enough to make it easy to work."

Judith stared at the sponge. How much?

Mary must have sensed her question. "Feel it. Add flour until it is less of a batter and more of a dough."

Judith added a little at a time until she felt the pieces pull together. "Would you check it?"

Mary felt around the edges with her hands and smiled. "You have done well. Now let me show you how to knead it." She whacked the sponge onto the floured surface, bunched her hands into fists, coated them with flour, and punched the dough. Judith jumped, and Mary laughed.

"Baking bread may be women's work, but it takes a strong arm." She worked the bread for a moment longer, folded it over, and invited Judith to try.

Judith stared at the dough, and at her hands. Resolutely, she balled her fingers into fists, coated them with flour, and pressed down on the dough.

"That's right. A little more pressure. Now turn the mound."

Five minutes into the experience, Judith's arms felt tired.

"How long do we continue?"

Mary laughed. "A good bread takes about half an hour. I'll take over for a spell." She coated her hands with flour and worked the dough. "I hope I am not being forward, dear Judith, but how much do you know about other aspects of housekeeping?"

Judith sighed. "I know how to clean. Father has always kept the lighthouse in tiptop shape, and I followed his example. I care for the clothes—laundering and ironing them—although I burned a few things before I learned how to gauge the heat correctly. But. . ." She gestured at the new curtains blowing in the window. "I know nothing of sewing beyond the ability to sew on a button or turn a hem. Any man who marries me will need to afford a housekeeper, for I am poor in the household arts." She took over kneading the dough.

"You have no need to worry. You learn quickly. You have shown a diligence and skill for cooking in the short time we have worked together. I will help you." Mary looked at her sideways. "Is there any particular man you have in mind?"

Judith colored. Had Sam told his mother of Father's rejection? How she loved this woman, like the mother she never knew.

"There may be." She wanted to say more, but to do so felt like a betrayal of her father.

"Piers Vanderkamp is a stalwart young man." Mary prepared five bread pans.

"Oh, Piers." Judith couldn't quite repress the frown that came to her lips at the thought of his persistent suit. "He has asked for permission to court me. Father likes him and thinks he is the perfect man for me."

"But you?" Mary asked, humor brimming in the gray green eyes so like her son's.

"He *is* a fine man. And I like him."

"But?"

"But I care for him as a brother. I cannot imagine spending the rest of my life with him. Yet I fear that if I do not accept his suit, I may spend the rest of my days alone."

At that moment, Judith heard Sam whistling as he entered the house after a call on a patient. Her frown turned upside down, and her heart sang.

"I doubt that." Mary cocked her head in the direction of the whistle and smiled. "God will provide."

Sam poked his head into the kitchen and sniffed the air. "Yeast. Are you making bread?"

"Yes." Judith became aware of the flour on her hands, her apron, in her hair. She must look a sight.

"I will look forward to lunch."

"Is young Johnny well?" she inquired.

"Well enough to return to work on the morrow. I see no reason for him to remain abed, praise the good Lord."

Sam came to the table and snagged a finger of dough. Mary slapped his hand. He rolled it around his mouth and swallowed. "I can't wait."

Judith giggled. "You have no choice. They have to rise again."

"You *do* know how to bake bread." Mary beamed. "And we are ready to put the dough into the pans."

"I can tell when I am an extra wheel," Sam said. "In any case, I need to write up my notes about the visit." He nodded his head in Judith's direction. "I will see you later."

Judith followed his departure, taking in his broad shoulders, the impossibly white cravat at his neck.

"Judith?" Mary's soft voice interrupted her thoughts. "Help me divide the dough." She touched Judith's hand. "God will work everything out."

Judith didn't know about that. Overcoming her father's prejudice would be a lot harder than learning how to bake bread.

Chapter 7

S am attended the next town meeting with a singular purpose. He reviewed the reasons for his proposal. The well-being of Judith Morrison mattered to him, as well as the safety of Capernaum's fisherman. He entered the meeting house, about a third filled with the men of the town.

"Dr. Hathaway! So good to have you join us." As always, Reverend Snodgrass welcomed him warmly. Lauder also shook his hand, and a healthy and hale Johnny smiled his thanks. Eli and Piers had already found a seat.

The meeting got under way a few minutes later. Sam waited until the floor opened for new business and then stood to his feet.

"Speak, friend." The mayor addressed Sam.

Sam looked across the gathered townsfolk, hoping they would give his recommendation a hearing.

"When I returned to Capernaum, I was pleased to see the lighthouse. For ten years, it has excelled at its job. It has protected men and ships at sea. Every night, I see the beacon from my cottage. Ten lamps shining strong and clear in the darkest and foggiest of nights."

Around the room, men murmured. What was his point?

Sam paused before continuing. "I live near the lighthouse, and I can see the effect of the weather on the structure. I have heard it creak in rainstorms and seen the wind blow out the lamps. A truly fierce storm would tear through the wood like kindling." He drew in a deep breath. "I propose that Capernaum build another, sturdier lighthouse of brick or stone."

Eli jumped to his feet. "The Rocky Point Lighthouse has survived every storm thrown at it for ten years. It cost this town two thousand dollars to build, and every penny was well spent. I check the building myself, year in, year out. There is no finer structure in all of Capernaum."

"I do not doubt that, sir." How could he help Eli understand? "But I have seen lighthouses in other places. On Cape Cod. Ones built of stone and brick. They do not sigh in the wind."

"Then why don't you go back to Connecticut or Massachusetts, where you belong?" Eli's face turned so red that Sam feared he would suffer from apoplexy on the spot. "Only a man afraid of the sea spooks at a little wind in the night."

"Give them time," Reverend Snodgrass advised Sam after the town meeting. "The people take pride in their lighthouse. It rises above the sea like the tower of Babel. And I fear people who want to tear down idols are not well liked." Snodgrass clapped Sam on the back. "I pray it does not take another tragedy for people to see the wisdom of your words."

∞

Tuesday, July the Fourth, opened with clear skies. Storms and catastrophes were far from Sam's mind. Today he would express his unity with the islanders by attending the town picnic in celebration of American independence. Mama and Judith had prepared food for both families, and he looked forward to spending more time with the lovely lass. Dressed in his army uniform, he hoped to make a good impression on father and daughter.

When Sam left the army, he would gladly have burned the uniform, along with the blood soaked into every fiber of the cloth. But today he would join with other veterans in display of patriotism. A white belt and vest and black gaiters adorned a plain blue coat and trousers. The scarlet sash and epaulettes indicated his rank as an officer. He would leave off the sword and the other folderol used for dress parade. Should he wear the tall, felt shako hat? Yes, he decided. It showed his regiment, and people might ask.

Mama came in as he cinched his belt. Not as tight as he used to wear it; he had regained some of the weight lost during long days and nights with little food and even less sleep. She drew in a sharp breath, and tears misted her eyes. "I prayed every day while you were gone that God would spare my son, since He had already taken my husband." She wiped at her eyes. "I am so glad He brought you home safely." She reached up and touched his cheek. "You look better now that I gave you that haircut."

He smiled at his mother fondly. "Shall we?" They walked out of the house. In the distance, a drum beat, and his feet moved in rhythm.

"Let's join them." All of a mother's pride shone in her eyes. If only Judith would look at him the same way. His pace picked up in his desire to arrive at the picnic. Mama had helped Judith prepare a traditional meal of poached salmon, peas, potatoes, and strawberry shortcake. They would share the fruit of their labors.

Several older men gathered in front of the meeting house, their demeanor proud in their fading uniforms from the revolutionary army. Sam's uniform looked new, almost gaudy next to theirs. Eli Morrison was the youngest among them, having fought as a young teenager in the battle at Yorktown. Sam straightened his back and marched in rhythm with the drum's slow cadence. He felt the people around him draw in their breath.

"Captain Sam Hathaway, reporting for duty, sir." He bowed in front of Capernaum's senior veteran, old Josiah Pepperill, who had survived Valley Forge with George Washington. Sam snapped off a salute.

The old man returned the salute and peered at his regimental badge. Sam was glad he had worn his shako. "I am proud to make your acquaintance, captain. You fought in the recent war with Britain?"

Sam gave details on his service to Pepperill. The town's mayor introduced each veteran. The gathered throng clapped enthusiastically when his name, rank, and service were announced. While the mayor continued to speak of the glory of God and country, Sam explored the periphery of his vision for Judith. She stood next to his mother, whispering to her. He pulled himself even straighter, the tassel from his shako blowing in the wind.

Reverend Snodgrass led a brief prayer that included a blessing on the food and then went down the line, shaking each veteran's hand. The townspeople fell in behind.

Last of all, the pastor came to Sam. "Well done, Doctor. We need a reminder of the recent conflict that preserved our freedom."

Sam leaned closer and whispered, "Sir. Why did none of the younger veterans join the parade today? I wondered if perhaps I made a misstep."

Snodgrass shook his head. "Rhode Island opposed the war. None of our men served in the last campaigns. But *you* did, and we thank you for it." He wrung Sam's hands.

Soon after, Lauder came along and congratulated Sam in ringing tones. "Well done, Doctor! We are proud to have a veteran of the war make his home in Capernaum." In a quieter voice, he added, "Not all of us agreed with Rhode Island's position on the war, but what could we do?"

Johnny stopped by next, and Sam smiled. Seeing the young man hale and hearty made his return worthwhile.

Even Piers shook his hand. "I would have fought if we'd had a regiment."

"There is no need to apologize. You show your worth here on Capernaum every day."

Toward the end of the line, Mama approached with Judith and Eli. Sam drank in the sight of the young woman. She was dressed in blue with red and white ribbons in her hair.

Judith appeared to return his regard. She studied him from the height of the shako and followed the line of his uniform to his newly shined boots. Her lips parted, and she shook her head. "You told me you had served in the army, but seeing you in uniform makes it come to life. Thank you for your service."

Mama nudged him. He realized he must have been staring. "You're welcome."

"*Captain* Hathaway." Eli came next.

Sam braced himself. He looked straight into the older man's eyes, a darker blue than Judith's, more like the color of the tricornered hat on his head.

"You will have to tell me more about your service." Eli's eyes took on a haunted look Sam recognized from soldiers revisiting a nightmarish experience.

He relaxed. Perhaps their common experience in the army would open understanding with Judith's father.

❦

Judith worked hard not to stare at Sam. He took her breath away. The uniform declared his patriotism and bravery in a way that needed no further explanation. Perhaps now Father would change his mind.

Piers spoke, interrupting her thoughts. "My sister-in-law has spread out our picnic by the rocks." He offered her his arm.

"We made other plans." Judith glanced at Sam.

A flush spread across Piers's face. "So a common fisherman isn't good enough for you?"

"Piers." Judith didn't want to offend him.

"Judith and I cooked together," Mary said, pointing to rolls in a basket. "But we can share a table, if you would like."

Judith quavered at the thought. A table shared by Sam, Piers, and Father would invite discord.

Piers stared at Judith, and then shook his head. "Sara has already set up our spot across the way. On the rocks." His voice dared Sam to join them.

"If you had asked earlier," Judith said, wishing to appease him.

"I assumed we would celebrate together, as we do every year. Never mind. I will see you on Saturday." Piers walked with stiff steps to his waiting family.

"I apologize if my presence caused difficulties." Sam removed the tall hat from his head and turned it in his hands.

"Oh, that." Judith threw him a saucy grin. "Piers assumes too much. Come, let's enjoy the afternoon."

Sam nodded. "Tell me about your experiences in the war," he said to her father.

Judith smiled. Father liked nothing better than to talk about his war campaigns. She had heard all his stories a hundred times. He would welcome a new audience.

"Help me finish cooking the meal at our fire." Mary cocked her head in the direction of the men. "Let them get acquainted."

She showed Judith how to wrap the salmon in cheesecloth and steam it in boiling bouillon. Around them, other family groups did the same. Yesterday, they had picked strawberries and baked rolls and shortcake.

"Have you ever made egg sauce?" Mary asked.

"Not without scorching it," Judith admitted.

"Well, let me show you. I boiled the eggs this morning."

As Judith stirred the sauce—no wonder she didn't excel at cooking: she lacked the patience needed to do it properly—she listened to snatches of the conversation between Sam and her father. They had each grabbed a roll and took one small bite at a time. They looked like two old soldiers sharing a frugal meal on campaign.

"And then the general said. . ." Sam threw back his head and laughed with her father at the joke.

A few minutes later, she heard, "Benedict Arnold—"

Father was pursuing another one of his favorite subjects. How could the man who turned the tide at the battle of Saratoga and perhaps even of the war have later betrayed his country?

"And those Frenchies, couldn't have done it without them." Father often spoke of his friendship with Louis Giguere, a French soldier who chose to stay on in Providence after the war ended.

Judith dropped two diced eggs into the sauce and strained to hear what Sam had to say. He might tell a fellow soldier things he would never tell her.

"Two hundred men. . ." Sam chopped with his hands, illustrating his point. "So much death."

Judith had seen death. Every island resident had. Men were killed at sea, women and children sickened and died, the elderly passed on to their reward. But she could not imagine the deliberate deaths of hundreds of men in battle. Father never told her those stories. She was glad he could discuss it with Sam.

Mary whipped cream for the shortcake. She dipped a spoon into the sauce. "We forgot the salt and pepper." She smiled. "That's easily fixed." She sprinkled in the spices, stirred it, and offered a taste to Judith.

"Perfect."

"And the fish has finished cooking. Help me make it pretty." They peeled the skin off the fish, placed it in the center of a large plate with peas and potatoes, then poured the egg sauce over the salmon. "Get the men."

Judith walked up behind the two men, heads bent in close conversation. "Father? Sam? Dinner's ready."

Father's head jerked up. "So soon?" He sniffed the air. "Lead me to the salmon."

A scant three quarters of an hour later, every bite of salmon and vegetables had disappeared, as well as the strawberries. A handful of biscuits and rolls remained for the afternoon.

"I have never had so delicious a poached salmon." Sam patted his stomach.

"That's because of the egg sauce that Judith prepared," Mary said.

"Did you, gal?" Father blinked his eyes. He turned to Mary. "You are a miracle worker, if you can make a housewife out of my daughter."

Mortified, Judith felt her face flaming with heat.

"Nonsense." Mary smiled. "She only needs the right teacher. She has learned a great deal in a short time."

"If today's meal is any indication of her skill, I'd line up for her cooking every day of the week." Sam bowed toward Judith. "It was truly delectable."

Never had Judith received so much praise for her cooking. A pleasing warmth surged through her from head to toe.

"I have overstayed my shift." Father yawned. "I must rest now, or I will never stay awake tonight. Come along now, Judith."

Judith didn't wish to leave. She felt languid, with the sun on her face, the pleasant stupor that follows a delicious meal, the agreeable company of the Hathaways. "Do you mind if I stay awhile longer?"

"I promise to see her safely home, sir," Sam said.

Father looked to Sam, then Judith, weighing his request. "This one time. It *is* Independence Day." He glared at Sam as if daring him to ask again and walked in the direction of the lighthouse.

Something tense inside Judith relaxed at this sign of a thaw in Father's mind about Sam. Shortly after Father left, Horace Wilson, the gangly schoolteacher, called for everyone's attention. The flag he held in his left hand, fifteen white stars on a field of blue and fifteen stripes of alternating red and white, fluttered in the wind. The town's best orator was about to recite the Declaration of Independence.

As he began the Preamble to the Declaration, Judith mouthed the familiar words along with him. " 'When in the course of human events, it becomes necessary for one people to dissolve the political bands which have connected them with another. . .we hold these truths to be self-evident, that all men are created equal, that they are endowed by their Creator with certain inalienable rights, that among these are life, liberty and the pursuit of happiness.'"

As he recited the words, the crowd grew as quiet as the quivering of leaves before a storm. The veterans of the War for Independence joined in a group, pride evident in the military bearing of their elderly shoulders. Light bounced off their uniforms, giving the illusion of the youth and vitality, patriotism and honor that had given birth to the United States. By the time Wilson reached the end of the document, Judith felt the spirit of those men gathered in Philadelphia during hot July days in 1776. Beside her, Sam saluted the veterans. A sheen of tears gleamed in his eyes.

" 'And for the support of this Declaration, with a firm reliance on the protection of divine Providence, we mutually pledge to each other our Lives, our Fortunes and our sacred Honor.'"

With the final words, a loud "hurrah!" went up from the throng.

"God bless America!" Mrs. Wembly raised the cry, and others joined in.

Judith touched Sam's arm. "Thank you for fighting to *keep* us free."

He bowed. "I was honored to serve."

Now that the solemn festivities had ended, the shopkeeper, who was handy with the fiddle, brought out his violin. Piers approached and, without apology, interrupted their conversation. "Judith, you promised me a dance today."

Judith searched her memory for the promise. He had mentioned the traditional dance at last Saturday's meal before his shift in the lantern room. She smiled apologetically at Sam and allowed Piers to lead her away.

Chapter 8

"I claim the honor of the next dance," Sam called after Judith.

She flashed a smile at him in agreement and followed Piers to the end of a line of ten couples. Wilson stood at the head of the line with Deborah Wembly, one of the fiddler's daughters.

Sam's foot started tapping when the music for the Virginia reel started. Piers and Deborah advanced four steps toward each other from their opposite ends of the lines, and then retreated. Judith and Wilson did the same. They continued with more advances and retreats, a do-si-do and a corkscrew that turned each man and woman in line to face the next. By the end, Wilson and Deborah walked under arched hands to the end of the line behind Judith and Piers. The steps repeated until at last they came to the head of the line.

Piers danced well, and the couple finished with a flourish. He held on to Judith's hand after the music ended.

"I have the honor of the next dance." Sam was thankful for the excuse to interrupt the moment between Judith and Piers.

Sam's rival scowled but relinquished Judith's hand. "May I have the third set?"

Judith looked from one man to the other, uncertain. "I will sit that one out. Maybe later."

Piers bowed and moved away.

Wembly called for the next dance, and this time they joined the middle of the line. Judith's feet tapped as the head and foot couples went through the formal steps. During the corkscrew, Sam caught sight of Judith swooping and swirling, all sunshine and gaiety. All too soon, the dance ended, and they went for a drink of water.

Piers arrived and claimed Judith for the fourth dance. Disappointed, Sam watched them take their places.

"There are other young women who would appreciate a turn." Mama appeared at his elbow.

"It is too late for this set, and I am dancing with Judith in the next."

Mama opened her mouth.

"After that, perhaps." She was right. Until he had Eli's permission to court Judith, he should not give her exclusive attention.

After today, he hoped Eli might change his mind.

The day seemed to last forever. Sam danced with three or four young ladies, but he managed to snag the last dance with Judith. Like the foxes portrayed in the reel, they darted in and out of cover, hiding and escaping, laughing and gasping.

The sun began its slow descent into night when the fiddler at last called an end to the festivities. Before the man set down his instrument, Piers made his way to Judith's side.

"May I escort you home since your father has left?" Piers's smile made Sam want to strike him, so confident he seemed of her answer.

Judith looked from Piers to Sam and colored. "There is no need for you to trouble yourself, Piers. Sam promised Father he would see me safely home this evening."

Piers's face turned as red as the flag. "I will see you in the morning, then, when I bring fresh whale oil." He backed away.

Sam tucked Judith's arm around his elbow and set out in the direction of the lighthouse. He loved the ocean on nights like this, when a light breeze provided relief from the midsummer heat and the surf made a soft *whoosh* against the rocks. They strolled, pausing now and again to look out at the ocean, calm as a mirror in the moonlight, not wanting the day to end. He remained quiet, allowing the peace of the day to speak for him. He began to hum.

"That's a spirited tune," Judith said. "I don't believe I've heard it before. Are there any words?"

"It's a song that became popular during the war. About the defense of Fort McHenry in Baltimore." He sang the first lines. " 'O! say can you see by the dawn's early light/What so proudly we hailed at the twilight's last gleaming.' "

"It is certainly stirring music."

Sam laughed. "I understand it was originally a British drinking song. Francis Scott Key wrote the words while he was imprisoned on a British gunship during the bombardment of the fort. After his release, someone else set the poem to music. It's hard to sing in places, though." He sang the chorus, his voice breaking when he reached "land of the free!"

"That's beautiful." He could see the tears in her eyes. "Do you know any more of the song?"

"The only other verse I know well is the last verse." Sam sang it for her.

" 'Then conquer we must, when our cause it is just.' I love that line. Teach me the chorus. Please." She sang, her voice soaring through the chorus in a lilting soprano. " 'Oh, say does that. . .' "

They sang the chorus together three or four times, their voices breaking the stillness of the night, ringing out over the land and ocean. " 'And the home of the brave!' "

As their voices rose with the final phrase, the lamps lit in the lighthouse and beamed on them. Judith lifted her face, all poetry and softness and joy. Sam took her hand and turned her to face him. With the smallest of movements, he bent forward and claimed her lips with a kiss.

∽

Judith looked across the expanse to the Hathaway cottage. Had a month already passed since the Fourth of July? She recalled every moment of that perfect day. The parade of veterans, the respect Father had shown to Sam—the kiss. She put her hand to her lips as if to seal in the touch of Sam's mouth to hers.

In recent days, Piers had redoubled his efforts to woo her. Every day he brought her wildflowers or little trinkets he thought she might like. She appreciated the sweet gestures but wished she could return his feelings. Why did her traitorous heart only feel truly at home when she escaped to the Hathaways' for a cooking lesson? Why did her heart sing when she heard Sam read Milton's poetry with such beauty and expression?

After the veterans' parade on Independence Day, most of Capernaum accepted Sam's worth. Only Father continued to belittle him, perhaps fueled by his fondness for Piers. At least his barbs held less animosity than formerly.

Today she would visit Mary for another cooking lesson, this time a dish to tempt Father's sweet tooth. Yesterday they had picked enough raspberries for a crumble.

At least Judith no longer needed to worry about berry juice staining her everyday dress. Mary had helped her fashion an apron. With her improved sewing skills, Judith had taken on a special surprise for Father, a quilt the colors of summer berries. Once cold weather settled in, he suffered from aching bones.

When she reached the door to the Hathaways', Sam looked up at her from his office desk and smiled a greeting. Then he dipped his quill back into an ink bottle and added to his notes. Judith hurried into the kitchen.

Mary had already set out a few ingredients. Over and over again, she amazed Judith with how many different dishes she could prepare from the same ingredients. This time, they had butter, flour, sugar, salt, and a bowl of berries.

Judith tied her apron behind her back. "Where do we start?"

"First, we need to crush the raspberries. By the time you get home tonight, your father may think you have injured your hands—they will be all red." Mary smiled. "But then you will give him a dish of crumble and cream, and he will forgive me."

If only raspberries had been in season when Mary began my lessons. Judith found blending the butter with sugar and flour until it resembled small pebbles a lot easier than kneading bread dough. But bread was the stuff of life, whereas berry crumble. . .that was food fit for a king.

They were about to put the crumble in the oven when a knock came at the door. Stefan Vanderkamp, Piers's father, waited on the step.

"The doctor. We have had an accident." His hands were red, covered with real blood. "They are coming from the boats."

Sam appeared at the door. "What happened? How many are injured?"

"A hook ripped through his chest." Stefan could hardly speak.

Is it Piers? Judith's heart skipped. She looked at Mary.

"It will not harm the crumble to wait," the older woman said. "Let's see if we can help." They rinsed their hands, stained red indeed with berry juice, and joined Sam in the surgery.

Judith watched Sam arrange his instruments on a tray. She recognized many of them by now. Lancets were used to bleed a patient. He set aside the dental instruments; broken teeth would be the least of the injured seamen's problems. He added tourniquets and frowned at the gathered lint needed for dressing wounds. Then he pulled out one last instrument: a saw.

Judith gulped. She prayed amputation would not be necessary. *O Lord, please let Piers be all right.*

"Mama, do you have any material we can use for dressings, if I run out?"

Mary nodded her head. "Judith and I will tear up some of the cotton we set aside for the quilt. How much do you need?"

"Wait until we see the extent of the injuries. You might want to heat up the iron."

Iron. Judith shivered. Heat cauterized wounds. She prayed again it would not come to that.

Stefan returned, carrying a man of much the same size and build of Piers. Judith's heart stopped beating. Then she saw Piers following behind, far behind, blood streaming down his face, leaning on the shoulder of his younger brother.

Judith slumped with relief, grasping the edge of the kitchen table for support.

∽

Judith's near faint registered with Sam, and then his attention riveted on the injured man—Stefan's oldest son, Piers's brother Martin.

A hole the size of a lobster's claw hollowed out Martin's back, sparing his heart by a few precious inches. No tourniquet or surgical saw could help a wound like that. Sam indicated that they should lay Martin face down. He prayed, then set to work.

First he placed his ear against Martin's back, not as reliable as the chest for checking the heartbeat, but he dared not risk turning the patient over. Martin's heart continued its normal rhythm, a little more blood leaking out with each beat. His breathing was another matter. He groaned in pain with each intake.

"Will he live?" Stefan asked in obvious distress.

Sam had no assurances to give. "I will do what I can. And you can do your part."

"Anything."

"Pray." He steered Stefan to a chair while he continued his examination.

Sam studied the mangled body of the seaman. He must clean the wound to stem the bleeding, but before he did that, he wanted to ease his breathing. "Laudanum."

Judith offered him the bottle. "I thought you might need it." She had regained her composure and had anticipated the medicine he would request. She looked at Martin, her face drawn. "Piers is also injured."

Sam glanced at the man who hoped to marry Judith. A flap of skin had fallen open above his eye.

"I can wait." Piers waved away the assessment. "Take care of my brother."

"Lie down," Sam told Piers. "Judith, place a clean dressing on that injury until I can tend to him." Not only would the action help Piers, but also it would keep her busy while he worked on Martin. While Judith was otherwise occupied, he debrided the wound, tied off a couple of small blood vessels, and packed it with a poultice of quinine bark.

"Doctor?" Martin roused briefly. He felt for Sam's hand. "Tell my wife that I love her."

"No last words. You're going to be fine." Sam would not voice his doubts to the patient. Martin's will to live might determine the outcome of the night. Sam listened to his breathing again—no noticeable improvement. If he was not doing better by eventide, Sam would have to bleed him a bit.

"Will he live?" Stefan's voice held the begging tone Sam had heard from so many, from husbands worried over their wives in childbirth to mothers watching children with ague. He ached for some assurance to give them.

"It's in God's hands. Martin will rest while I take care of Piers."

Judith stroked Piers's hands, looking as gentle and concerned as his mother ever had, and jealousy surged up within Sam. He reminded himself of his oath—"first, do no harm"—and prayed for God to rid him of the ugly attitude. Then he saw Piers's frightened expression, a mirror of Sam's own fright whenever he entered a boat, and his heart softened. He knew he would do his best for this man.

"Are you in pain?" Sam asked first.

"Only on the temple." Piers touched his wound.

"No other injuries?"

Piers shook his head.

Sam lifted the dressing. The cut itself wasn't serious. One inch long and a half inch across, it looked worse than it was. As always, infection was the deadliest enemy. He would clean it and stitch the skin, then pray for the best.

"I need to stitch it up. Do you want laudanum before I start?"

Piers curled his lip. "That's not necessary."

I expected that answer. "Very well." Sam reached beneath his cabinet for a bottle of whiskey he kept there. If Piers would not *drink* a painkiller, Sam could at least deaden the site of the wound. He soaked a cloth with the spirits and pressed it to the cut.

Piers's facial muscles contorted with pain, but he didn't speak. Judith stroked back his hair.

After a few minutes, Sam threaded a needle, then paused. "Judith, please hold Piers's head still."

"I'm not a baby. I won't squirm," Piers protested.

"It is a natural reaction when you feel the metal against your flesh." Sam forced himself to smile. "Besides, how often do you get to have a beautiful woman hold your head in her hands?"

Judith placed her hands—red from the berry crumble—on either side of Piers's head. She kept them steady and gentle in circumstances that would frighten many men. Sam prayed he would remain as steady, and he pierced the left side of the cut with the needle.

Piers's eyes widened, but otherwise he didn't move. He tightened his lips in a straight line, as straight and thin as the tiny stitches Sam used to close up the wound. He worked in silence, determined to do his best work. In the end, a right angle of neat black stitches held the flap of skin in place. He wound a dressing around Piers's head. "Change the bandage every day," Sam warned his patient. "Other than that, you are free to go."

"I will stay with Martin."

Sam nodded.

"Sam?" Mama called from the door. "I have prepared some beef broth for you. You must be tired." She carried a tray. "I brought some in for you too, Mr. Vanderkamp. I know you want to stay by your son's side."

"I'll get some for Piers as well." Judith rose from the seat she had taken by his side. "Then I'd best be gone home. Father will want to know what has happened."

Sam looked out the window, surprised to see that the sun had passed its zenith and the noon hour had long since ended. Hunger he had not realized made its presence known. He placed a hand on Stefan's shoulder. "I have done all I can for now. Call me if there is any change."

After Judith brought a bowl of broth to Piers, Sam walked her to the door. "You were a wonderful help today."

She looked pained. "I wish I could do more. How dreadful."

"Piers will be fine."

"But Martin?"

Sam shrugged, unwilling to commit himself. "I will do what I can."

"Father and I will pray." She carried a bowl, aromatic with cooked berries, under her arm.

Sam watched her departure and wondered at the degree of concern she showed for Piers. Perhaps the accident had forged the attachment her father longed for between them. Sam gritted his teeth.

Mama set the table with the promised broth, as well as bread and butter. He ate with good appetite and prepared to return to the surgery. Their daily Bible reading would wait.

"Not before you taste Judith's berry crumble." Mama pushed him back into his chair and placed a bowl covered with cream in front of him. "I have a suggestion."

"What is it?"

"*Rest.* You will be up throughout the evening with Martin."

Sam chuckled. "Do you know how many sleepless nights I passed during the war?"

"No one needs your services at this moment. Rest while you can, so your wits will be sharp tonight."

Sam considered her suggestion. "Half an hour. No more." He climbed the stairs and fell into instant slumber.

∞

All the way home, Judith debated whether or not to wake Father to tell him the news of the accident. The Vanderkamps were like part of their family. But a good two hours remained before he needed to arise for his night's work.

She needn't have worried. When she arrived at the lighthouse, she heard her father upstairs, whistling in the lantern room. He sounded so happy. This news would break his heart. She placed the crumble in the warming pan.

"Judith? Is that you?"

She forced a smile on her face and prayed to God for strength.

"Yes, Father. I am coming."

Father met her on the landing. "Isn't that Vanderkamp's dog by the Hathaways' cottage?"

"Oh, Father." Judith's eyes filled with tears. "Something awful has happened."

"What is it?"

She shook her head and pointed down the stairs. "Let me tell you about it while I fix you some supper." She kept her tears in check while she spoke of the slip of the fishing gear, the way it tore through Piers's skin and then impacted Martin in the back. "He looked so awful. I don't see how he'll live."

"I'm going over."

"No, Father," Judith protested. "He's too weak."

"But the doctor will be able to fix him, won't he?"

"I don't know," Judith acknowledged. "Sam seemed uncertain. I promised we would pray."

Father looked as though he had aged ten years in the few minutes since he heard the news. "And Piers?"

"Sam stitched up the wound. There may be a scar, but otherwise, he is fine. He is concerned about Martin."

"Then pray we must." Father pushed aside the plate of sandwiches she had prepared and knelt on the hard floor by the fireplace. Judith joined him. Nothing less seemed appropriate. "Almighty God and heavenly Father, Thou who madest earth and sea and everything therein, we come before Thee today, bringing our petitions...."

Father's wordy prayers, which often lulled Judith into a somnolent state, lifted her up today. With every phrase, her spirit cried, "So be it, Lord!" When at last he said "amen," an hour had passed.

The evening dragged by. First she thought of Sam, of his sure hands as he tended to the injured. Then she thought of Piers and the way her heart cried when she saw his injury.

Perhaps Father was right all along. Perhaps she held more feelings for Piers than she had realized.

Chapter 9

Judith didn't rest well that night. After an hour or so of sleep, she awoke to the memory of the torn bodies of Martin and Piers. She prayed and returned to sleep, only to have the dream recur. When she came to awareness shortly before five, she arose.

She was browning the last slice of hasty pudding when Father came down the stairs.

"We will go to the surgery this morning." His voice didn't allow for any argument.

"Yes. But first we will eat." She dished out the hasty pudding and put crocks of butter and molasses on the table.

They ate in silence. Judith wondered if Father would persevere with the daily Bible reading. Probably so. The hour had barely passed six, still too early for a call. Today's reading came from Ecclesiastes. He read at double speed, stumbling over some words, until he reached the third chapter. " 'To every thing there is a season, and a time to every purpose under the heaven: A time to be born, and a time to die.'" He paused, cleared his throat, and continued.

Pray God, not that.

Father led in prayer, shorter than the previous evening, but no less heartfelt. By seven, they headed down the path to the Hathaways' cottage. A scream erupted from the surgery as they neared the dwelling, a cry of pain that stung Judith's flesh like black fly bites, as fatal as a snake's fangs.

Mary opened the door before they could knock. "Judith. Eli." Her face crumpled like bacon cooked too long in the pan. "Come in."

Piers filled the doorway to the surgery. "He's dead!" His bellow probably could be heard in the center of town. His face flushed so red that Judith feared he would burst the stitches on his forehead. "You said God called you to heal the injured seamen of Capernaum, but you couldn't save my brother."

Martin!

Sam stood in front of Piers, head dropped to his chest, hands hanging loosely by his side, not defending himself.

Stefan's voice interrupted Piers's tirade, murmuring something too low for Judith to understand the words.

"You're a worthless good-for-nothing." Piers wouldn't let it go. "No good at sea and not any better in the surgery. Go back to Connecticut. You can tend all the sprained ankles and broken fingernails you want." Piers stormed out the door. Stefan mumbled something that might have been an apology to Sam, then stumbled after his son.

Desolation closed down Sam's face, a look of failure and despair and hopelessness. He stared at Piers, who ran in the direction of his home.

Judith didn't know for which man she felt more compassion.

∞

"You must eat." Mama brought Sam a slab of bread and butter with molasses.

Sam waved her away. Neither eating nor sleeping mattered. The only thing of consequence was his failure to save Martin's life.

"It's been two days. You help no one by acting this way."

Sam sighed and bit into the bread. When the molasses hit his tongue, his stomach growled with hunger. Mama smiled with satisfaction. "I will cook you some eggs." She turned around at the door, shaking a finger at him as if he were still a small child. "Fifteen minutes. That should give you sufficient time to shave."

Sam ran a hand over his chin, two days' bristle scratching his skin. He climbed the stairs to his bedroom, lathered his face, and took a razor to the growth. The cold water in his basin seemed fitting for what amounted to an act of penance.

Exactly a quarter of an hour later, he walked into the kitchen. Mama set a platter of eggs, bacon, and toasted bread in front of him. He drank deeply of fresh milk and cleaned the plate.

"Good." She heaped more bread on his plate. "Today Judith and I are bringing a meal to Martin's widow. I want you to join us."

Sam started at her suggestion. He had failed in spite of his best efforts. At least he could apologize to the grieving woman and offer what comfort he could.

"You should have adequate time to finish your ablutions and perhaps rest while we prepare the meal. Now go, before Judith sees you in your present state."

Sam looked at himself. In spite of his newly shaven chin, he was still a mess, dressed in the same blood-spattered shirt he had worn while operating on Martin. He stank like an animal. Even he could smell it. "I will."

In his room, he stripped down to the skin. He scrubbed every pore and tore a comb through his hair until he felt he was pulling himself apart. "God, forgive me for my failure," he prayed. "And let the Vanderkamps forgive me as well." His bed, unslept in for three nights, beckoned to him. He dropped his head on the pillow. *Just for a minute,* he thought.

The sun was high in the sky when he awoke, and the aroma of stewed chicken wafted up the stairs. Mama had retrieved his dirty clothes and laid out a newly pressed shirt and trousers. He donned the clean outfit eagerly, as if the fresh air and soap could wash away the stain of his failure. As he dressed, he heard the murmur of conversation from downstairs. *Judith.* He hurried, keen to bask in her calm warmth.

His steps slowed as he reached the bottom of the stairs. What if Judith's regard for him had dropped, now that he had let Martin die? He couldn't endure it if she snubbed him or showed even a hint of the contempt Piers had expressed.

"Sam!" Judith looked up from the table where she was peeling potatoes. A smile split her face, joy mixed with relief. "I am glad to see you up and about."

He relaxed. "I feel much refreshed." He nodded to his mother in a gesture of silent thanks.

Judith dropped the potatoes in boiling water. "I cannot express my amazement at your efforts with Martin. You truly are a gifted surgeon."

He looked into her eyes, as blue as the summer sky. She meant what she said. He fumbled for something to say in return.

"And you were an invaluable assistant. I could use your help more often, if your father will agree."

Judith colored, and he knew his suggestion had pleased her. "I would be honored to attend your patients, if you think my service would be of value." Light sparkled in the depths of her eyes.

"I would appreciate your presence any time you are free." Sam hoped she knew he meant more than his surgery.

Judith broke eye contact and threw the peelings into a bowl for further use. "Your mother kindly agreed to help me cook for Martin's family. I would not trust myself to prepare a meal on my own."

Judith often said things like that. True, her biscuits at the oyster festival had been almost inedible. Since then, she had learned so much so quickly; he didn't know why she fussed so. Her cooking would provide nourishment for a family, and she offered so much more. If only he could help her understand. She was so unlike himself, who had failed at the one thing he claimed to do well.

After the potatoes cooked, Mama helped them pack the chicken, potatoes, bread, and boiled cider pie into a picnic basket. She added a few crocks of fresh milk and butter. "You two go on." She shooed them out of the house. "I will stay behind to clean up."

Instead of taking the path to town, Judith headed across the meadow behind the cottage. They followed a path in the grass marked by frequent passage, probably worn by Piers on his daily trips to the lighthouse. Such a small thing, but nonetheless Sam felt a pang of jealousy at the familiarity it suggested. Piers was the better man for Judith; Sam should not accompany her on this visit. He should leave the way clear for the man her father had chosen.

"Sara—that's Martin's widow—lives by the sea. Next door to the Vanderkamp home." Judith's voice interrupted his thoughts.

Sam searched for a reasonable response. "Are there children?"

Judith glanced up at him. "A girl of three or four. And Sara is. . ." Her face grew pink.

"Ah." The timing of Martin's death couldn't be worse, if his widow carried his child. At least Sam had known his father before his death. Guilt struck him again. *Heavenly Father, forgive me.*

"Sam." Judith paused and looked up at him, eyes full of concern and faith. "You did all you could. Life and death are in God's hands." She glanced to the side, as if unsure how to continue. Then she looked back, her face a mask of determination. "You must have lost patients during the war. Martin cannot be the first man you have seen die."

Sam shook his head. "You expect death in battle. I thought, when God called me here, that it would be different. I didn't expect to keep everyone alive. Perhaps I expected that I would be able to heal those who were young and strong, with so much life ahead of them."

"No one expects that of you. Least of all God." She gestured behind them. "Take the lighthouse for example. It has saved many lives since it was built. Men see the rocks and steer clear of them." Judith began walking again, taking care to keep a distance from the rocks. "But not all. At least one boat has come ashore on the rocks since it was built. Father went through similar doubts."

Eli doubted himself? Sam had a hard time imagining the older man ever questioning his calling as lighthouse keeper.

Sam breathed in the air, as if the salt could purge his head of unwanted worries. "This must be the place." He quickened his pace to reach the cottage perched at the edge of a dock. He sent up a wordless prayer and stepped forward to knock on the door.

∽

Piers opened the door. Judith sucked in her breath, distressed at his disheveled state. He could have modeled for Job sitting in the ashes.

Piers looked Sam up and down, frowned, and then noticed Judith. A small spark of life gleamed in his eyes.

"Who is it, Piers?" A woman's voice called from the back of the room.

"Judith. And the doctor."

"Bring them inside. No need to let all the flies in."

"Go ahead in. I was just leaving." Piers motioned them in and then left.

Sara Vanderkamp sat by the fireplace, body awkward with child; her face calm in spite of her unkempt hair and dirty apron. Young Abigail played at her feet, turning her corncob dolly over and over. Always petite, Sara seemed to have shrunk to an even smaller size, back to a girl or perhaps a wizened wise woman. When she saw the basket in Judith's arms, she struggled to rise.

"Food! I must make some tea for you to drink."

"No, no, you mustn't trouble yourself." Judith placed the basket on the table. "Mary Hathaway helped me prepare you something to eat. Enough to get you through a few days." She moved to the kitchen area to put away the foodstuffs.

"Dear Judith, sit down. I would like to visit with you. We'll take care of the food later." Sara pointed to the seat across from her. "And Dr. Hathaway. I haven't had an opportunity to welcome you back to the island."

"Mrs. Vanderkamp—I can't tell you how sorry I am about your husband's death. He asked me to tell you—that he loved you."

Sara dabbed at her eyes. "Thank you for telling me that."

"I didn't know Martin well, but he seemed to be a fine man. A loss to the community."

They spoke of the injuries and what had happened. Abigail swung her dolly in larger and larger circles, agitated by the conversation. Judith called her to a corner to play.

"What is your dolly's name?" Judith studied the scrap of cloth wrapped around a corncob.

"Martin."

"Oh?" Judith fought to keep her voice steady. "I thought it was a *girl* dolly."

"It used to be. But then I added a hat."

Judith noticed a knitted scrap sitting on top of the cob. "I missed that."

"I named him after my papa. He's dead."

"Yes, I know. You must be feeling sad."

"Oh, I'm not sad. But Martin, he feels bad. He says he's hurting. See?" She showed Judith a place in the cob where a nail had been driven into the side. "If someone doesn't fix him soon, he'll die, too."

Oh, Abigail. Judith's heart went out to the little girl.

"Do you think Dr. Hathaway can fix my dolly?"

Judith glanced at Sam, deep in conversation with Sara. Would he think her request foolish, beneath his dignity? Before she could respond, Abigail jumped up and leaned against Sam's knee.

"Doctor?" Abigail held her dolly up for his inspection. "My dolly is hurt. Can you help him?"

Judith needn't have worried. Sam lifted the girl onto his lap and took the corncob in his large hands. "Let me look." He found the offending nail hole. "We'd better stitch her up. Do you have a dressing I can use?"

"The dolly is a *boy*. Why does everybody think he's a girl?" She rummaged in her mother's rag box beside her on a table and removed a square of red cloth. "Can he use this, Mama? Please?"

"A boy, huh?" Sam studied the cob. "Now I see." Sam turned to Sara. "Do you mind? I only need this much." He held his fingers about a quarter of an inch apart. "And if you have scissors and needle and thread—"

Moments later, Sam applied a tiny square across the hole in the doll and pushed the needle in and out of the cob's harsh surface. "This is the first time I've ever performed surgery on a doll. You'll have to forgive me if I mess up."

"He's all better!" Abigail squealed and showed the doll to her mother. "Look, Mama, Martin is all better!"

"There is nothing to forgive." Sara looked at Sam with meaning. "You did a wonderful job."

Judith only hoped Sam would believe it.

∞

"That was so sweet. The way you fixed Abigail's dolly."

"What?" Judith's word brought Sam out of his reverie. "Oh. The dolly. She named him Martin, did she?" He shook his head. "I only wish I could have repaired her father so easily."

"Oh, Sam." Judith sighed. "Can't you see how grateful they were that you were there with Martin at the end?" She dawdled and stared out at sea, at the boats returning to dock after a day's fishing.

The white sails made a pretty sight against the sky, pretty until he had to sail on one, that is.

"I'm so thankful your mother helped me fix the lunch. They might have refused to eat it if they thought I had prepared it by myself."

"Why do you worry so about that? People know your good qualities. There is so much I admire about you. The way you noticed Abigail's distress and helped her, for instance. You should not worry about your housekeeping."

Judith's mouth straightened into a thin line. "So you don't think I can cook, either."

"That's not what I meant at all!" Sam wanted to tear at his hair. "I have enjoyed everything you have prepared with Mama. I only meant—" A glance at her sour face told him his explanation only made matters worse. "I will enjoy anything you choose to serve to me."

"Even if it's underdone or burnt?" A small smile curved Judith's lips.

"I'm sure that won't happen." *And if it does, I'll eat every bite and pretend I don't notice.*

Chapter 10

September 23, 1815

"J ust one more push, and it will be over." Sam reassured the Widow Vanderkamp.

The local midwife was attending another birth, and she had recommended Sara call Sam in. Sara had been in labor throughout the previous day and the long night. For a time, he had feared he might need to use forceps or even perform the dangerous caesarean section. At last Mrs. Vanderkamp had entered the final stages of labor.

"Take a deep breath. Gather your strength." Judith wiped a wet cloth across Sara's damp forehead. She had insisted on accompanying him when the call came to attend the birth. He hesitated to agree because, to the best of his knowledge, Judith had never assisted in childbirth before. She had proved an excellent assistant.

A scream tore from Sara's throat. Her womb heaved. Out slid first a head, then chest, then. . .

"It's a boy!" Sam called. At times like these, he shared some of the euphoria that fell on new mothers and fathers. This infant was full-sized and healthy. As soon as Sam's hands touched his skin, the baby bawled.

"Let me see him."

Sam cut and tied the cord, wrapped the baby in a flannel cloth, and handed him to his mother.

She patted his head, uncurled his tiny fists, and counted his fingers. "Martin," she whispered. "Thank You, God."

A pale-faced Abigail ran into the room and stopped. "Mama!"

"I'm fine, Abby. Come and see your brother." Sara beckoned her daughter.

Abigail approached and peered over the edges of the flannel. She wrinkled her face. "He's *dirty*."

Judith laughed. "Then let's clean him up, shall we?" She gestured to Sara. "May I?"

Sara kissed the baby's head, then handed him into Judith's waiting arms.

"I have warm water waiting, just as you requested," Judith told Sam. "I know what to do."

Sam used the break to examine Sara and make sure nothing further needed to be done. He patted her hand. "A good night's work." He smiled at her. "You have a fine, healthy boy."

A few minutes later, Judith returned baby Martin to his mother. Sam saw the family group, mother and children, and felt anew the loss of the fisherman. The people of Capernaum would care for the family. They would not go hungry. But no one could take a father's place.

He looked at Judith, who hung back now that their job was done. He imagined her with children clinging to her skirts, children with her soft blue eyes and his dark hair. *O Lord, let it be. Some day.*

Someone knocked at the door, and Stefan stuck his head through the open door. "Any news?"

"Come and see your grandson!" Sara called.

Stefan entered, followed by his wife. "I can only tarry a few minutes. The fish were practically jumping out of the water yesterday. We want to catch as many as possible before the storm hits."

Piers arrived a few minutes later. He glanced at Sam as if questioning his presence.

"I'd best be going." Sam decided to make his departure. "My work here is done."

"Just a moment. Father will be expecting me." Judith gathered her shawl around her shoulders and walked with him out the door. She peered over the rocks at the eastern sky, where the sun began to rise. A light breeze caught her hair, somewhat undone after the night's efforts. It made no difference. She was as lovely as ever.

"I don't like the looks of that sun."

Dawn looked more beautiful than ever that morning. A golden haze gave it a halo effect. Sam knew some people considered it the sign of a coming storm.

"Do you really think it will rain?"

"Didn't you hear Stefan say the fish were jumping out of the water?" She mentioned another sign of a storm. "And the cow seemed restless when I tried to milk her yesterday morn."

Sam looked at the maple tree, a red leaf sparkling here and there among the branches. "And the leaves are turned upside down. It will rain today." He suppressed the shudder that the thought of a bad storm always created in him. The earth needed moisture. He could not fear rain every time it fell.

"What a wondrous event." Judith returned to the topic of their night's work. "I know she was hoping for a boy. How good God is."

If God is good, then why did He let Martin die? Sam kept the question to himself. Some questions were unanswerable, except to believe that God was good and would work everything together to create something good.

To the east, fishermen went to sea. Two figures climbed into a boat at the end of the Vanderkamps' dock. Another day of work lay ahead. Sam hoped no patients would need his attention for a few hours so that he could get some rest.

"Join us for breakfast," Judith invited Sam as they approached the lighthouse. "If you meant what you said about enjoying everything I cook."

"How can I refuse an offer like that?" Sam smiled. "But what about your father?"

Judith tossed her head. "He is foolishly protective. If he could have seen you last night. . .I have never seen a more noble act."

Sam shook his head. "He only wants what is best for you." He sighed. "And I'm not it."

"He doesn't *know* you. And as long as you refuse my invitations to the lighthouse, he never will know more of you than he sees at Sunday meeting."

"Very well. This once." He glanced up at the lantern room, where first one, then two, then all ten lamps went out. "We'd best hurry. How can I help?"

"Our cow will need milking. I'll fix porridge while you take care of Daisy."

Sam entered the barn. Even in the semi-darkness, the cow's eyes gleamed white, open wide in obvious distress. Sam reached for the milk pail and opened the stall door. "Easy, girl."

Daisy bumped against him, as if anxious to leave the safety of the barn. She mooed.

"Wow, girl. Let me help you." He sat down on a stool and worked her teats, enjoying the rhythm of the milk squirting into the pail. She stood still long enough for him to empty her full udder, then cried again for release. He rubbed her ears. "I'll tell Judith that you are anxious for the meadow today."

Eli came down the stairs when Sam reentered, carrying the milk pail.

"Doctor. What are *you* doing here?"

"I've been milking the cow."

Before Eli could question Sam further, Judith placed a pot of porridge on the table. She poured tea into their mugs. "Leave the pail by the back door, and I'll take care of it after breakfast."

Sam carried the pail to the back as Judith requested. The lighthouse timbers moaned. The wind must have picked up. Once again, he felt and dismissed his unease at the approaching storm. From the kitchen, he heard father and daughter talking.

"What is *he* doing here?" Eli sounded upset.

"I'll explain over breakfast. The food is getting cold."

Sam took a deep breath and returned to the main room.

Judith smiled and seated herself at the table. "Father, do give thanks for the food."

Eli acquiesced without further grumbling. "Today You are commanding and raising stormy winds. You are lifting up the waves. We thank You again for this lighthouse. We pray that You will use it to protect the men of Capernaum. In the name of Jesus Christ our Lord, amen."

Even the lighthouse keeper seemed a little uncertain about the approaching storm. Sam took a bowl of porridge. *Delicious.* Judith had added a splash of maple syrup. She must have remembered his preference for the sweetening. He added cream and stirred it in, smiling at Judith to let her know his appreciation for the meal.

"Now, Doctor, if you will be so kind as to explain why you kept my daughter out all night." Eli had waited, as Judith had asked, and he would not stomach any further evasions.

"Sara—" Judith began.

"I asked the doctor." Eli's stony blue eyes demanded an answer.

"Judith was kind enough to offer to accompany me when Mrs. Vanderkamp's time came."

"I sent you a message, Father, explaining where I was."

"But all day and night? Such things do not ordinarily take so long."

"Sometimes they do. Mrs. Vanderkamp delivered a healthy boy shortly before dawn." Sam allowed himself to smile. Nothing felt better than seeing a healthy child born into the world.

"I don't understand why she asked for your presence at all," Eli grumbled. "Mrs. Wembly has served as the midwife for all the women of Capernaum for years."

"Father." Judith rapped her fork against the table. "Mrs. Wembly was attending another birth. She knew that Sara had a difficult time with Abigail; she believed she would benefit from a *doctor's* expertise. And she did." Judith turned those brilliant blue eyes on Sam. "Young Martin is as fine a lad as I've ever seen."

"Praise be to God." Eli lifted his eyes to heaven.

"Judith was a great help to Mrs. Vanderkamp, sir." Sam wanted to support Judith, to let her know—and her father—how he valued her assistance. "She calmed Mrs. Vanderkamp's fear and made the birthing easier. She has a real gift for helping the sick." He paused, wondering whether to add the last bit. "Perhaps it is even her calling, sir, if I may say so."

"Her calling is to take care of her family and home." Eli didn't seem to appreciate Sam's comments. "Which for now is with me."

But one look at Judith's shining eyes told Sam how much she appreciated the compliment. That was all he needed to know.

∽

"Don't dawdle, gal!" Father's voice called Judith from the lantern room.

Judith pushed herself out of the reverie that had halted her steps. Halfway up the stairs, she had paused by the window, watching Sam's progress home. He clapped his hat to his head and bent over, fighting the wind. Tree leaves danced in the wind, their branches swaying in an eerie country dance. She turned away from the drama unfolding before her and hurried up the stairs. "It looks like we're in for a bad storm."

Eli grunted. "Let's clean the lamps and relight them. We'll need to keep them going today."

As soon as Judith polished one lamp and reflector, Father relit the wick. They sped through the process.

"Father, you must rest. You've been up all night."

"As have you." His eyes leveled on hers. "We will discuss that further, after this storm has passed." His stern expression relaxed. "Now go. Rest, gal. I will keep the first watch. Perhaps Piers will return. He will know we must keep the lamps burning."

Judith knew she could not convince her father otherwise. She kissed his cheek and trotted down the stairs. From the landing, she saw a line of animals—a couple of dogs, a fox, even a rabbit—crossing the meadow away from the water.

A few minutes later, Judith settled in her bed to rest. But how could she? The exciting events of the previous night replayed in her memory. She had never been present at a birthing before. When Sara held baby Martin in her arms, Judith could tell that all the pain and work to bring him into the world disappeared from her mind. Someday, God willing, that would be her, holding her own baby. Would he have downy blond hair like Piers, or dark curls like Sam? Her face burned. Should an unmarried woman entertain such thoughts?

Judith had drifted into a light sleep when a tremor awakened her. She sat bolt upright in bed. The house moaned and groaned, unhappy with the stress the wind placed upon it. She couldn't return to sleep and was pulling on her day dress when she heard a knock.

Sam stood at the door. Rain slashed against the meadow, flattening the grass. "I came to take you to the church with us. You and Eli."

The church bell tolled from the center of town, a community-wide emergency call.

"Father is in the lantern room. He wants to keep the lamps burning through the storm."

"Yes, we saw the lights. But it will not be safe here."

"He will not leave." Judith shook her head. "It is his responsibility to make sure no sailors come aground on the rocks."

"We have seen fishing boats coming in for the last hour. No one is fool enough to stay out in this storm."

"I doubt he will agree." Judith gestured helplessly.

"May I?" Without waiting for an answer, Sam bounded up the steps two at a time. Judith followed at a moderate rate.

"You must leave, sir." Sam stood in the middle of the lantern room.

"Nonsense. I need to keep the lamps burning. Now be gone with you. I have work to do."

"Sir. This is no ordinary storm. Look at the sea." Sam moved to the window, pointing to the east. Judith joined him.

What she saw made her draw back. Waves higher than a man's head crashed upon the rocks, water spraying as high as the sides of the lighthouse. A tree bent over and snapped, its branches falling to the ground. When the wave receded, water had crept halfway from the high-tide mark to the lighthouse door.

"The waves sprayed on us as we crossed the meadow, sir. It will only get worse."

Eli shook his head. "You may be afraid of a little water, Doctor. I am not. I will remain."

Sam paled. "There is such a thing as unreasonable fear, and then there is stubborn pride. You are endangering not only yourself but your daughter." He turned to Judith. "Will you at least listen to reason?"

Judith looked between the two men, both of them so near and dear to her. Father already looked exhausted, and she knew he would not leave. The lighthouse was a part of him, and as long as it stood, he would not abandon it. Neither could she.

"I. . .cannot." With her eyes, she begged Sam to understand. *He's my father. I cannot abandon him.*

Sam looked at Eli, then at Judith. "I cannot make you go against your will. If you change your mind, people are gathering at the church, since it is the high point of the island." He nodded in farewell. "I will pray for you."

The pounding rain enveloped Sam's figure within seconds. Judith stared into the storm, wishing they could have gone with him.

∞

An hour later, Judith watched the windows bend as the wind battered them and cresting waves threw water against them. The roof groaned and creaked and shuddered every few seconds.

Father refilled the lamps with whale oil and then joined her by the east-facing window. He placed a hand on her shoulder. "Judith."

She turned to face him. Father *never* called her by her given name. Something serious was bothering him.

"What is it?"

"The Almighty God is lifting up the waves higher than usual today." He managed a half-smile. "It makes me think on eternity."

As he spoke, another wave crest rattled the room. A lamp went out, and he relit it. Then he spoke again. "Years ago, I invited Jesus Christ to be both my Savior and my Lord. I do not fear what will happen to me. But you, my dearest daughter. What say you?"

Judith studied her reflection in the mirror, warped into a foreign object. "You know I went forward in meeting when I was ten."

"I know. But are you *sure*?"

Judith considered the question. She had believed in the God who commanded wind and wave since before she could talk. Later, when she realized that she was a sinner who needed a Savior, she had asked the Lord of the universe, who came to the earth as a baby, to forgive her. She had never doubted her salvation.

But in the last few months, she had felt the breath of death while tending Martin and Sara. Was that only last night? It felt like a lifetime ago, in this day of cloud and rain and never-ending gray sky. If God called her home today, was she ready? Another spray hit the window, and she flinched as if the moment was upon her. The familiar words from John 3:16 came to mind and reassured her. *"Whosoever believeth in him should not perish, but have everlasting life."*

She felt for her father's hand and squeezed it. "Yes, I am sure."

"Thank God." His face relaxed, and a yawn escaped his mouth.

Judith felt badly, once again thinking of his long night's work and constant efforts of the morning. "I will prepare us some lunch. Then you must rest. I will keep the lamps burning." She kissed his cheek and went down the stairs. This time at the landing, she couldn't see out the rain-coated glass.

She considered cooking something hot but decided against it. Hot tea with ham sandwiches would have to suffice. The boards creaked and groaned as she worked. *Lord, keep us safe. Keep the lamps burning. Bring the men home safely from the sea. Give Father strength; keep him alert as he works night and day.*

Judith called up the stairs but realized Father could never hear her voice over the howls of the wind. She put the sandwiches and tea on a tray and ascended the stairs. The steps trembled beneath her feet, and she fought for balance. At the point she reached the landing, a fierce blow pummeled the tower.

Crack! A new sound thundered down the stairs, followed by her father's scream.

Chapter 11

Water hit Judith's face before she reached the top step. The familiar lantern room had disappeared. Rain poured in through a gaping space in the roof. Planks and shattered glass lay scattered across the floor. Wind buzzed as if a swarm of a million bees drove the water from sea to land. On the opposite side, part of the roof remained intact and four of the lamps continued burning.

Judith spotted her father lying still beneath a section of the broken roof. With a cry, she darted forward.

"Don't come any closer. Glass. . .everywhere."

Judith ignored his command. Sturdy shoes protected her feet. A thousand shards of glass, some no bigger than a needle, others as sharp and wide as a meat cleaver, coated the floor. She could not kneel to help him without cutting herself. She could not help Father if she injured herself. She pulled on heavy gloves and grabbed a broom, then swept rain and glass aside to make a space large enough to take a place beside her father.

"Are you injured?" Judith could not see anything below her father's waist. "Can you move?" Removing the gloves, she ran her hands over his face. The flying glass had nicked him here and there, but she didn't notice any bad cuts.

Father shook his head. "The roof is pinning my legs down. I can't get out. And I think my arm may be broken. I can't move my fingers."

"Let me help." Judith tried to heave the plank nearest to his waist, but she could no more move it than she could carry the world on her shoulders like Atlas. Too many other boards lay on top. She studied the configuration, seeking the top piece. There it was, at an angle from one of the extinguished lamps to his feet. She began to shift it and cried when glass pricked her thumb.

"Be careful!"

"I will." She pulled the gloves back on and moved one plank, then another. When it fell to the floor beside Father, it knocked more debris loose onto her father's chest. If only Sam were here.

I can't do this by myself, not without risking further injury to Father. Almighty God, who is there to help me?

As in answer to her prayer, the wind took a breath, quieting enough to hear the church bells ringing. The people of Capernaum were gathering at the church. Sam was there with them. Her heart relaxed.

Did she dare leave Father alone while she went for help? What if more of the roof caved in, or the wind blew debris in? She gnawed on a knuckle. *Think, Judith.*

"I must go for help. But first let me try something." She nailed a tarp to the remaining roof beams in an effort to protect the remaining lanterns. That was all she could think of to do.

"Check the lamps."

Judith wanted to forget about the lighthouse, about his job, but she knew he would not rest if she ignored his plea. She added fresh oil to the wicks.

"I feel so helpless," Father said. "It's my job to protect *you.*"

Judith knelt beside him. "You have the hardest job of all. You must watch and wait. Pray for me as I go to town."

"My brave girl." Father smiled. "Thank you for giving me something to do."

Judith ran downstairs and tugged an oilskin over her dress, although she doubted it would offer much protection against this gale. Not that it mattered; her exposure in the lantern room had already left her drenched. She opened the door.

The once-familiar landscape had been transformed. The line of trees that offered a windbreak between the lighthouse and the Hathaway cottage had broken in half. All familiar landmarks had disappeared. In this weather, would she lose her bearings, wander onto the rocks rather than to the town center? Even in the entrance, the wind pushed and pulled at her.

God, help me. She took a single step away from the door.

Over the wind and rain, she heard the church bells. As long as the sound made itself heard, she could follow it. She looked back at the lighthouse. Four lamps burned bravely against the darkened sky. Forward to the bells; away from the light. She could find her way.

∞

" 'Be strong and of good courage; be not afraid, neither be thou dismayed; for the Lord thy God is with thee whithersoever thou goest.'"

Sam listened as Wilson, the singing master, quoted from Joshua. Several other people in the congregation had already shared verses speaking to faith in the Master of land and sea and about courage in the face of danger. God's challenge to Joshua was one of Sam's favorites, as well. He thought of it every time he performed an operation or entered a battlefield. If only the same assurance that steadied his hands would calm his heart now. This terrible storm felt as though the end of the world had come to the island. He looked at the satchel he had carried for Mama, wedged between his feet. Perhaps he should have brought his medical bag instead. *No point in worrying. It's too late to go back.*

"Next let us sing 'Wisdom.'"

Sam knew the hymn, based on the eighth chapter of Proverbs. His breath caught in his throat as they began the second verse. "God swathed about the swelling of Ocean's mighty flood." Could the God of storm and ocean "be delighted with creatures such as we," as Cowper stated? Was this great gale God's way of measuring men's worth, their trust in Him? If so, Sam feared he would be found lacking.

A scuffle broke out behind him. Children couldn't seem to contain their excitement. Little Abigail Vanderkamp squirmed in the seat next to her mother, who had traveled to the meeting house with her newborn. The little girl bent her head as if to hear the moaning of the boards better. Oh, to have the faith of a little child, who viewed the entire experience as a grand adventure. When else would they be dismissed from school in the middle of the day?

Sam counted the seamen and their families who filled the benches. He didn't know everyone in the village, and he saw some people he had not yet met. Piers and Stefan Vanderkamp sat with Sara and Abigail. For Judith's sake, Sam was pleased they had returned to safety from the ocean.

Judith. The Morrisons were among the very few people *not* at the meeting house. She wouldn't leave the lighthouse as long as her father insisted on staying. Sam prayed for her safety.

"Let us pray." Reverend Snodgrass took over from the singing master. He petitioned God to give them a measure of the wisdom present at the creation of the world. He thanked God for the safety of those who made it to the meeting house. He named a vessel still at sea, a family Sam didn't know. Last of all, he prayed for the lighthouse, for Eli and his work.

A chorus of amens rolled across the congregation. Wembly stood to his feet. "The gale is not decreasing. I fear that if it continues, the flood waters will reach even this meeting house."

Worried murmurs erupted from the crowd.

"I propose that we move to the mainland while we still can."

"But. . .the waves," some murmured.

Sam grew seasick thinking of such a journey. Yet the storekeeper had a valid point.

"I am not a sailor," Wembly added, "but I believe the island may provide a small buffer from the winds."

A few fishermen around Sam nodded.

Lauder stood to his feet. "I agree. The trip from here across will be far safer than going out into the ocean. And I agree with Mr. Wembly. Travel to the mainland will be safer than trying to find a high point on this island."

More folk nodded. Others sat in stunned silence. Piers stood to his feet. "I, for one, am willing to take the risk. We have room in the *Sea Maiden* for our family and six more. Who will come with us?"

"I would accept your offer, but I must stay until everyone has left. Perhaps— would you escort my family?" As usual, Snodgrass took the lead. His words encouraged others to speak out. Soon the congregation broke into groups assigned to different boats.

"Sam?" Mama came up to him. "I have taken a seat in Mr. Lauder's boat. You?"

Sam gritted his teeth. He had looked at the lighthouse and seen the diminished light. Mama would not like his decision. "We have not heard from the Morrisons since early this morning. And several of the lamps have gone out. I must check on Judith's safety before I can leave."

"You will not convince Eli to leave." Snodgrass must have overheard his statement. "His work is more important today than ever."

"But Judith—" Sam was determined he would not depart without one final attempt to make her listen to reason. "She should come with us. I must try again."

Snodgrass nodded his head. "Lauder has agreed to wait until everyone has left the island and to take me on the last trip. I will go with you and add my pleas to yours." He laid his hand on Sam's shoulder. "But I do not expect her to come. She will want to stay as long as Eli remains on duty."

The rain had slackened slightly as they walked through the town. They made slow progress, slogging through mud and debris. Each plop of Sam's boots taunted him, urging him to speed while sucking him into the earth. This once, he wished the lighthouse wasn't so isolated on the point. They could not make the trip quickly. By common consent, the men didn't speak as they walked. They saved their breath for the task at hand.

As the wind rose and fell, Sam sought familiar landmarks. Water crept up the steps of the cottages lined along the docks. In the distance, his home formed a dark mound. At times, the only guidance came from the lighthouse, where just four lamps appeared to burn. Sam struggled to put his finger on what troubled him, beyond the obvious loss of lanterns. The light burned continuously, that was it; it wasn't blinking on and off in its normal rhythm that differentiated the Rocky Point Lighthouse from others along the coast. Something had happened in the lantern room or to Eli.

Sam didn't waste energy explaining his concern to the pastor, but he picked up speed. Snodgrass fell behind by a step. Sam didn't care. He wanted to discover the fate of those left behind. He struggled up a small incline, the last before the pastures leading to his cottage.

A few short yards away a figure in an oilskin coat struggled through the mire. *Judith.*

∞

Judith felt she could not walk much farther. She had already fallen down twice. The wet grass tugged at her skirts and the mud sucked off her shoes, so that rocks and branches had bruised and torn at her feet. Only a determination to reach town, to get help for her father, kept her going.

At least the wind had slackened a little. She no longer had to fight so hard to avoid being pushed back toward the lighthouse. With the lighter rain, she had made out the Hathaway cottage as she passed it. Even as she moved away from the shore, the roar of waves rending rocks filled her ears.

Wait. Judith halted as she realized she had not heard the church bells for a solid quarter of an hour. Had the meeting house been destroyed? Had the people left the island, assuming Eli would stay with the lighthouse? She wanted to weep. She could not bear the thought of finding no one to help free her father and of facing this terrible gale on their own.

Oh, heavenly Father, help me. Help us. She debated the wisdom of continuing into town. What if it were deserted? How far did she have left to walk? She cupped her hands around her eyes in a vain effort to protect them from the rain's assault and peered into the distance.

Two men appeared at the edge of the field, the taller one running toward her. *Sam.* She gathered the dregs of her strength and rushed into his arms.

"I'm glad I found you here." Sam spoke first. "You must come with us. John Lauder has saved us a space in his boat."

Judith shook her head. "Father is trapped beneath the roof. The wind blew it in. I need your help."

Reverend Snodgrass caught up with them while they spoke.

"Eli is hurt?"

"We think his arm is broken. I couldn't move the boards to check." Judith wanted to scream, but the wind did it for her. "I fear the wind will blow down more of the roof. Hurry!" She headed back in the direction of the lighthouse, her path eased by the arrival of help. She didn't wait for an answer. She knew they would follow. God had heard her prayer.

Sam passed her and arrived at the lighthouse first. Snodgrass helped her walk the last few steps, or perhaps she was helping him; together they made the trek. Sam had already disappeared up the stairs when they pushed at the door. The wind caught the door and threw it against the wall.

"Your feet. My dear Miss Morrison—"The pastor looked horrified as he saw their condition, bloodied after she had lost her shoes to the mud.

"I will be fine. Go up to the lantern room." Grateful for the shelter of the lighthouse, Judith shook some of the excess water from her head and followed behind him.

"I might have known she'd bring you." Father's voice sounded weaker than it had when she had left. She shot a stern look at him, and he added more graciously, "Thank you for coming."

"I met them on the way, Father." Judith pushed her way past the tarp. God had been with them; as the winds had lessened, the tarp had remained in place. No further damage had happened to the roof. *Thank You, God.*

Sam paced the floor, studying the placement of the planks.

"Let me see." Reverend Snodgrass pushed beneath the tarp. "Before God called me to the ministry, I worked as a carpenter. I have some experience with stacking wood." He studied the mess the wind had made of the roof. "We should start here." He pointed to one of the boards across Eli's feet. Sam found the other end and eased it out of its place in the stack.

Judith tried to help but decided she made things worse. She found a place to stand in the far corner of the room. No one had refilled the lamps for hours. Of course not. Father could not, and she had been absent. She climbed down the stairs for more oil and heated water for tea. The men needed something warm after the clinging cold of the rain and waves, if she could convince them to drink a cup. Then perhaps they could all leave. If the fishermen had returned to town and now sailed to the mainland, the lighthouse was not needed. She prayed that everyone was safe.

When she returned to the lantern room, they had succeeded in freeing Father from the wreckage. Sam bent next to him, moving his sure hands over Father's arms and legs. He cupped his ear to his chest. "Your lungs and ribs escaped damage." Judith could hear the relief in his voice. "But your arm is broken." He grabbed a cleaning cloth and fixed a sling for Eli's arm. "You must leave with the boats, while you still can."

"I can still walk, can't I?" Father stood to his feet. "I told you before. I won't leave. I have to keep the lamps burning. Reverend, didn't you say there is still a boat at sea?"

Judith's heart burned. Father would never agree to leave as long as men remained in danger.

"Eli, you must leave while there is still opportunity." The pastor added his pleas. "No one anticipated a storm like this when the lighthouse was built."

A mulish look appeared on Father's face, and Judith hastened to intervene. "I brought tea. And sandwiches I made earlier." She used a mother's voice, the one she heard Sara use with Abigail, and even Mary with Sam on occasion. "We can think more clearly after we have some refreshment."

Sam swallowed his sandwich whole—the three sandwiches she had made for Father allowed for one for each man—and gulped the tea. She refilled his cup and handed it to him, silently insisting that he drink it before he restarted his argument. Judith took her time, chewing each bite as if it might be the last she would eat that day. It probably would be.

As soon as she swallowed the last of her tea, Sam burst into speech. "Judith, you at least must come with us to the mainland." He gestured at the tarp. "It is only a matter of time before the rest of the roof goes. Then the lamps cannot burn at all, and you will have placed yourself in danger for nothing."

As if in answer, the wind picked up and threw waves against the outer wall.

"If we tarry much longer, Lauder may have to leave without any of us. We do not have time for this argument. Judith, you are coming with us." Sam made it a statement, not a question.

She glanced at the shadows that danced against the tarp and prayed for wisdom. "Father should go. I must stay."

Chapter 12

"Judith." Her name came from three sides. None of the men agreed with her decision.

"Where is Piers? He can help me with the lamps." Father wouldn't budge. "He was the first to offer to take people to the mainland," the pastor explained. "The Vanderkamps have long since left."

"Then I will stay. Eli and Judith can go in Lauder's boat." The words sounded as though they came from the depths of Sam's soul. "I don't know much about lighthouses, but I do know how to light a lamp."

"Stop it. All of you. You are wasting precious time." Judith prayed they would listen to reason. "Father, you must get to the mainland. Sam, you must go with him and see that his arm is set correctly." She refused to give in to fear. "Besides, Sam, you don't know enough about the lighthouse. I do. The best thing you can do to help me is to make Father get to the boat. Carry him, if you must. That is your job." She lifted her chin. "Mine is here."

Sam looked at her a long moment, his uncertainty clear.

"The Lord will be with us both. We don't need to be afraid." Judith prayed he would understand.

"Amen." Reverend Snodgrass chimed in. "Let us say a brief prayer to the Almighty and move quickly." As good as his word, he prayed for Judith's safety and for that of any men left at sea.

Sam lingered for a second. "I will go, since you insist." He stared at Judith, as if seeking the words to unburden his heart. "I love you, Judith." He said it as if he couldn't help himself, heedless of her father's presence.

Judith's heart leapt with joy, instead of the fear that had governed the day.

"I have told you—" Father's voice gathered some of its usual strength.

Sam faced him, determination etched in his features. "I will not leave without speaking my mind." He turned back to Judith. "And once we have settled your father where he is safe, I will return. You should not face this alone."

"I—" Judith didn't know what to say. She didn't want to encourage him to cross the treacherous waters twice. This was not the time to exchange words of love. Or maybe it was. "Sam, you know I care for you. Do what you must. I will be praying for you."

Between them, Sam and the pastor lifted Father against his protests and carried him down the stairs. A few minutes later, she heard the wind slam the door shut.

All alone, she was left to face the worst storm in the history of Capernaum Island.

⟨∞⟩

Sam paused at the entrance, debating the best route to the boats. Progress across the field carrying a man would not come easily.

"The most direct route to the boat will be that way." Reverend Snodgrass pointed along the leeward shoreline extending from the point. "And perhaps we will find better footing among the rocks."

Sam stared at the forbidding rocks and straightened his shoulders. Funny how he would rather go at the head of the army into battle than walk near wind and wave.

"Don't be daft, Reverend. Sam won't let himself that near the water." Even in these circumstances, Eli taunted him. "He'll faint before he gets into a boat."

Perhaps Eli's jibe was God's gift to make Sam move. A desire to prove himself moved his limbs where sheer willpower faltered. "God will lift you up on eagle's wings, Eli, or we'll carry you with an eagle's talons if we must. Now I know this will hurt"—it had to, the way Eli's arm dangled at such an odd angle—"but we will get you there as quickly as possible." Without allowing himself to think about the rocks or the waves that crept ever closer, Sam matched his stride to that of Snodgrass and headed as the crow flies for the Lauders' boat.

The wind threatened to pick them up and toss them wherever it willed. Yet Sam could tell it had lessened ever so slightly. Otherwise, he suspected they would not keep their footing. Tree limbs obstructed the path he had walked with Judith only that morning in the joy of a new birth. They walked around obstacles and passed the Vanderkamp cottage. The Lauders' home lay straight ahead.

A brief respite allowed for speech. "Put me down!" Eli demanded. He glowered, a grimace contorted by pain. "We will move faster, and there's nothing wrong with my feet."

"If you try to return—"

"I won't." Eli took a step forward to prove it.

The wind tore any further words from them and hurried them across the small patch of sand to the waiting boat.

"Where's Judith?" Lauder shouted over the noise.

Sam pointed to the lighthouse, where four lamps continued to burn, now blinking in turn. "Eli is injured, and she chose to stay."

Lauder looked as though he would argue the point but decided against it. "Get in the boat. I dare not wait any longer."

"I should go back." Eli's obstinacy returned.

Not now. Sam gritted his teeth. "If you don't get in the boat, I'll pick you up and put you in myself."

"Come, Eli, be reasonable. We have already decided." Snodgrass intervened before another argument erupted. He extended a hand and assisted Eli into the boat. Mama and the Lauder family dashed from the cottage and took their seats.

Only Sam was left. He took a deep breath that filled his mouth with rain water, spit it out, and forced himself to lift a leg over the bow. He found himself on the middle seat beside Snodgrass, facing young Johnny and Lauder. Mama sat in the stern, next to Eli, her head bowed. Of all people, she knew Sam's heart best. She looked at him long enough to smile encouragement, then returned to her prayers.

Eli glowered at Sam before turning to face the lighthouse. They had both left their hearts in the lantern room. Twisting around, Sam could see Lauder's wife and daughter. The boat was well balanced.

The lee side of the island protected them from the worst of the storm, but wind and wave still rocked the boat. The sandwich Sam had eaten threatened to reappear. If not for his promise to Judith, he would rather face down the jaws of the storm on the island than to venture out in this small vessel.

"Take an oar, Doctor. We want to make quick progress while the wind has died somewhat," Lauder shouted into his ear.

I can do this. Sam sent the message to his quivering knees. What did they matter? He didn't need steady legs to sit and row. He grabbed an oar. When the next wave lifted the boat, they pushed off into the sea.

The men didn't speak, concentrating instead on developing a rhythm. No longer the puny teenager who could barely lift the paddle on his father's boat, Sam kept pace with the two fishermen. Snodgrass struggled.

"I will take both oars," Sam shouted into the reverend's ears. He nodded.

"I believe my time is better spent in prayer." Snodgrass clasped Sam's shoulder and huddled in a puddle at the bottom of the boat.

Could Sam have saved his father if he had been a man, and not still a child? If he had rowed harder and faster, could they have avoided the accident that landed them on the rocks? He knew what his mother would say. Life and death were in God's hands, and he shouldn't blame himself. But the question lingered. Today not one, but seven other lives depended on his skill. He prayed he was up to the task.

On the open water, waves as large as horses galloped toward them. Sam closed his eyes and rowed. What he couldn't see might not bother him. The boat fell lengthwise, as if tossed over a cliff. He opened his eyes in time to see them glide down from the crest of the wave. There was no way of escaping the motion of the boat. This gale surpassed the storm that had killed Sam's father, in the same way a bull dwarfed an ant. No one alive had seen its equal.

In the bow of the boat, Eli clutched his arm and grimaced. Mama cupped her hands to his ear, speaking encouragement, Sam was sure. He wished he could have set Eli's arm before they started, but they couldn't waste even a second. Sam knew the arm must be tormenting Eli.

The lighthouse lanterns broke through the torrent, illuminating their progress. The rocky point that had claimed the life of Sam's father lay behind them. But Judith remained on that spot of wind and destruction, with only the thinnest of protection. He longed to be with her.

Before that could be, he must complete the job Judith had given him to do: *Take care of my father. Make sure the man who thinks you have less courage than a fly is safe before you come back to me.*

Judith had offered Sam a test of both his courage and brotherly love. He looked once again at Eli. The man had closed his eyes and slumped on the seat. Unconscious?

He threw himself into the oars, willing them to move faster, farther. He could return to Judith only after he had done everything possible to save her father. Only then would he have proven himself worthy of her love.

∽

Judith strained to hear the footfalls of the departing men on the stairs, but wind made her deaf to any sound except its constant blow. She hoped Sam hadn't sensed her fear at remaining behind alone. Had she done the right thing in insisting he accompany Father to the mainland? *Yes,* she decided. Father never would have left unless forced.

The wind blew across the lamps, and their lights flickered. *I must not give in to fear. There is too much to do.*

If the lamps went out while the men were in sight, they might dash back to the lighthouse, afraid for her safety. She could not allow that to happen. What could she do?

The tarp remained in place, although wind battered it with every blast. What else could protect the lamps? *The windows.* If she covered them completely, the light would not be seen. Perhaps she could cross beams in an X pattern? Now that Sam and Reverend Snodgrass had sorted the wood from the fallen roof, she could pull pieces across the floor.

Moving enough planks to cover the windows took more energy than Judith thought she had. She grabbed a mug of cold tea and downed the liquid. Renewed by the sweet drink, she bent into her task. The area under the windows where Father kept the hammer and nails was bare. Wind had blown the tools around the room. She wasted more minutes while she poked and prodded through the wreckage. *Aha, there they are.* She tucked as many nails as she could find into the pocket of her apron and took hold of the hammer.

She lifted the first board into place. In the quarter of an hour it had taken her to assemble supplies, the gale had done further damage. She could no longer see the Hathaway cottage. She prayed that it remained intact. The trees that surrounded the base of the lighthouse lay battered, either broken in half or torn up by the roots and thrown across the forest. While she watched, an unseen hand lifted a tree out of the ground and crashed it into the base of the lighthouse. She felt the wood shudder all the way to the top.

O God, how shall I survive? And what about Sam and Father and the others, who had delayed their departure to check on her safety? The windows of the lighthouse looked out to sea. Even if rains and clouds lessened, she could not see the boat on its way to the mainland. *God of sea and sky, may they find calmer water on the lee side of the island. Bring them to land safely.*

Another gust of wind blew at her, carrying ocean water with it. She choked on the salty mist. Enough thinking. She hammered the first board into place, then the second. The next gust hit her shoulders with water, but the boards did block some of it.

Turning around, she saw that one of the lamps had gone out. She prayed that Sam and the others didn't notice. The flint remained dry and safe, thanks to Father's careful provisions. She lit the wick and returned to her task of boarding over the second window.

The view out that window was even more frightening than the view from the first. The familiar rocky shore disappeared under waves carried far higher than the high-tide mark. It crept within yards of the base of the lighthouse. She shivered. *I must trust God to protect me from the wind and waves.* If God brought her—and the seamen she sought to protect—safely through this gale, she would serve Him with every ounce of her being for the rest of her life.

The wind fought her. The board bowed back as she tried to hammer it, knocking her shoulder. Frowning, she knelt to hammer the lower end first. That gave her enough of a foundation to hammer the top in place. The second board went up more easily.

Wind pounded the boards. The room swayed in its path. But less rain fell in the room, the lamps continued burning, and Judith allowed herself to slump to the floor. She forced herself to think of something else.

Her thoughts jumped to Sam. He had said he *loved* her. He had shown it every day since his return. The way he ate every meal she attempted with Mary's help. His words of appreciation when she helped in the surgery. The confidence in her he showed by inviting her to assist with the birth of young Martin. Could that really have only been this morning, scant hours ago?

What had happened to Sara in this storm? A woman lying in from childbirth should not move. Well, she trusted Piers had taken care of her. Reverend Snodgrass had said the Vanderkamps were among the first to leave. Still, Judith prayed for the widow. If anything should happen to mother or child, multiplying the tragedy the family had already experienced this year. . .she prayed for their safety and for peace for the entire family.

Piers. As she held him up to God, she realized she prayed for him as she would for a brother. He was a good man, but he was not the man for her. Why couldn't Father see that? After the Fourth of July picnic, she had hoped for reconciliation between him and Sam, but Father's animosity continued. Why did the two men she cared for more than anyone else in the world have to dislike each other? She prayed again that they would work together against their common enemy, the storm. That Father would recognize Sam's courage as he did what was right in spite of his fear.

Judith could never marry Piers. She knew that now. Not when she held such strong feelings for Sam. If God brought them all through this storm, she would tell them both.

Chapter 13

D octor!"
Eli's frantic voice broke into Sam's reverie. So the man had come to consciousness. Good. "What is it?" He could not leave the oars to check.

"The lighthouse. One of the lamps has gone out."

Judith. Fear squeezed Sam's heart. "Only one?"

"Three are still burning." Eli managed a smile. "And she has returned them to their on-and-off status so that boats can tell which lighthouse is signaling." His smile faded. "But I worry for her safety."

As do I.

"I should never have left." The words tore from the older man's throat. "What kind of man am I, to leave my daughter in such danger?"

"She didn't give either one of us a choice."

"But I should..."

Sam didn't answer for a moment. How could he? The same sense of having failed Judith assailed him with every stroke of the oar. He had abandoned the woman he loved to the storm.

"You stubborn old fool." His frustration spilled over at Eli. "She *made* us leave, or don't you remember? She loves you. Your safety, and that of any men still at sea, matters to her more than anything else."

Eli grunted, shifted in his seat, and grabbed his arm. He needed more care than the impromptu sling Sam had fixed. The sooner they reached shore, the better.

Sam's strokes had slowed down as he exchanged words with Eli. He put all his strength into the oars. As they crested the next wave, followed by the precipitous drop he had come to expect, he saw it. The promised land. *Shore.* He renewed his efforts, and the wind pushed them onto the beach.

A handful of men remained on shore, Piers among them.

"Where is everyone?" Sam demanded as they pulled the boat onto the beach.

"Gone to seek higher ground. The wind is pushing the ocean farther inland." Piers peered at the boat, naming the occupants. "What is Eli doing here? Where is Judith?"

Sam took a deep breath. "Eli was injured. Judith stayed behind to keep the lamps burning."

"And you let her?" Piers seemed to expand with anger.

"Someone had to keep the lighthouse going." Eli gestured with his uninjured arm and grimaced. "I am a useless old man."

"But someone should have stayed. . ." Piers's voice trailed off.

"She asked me to make sure Eli was safe. She needs me to set his arm. Is there any place we can find out of this wind?"

Piers laughed, a bitter sound that echoed the buzzing of the wind. "The people of this town have gone farther inland. They fear flooding."

The significance of Piers's presence registered on Sam's consciousness. "What about Sara? The baby?"

"With Father and Abigail, farther up the road."

Sam breathed a prayer for the new life.

"Sam, Piers." Reverend Snodgrass laid a hand on both their shoulders. "Now that we have all arrived, we should move. They tell me there is a doctor in the next village."

"I promised Judith—" Sam started to speak.

"I must return—" Piers interrupted.

They glared at each other.

"I know the sea. I know the lighthouse. I should go." Piers stood, hands balled into fists, ready to fight anyone who disagreed. "And *you* can set Eli's arm and make your way to safety. Where you belong."

With the old men, women, and children. Piers's implication was clear, and anger surged through Sam, making him forget his aching shoulders and surging stomach.

"Enough!" Eli thundered. "You are wasting your time. Piers—your family needs you. Sara needs you. Martin needs you to take care of his young son. You can come with me."

That meant—Sam couldn't believe his ears.

"Sam, you have fulfilled your promise to Judith and brought me here. The village doctor can set my arm." He looked straight at Sam. "Judith means more than life to me. I know you love her. I know you will do everything you can to keep her safe. Please—return to the island. Not for my sake. For hers."

Piers glared at Sam for a long moment, ready to object again.

"Come, Piers. We'd better be going." Reverend Snodgrass placed a hand on his shoulder.

Piers blinked and relented. "Take this." He handed Sam a bag of tools. "In case you need them."

Sam didn't wait for a second invitation. He sprinted to the boat. "Pray for us!" he called over his shoulder. He pushed the boat into the water before Piers could stop him. Only one thought filled his mind. *Judith.*

The wind that had carried them every stroke of the way now blew him back, refusing to let him budge the boat into the water. Seaweed flew around his head.

How could he ever make his way back to the island?

He waded into the waves, pulling at the boat. Snodgrass helped him shove off and then joined the small group walking down the road. Sam prayed for their safety, refusing to consider his own.

He looked up, the pulsating beam from the lighthouse breaking through even the pounding rain. A beacon of hope, of trust, of faith. . .of love. The love of Judith, and yes, even Eli, for the people of Capernaum. The love of Judith for her father, and his love for her. The love of God for His people, not wanting any to perish. The love—Sam's heart pounded with the weight of it—he held in his heart for Judith.

Wind pushed him against the bow of the boat. In this gale, he could smash on the rocks as surely as his father had. Fear tightened his grip on the oars. He prayed, as he had so often throughout that day, *O Father, You once stilled the wind and waves when the disciples feared for their lives. I don't care about myself, but Judith needs me. Bring me to her safely.*

No change came in the sky. Sam sucked in his breath, yanked the boat from the sand with all his remaining reserve of strength, and climbed aboard. Grabbing an oar in each hand, he bent against the wind and dug deep into the water. He would row back to the island, or die trying.

As suddenly as the waters of the Jordan River parted when the soles of the priests' feet entered the water, the wind stopped. Waves that towered over him only moments ago now gently rocked the boat like a cradle. Could the storm have passed so suddenly? Had God miraculously intervened?

Sam didn't understand the abrupt cessation of the storm, but he rejoiced. Renewed energy surged through his limbs. He pulled on the oars with all his strength. In calm seas, a lone oarsman could manage the trip in half an hour.

The sky remained a washed-out gray, yet the sun broke through the hovering clouds. Good. Perhaps its rays would dry out the water-logged coat that hung heavy from his aching shoulders.

A seagull took off from the water, soaring into the sky that was its God-ordained element. In the distance, the group on shore raised jubilant cries. The normal sounds of the sea returned—waves lapping at the boat, oars slapping into the water. Small sounds Sam missed in the cacophony of the storm. God had inserted a rest in the midst of the storm's song.

A rest? No, God had put a full stop to the gale. Sam saw no signs of the storm's return in the sky. With each pull of the oar, the island appeared closer. He saw the lighthouse, still standing tall and strong. Prayer flowed from his lips as he prayed. *Thank You for the passing of the storm. Thank You for this miracle. Thank You for sparing the lighthouse—Judith—all those I love through this storm.* He felt light at heart. Fish leaped out of the water at the sides of the boat, as if they were rejoicing with him.

Sam made the mistake of looking past the fish into the depths of the water. Those depths could still kill him. If he fell over the side, he would fall down as surely as if a rock were tied to his foot. His sodden coat would drag him down. He wished he had removed it back on the beach, but at that time, he still needed it for the small protection it offered against the constant rain.

Sam fought the fear. The boat remained stable in the water; no waves thrashed him to and fro. He had no reason to be afraid, if only his heart would agree.

Focus on the light. Sam stared at the lighthouse, counting the pattern of the lamps as they blinked on and off. *Keep your eyes on Jesus. . .and run the race.* As long as he kept his eyes on his goal and didn't stare into the depths, he could manage.

One stroke at a time.

Judith couldn't believe it. The tarp that had whipped wildly only moments before hung without moving. The boards covering the windows didn't bend or creak with the wind. Through the open spaces, she could see sunshine. *Sunshine.* Could the storm have passed so suddenly?

She took advantage of the quiet to tack the boards across the few unbroken windows again and to refasten the tarp. She also swept water from the floor. Did she need to keep the lanterns burning? In spite of the sunshine, the sky remained gray. She would keep them going. Evening could not be far off. Instead, she grabbed the almost-empty pail of whale oil, refilled it, and headed back upstairs.

She set down her burden on the landing to stare at the transformed landscape. A good third of the trees in the forest had fallen or blown into the clearing around the Hathaways' house. Their chimney had disappeared. Ocean water still lapped around the foot of the lighthouse. She had never even heard of such a storm. The people of Capernaum would return to massive destruction.

She stared once again at the Hathaways' cottage. The roof appeared damaged. *Oh, Sam.* Had Lauder's skill been enough to bring them to the mainland safely? Could the wind have carried them off course, away from the safety of the sandy beach and onto the treacherous rocks that existed even on that coast? She prayed not.

She prayed for her father as well. How he fought to remain, even when in such pain. She prayed for peace between him and Sam. If they could not forget their differences in the face of this gale, they might never reconcile.

She had dawdled long enough. She dragged her feet up the remaining stairs, repeating her rhyme to spur her forward. *"Four, five, six, boats of sticks."* O God. *Boats of sticks.* She thought of Sam's promise to return to the island once he settled Father. She prayed he would not be so foolish. What if the storm started up again? Would he be incautious enough to attempt the crossing alone? *Please keep Sam, Father—all of them—safe!* *"Seven, eight, nine, light sublime."* She allowed herself a smile. The lighthouse—or perhaps she should say the lighthouse keeper—had done its job during the storm.

A few minutes later, Judith had refilled the lamps and made certain the lights didn't flicker. Exhaustion struck. More than a day had passed since she'd last slept, and she faced another all-night session in the lantern room. She would rest before night fell.

She returned to the bottom floor, carrying the flint with her, wrapped in waterproof cloth next to her skin. She wanted to keep it as dry as possible. A thin river of water ran across the floor. They had never experienced any flooding inside the structure in all their years at the lighthouse. Everything she touched was damp, including her bed. She wrinkled her nose. *Think, Judith, think.* She was too tired to think. Perhaps a cup of tea would revive her enough to make some decisions. A cup of tea, and a few hours of sleep in her bed, whether damp or dry. She was too tired to care.

While the tea steeped, Judith removed a loaf of bread—had she baked it only yesterday, all on her own, after Mary's careful tutelage?—and cut a couple of slices. She put the bread on a toasting fork and held it over the fire. Finding a crock of apple butter, she spread some of the preserves across the browned slices and sipped at the tea. The warmth spread into her bones. She found a blanket tucked away in her chest, only slightly damp, and laid across the top covers of her bed.

A single thought floated through her mind as sleep claimed her. *Sam.*

Bang. Judith's eyes flew open. Only short minutes had passed. Something slammed into the outside wall, sending shudders through the bed where Judith lay. The storm must have started again. But wait. Before the storm hit them from the other side of the lighthouse. Had the wind switched directions? Could the lighthouse withstand another beating like the hours that had passed before?

God, give me strength. Keep me awake. Judith sat up, her feet landing in a thin sheet of water on the floor. She retracted them and reached for a fresh pair of woolen socks. As she pulled them over her feet, wind pummeled the sides of the building. She began the climb to the lantern room.

∞

Sam focused on the small, sandy patch, maybe five minutes away. He was more than ready to get out of the boat and walk on dry land again.

He renewed his efforts and felt a push at his back. Rain sprinkled his face. The storm had returned, this time blowing him toward the island instead of away. He didn't care. A mild wind would bring him to shore more quickly.

A moment later, he knew he had misjudged the rain. The gale had returned full-force. Waves lifted the boat and thrust it onto the beach. The bow hit something hard, and it cracked. Water began to seep around his feet. The vessel was ruined. They could not leave the island even if he could convince Judith to leave. All the other boats had been used to transport people to the mainland.

SEASIDE ROMANCE

Judith. The lighthouse lamps burned as brightly as ever, tantalizingly close. Sam couldn't wait to reach her, and he broke into a trot. The wet sand sucked at his feet, slowing him, trying to trip him. He looked toward the rocks. They, at least, would not pull the shoes from his feet. But the rain would make them slippery, and he could do no one any good if he fell and broke a leg or an arm as Eli had. He struggled across the sand and onto the path leading to his cottage and the lighthouse.

A few yards into the intervening forest, it became obvious that the path no longer existed as such. Every few feet, Sam had to make his way around tree limbs. Trees he had climbed as a child lay scattered like broken twigs on the ground. Without the path, with the wind howling like a mythological siren, he lost his sense of direction. *Help, God.* He returned the way he had traveled, back to the beach.

A towering wave rushed toward him, as tall as most buildings on the island, taller than anything he had ever seen before. He did the only thing he could think of. He grabbed the lowest branches of the nearest tree and scrambled up the trunk. The wave struck the forest. Sam's tree snapped back and forth, tossing Sam like a ball on a string. He clung to a branch with both arms and legs, feeling it tear his skin in the effort. The wind beat at his head, blinding him. Branches whipped across his face, bruising his forehead and cheeks. His knees dug into the branch and held on. The action was a prayer without words.

Slowly, agonizingly, Sam became aware that water no longer pushed at the roots of the tree. Wind pulled at his perch. Rain sought to push itself under his skin. He chanced a look down. Water stood above ground, to be sure, but he didn't think it was more than a foot deep.

In the terror of the last few minutes, he had made his way to the top of one of the tallest trees in the forest. He looked out across the wasteland created by wind and wave, looking for some discernable landmark in the whirlwind of water and debris. To his left, he could see the battered remains of the boat. That meant the lighthouse should be straight ahead. He searched for beams of light piercing the storm, assuring him Judith was safe.

No light. Perhaps he had turned around and the lighthouse stood behind him. He twisted his body as far as he could. Still no light. His eyes sought the line of broken rocks that identified the point of the island. They were still there, as jumbled as ever. But the lighthouse. . .

Snapped beams formed a rough circle. The lighthouse had broken in half.

Chapter 14

Halfway up the stairs to the lantern room, Judith heard glass shatter and boards snap. She ran up the remaining stairs, pausing when she saw the last step had snapped, two halves held together by a few splinters of wood. She extended her leg and took the double step to peer into the lantern room.

Splinters of glass and wood covered the floor. All four remaining lamps had shattered, plunging the room into eerie twilight. She didn't know the time, if it was mid-afternoon or the dead of night. This one single day had lasted long enough for several lifetimes. She had to face the fact that no matter how much she wanted to, she could not keep the lamps burning. There were no more lamps.

She wanted to sit and cry, but she would injure herself if she sat on the glass strewn across the floor. Rain plastered her hair against her face, darting at her eyes. She didn't care.

Another gust of wind reminded Judith she should leave this exposed area. Lifting her skirts, she reached past the gaping hole to the next step with her foot. It found solid footing, and she lowered the rest of her body. She took her time walking down, wondering what else she could do to keep a light going. Slowly and deliberately, she descended the stairs with the cadence of an infirm person.

She paused at the landing, scanning the island for a place where she could build a signal fire of some kind. Did any place on the island offer some kind of natural protection? She recalled a hillock beyond the Hathaways' cottage. Perhaps she could do something there. At least she had the materials needed to start a fire. She touched the flint still tucked beneath her dress. Tinder could be picked up downstairs.

Judith gathered her skirts to descend the remaining stairs when she caught sight of the ocean. A gigantic wave, unlike anything she had ever seen, even on this nightmarish day, galloped across the surface of the water and headed straight at her. Judith flew down the stairs, skipping two steps at a time, and ran for the only cover she could think of.

∞

Sam shinnied down the trunk of the tree. His estimation of the depth of the standing water was a little off, more like six inches than a foot. What was the quickest route to the lighthouse? To Judith? *O God, please let her be alive.*

The rocks. He must go by the rocks. Branches hidden in the water snagged his legs and slowed him down. He turned the curses that came to his mind into prayers, asking God to guide his feet. God answered, as He had so miraculously calmed the storm long enough to allow Sam to return to the island. Sam picked his way through the debris and found his way out of the forest.

A few planks from Lauder's boat bobbed in the swash where the beach had been. He didn't know what had happened to the rest of it. But Sam couldn't worry about that destruction right now. He turned to his right and studied the rock-strewn shore before him. Perhaps even here God had prepared a path before him. The big wave seemed to have shifted even the largest boulders, and had smashed others. It had transformed the beach into a giant's rock garden, with plenty of room for a mere man to walk through. Sam set his eyes on the first boulder for a landmark and walked toward it.

Five minutes later, Sam tried to straighten his body long enough to locate the next landmark. The wind kept pushing him off course, wanting to pick him up and crush him against rock and tree. Would he have better luck crawling on all fours? He would slither on his belly like a snake if that would help him reach Judith. He looked at his hands, now skinned and bloodied. He would attempt to remain upright. Shallow breaths seemed to work best. Great gulps of air brought rain into his mouth.

About a quarter of an hour later, his efforts were rewarded with the sight of the remains of the lighthouse.

⌒

As the wave hit, Judith flung herself beneath the stone bench Father had placed in the kitchen. The door buckled and then crashed to the floor. Water rushed in over her, around her, past her, time and again. She opened her mouth for a deep gulp of air every time the water subsided, only to be submerged again. Mugs and boards and crocks bumped into her shoulders, her legs, her forehead. The bench didn't move, as solid as Plymouth Rock, God's rock for her personal salvation.

Gradually, the water level around Judith subsided. She no longer had to gulp for air between submersions. It fell below her chin. . .her knees. . .her ankles. A few broken dishes floated by her. Broken pieces of wood—the table? A chair?—blocked her view. She felt around on the floor, checking for anything sharp that might cut her. Not finding anything, she pushed the wood away and climbed to her feet.

Judith didn't know what she expected. She saw that the door had given way and noticed broken furniture and possessions. But this. . .

Where once four solid walls had reached thirty feet into the sky, now the ceiling gaped open. Half the tower had blown away. The wind had not abated in the slightest. As she took in the damage, the wind tugged another board free and flung it into the air. She flinched. At her feet, a sea bass thrashed for air, the depth of water in the room not enough to keep him alive. She wanted to help, to scream, to do anything to keep it alive, as if its survival was a mirror of her own. She wished she had listened to her father, to the preacher—to Sam. She had stayed on the island for nothing. Had the wave reached the mainland? How far did it push? She felt as lonely as Noah and his family must have felt when they looked out from the ark after the flood. Lonelier, perhaps, because he had his family and a boatload of animals demanding attention.

Judith pushed her way through the water—not deep now, not much deeper than before the wave—and past the remains of what had been her home for ten years. The dishes, the only thing she had left from her mother, floated in pieces in the water. The Bible and *Olney's Hymns* lay facedown in the muck. She lifted them up, crying when her eyes took in the open page of the hymnal. "God moves in a mysterious way/His wonders to perform/He plants his footsteps in the sea/ and rides upon the storm."

This storm was one wild ride. She started to laugh and then stopped herself. She would not help herself by becoming hysterical. *God kept me alive!* She shook herself—not even a single broken bone. She was not alone in the world. The storm would pass. People would return to the island. And she still had a job to do. If she could get to the hillock by the Hathaway cottage, perhaps she could start a signal fire. That's why she had stayed behind. To keep the lights burning.

The tarp that had protected the lamps for most of the gale floated by. She could use it to haul logs or whatever else she might need. No, she couldn't take anything heavy. The tarp to offer what small protection it could—little enough in this wind. The precious flint, something to eat if she could find it. Surely this storm would pass. Then she considered how the wind skipped everything from mugs to tree across the ground and decided to take her family Bible. She longed for the book of hymns, but that added weight. She tied the few items inside the tarp and maneuvered her way through the room, as uncertain of her way as if in a maze.

At the door frame, she closed her eyes, unwilling to look upon the devastation that the wave had brought. *God, give me strength.*

When at last she opened her eyes, she saw the one thing she didn't expect. The one person she had prayed for most earnestly.

Sam ran toward her, his legs moving as if propelled by the wind.

∽

Judith! Sam breathed a prayer of thanksgiving when he saw his beloved silhouetted in the doorway. The sight of her gave fresh energy to his tired limbs, and he weaved through tree branches and rocks to her side.

Unmindful of the storm, ignoring the proprieties that dictated their ordinary existence, he clasped her in his arms and kissed her. A kiss as wild and desperate as the wind and rain that continued to rage around them. He broke away when he became aware of a bundle with sharp edges she held between them.

"Sam. I thought I'd never see you again." Judith hiccupped a sob. "I thought I might never see anyone again. I felt as alone as Elijah on Mt. Carmel."

"Judith." Sam cupped her chin with his hands. "I promised I would return. And God calmed the sea long enough for me to cross." He wanted to kiss her again, but they needed to find shelter—any shelter—whatever might protect them until the storm passed.

She must have read his thoughts, for she took a step forward. "The hillock by your cottage. I want to get a signal fire going if it's at all possible."

A signal fire? Even now, after the great gale had torn apart the lighthouse, she was determined to do her duty. Sam shook his head but didn't argue. Instead, he turned in the direction of his cottage, always visible from the point of the island.

"Earlier I saw that the chimney had gone. . . ." Judith's voice trailed off. "The wave must have washed away your home." She said the words almost under her breath. "I'm so sorry."

"Come." A pang hit Sam; the loss of the cottage represented more than the loss of a few odds and ends. He couldn't stop to think about it now. They needed to move, to reach higher ground before the water that lapped around their ankles rose any higher. "I know the way." He took the bundle from her arms and led them on.

A quarter of an hour later, they had made slow progress. Branches he could step over proved insurmountable obstacles to Judith in her skirts. Water had risen past their ankles. They dared not continue at this slow pace.

Sam placed a hand on Judith's arm. "Pardon me, but I feel I must do this." He retrieved a knife from the bag of tools Piers had handed him and cut the skirts and petticoats down to her knees. He caught sight of a jagged tear running across her knee. His stomach clenched. All the more reason to hurry.

She gasped and stared at her bare legs as if she had never seen them before.

"Try walking."

She took one step, then two, and then extended her stride as her legs found freedom of movement. "That was wise," she admitted as he helped her over a fallen branch.

Soon they approached the spot where the Hathaway cottage had stood for all of Sam's life. Sam fought the urge to stop and look. The hillock lay straight ahead.

Climbing the hillock proved harder than Sam thought possible. He bent into the wind, took a single step, and then helped Judith up the slope. After a couple of feet, the wind pushed them back down, head over heels like Jack and Jill, to the bottom.

"Why"—Sam fought for breath to speak—"the top of the hill?" He remained on the ground.

Judith took several deep breaths before answering. "Because it's the highest spot I can think of. A signal fire." She struggled to her knees and grimaced. Sam remembered the gash. "Stop."

She remained on all fours, swaying back and forth like a child learning to crawl. "If I stop too long"—a deep inhalation made her choke—"I won't be able to move again."

Think, Sam, think. "There's an overhang on the other side. About halfway up."

"I want the top."

Sam shook his head. "Even if we can make it, the wind will blow out the fire as soon as you light it. The overhang might provide enough protection. The wind will be blowing from the other side of the island, not in our faces."

"And we'll still be facing the sea." She sat on her haunches and wiped her muddy hands on her dress. "A good idea. Point me in the right direction, sir."

He stood up and gave her a hand. "This way."

Progress up the opposite side of the hillock eased only slightly. Wind whipped around the obstacle and attacked them from the side. At one point, Judith dropped to her knees and crawled for a few yards. It felt like hours passed from the time they first set out from the lighthouse before Sam reached the overhang and helped Judith into the tiny recess. The ground was still damp but not flooded like the rest of the island.

They both lay down, blowing in and out like whales sneezing through their air holes. Sam had never felt so spent, not even in all his time with the army, yet the hardest task lay ahead of them. He would have slept and encouraged Judith to do the same, if they could sleep with the wind howling in their ears, but he didn't speak. She would never agree.

"Look, there are twigs in here, as if someone had gathered kindling." Judith found a bundle in the corner. "A little damp, but not too bad."

"So local boys still spend the nights here. I used to when I was a lad." Sam had known Judith would want to start the signal as soon as possible. "I will see to the fire. But first, I must tend to your knee."

"It's nothing."

"I'm the doctor," he said. "Let me look." He cut away the remaining cloth that rain and blood had stuck to her skin. As he feared, it cut close to the muscle that allowed the leg to move. He had seen cuts like this in the war—he had seen what could happen. *O Lord, not that!* He feared that only the great Physician could prevent infection and gangrene from setting in.

He prayed without words as he debated what to do. "Water," he grunted. At least on the battlefield he had ready access to fire and water. That was not the case here. They had no pan to catch the rain, and even if they did, sea salt would taint what fell from the air.

Judith pawed through the belongings she had carried in the tarp and handed him a small bottle. "'Tis only a small flask, but—"

"Bless you!" Next step. Where could he find a clean strip of cloth? Judith had already sacrificed her dignity with her skirts, and mud coated what remained. His clothing was not in much better condition. But perhaps. . .he removed his coat and shirt. Wind blew into their small refuge and sent shivers across his exposed skin. As he expected, his undershirt was relatively clean, if wet. He paused a moment. What he proposed crossed the line into impropriety, but he had no time to waste on such matters. He pulled the undershirt off and replaced his shirt. After he cut the undergarment into strips, he tucked all but one into the tarp. He considered using the water in the flask, but decided against it. Rain had already soaked the material.

"I'm sorry—this may hurt." Sam applied pressure to the wound.

Chapter 15

Judith fought back tears. Sam dabbed and prodded and wiped at the wound, going through three strips of cloth in the process. That was bad enough. Next he took his knife, ran his finger along the blade, and glanced at her, silently begging her forgiveness. Then he cut at the edges, removing debris that had embedded itself during her crawl up the hill. She whimpered. She couldn't help it. *Please, God, help me be brave. Thank You that Sam is here. It hurts, it hurts, it hurts.*

Judith distracted herself by looking at Sam's back. How broad his shoulders were, how strong his muscles seemed. This man could protect from anything.

"I'm almost done," Sam promised. He cleaned away the blood accumulated during the cutting and wrapped a long strip around her knee. Regret clouded his eyes. "Once we get the fire going, I need to cauterize the wound. It's the best I can do in these circumstances." He gestured helplessly at the wind that continued to roar, the rain that blinded any sight beyond the edge of the small ledge where they sat.

Judith blinked back tears of pain. "Thank you, Sam. I. . .needed you today."

He flashed a smile at her, the only white spot in a face covered with mud, brilliant and full of joy. "I promised to come back, didn't I?"

"Yes, you did." Sam had come back, fighting the storm, fighting her father. Sam, not Father, not even Piers. She returned his grin with one of her own, the effort painful as if the events of the day had taught her face never to lift in a smile again.

"I want to hear all about the crossing." And she did want to, every scary inch and word and sound. "But first, the fire."

"Of course." Sam's mouth twitched, the smile not quite as brilliant but full of mischief instead. "I'll just find us a dry log or two."

Judith's heart sank. He had put her fear into words. Even if the rain would not snuff a fire out, how could they get one started? She doubted there was a dry log left on all of Capernaum Island.

Sam turned serious. "Don't fret. I learned how to start a blaze in spite of rainfall while I was in the army. Not in a storm like this, mind you—but I know a few tricks. I see quite a bit of tinder in the back there. I'll look for several good-sized branches while you get the fire going."

"Shouldn't we build a cairn first? Of rocks?"

Sam shook his head. "You have enough sticks there to build a good, hot bed for the fire. You know how?"

Judith nodded her head. "I take care—took care—of the fireplace at the light-house."

"And you brought flint?"

Judith nodded her head again. "I know what to do." She stared out the opening. "Oh, Sam, I hate to ask you—"

"You're not asking. I'm volunteering." He saluted. "I'll be back before you can finish singing 'Contentment.' Okay, maybe twice through."

Once again, he made her smile. The hymn he referred to had eight verses.

"I will return. And that's a promise." He kissed her cheek. She breathed his scent. A moment of delicious dizziness passed over her. Then he gathered his shirt and coat around him again. He disappeared into the sheet of rain that separated her from the storm.

As soon as Sam disappeared into the gale, loneliness returned. Judith felt more alone than she had in all the hours she had spent in the lighthouse. Gritting her teeth against the pain in her knee, she set to work gathering pine needles and small twigs from their resting place at the back of the overhang. The words of the hymn Sam had mentioned sprang to her lips. "Fierce passions discompose the mind/As tempests vex the sea." Fierce passions of fear and loneliness threatened to discompose her mind in this storm. Those emotions vexed her soul as surely as the great tempest vexed the ocean, transforming familiar tides and waves into monsters. Cowper had supplied the answer with the rest of the first stanza. "But calm, content and peace we find/When, Lord, we turn to Thee." She continued singing the words as a prayer, an affirmation that God's peace would see her through the storm.

Sam said they didn't need a cairn, but she built a small wall to protect the fledgling flame from the wind. She sang the second stanza of the hymn while she piled a few rocks together at the midpoint of the overhang. She struck her flint against the knife left with the kindling. By the time she finished the third verse, a spark had caught the pine needles. She stopped singing long enough to blow the spark into life, and a small flame licked at the edges of the kindling. Through the fourth and fifth verses, she added more needles and twigs to feed the fire. The wind blew over her back, over the rocks; but though the fire eddied, it didn't go out. She had finished the last verse—"Taught in my Savior's school of grace have learnt to be content"—by the time she was ready to move on to the next step.

Wonderful how much difference the bright flame made. It offered hope and comfort, if little heat. The fire, and the hymn offered as a prayer, had cheered her soul. She continued to feed the flame while she crisscrossed small branches over the fire, building a foundation for the wood Sam would bring. *Sam.*

Judith strained for some sign of his approach to the cave, worried about him out in the wind. A tenor voice warbled, "Have learnt to be content." Sam parted the rain curtain, splattering water on the ground, an armload of branches wrapped in his coat.

"I told you it would only take two times through." He smiled broadly, as if he had gone on a pleasant stroll through the woods instead of fighting wind and rain for lifesaving firewood. "That's a good fire." He chafed his hands over the flame, then unwrapped his coat. "I found these under a tree that fell down. They're only slightly damp. If we dry them by the fire for a while, they should burn." He ranged branches of various lengths around the ring of fire.

Judith moved so that Sam could take her place by the fire. If possible, he appeared more soaked than he had when they'd first arrived at the overhang. He didn't seem to mind it any more than when he had dashed through puddles as a boy. Dark curls dangled around his face, framing those gray-green eyes as merry as Christmas morning. "That's better." He spread his hands over the growing flame. Judith wanted to reach out and touch the curls that bounced around the nape of his neck, but she resisted the urge.

God had brought Sam back into her life and back to her through this gale. He would surely see them both through to the end.

∞

Sam watched Judith settle down next to him. He longed to pull her into his arms, but instead, he reached for the log at his feet. It felt warm to the touch, dry enough to burn. He tipped it into the fire, which flared into the air with a shower of sparks.

"Well done!" Judith's face took on a cheery glow. "I didn't think it would be possible to start a signal fire."

"God works miracles." Sam still marveled at the storm's eerie calm that had allowed him to cross the water on his return to the island.

"Tell me about the voyage. How is Father? Did you see the Vanderkamps?"

Piers. The rosy feeling inside of Sam vanished. "Eli slipped in and out of consciousness in the boat. They promised to take him to a doctor in a nearby village." He prayed the wave that had washed over the island had not reached the mainland.

"And Sara? Do you know what happened to her and the baby?"

Judith was inquiring about the new mother, not Piers. Sam relaxed. "Piers said they had gone ahead. They made it across safely." He checked a second log. It had dried enough to add to the fire.

Judith tucked her legs under her and grimaced as the gash on her knee hit the ground. Blood had already seeped through the binding. Professional concern took over. He took the knife from its sheath and placed it at the edge of the fire.

Judith noticed what he was doing and cringed. "Is that really necessary?"

Sam pointed at the blood-stained bandage. "Your wound is still bleeding. We want to stop it before infection sets in." His mouth set in a thin line. He had seen too many wounds turn into deadly gangrene. He would not, could not, allow that to happen to Judith.

While the knife heated, Sam removed the bandage and cleaned away the accumulated blood. He breathed a prayer of thanks when he saw no puss or swelling. When he judged the blade was hot enough, he said, "Turn away, and close your eyes."

Judith cupped her chin against his shoulder, scrunched her eyes shut, and began reciting, " 'The Lord is my shepherd, I shall not want.' " She stumbled through the words, repeating them over and over.

In a single swift movement, Sam inserted the knife into the gash. Judith jerked once, screaming. Then she stilled. The odor of burned flesh permeated the overhang. He lifted the blade. Mission accomplished: The edges of the wound had cauterized. He wrapped a fresh bandage around the wound and sheathed the knife.

Judith sobbed. Tears fell down her cheeks, and she rocked back and forth. He pulled her into his arms, tucking her head under his chin. "I know it hurts." His own voice broke. "I had no choice."

"I know." She burrowed into his chest and didn't speak again.

Was there something, anything that could take Judith's mind off the pain? He had no laudanum. A flask of water, but no pot to warm it in. Hadn't she brought a Bible from the lighthouse? Scripture might calm her. He turned to the middle and began with the first psalm. " 'Blessed is the man that walketh not in the counsel of the ungodly. . . .' "

Judith turned her head, her mouth forming the words as he read, slowly relaxing.

By the time he reached the third psalm, she had closed her eyes, and her breathing had slowed. " 'I laid me down and slept,' " Sam read, looking at the precious face so close to his own. He finished the chapter as he eased her onto the ground. Hands clasped in prayer over her body, he recited the last verse. " 'Salvation belongeth unto the Lord: thy blessing is upon thy people.' " He had done what he could; the rest lay in God's hands.

Sam checked the fire bed Judith had prepared and added another log. Was there any point in maintaining the fire? Could anyone at sea see the blaze through this rain? He prayed they could. At the very least, the overhang offered some shelter from the rain, and the flames gave warmth to ward off chills and illness.

Lord, You promise to be a refuge, to bring salvation to Your people. He looked out at the curtain of water that continued to cascade from the overhang. *Isn't it time for this storm to end?* The wind howled in reply, and the flame danced. God had not saved them from the storm, but He would save them through it.

Throbbing pain roused Judith from sleep. She looked at the knee that created such discomfort. *No blood.* Praise God. Thank Him for Sam's presence and care.

Next to her, the fire burned low. Sam's head bent against his chest, and his lips fluttered as if snoring, not that she could hear it above the wind that continued to rush by the overhang. She sat up and stirred the ashes, adding another log. The fire flared into life again.

Judith's stomach twisted in a way that reminded her of the long hours since their last meal. She thought about the biscuits she had carried from the lighthouse. *No. Not until Sam has awakened.* She had no desire to rouse him from his sleep. He had remained awake for a night and a day, and had spent himself rowing to and from the mainland. He needed to rest.

What further damage had the gale brought? Judith stood up, bending over in the small area, and crept to the edge of the overhang. The dull gray sky had not changed color since the storm began, and clouds obscured the heavenly constellations. She couldn't tell if it was the night of the same day, or whether a twenty-four-hour period had passed.

When would this storm ever abate? She thought of another one of Cowper's hymns. "Though tempest-toss'd and half a wreck my Savior through the floods I seek." *Tempest-tossed, wrecked, flooded*—all those words and more applied. But her faithful Lord had kept her alive, and more than that, had allowed her to keep a signal fire burning. Had all her work helped even one sailor? She would have to trust God with the results.

They needed more wood. Her knee protested when she straightened her back, but she walked through the cascading water into the storm. Wind immediately bent her over double and swung a tree at her head.

She ducked, and the tree missed her by several feet. Praise the Lord. The gale showed no signs of lessening. She turned to be sure she could see the fire, glad to notice that its flames shone clearly in spite of the rain. Perhaps men at sea could make out a faint glow, at least.

Certain she could find her way back, she plunged into the darkness. She reached a fallen tree and set to work. A couple of tries convinced Judith the task required a man's strength. She settled for gathering branches, moving farther away from the overhang with each step.

"Get back inside!" Sam's voice growled behind her. "I'll get more wood."

Startled, Judith dropped a couple of the branches from her arms. She wanted to cry. She didn't have the energy to pick them up again.

"Go!" Sam repeated.

Mud sucked at Judith's feet and splashed on her knee. It ached as though another cut had opened. She pried her feet loose one at a time, and she dropped another branch. By the time she plunged through the rain curtain into the relative warmth and comfort of their shelter, she had lost half of her precious bundle.

How much longer could they keep going this way?

Chapter 16

Judith lost no time spreading the wet branches around the fire, as Sam had done on the previous night. She didn't know if the fire could dry them out. She doubted a spot on the island remained where water hadn't soaked through the soil to the very center of the earth. Only the dirt in the immediate area around the fire felt dry to the touch. She checked the tarp. It had kept the last precious biscuits dry. When Sam returned, they would eat.

Seeing the fire had gone down, Judith added another log. Only one more dry piece remained. She prayed the new wood would dry enough to burn.

Humming announced Sam's return. He managed a full armload of branches, piled as high as his head. "I think the wind has died down some." He smiled, *smiled*, as if he had gone for a stroll along the beach. "The storm can't last forever. Not unless we're reliving the days of Noah."

Sam's statement reminded Judith of Jesus' warning about His return. "What if Jesus did come back today?" Judith blurted out the words. "I'm a Christian. I have been since I was a little girl. But. . .I'm not ready for my life to be over." She whispered the last words. Was it shameful to want to know a man's love and to experience the joy of raising children before she went home to be with the Lord?

"That's good, because you should have a good long life ahead of you." Sam sat next to Judith and took her hands between his own. His eyes, a serious gray, studied her. "I have seen death. No man chooses it, and you're right, there are times when death singles out an individual. But that's not going to happen to us. We—you and I—will have a lifetime together." He brushed her mouth with his.

Judith was savoring the contact when he pulled away. "We must be careful with the fire."

He gestured at the still-wet logs, but Judith suspected he was referring to more than one kind of fire. She allowed him to withdraw but kept a finger on her lips where he had touched them.

"Do you think these logs will dry enough to burn?" She struggled for a normal tone.

Sam shrugged. "We should let the fire burn low, in case the branches will not catch fire. We will help no one, not even ourselves, if we allow it to go out altogether. Conserve the fuel."

Judith nodded. She had seen the possibility coming.

"I need to check your knee."

Judith extended her leg, and Sam pushed the edges of her skirt up an inch and examined the wound. "When you went outside, you coated it with mud again." He sounded like a scolding mother, fussing at her children for their misbehavior. "I'll need to change the bandage." He removed the strip of cloth, gently pulling it away from the wound where it stuck.

Judith held her breath. Her few steps across the hillside had caused her knee a great deal of pain. Cold air blew across the burn, and she shivered.

Sam frowned and pressed a hand against her forehead. "You have a fever. What I wouldn't give for my medical bag." He forced a laugh. "I expect it's floating somewhere, all my vials of medicine mixing with the ocean water. At least the fish will be healthy. What you need is willow bark tea. It helps lower a fever."

"Don't trouble yourself. I can't offer tea." Judith smiled. "But we do have water left, and biscuits." She produced the handful she had wrapped in a napkin when she left the lighthouse hours ago. "This is as good a time as any to eat our last supper." She giggled, and she wondered if she were slipping into delirium.

Sam looked at the biscuits as if she had offered him plum pudding on Christmas Day. "Bless you, woman." He studied the three mounds in the napkin. "Shall we each take one now, and save the last for later?"

Judith shook her head. "They are getting harder by the hour. If we wait much longer, we may break our teeth trying to eat them." She snapped one in half and handed it to Sam.

He nibbled at it, and then looked chagrined. "We should pray."

Judith had another idea. "Father began reading Hosea this morning. Yesterday. Whenever." She opened the tarp and extracted the Bible. "I'll read the rest of the book, and then you can pray."

What a strange place to feel cozy and comfortable, reading the daily Bible portion like an old married couple: in a dark overhang against the everlasting rain for a backdrop, with a fire to warm them and dry biscuits for breakfast. Judith put herself in the place of the prophet, giving drama to his dire warnings. By the time she reached the last chapter, she neared tears.

" 'They that dwell under his shadow shall return; they shall revive as the corn, and grow as the vine: the scent thereof shall be as the wine of Lebanon.' Oh, Sam—it's as if God is promising to bring back our loved ones. Capernaum will be rebuilt." Tears glimmered in Sam's eyes as well.

"Let's pray." He cleared his throat. "Our heavenly Father, we thank Thee for seeing us through the storm. We pray for this land, and our people. May we return to Thee with our whole hearts." Sam prayed for each citizen of Capernaum by name. "I thank Thee for Judith. I pray that Thou wilt open Eli's heart to our courtship." Almost as an afterthought, he ended with thanksgiving for the food they were about to eat.

"Amen," Judith chimed in. "Shall we eat?" She broke off a tiny piece of the biscuit. She wanted to savor every morsel. Who knew when they would dine again?

"This is like the last supper, you know," Sam said. He held up the remaining bit of his half biscuit. "Like the body of Christ, broken for us." He pointed to the flask. "Water to wine. The blood of Christ, shed for us." He closed his eyes as if in prayer. "We thank Thee, O Lord, for providing for our salvation."

In Sam's company, the few bites of biscuit accompanied by even fewer swallows of water satisfied Judith more fully than any feast she had ever enjoyed. She stared at the rain curtain with renewed hope.

She and Sam would face the post-gale world, recreated into something new and wonderful, together.

Chapter 17

A hiss and sizzle brought Sam to wakefulness. *I dozed off again.* He chided himself. Judith counted on him to keep the fire going. He lifted the least damp log onto the fire and willed the fire to take the wood. Sparks flew and snapped, and flickers of flame licked the branch. It would burn. Thank the Lord.

In the corner, Judith's chest rose and fell in a steady rhythm, and she snored softly. Her face was flushed. Once again he wished for willow bark tea. Instead they had a meager amount of water left in the flask.

Behind him, water dripped against the ground. The various things he heard coalesced into realization. The water *dripped*. He heard Judith's snore and the snap of sparks from the fire. When he'd fallen asleep, the storm had drowned out all sound. They had worn out their voices with loud speech.

He turned ever so slowly, fearful that reality would dash his hopes. Blue sky welcomed him beyond the droplets of water that continued to pour from the overhang.

"Judith! Wake up!" He didn't wait for her to answer. He left the shelter and leapt in the air. Small puffy clouds floated through the daytime sky, as pretty a day as he had ever seen.

"Praise be!" Judith joined him on the grass. "God brought us through the storm." She moved her legs in a dance of joy but stopped and grabbed her leg.

Overhead, seagulls swarmed in a chorus, their cries a heavenly anthem of thanksgiving. They dived as a group to the ground.

Sam followed their flight, and froze.

"It's all gone." Judith spoke, echoing his thoughts. She turned in a slow circle. "Not a building is left standing."

Here a chimney still stood, there a fence post, as well as a good many trees; but the gale had left no place untouched. Sam turned south to the lighthouse. The wind had demolished another wall, but the foundation remained. They could rebuild it, with stone or brick this time.

Boulders pockmarked the shore where the waves had lifted and scattered stones as if a giant had played a game of ninepins. Sam scanned the shore, seeking the fishermen's docks.

"Do you see any sign of Lauder's house?" Sam looked north for the red building, the most recognizable dwelling on the beach.

"That might be it." Judith pointed to a patch of red lying on the sand.

"But that's not—" Sam squinted at the patch of sand, the contours he had memorized in childhood. "That's not where the fishermen's docks are located. Did the wind carry it so far?"

He continued circling, seeing the mainland, visible now in the daylight, then again the ruins of the lighthouse on the rocks, until he once more faced the only sandy spot on the island.

"God has reshaped the shore." Judith spoke in an awed voice. "The beach we knew is gone."

Sam fought the sense of disorientation that the changes thrust upon him. Not a stone was left unturned, a leaf untouched, a building undamaged. More than that, he didn't recognize the contours of the island. He felt as if the gale had carried them to some faraway place. *This must be what Noah felt like after the flood. The world as he knew it had been transformed, reshaped.* At least, unlike the patriarch, he and Judith were not the only people left alive.

When people returned—if they returned—they would have to start over. Some might choose to remain on the mainland, where the gale could not have done as much damage.

"Oh, Sam." Judith tugged at his tattered sleeve. "I have never seen such a glorious day." She lifted her face for the sun's kiss. Bright spots in her cheeks marked her otherwise pale face.

Fever. Her leg. The chilling rain.

Any joy Sam had felt in the end of the storm fled away.

∞

Judith danced inside. This was a morning to celebrate, to offer thanks to the Lord for bringing them safely through the storm. Excitement burned through her. If they had survived this terrible gale, so must everyone they cared about. And God had brought Sam to her side when she needed him most. He had aided her, cheered her, and tended to her injured leg. God was good. She laughed, but her laugh became a cough.

"Judith."

The worry on Sam's face dampened Judith's jubilation.

"I want you to go back to the overhang." Sam nudged her in that direction.

The overhang? On this day of sunshine and gladness? She had spent enough time in the old camping spot to last for years.

"Not now." She wanted to explore this new world, even if it meant walking through water. Waves still lapped the bottom of the hillock, like the flood that had covered all mountaintops except Ararat. Too bad they didn't have a dove they could send out to check for dry spots. She giggled and took a tentative step down the hillside. Her bare feet slipped on the slick grass, and her injured knee wobbled. She fell down.

"Judith!" Sam caught her in his arms. "I didn't think you would be so foolish."

The short hairs on Sam's arms tickled Judith's bare legs. It felt strange—good. She giggled. She couldn't help it. It was utterly improper and hilarious and full of the promise of new life, all at the same time.

"Stop laughing, will you now? I'm serious."

"Yes, Punch." And Judith laughed again. A small part of her realized her hilarity was inappropriate to the situation. More than sheer joy at finding herself still alive after the storm lay behind her euphoria. She wrapped her arms around Sam's neck, wishing the distance to the overhang was farther. No sooner had she relaxed in his arms than he bent over and laid her next to the fire.

All her energy spent, Judith didn't move or speak. She watched Sam putter around the back of the shelter. Her side nearest the fire felt overly warm, while the rest of her shivered. Sam saw the movement and frowned.

"Let me look at your leg." He untied the bandage and studied her knee, creases appearing between his eyes. Judith struggled into a sitting position and looked as well. Below the mud-and-grass-stained tatters of her dress, she could see the knee had swollen and reddened.

"Is it—infected?"

Sam pressed the still-tender skin. She struggled not to wince. He cleaned the wound and bent his head to look at it closely. She felt a little uncomfortable with his close inspection. At last he raised his head. "No infection. I think muscle damage has caused the swelling." He hesitated.

"What is it?" Judith wanted to know what was troubling Sam.

"Although I see no sign of infection, you have a fever." Sam knelt beside Judith and took her hand between his. "My dearest love, I fear for your health. I am going to search the island. See if I can find a pot or two, some fresh water, food if possible." He piled a few small branches to form a shelf and laid out the items she had brought in the tarp. Then he took the heavy material and pulled it over her.

"While I am gone—" Sam's cheeks pinked. "Remove your clothes and lay them by the fire. Do not put them back on until the water has left them."

Judith felt herself flush, and knew it wasn't from fever. She sputtered. "I never—"

"Don't fret, my dearest." Sam lifted her hand to his mouth to kiss it. "I will call out before I come back in." His face scrunched with concern. "Can you manage the buttons and hooks?"

Judith grinned with a faint echo of her earlier smiles. "Yes. But I wish I could go with you."

"None of that." Sam let go of her hand. "Let me take care of you. Your father trusted me with his most prized possession. He will not like it if he returns to find you sick."

Sam smiled farewell and walked out from the overhang. Delicious delight spread warmth through Judith's body, whether from the heat of the fire or the depth of Sam's regard—or both—she couldn't say.

∽

Sam prayed for Judith's health as he made his way down the hillock, wishing he could race through the grass the way he had in childhood. Not today. A single misstep, and he would plunge his foot onto a board with a nail in it or stab himself with a broken branch. Sam bit his bottom lip and sent up a prayer. He felt helpless. They needed food and a way to collect and heat water. If only he could fix Judith some tea, even if just from pine needles. . . .

He reached the bottom of the hillock and stepped into the lake that had been Capernaum Island. Cold water rose past his ankles and halfway up his calves as he sloshed through the muck. His own cottage lay closest, so he headed in that direction. He didn't expect to find foodstuffs lined neatly on shelves; but perhaps he could lay his hands on a few things. In any case, it was a place to start. God willing, he would even locate some of his medical instruments.

He walked through the clearing and past the old maple tree stump that refused to be uprooted in all the years of working the farm. It remained there, too stubborn to let even the storm lift it away. He was glad to know the wind and rain had not reached to the depths of the root systems of the island. He pushed through corncobs and wheat stalks floating in the water.

When Sam approached his home, he halted. Half the roof sank into the muck, like a child's play house. A few beams from the north wall were left, but the wind that had started blowing from the east and then shifted to the west had taken three walls hostage, hiding them who knew where. All the memories. . .

Sam shook himself, wanting to rid his mind of those thoughts. *Keep focused on your mission.* The few remaining beams stood around the surgery. Perhaps they had provided enough shelter to keep a few things intact. He prayed it was so.

The debris underfoot increased the nearer he drew to the ruin. Something clanged when his boot hit it. A pot? Sam reached down and found Mama's favorite kettle. *Praise be.* He leaned over and ran his hand through the water, hoping to find one more pot. *There.* The handle was broken and the sides bent, but it could still be used. A spoon floated by, and he grabbed it.

Next stop, the surgery.

Chapter 18

In the area that had once housed Sam's surgery, broken tables and glass and soggy paper pulp mixed with water and turned it into mush. He fought his dismay, his eyes scanning the area for anything useable. Bobbing in the far corner, where two boards remained together, he spotted his medical bag. Joy jumped inside him.

Next, Sam considered the problem of food. The storm had sprinkled flour and cornmeal throughout the house. He found an uncorked crock of something. He opened it and sniffed. Molasses. He added that to the growing pile in his arms.

But how to get fresh water? Underfoot, rain had mixed with the sea water that had washed across the island. Did the pump still work? He waded through the debris to check and primed it once, twice, three times. At first mud and slush pushed out, but finally sweet, clear water appeared. He filled the large kettle.

Sam prepared to return to the hillock when he spotted a barrel some distance away, in the direction of the Wemblys' house. He decided to check it out. Balancing the kettle and other items in his arms, he set out down the road. Everything he was carrying made progress even slower. He could have used the tarp, but Judith needed the warmth. If necessary, he could make a second trip.

The barrel contained salted fish. *Food.* He licked his lips, his stomach growling in anticipation of something to fill it. The barrel had not belonged to him, but the owner—whoever he was—wouldn't mind, under the circumstances.

How could Sam get the barrel back to the hillock, along with everything else? He felt as though he had as few tools as Adam had in the Garden of Eden. In other words, none. Even if he had a wheelbarrow, he couldn't push it through the mud. Well, the barrel was shaped like a wheel. He could roll the barrel with his feet while carrying the other items in his arms. He frowned. That could take hours. He wouldn't make it back to the hillock before sundown, and he needed, *wanted,* to return to Judith long before then.

A row boat. Push it along with an oar like a punter. That might work. But where could he find one? The thought died as soon as it formed. The Hathaways had not owned a vessel of any kind since his father's death. Even if they had, the gale would have torn it to shreds.

Although Sam had avoided boats since his father's death, today he longed for one. It seemed the speediest way to cross the standing water to the hillock where Judith waited. Waves and rocks and dangers didn't enter his thinking.

In the cauldron of the storm, his fears of the ocean and travel at sea had disappeared.

Sam wanted to skip, jump, clap his hands. He couldn't without losing the precious clean water. Instead, a wide smile stretched his facial muscles, as if the edges of his lips could touch each ear, cracking the salty residue on his face. God did indeed work in mysterious ways His wonders to perform, if He used a great gale like yesterday's storm to undo Sam's greatest fear. He couldn't wait to tell Judith.

After the spurt of jubilation, reality returned. The problem of moving the barrel remained. Sam turned the barrel on end. If he slipped his medical bag over his arm like a satchel, the remaining items would fit on top of the barrel. His arms could hold it well enough to carry it.

Sam bypassed the cottage on his way back to the hillock, his desire to return to Judith guiding his feet to the safest footing. The water level had fallen during the past few hours. In much less time than he considered possible, he had returned to the overhang.

∞

"Judith?" Sam's voice roused Judith from her quiet thoughts. "Are you decent?"

"Yes, sir." The clothes had dried in no time at all next to the fire. She pulled the tarp over her bare legs.

Judith gasped at the sight of the apparition that pushed into the shelter. How had Sam ever managed to transport so much?

"Fresh water!" Sam set the kettle down carefully. He didn't want to waste a single drop. He withdrew a crock jar from his pocket. "Molasses. And my medical bag!" He grinned. "God hid it in the place the wind was least likely to throw it around. Of course, the instruments may be broken. I haven't had opportunity to check yet." His face momentarily sobered, but he couldn't suppress a smile.

"And last of all—food! I found a barrel of salted fish." Sam lifted the cover from the barrel. Judith breathed in the heavy scent like lilacs on a spring day.

He gestured at the brimming contents. "Care to cook some breakfast?" He proffered a pan. Sam seemed younger, lighter, somehow, as if he had found more than survival items in his search.

Judith laughed. "I may burn them."

"I will eat them even if they are charred to the bone. I would even eat them cold, but you need the broth."

Judith screwed up her face. "Broth. If only I could steam them, but we have no covering."

"Leaves," Sam announced. "That's what we use to steam lobsters."

Judith nodded. She used the pan to take a modicum of water from the kettle, wrapped the fish in leaves, and placed it over glowing ashes at the edge of the fire.

"What happened?" she demanded.

"I found what we needed," Sam said. "God was good."

"It's more than that. You're different in some way I can't place."

"Oh, that." Sam dipped the water flask into the kettle to refill it and drank from the mouth. "When I was figuring out how to get the barrel here with everything else, I wanted a boat."

Judith stared at him blankly, her mouth forming his words. She repeated them out loud. "You wanted a boat." A smile stole around her mouth, and she repeated them again, shouting this time. "You wanted a boat!" She flung her arms around Sam's neck and kissed his cheek. Judith leaned back, her face wreathed in smiles. "You've always been brave. But now—you're not afraid anymore."

Sam nodded his head. "I guess the storm cured me of the problem." Laughter ripped through him, a sound that came from deep inside. "With God's help." He thought about what Judith had said. "You think I was always brave?"

"Isn't that what courage means? Acting even when you're afraid?" Judith peeked at the fish in the pot, a blush coloring her cheeks. She faced him straight on, holding Sam with her gaze. "You never let your fear keep you from doing what was right. You came back to Capernaum. You faced those monstrous waves. For me. I will always treasure that memory in my heart."

Sam wanted to capture those pink lips with his own, but he dared not. "Thank you."

Judith lowered her gaze. "You're welcome." She pierced the steaming fish with the knife. Flakes of white meat showed on the utensil when she lifted it out. "It's ready." She lifted the pieces out on their beds of leaves and offered him the spoon to sip the broth. "I considered taking the food outside, but without bowls or mugs, we'd best eat here. We can go out later."

The fish fell apart in their hands, and the broth satisfied a hunger Sam had suppressed for too long. They finished one flask of water between them. They drank a second slowly, extracting every morsel of fish from the bones. Never had such plain fare tasted so good. "Never let anyone tell you that you can't cook." Sam sat back and rubbed his belly.

Judith smiled and refilled the flask. "Why, thank you, sir." She left the pot in the ashes. "Shall we go out on the hillside? I'll take the tarp." She walked onto the grassy hillside and patted the ground. "The ground has already dried somewhat." Overhead, the sun had started its descent into the west. "By tomorrow, perhaps the standing water will be gone."

"But not the mud." Sam suspected the ground would not be firm again for a week or more.

"When do you think the islanders will return?" Judith asked while Sam helped her spread out the tarp and settled her on the covering.

He looked out to sea. "I doubt they'll come today. Maybe tomorrow."

Ducking back into the overhang for his medical bag, he then sat down next to Judith, his hands clasping the bag uncertainly. Judith's health didn't worry him as it had earlier. A good rest and a decent meal had restored her normal vivacity. Her knee—which he had studied while she moved about, fixing dinner—hadn't worsened. He would clean the wound and leave it be. No bindings were left.

He felt small hands cover his, over the closure of the bag. "You can replace your equipment. It's what you carry inside of you that makes you a doctor—not what you had in your surgery. Look what you did for me with naught but a knife and fire." She lifted the edge of her skirt, so he could see the wound clearly. The redness had lessened. Judith twisted it from side to side. "It hardly hurts when I move it."

Sam set his bag aside. He would check it later.

"Look! There's the first star of the night." Judith pointed to the deepening turquoise sky.

"I've heard that if you make a wish on that star, you'll get whatever you want." He smiled wryly. "I'm not a superstitious man, and God has already given me everything I could wish for."

"Our lives." Judith nodded.

"Our future." Sam took a breath. "Do you know what your father said to me before I came back to the island?"

Hope jumped to Judith's face. "Did he"—she swallowed—"change his mind? About you—about us?"

"As good as. He told me that you mean more than life to him."

"Oh, Father." Judith bit her lip.

"Then he said, 'I know you will do everything you can to keep her safe. Please—return to the island. Not for my sake. For hers.'"

"Oh, Sam." Tears glistened in her eyes. She leaned in to him.

He accepted her implied invitation and caressed her lips with his own.

∞

Morning sun stabbed the overhang. Judith rubbed her eyes. She and Sam had stayed up talking until the sky turned dark as midnight. The hours sped by while they pointed out constellations, made up a few of their own, and shared stories about the years Sam had spent away from the island.

Judith insisted they keep the signal fire burning throughout the night, and Sam took the first watch. Today, they could build a cairn that could be seen better from the sea. She thought she was too excited to ever get to sleep, especially with Sam only on the other side of the fire bed, but the flickering flames lulled her into drowsiness as she recited as many Bible verses as she could remember. When sunlight awoke her, she realized Sam had never roused her for her turn at watch.

Judith felt every aching bone, and her knee throbbed, but she didn't care. She glanced in Sam's direction. He must have fallen asleep when daylight fell. She moved quietly onto the hillock to avoid waking him. She stretched her limbs, reaching to the sky in a gesture of praise to God. She rotated in a circle, praising the God of north and south and east and west.

When she turned in the direction of the beach, she let out a yelp. "Sam!"

He dashed out of the overhang. "What's the matter?"

"Look!" She pointed.

Several boats pulled up on the beach, and people were disembarking. "They're back!" She started down the slope.

"Wait!" Sam ducked under the overhang and returned with the most essential items from their campsite. "We probably won't return here tonight." He looked her up and down and chuckled. "Eli may demand a wedding when he sees the state you're in."

Judith looked down at her scandalously shortened skirt. Surely people would understand, but...she frowned and grabbed the tarp. The multiple-purpose item proved useful once again. She tied it around her waist. It met in the middle with a gap that widened as it spread over her skirt. The effect was a bit like an old-fashioned gown parted in front to show layers of petticoats.

"I'll walk in front," Sam promised. He picked his way carefully, mindful of her still-bare feet. A few minutes later, he announced, "They've seen us! Or maybe it's the fire they noticed. They're headed this way."

Now that the ground had absorbed the standing water, and with the sun illuminating obstacles in their path, they made quick time. Piers reached them first.

"Where's Judith?" he demanded.

"Here." Judith stepped out from behind Sam. "Praise God you're safe. Your family? Sara? The baby?"

Piers gaped at Judith's strange attire. Then he came to himself. "They are well. They will wait a few days more before returning. We thought it wise to check for damage." He gestured. "Nothing of our home remains."

"We're New Englanders. We will rebuild." Sam clapped Piers on the back.

"Did everyone from the island make it to safety?" Judith wanted to know.

"Yes! Praise be. One last boat made it to land during that strange calm. He said the lighthouse beacon kept him safe during the storm."

Judith relaxed and praised God. Their efforts had mattered, after all.

Piers looked from Judith to Sam and back again. He extended his hand. "You're a good man, Sam Hathaway. I'm not ashamed to admit it." He bowed in Judith's direction. "You will hear no more from me."

"Piers." Judith pinked, and unexpected tears came to her eyes. "You will always be my dear friend."

Piers's mouth twisted. "I do not expect anything more. Come, let me take you to your father."

"He's here? I thought—I feared—" She made a helpless gesture. "He broke his arm."

"A broken arm couldn't keep your father down for long. You must know that." Piers led them back the way he had come. "The doctor in town set it. He wanted Eli to remain behind, but you know your father. He had to return to you." He shrugged. "His heart is breaking to see what happened to the lighthouse."

The three of them chatted as they walked, gone the discomfort that had marked their conversations to date. Minutes later, Judith found herself on the beach.

The same soft sand tickled her toes, and the same blue sea greeted her eyes. Everything else had changed. She didn't care. She ran to Father, who sat on an upturned boat, talking with Reverend Snodgrass.

"Judith!" He stood to his feet and embraced her with his free arm. "Thank God you are alive." Then he noticed her unusual attire and cocked his head to study her knee. "What happened to you?"

Judith felt heat flood her cheeks. "It's nothing. I cut my knee, and Sam tended to it. I am well."

"The doctor, heh? Come ahead and join us, Sam." He gestured for Sam to join them.

Sam stepped forward. "I took care of her, sir, just as you asked."

Judith felt Sam reaching for her free hand.

"So that's how it is." Father started to proffer his right hand, but a sling held it in place. "I know you did, son. You have my permission to court my daughter. There's not a better man on the island."

Judith smiled through her tears. The great gale had blown a fresh wind of love and grace across Capernaum Island.

Epilogue

September 21, 1816

Judith took out the pumpkin bread dough she had shaped into biscuits earlier in the morning. Father had told her not to bother with a fancy breakfast, but she wanted to provide him with the best she could prepare on this last day. She thrust the pan into the oven when she heard footsteps on the stairs.

"Smells good." Father beamed. He smiled a lot these days. Over the spring and summer, he had overseen the construction of a new lighthouse built of stone and mortar. Most islanders had returned. The men of the village pitched in after they finished rebuilding their homes. Piers was one of the volunteers, of course, as well as Sam. Dear Sam.

"We should have time to read our Bible portion while the biscuits bake." Judith poured two mugs of coffee and sat down, ready to hear from one of the minor prophets.

The Bible was water-stained and some pages blurred, but Judith treasured her memories of its promises during the gale. Father surprised her by turning to the family record in the middle of the Bible. "Look." He turned it in her direction.

Beneath the record of her mother's death, she read "Samuel Hathaway Jr. united in holy matrimony with Judith Morrison, September 21, 1816."

"Now don't let too much time pass before I add grandchildren to the record."

"Father!" Judith blushed.

Eli turned to the New Testament. "I know the wedding ceremony includes 1 Corinthians 13, but I wanted to read it this morning, as well."

Reverend Snodgrass planned to preach from the thirteenth chapter of 1 Corinthians during the ceremony, but Judith would never tire of hearing the familiar words.

" 'Charity. . .beareth all things, believeth all things, hopeth all things, endureth all things. Charity never faileth.'" Father recited the words with unusual feeling. He looked up from the Bible. "Remember that, child. The tender feelings you hold for Sam today may falter, but love, true charity, will not fail. Let us pray." He offered a shortened version of his usual prayer, as if he was as excited about the day ahead of them as she was. He sniffed the air. "Now, are those biscuits done yet?"

Judith set out fresh-churned butter and pulled the pan of biscuits from the oven. Plump and evenly brown, they testified to her improved cooking skills.

After breakfast, Sara Vanderkamp arrived at the door with her children. She would stand up with Judith. Young Martin hoisted his short legs over the doorsill and ran to Judith. Sara followed, a covered basket dangling from her left arm.

"Go. I'll clean up." Father looked a bit forlorn. "It won't do for my daughter to be late for her wedding."

Judith hugged him. "Thank you for everything." Abigail played with her little brother while Sara followed Judith into the curtained corner where her bed sat.

A new dress draped across her bed covers.

"I've never seen anything so fine." Sara fingered the mauve muslin material.

Father had insisted Judith make a new dress for the wedding. She copied the latest fashions, with a high waistline, ruffled neckline, and double-yoked collar. She couldn't wait for Sam to see her. "It does seem like a waste, although I will wear the dress to Sunday meetings after the wedding."

"You will be lovely. Oh, and I brought flowers." Sara uncovered her basket. "I spotted a patch of wildflowers last week and returned there this morning. I know they won't bring good luck—"

"They're beautiful." Judith sat down. "It's my wedding day." She still couldn't believe it.

∞

The bell, found mired on the beach after the great gale, rang brightly in the newly constructed meeting house. Sam stopped pacing the parsonage floor. "Is she. . .?"

Mama peeked out the window. "I see her. She will be here in moments." She crossed the room to Sam and straightened his cravat. "You are very handsome." She wiped at her eyes. "I promised myself I wouldn't cry."

"You are not losing a son."

"I know. I love dear Judith. These are tears of happiness."

Reverend Snodgrass poked his head in. "It's time."

Mama entered the church first to take her place on the front bench. The pastor went next, and Sam last of all. He had only enough time to spot Sara Vanderkamp on the bench opposite his mother before the music swelled and the doors opened.

The setting sun silhouetted Judith, creating a halo around her face. No heavenly being could be more beautiful. This precious woman had beamed love into his broken and fearful heart and made it whole.

Whatever the future held, Sam would cherish Judith every day for the rest of their lives.

Award-winning author and speaker **Darlene Franklin** recently returned to cowboy country—Oklahoma. The move was prompted by her desire to be close to her son's family; her daughter Jolene has preceded her into glory.

Darlene loves music, needlework, reading and reality TV. Talia, a Lynx point Siamese cat, proudly claims Darlene as her person.

Seaside Romance is Darlene's tenth title with Barbour Publishing. Prodigal Patriot, a historical romance set in Vermont during the American Revolution, is currently available from Heartsong Presents. Visit Darlene's blog at www.darlenefranklinwrites.blogspot.com for information on book giveaways and upcoming titles.

THE MASTER'S MATCH

TAMELA HANCOCK MURRAY

Dedication

With special thanks to my parents, Herman and Ann Hancock.
You both have always given me your love and support.

Prologue

Providence, Rhode Island
1838

Ten-year-old Becca Hanham could not go home until she sold enough lucifers to buy bread. She pulled a ragged shawl around her tiny shoulders, but the motion did little to ward off the cold of a December evening in Providence. Standing by the tavern, she heard piano music, laughter, and singing from within. No wonder each night Father escaped to the light and warmth of such a place. At home Mother always looked sad, and Becca's brothers and sisters filled their cramped rented rooms with yelling and crying. Still, Becca yearned to go back. Whistling wind bit her bare legs.

She peered down the familiar street of Providence, hoping for customers. At the first cross street, a tall man wearing a stylish hat and unblemished outer coat walked alongside a woman donned in a fur-trimmed cape. Looking into each other's eyes, they laughed and talked as they approached.

What would it be like to be so happy? Becca wondered.

Soon the couple drew close enough to hear her. "Lucifers, sir?" Her hand shivered as she held the matches out to him.

He shook his head.

Knowing better than to pose her question to the lady, Becca set her gaze on the street and returned the lucifers to the small reed basket hanging from the crook of her arm.

"The poor little thing," she heard the woman mutter as they kept strolling. "Oh, Thomas, can't you buy some to help her? Your servants tend many fireplaces at your estate."

"You are too kindhearted, Elizabeth. If I bought goods from every street urchin, I'd soon be living alongside them. And so would you, after we're wed. You wouldn't want that, would you?" Even his thick topcoat didn't hide a shudder.

The woman glimpsed back at Becca. "No, I suppose not."

The first time Becca had heard similar observations, she felt a bite deeper than the cold, but since then she had grown too resilient to let such comments bother her. Why should anyone want to change places with her? A quick look at her reflection in a dark window confirmed that a washed face and clean clothes couldn't conceal her ragamuffin status.

Another couple, this time appearing to be mother and son, approached. Becca held out her wares and offered them for sale, but they kept their gazes from touching her.

The little girl fought discouragement. *If I can sell but a few more, I'll have enough money. Oh, it is so cold! Father in heaven, please send me a buyer soon.* She peered at the matches in her basket. If only there were a fireplace with blazing logs nearby. Then she could keep warm. But the nearest fireplace burned in the tavern, and children weren't welcome there. Thoughts of lighting a lucifer on a cobblestone visited her, but such a tiny flame wouldn't keep her warm long. Why, it would hardly warm her at all. How many times had Mother told her not to light matches since any she used would eat into their profit?

So cold. So cold.

With no one in sight, she couldn't resist. She had to light one. Kneeling to reach the cobblestone, she struck it hard against the surface, inhaling the strong odor of sulfur. How terrible hell must be if the doomed must smell sulfur forever. She shook. Still, the warmth against her palms helped, if only for a moment. She let the stick burn as long as she could before dropping it. Then there was no light and no warmth.

Dismal thoughts of the condemned left as she spotted a young man, just in his teens, rushing up the street toward her. His face looked the way she imagined young David's in the Bible—the courageous youth who beat a giant with a mere sling. Mother described him as comely. To Becca's eyes, that adjective fit the approaching figure. Her gaze took in his mode of dress. A stylish overcoat and fine leather boots told her he wasn't a servant, and he was too young to worry about keeping a fire lit. Discouragement visited. He wouldn't buy any lucifers. Still, she had to try.

He had almost passed her before she summoned the courage ask, "Lucifers, sir?"

To her shock, he stopped. Looking down at her, his brown eyes not only caught her gaze but also filled with compassion. He nodded. "It's terribly cold tonight. A girl like you shouldn't be out."

A blush of embarrassment warmed her face but gave her no comfort. "My family needs to eat, young master."

"Of course. Well, we have lots of fireplaces at my house. Cook will be happy to see a new box of lucifers."

"A whole box, sir?" She tried not to gasp with happiness.

"Yes." He extended his gloved hand. "May I have the lucifers, please?"

Wary, she nodded and handed them to him, then watched him place the container in his coat pocket. She prayed she hadn't been duped, that as a joke he would run off with her wares without paying. If that happened, Father would whip her for sure. She swallowed.

He remained in place and took off a black leather glove. She couldn't help but wish she had gloves to cover her bare fingers. "Hold out your hands, please."

She extended one hand.

He smiled. "No, both. If you will."

"Both?" Yet she complied.

He reached into another pocket and withdrew a number of coins, then placed them in her open palms.

She gasped, noting most were ten-cent coins. Never had she been so grateful to see an engraving of Lady Liberty with a star for each of the thirteen original colonies surrounding her image. "But this is too much, sir."

He slid his fine glove back over his hand. "Perhaps you might buy a pair of mittens."

She would never be permitted to spend money on herself but didn't want to point out the fact. "Really, sir, I must charge only what's fair."

"I don't want any of it back. Please. Keep the money in the name of Christian charity."

Christian charity wasn't unknown to her, but such generosity was, even in the name of Christ. She tried not to gasp. "Are—are ya sure?"

"I've never been more certain of anything."

She'd never held so much money in her life. "Thank you, sir. Thank you from the bottom of my heart." Clutching the money, she hurried to buy the bread so she could rush home and warm her toes by the fire.

"Lord, I know that stranger didn't need so many lucifers. He bought them out of mercy. I didn't know there could be so much kindness—at least not for me," she muttered. "I'm so glad he belongs to Thee. Please, keep him in Thy protection forever."

Chapter 1

1848

How much longer will that triflin' Abby girl be gone? I'm hungry." Father's voice bellowed from the room he shared with his wife and the babies.

Up to her elbows in dishwater, Becca shuddered. She recalled her days as the family's match girl and Father's wrath if she didn't sell enough lucifers to keep the family fed. If only he could get his job back at the factory, but he loved the bottle more than any work, and even the most patient boss couldn't afford her father's drunkenness and absences. The brother who did manage to keep a factory job had wed, so his earnings supported his wife and their new baby girl.

What little income their household earned came from sporadic odd jobs she and her younger siblings could pick up now and again. Two older sisters had married as quickly as they could to escape and now had their own homes to manage. In the meantime Becca, now the oldest of the remaining siblings, spent her waking hours helping Mother with Becca's brothers and sisters. One could almost set the calendar by the arrival of a new Hanham baby each year. With so many mouths to feed, they were forced to squeeze the most out of every cent.

Wiping a dish without setting her mind to the task, she recalled that bitter evening so many years ago. Each day since then she had prayed for the safety of the young man who had bought lights from her when she was at her most desperate point. If he hadn't shown her such mercy, she wondered how long she would have suffered in the unusually bitter and miserably cold night.

"Becca!" Father's voice punctured the air as he entered the front room that served as the kitchen and parlor.

She let the semiclean dish fall back into the water and turned halfway toward him. "Yea, Father?"

"Look at me when I speak to ya." A tall figure, he appeared imposing even when he wasn't in a foul mood.

"Yes, Father." Without stopping to swipe water from her hands, she faced him.

"Where is that Abby girl?" He sat at the table, the burden of his weight causing the old pine chair, most of its varnish long worn off, to creak.

"Little Abby? I'm sure she's still out sellin' lucifers, Father." Becca looked

118

outside. "It's still mornin'. She has hours left. Oftentimes I had to sell well into the night, remember?"

He grunted.

"I just hope she doesn't have to stay out too long today. This January weather chills to the bone."

"I doubt she'll stay out all night like you did," Father observed. "She's a shirker, that's what she is. Ya always brought in enough fer us." He eyed a nearby pitcher. "Pour me some ale now."

She wanted to defend little Abby but knew that argument would do more harm than good and increase Father's ill temper. Instead she remained agreeable and picked up the pitcher. "Yea, Father."

Poor Abby. Memories of how difficult being a match girl was flooded her, bringing her angst. As soon as Father swigged the portion of ale Becca poured, she returned to her dishes. At least the numbing drink would keep him occupied and quiet for a few dear moments.

The next instant, Mother came back from errands, a tired expression on her face. When she entered, a blast of cold air followed her through the open door.

"Shut the door, woman," Father said. "It's cold enough in here as it is."

Becca couldn't argue that. In winter the house never felt warm enough.

"I'm sorry."

Becca looked at the reed basket Mother used for groceries and realized it held precious little.

"Where's the food?" Father asked. "Seems like ya didn't hardly bring us nothin'."

Setting the basket on the table, Mother apologized in a small voice. "I bought what I could with the pennies I had. Mr. Sloane says he won't give us no more credit. We have to pay up our bill."

Father snarled and set down his mug with enough force to bang against the table. "Is that so? Why, I oughta go right there and give 'im some o' this, I should." He pounded his left fist into his open right palm.

Mother rushed to his side and placed a restricting hand on his shoulder. "Please don't. Not now. Especially not now with the new baby on the way."

Though the announcement didn't come as a surprise, Becca suppressed a groan. She chastised herself for her feelings, but a new life would make things even harder for the family. "A—another baby? But Bennie is only three months old."

"Shut yer mouth, girl. A new baby's a blessin', I tell you, if it's a boy." Father puffed up his chest. "Soon the children I sire will be enough to fill all of Providence. I'm sure this new baby will be a healthy boy."

Thoughts of two lost siblings sent a wave of sadness through Becca. Obadiah had lived only a day after his birth. A passive little thing, he'd withered away and died. Why, they did not know. Five years ago another little boy, Manny, had been run over and killed by a horse when he was crossing the street trying to reach a customer wanting a newspaper. They lived in a dangerous world, and only cautious children with strong constitutions survived to adulthood. Becca prayed the new life in Mother's womb was already endowed by God with both of those traits.

"A baby's a blessin' whether a boy or girl." Mother frowned. "But I hate bringin' a new life into a place where there ain't enough money to pay fer food. What will we do?"

"I know what we can do." Father set his gaze on his daughter. "Becca, ye're a good worker. It's past time fer ya to get a job that pays a wage."

Mother paled. "But what will I do? I need Becca here to help me."

"Enough, woman. Ya don't need to be such a sloth. Time for ya to take on more work so we can feed this family." Pride filled his voice. "Yea, it's a good thing for a man to sire a brood o' twenty and countin'."

Mother remained at Father's side but turned her face to Becca. Wide eyes and a distressed line of her mouth told her she wanted help convincing Father that their daughter shouldn't get a job.

A fortifying breath gave Becca courage. "Father, I want to stay here and tend to me brothers and sisters."

"Enough of that. If ya don't want to work in town, ya can always wed. At least then with ya married and out of the house, there'll be one less mouth to feed. Just think o' yer older sisters and brothers, all with husbands and wives of their own now. And with Deb havin' a little one o' her own soon, I'll be a grandfather again. Six and countin'. Why don't ya do me proud, too?" Father rubbed the salt-and-pepper stubble on his chin and rocked his chair back against the wall. "Ya know, I've seen how Micah Judd looks at ya. Maybe the two o' ya could make a go of it."

The image of a rotund, unkempt boy who couldn't utter a thought without cursing came to mind. "That foul oaf?"

How Father managed to look offended, she didn't know. "He ain't so bad now. What's the matter? Think ya can do better—mebbe get a wealthy gentleman?" His laugh sounded ugly.

"You might not believe me, but money ain't me goal."

"And that's a good thing, too, since there ain't no money 'round this part o' town." Father chortled.

Becca remained serious, facing her father as she leaned against the counter. "I don't fancy Micah because he's not a godly man. And I don't love him."

"Love him?" Father's chuckle had no mirth. "There's more to marriage than love." He looked to Mother for confirmation. "Ain't that right, woman?"

"Love is a nice thing to have. That's why I'm still here." Mother's quiet voice matched her meekness as she stared at the tabletop.

"Is that right? I don't believe it. No, ye're here because I kept ya and yer kids fed and clothed all these years." Father folded his arms and cleared his throat.

Mother surveyed her cotton dress, thin with wear and mended more than once, before her gaze shot up to meet his. "We started out in love. Remember those days?" Hurt mixed with wistfulness colored her voice.

"Sure I do." His voice was devoid of emotion as he dismissed his wife and turned to his daughter. "Now, girl, ya can make a good life with Micah. No doubt about it."

Queasiness stabbed at her gut. "No, Father. I'll find me a job."

"So ye're serious?" Mother's eyebrows rose, and her mouth slackened in alarm. "Where?"

"I don't know, Mother." How could she know? She hadn't considered the possibility until moments ago. "I—I ain't got no skills, 'cept the ones I learned at yer knee."

"Yea, ya know how to run a household better than anyone else I know," she agreed. "Surpassin' even meself, I'd say."

"There's no better place to use what ya learned here than in a position as a wife." Father shrugged. "But if ya can find a job, suit yerself. That will be more money to line me pocket. Mebbe Mr. Whittaker would hire ya at the tavern. I could put in a good word fer ya."

Becca imagined if she took such a position she'd be ogled and prodded by drunken men, young and old alike. Not to mention Father would expect her to pour him ale for free when the owner wasn't watching. "I—I'd rather work somewhere else."

He scowled. "Where, Miss High Horse? Like ya said yerself, ya ain't got no trainin' fer a good job."

"Maybe one of the factories will take me."

Mother pursed her lips. "No doubt they will, a hard worker like you. But ya know from yer brother's experience that the hours are long and the work can be dangerous."

"The pay is good," Father said.

"Yea, but I think ye'd be happier doin' somethin' else." Mother brightened. "I know. Ye're wonderful with yer brothers and sisters. Mebbe ya can be a nanny for some upper-crust folks."

"That's it! Why, I don't mind helpin' ya here around the house. So why should I mind helpin' out some society woman? I'd think she'd have less children than we have runnin' around here." Becca spoke faster as her excitement increased. "Yea, I think I could do that." Without considering the consequences, she took off her tired apron, threw it over a kitchen chair, and headed to the tiny room she shared in discomfort with eight sisters.

Mother followed her. "What are ya doin'?"

"I'm takin' ya up on yer suggestion, that's all. If I'm a-thinkin' I'll get me a job,

I'd better look me best. So I'm washin' me face and hands." A quick lean toward the mirror told her she looked presentable enough, even under close scrutiny. Behind her, she caught Mother's reflection. The graying woman's shoulders stooped more than usual, making her seem even older than her forty years. Any trace of happiness had vanished from her face and demeanor. Sighing, Mother crossed her hands over her chest. She looked at the straw-stuffed mattresses on the floor as though she considered sitting on one but seemed to think better of it and remained standing.

Becca didn't turn around. Instead she twisted her coffee-colored hair into a flattering upward style as she consoled her parent, leaving a few ringlets to fall loose around her face. "Don't be sad, Mother. Think of this as a new adventure. Fer me, fer all of us. Maybe the whole Hanham clan will be better off because I went and worked fer some society folks." Becca retrieved her best dress—the one she wasn't wearing at present—out of the oak wardrobe that Grandfather had made for Mother on the occasion of her wedding. The old and simple garment was no longer considered fashionable, but it would have to do. She slipped off her old dress and slid the clean cotton frock over her petticoats, grateful that she made a point of keeping one step ahead in the ongoing battle against mounds of dirty clothes.

"But I didn't think ye'd be taking action so soon," Mother protested to the point that she whined.

Unaccustomed to her mother complaining, Becca winced. "I'm sorry, but I can't marry Micah, and if I don't do somethin' to earn money quicklike, Father will have us at the altar before we can take in a breath." She touched her mother's shoulder. "Ya don't blame me fer not wantin' to hitch meself to Micah, do ya? Please say ya don't blame me."

"I don't. I want someone better than Micah for ya, too, even if he does have a good position at the silver factory. But a job fer me Becca now? I thought we was just talkin' before."

One of Becca's brothers, Samuel, ran in and put his face in his mother's skirts. Concerned about his own problems, the boy didn't notice he had interrupted a critical exchange between his mother and sister. "They won't wet me pway wif 'em," the little fellow wailed.

Both women knew "they" referred to his older siblings and assorted neighborhood children. Mother stroked his curly blond locks. "Tell yer brothers and sisters I said to let ya play with 'em or I'll make 'em come in the rest of the day. Run along now."

He lifted his face, smiled, and nodded. "I'll tell 'em."

Mother watched him run out. "Ah, to be young. Ever'thin's right with the world in a minute."

"If you're a boy around here, that's so." Becca sighed. "At least Father let Laban choose his own wife."

"Yea, but who can object to Lizzie?"

The image of a green-eyed beauty popped into her head. Lizzie made Laban happy. What more could anyone want? "She's one of my favorites, she is. I wish she had a brother older than ten," Becca ventured in half jest.

Mother's laugh brightened the room. "There's plenty o' crop around here. Maybe one of the other fellas caught yer eye? Ye're pretty enough to have any boy around. Peter, maybe?"

He appealed to Becca more than Father's choice of Micah, but not enough to wed. "No, Mother. There ain't nobody I want. At least nobody I've seen around here. I'd rather be an old maid than be unhappy in marriage."

Mother gasped. "An old maid! Ya don't mean it!"

"I do. I won't marry someone I don't love. You love Father, and your marriage is hard enough."

Mother looked at the floor. "I can't deny it."

"I'll do as Father says and get me a job. Today is as good a day as any to get started." She peered outside the window to eye the midmorning sun cutting the rising fog over the Providence River. "It's early yet. I have the whole day ahead o' me. I 'spect I'll have a job by noon." She took her coat out of the wardrobe.

"That wrap looks mighty worn. If I'da known you'd be lookin' fer work, I'da sewn ya a new one."

Becca fought the impulse to ask Mother how, considering they lacked for grocery money and probably were behind on rent, too. A new coat would be an ambitious sewing project requiring much fabric. Instead Becca whipped on the gray garment she already owned and buttoned it to the top. "This coat has come in good, and it's still more than warm enough to fight the Narragansett winds. At least it don't usually get as chilly here as Aunt Hilda says it gets in the Berkshires."

"We can thank the good Lord for that." Mother paused, and her eyes grew misty. "I don't want ya to go. Let me speak with yer father. I can talk some sense into him."

Becca had seen her mother's pleas for any favor ignored too many times by her father to believe such a brag. "I knows ya need help, Mother, but Mary can take over some of my load. And her chores can go to Sissy. And Naomi's already doin' more than her share."

"I can't argue none of that." Tears flowing from her mother's eyes betrayed her sense of helplessness.

Becca embraced her mother. "Aw, it ain't as bad as all that. In a way Father's right. It's time I made my way in the world. And don't worry. I ain't goin' far. I'll try to work close enough that I can come home ever' night."

"I ain't sure about that. Babies wake up in the night, ya know, and their mothers want the nanny to tend to 'em. Don't count on seein' much of us if ya get a job as a nanny." Mother choked but composed herself enough to offer Becca a close-lipped half smile. "Then you'd best take your other dress and personal necessities along with ya."

Becca packed as her mother suggested, then donned a woolen bonnet before giving her mother one last embrace. "I'll be fine. Don't ya worry, now."

"I hope so. Ya know, there's been talk of bank robbers strikin' in the better parts of town. I want ya to stay safe, ya hear?"

"Oh, Mother. What would a bank robber want with me? I don't have nothin' of value on my person, and I ain't got no reason to go near a bank. Ya worry too much." She picked up a cloth bag she had embroidered for herself, a small luxury she felt added a bit of fashion to her plain style of dress.

"Mebbe I do. I'll try not to so much." Mother squeezed her one last time before letting her go. She wouldn't let her gaze meet her daughter's. "I—I'd better get to my dustin'. And there's lunch to think about. Another burden fer me, now that ya won't be here."

"Remember, there are sisters behind me to take me place. Why, ya won't miss me a'tall."

Mother sniffled.

Forcing herself to leave her mother behind, Becca went through the front room. Her father hadn't moved from the table.

He looked her over and then eyed the satchel. "Goin' outside, eh? What's that ya got there?"

"My clothin'. I might not be able to come back ever' night. But I promised Mother I'll try."

"So ye're really goin' to get a job at some rich woman's house." He let out a grunt. "I wish ya luck." His tone indicated he thought her chances were as good as walking a city block without encountering horse manure.

She decided to remain cheerful. "Thank ya, Father."

"Ya just be sure to bring yer money to me. Ya got yer family to feed. Ya don't need to buy perfume and dresses and hats fer yerself."

She'd never been free with what little money she ever earned—not even the hands full of change from that young man so long ago. Why Father gave her such admonition, she didn't know. "Yea, Father."

"And another thing before ya go."

She looked at him with more hope than she meant. Perhaps he would offer a few kind words to her before she left. Maybe even an embrace. "Yea, Father?"

"Pour me another portion o' ale."

∽

Nash Abercrombie sat at the desk in his study, mulling over a stack of correspondence in need of urgent tending. He'd been abroad, and the number of papers in the pile overwhelmed him. Though Nash's official period of mourning for his father, Timothy Abercrombie, had slipped away in a sad blur, many of the letters and notices concerned matters regarding the estate. Addressing them felt painful. Not a day passed when Nash didn't grieve over his loss. He had always felt badly enough that he never knew his mother, but why did his father have to be taken away much too early—and in Nash's absence when he couldn't be at his deathbed to tell him good-bye? Father and son knew they loved each other, but Nash wished he could have told him one last time on this side of heaven. His father had been manly, yet gentle and kind with a ready laugh and a God-fearing spirit. The world suffered more without him.

His faithful old butler knocked.

"Yes?" Nash answered.

"Pardon me, sir," Harrod said. "Cook asks if you would like her to send Jack to the Providence Arcade for lobster. She suggests it for dinner tonight."

He smiled. "The thought is kind of her, but really, I am dining alone and don't require such extravagance."

"Cook knows lobster is your favorite, and she wants to celebrate your arrival. We all celebrate your arrival, sir."

The notion of such a delicacy tempted him, but the reality of eating alone, along with the price of lobster in winter, left him without an appetite. God had provided him with more than enough wealth, but squandering money seemed unwise from both a spiritual and practical standpoint. "Perhaps I can indulge in lobster this spring when I can host a proper dinner party. Tell her I appreciate her consideration, but tonight I'd love some of her delicious vegetable soup and herb bread. And a bit of cheese, if she has it on hand."

"She'll be disappointed, but I commend you on your frugal ways. Your father would be proud, sir."

Nash dismissed Harrod and swallowed a lump in his throat as the old servant took his leave. Harrod had been Father's valet and butler and now served Nash in the same capacity. Harrod's good opinion meant something to him.

Tapping his ivory stylus on the top of the desk, he couldn't help but think of Hazel Caldwell. In her eyes a modest soup would hardly be considered an adequate first course for a light luncheon. In his mind he could hear her chastising him for dining as a pauper would. He would hate to see the bills Hazel's future husband would be forced to pay.

He prayed someone would talk sense into Hazel so she wouldn't hold on to the dream of their marriage. He might not have told Papa he loved him before he died, but Nash did tell him his desire was not to wed Hazel, no matter how prestigious and important her family name and connections. Nash and the Abercrombie wealth were nothing more than a means to her social ends. Judging from the way she treated him—never taking an interest in him as a person and every discussion involving extravagance—her love for him could be contained in the tip of a hummingbird's beak.

He set down his stylus and rested his face in his open hands, thinking. Nash was no fool and knew about loveless matches in his circle. All would be well and proper on the surface. Wives chosen for beauty, prestige, or fortune—or some combination thereof—fulfilled their duty by providing heirs as soon as was proper after the wedding day. Then they took consolation in discreet love affairs, profligate spending, or both. Meanwhile the husbands took a mistress—or two. The idea of such an unbiblical arrangement sickened him, and never would his father have asked Nash to live his life in such a way.

Of course some of his friends and acquaintances had found love within their marriages. He wanted to be among their number. And that meant convincing Hazel that she would make a better match with someone else.

He smiled, knowing the expression held no joy. *She needs someone else indeed. Someone who can love her.*

He put his hands together in prayer. "Lord, give me the strength and courage to follow Thy will and my heart."

Chapter 2

Cloth satchel stuffed with everything she owned in the world on her arm, Becca set out with a determined step. The wealthy people's houses were up the hill, and up the hill she planned to go.

Frigid wind rubbed at her cheeks, but she tried not to think about the cold. She hadn't told her mother a fib about the warmth of her coat. As long as she kept walking, she stayed passably comfortable except where the coat didn't quite cover her skin. She'd worn the wrap several years, and the sleeves fell a bit short. But the mittens Mother knitted for her this past Christmas warmed her hands, and remnants of rags stuffed in her boots shielded her feet where the soles were worn through.

As she walked into the wealthy part of town, the atmosphere and scenery changed. Boisterous crowds couldn't be heard, and leering men didn't loiter in this part of town. Ramshackle, unpainted dwellings gave way to fine homes where, judging from appearances, inhabitants lived in luxury—or at least comfort. Self-conscious from the occasional curious stare aimed her way, she tilted her chin upward to show she indeed belonged there. After all, she was on a mission. She had just as much right to be there as anyone else.

Though she had entered a neighborhood on Benefit Street where ladies could afford nannies, she kept walking. No house looked more welcoming than another, and no reason presented itself as to why she shouldn't start knocking on doors. She stalled out of nervousness, despite her attempts to appear otherwise.

"Lord, where do I go?"

Gray clouds drifted over the sky, taking with them the brittle warmth from the winter sun. The time to start her search in earnest had arrived. Reaching a corner, she read the post. WILLIAMS STREET.

She smoothed her skirt and hair. Straightening her shoulders, she strolled to the front of a well-maintained house with a pretty wooden door and knocked.

A butler answered and inspected her with a keen eye. "How dare you, girl. Don't you know the help goes to the back?" The door banged shut.

She had never entertained illusions about her importance in society's ranks—her rung on the ladder hovered near the bottom—but she hadn't expected to encounter such rudeness, especially from a servant. She lingered at the door and gathered her thoughts. *He called me "the help." Come to think of it, I sure am the help. At least I hope I will be by the end of the day.*

127

Within minutes she found herself at the back door. Temptation to report the butler's unpleasant manner visited her, but she dismissed it. Snitching on a servant as Samuel tattled on his siblings would gain her no respect. She widened her eyes and set her mouth in a slightly upturned bow so she wouldn't show she'd already been treated in an abrupt manner. She took off the mitten on her right hand and knocked.

"Ye're late!" The shrill voice whizzed into the air before the door opened.

"I'm late?"

By this time an obese woman wearing a white cotton bonnet and apron splattered with melted lard stood before her. "Oh, I thought ya were the delivery boy. Who are ya, and what da ya want wif us?"

Becca didn't think the cook would be much help, but there was no reason to be rude—even though the butler had slammed the door in her face. "I'd like to speak with the mistress of the house, please."

"Ya would, would ya?" The woman eyed her. "Concernin' what?"

"I'd like a job. As a nanny."

The woman laughed so loudly Becca jumped back. "There ain't no need for a nanny here. Mistress is nearly sixty, and she lives alone wif nuffin' but us servants. Off with ya now. I've work to do."

"But—but surely there must be someone in one of these houses nearby needin' a nanny."

"How do ya expect me ta know such a thing? I come here to work, not gossip. Off with ya, I say." The woman banged the door shut in Becca's face.

Not about to let the grumpy cook get the best of her, Becca tried one house after another, trekking from one street to the next. Between each unsuccessful encounter, she watched the weather, hoping she could take shelter should snow start to fall.

At the seventeenth house, a pretty young maid answered. "A nanny? Why, yes, we're looking for a nanny. Mr. and Mrs. Gill are the parents of three girls, ages two, four, and five. And we are expecting a new arrival later this year."

Becca almost jumped up and down with glee. "That sounds wonderful."

The maid's eyebrows rose. "Really? You'd be surprised how many girls run away nearly screaming at the thought of three small charges and a new infant." She gave Becca a knowing grin. "I think she'll see you."

Becca's heart beat with anticipation as she followed the maid. Their little family sounded easy to tend in comparison to caring for her many siblings at home.

The maid escorted her into a small sitting room upstairs. On the way she couldn't help but drink in the sight of life-sized portraits painted in oils, ornate furnishings, and elaborate draperies. She imagined even a small table cost more than her family earned in a year. What would it be like to work in such a fine residence? She hoped to find out.

The sitting room proved simpler, but the woman did not. Donned in a morning dress that would have suited most people for church, she looked down her nose at Becca from her position on a settee and did not offer her a seat despite the availability of two chairs. "You don't look like a nanny."

"What does a nanny look like?"

"I don't know." The woman shifted in her seat, clearly taken aback that Becca had posed a question she couldn't answer without some thought. "More educated, I suppose. How much schooling have you had?"

"Hard to say, ma'am. Mother taught me how to read, write, and cipher numbers. She says I catch on real fast."

"I see. So you haven't had many advantages in life." Her tone reminded Becca of the long icicles hanging off the woman's front awning.

Becca's mouth fell open, embarrassing her. "How'd ya know?"

"I catch on real fast myself." The woman's slight smile told Becca she fancied herself funny, but Becca felt the joke had been made at her expense. "So where is your letter of recommendation?"

"Letter of recommendation?"

"Yes. Surely you have references to approach me in such a manner."

"References?"

Mrs. Gill breathed out once before speaking. "People who can tell me you'll be a good nanny."

"Oh. Well, Mother told me that's what I should be. I've helped take care of me brothers and sisters ever since I can remember."

"And how many do you have?"

"Nineteen, with another one on the way."

The woman gasped. "I suppose I could count that as experience with children. What caused you to visit me looking for a job as a nanny?"

How could she answer such a strange question? Mrs. Gill's house had been next in line, that's all. Becca had a feeling such an answer wouldn't impress the formidable woman. Honesty appeared to be her best option. "Me father said if I don't marry, I have to work."

"Oh. Is that the only reason?"

She took in a breath. "The only reason I'm a-lookin', yes, ma'am."

"I see. And someone who knows your father knows me? One of my lower-ranking servants, perhaps?"

Tired of this line of questioning and its implied insults, Becca laid out the whole truth. "I don't think so. I just walked till I found a street with pretty houses and started knockin' on doors."

Mrs. Gill clutched at her throat. "My, but that is unorthodox."

Becca wasn't sure what that meant, but she thought it best to nod.

Her interviewer stiffened. "So you have no formal credentials, no experience, and you know no one other than your parents who can recommend you?"

"Nobody as rich as you are."

Becca thought she discerned the slightest hint of a genuine smile touching the woman's lips, but that instant soon passed. "Someone in my position cannot entrust anyone without references or formal experience with the care of my precious children. I require someone far more cultured." She called for the maid.

Becca wasn't sure what to say next, but she did know from talking to other girls in her neighborhood who'd been servants that no matter what, you had to seem grateful. "Thank you, ma'am."

The maid arrived before the words left Becca's lips. "Escort her out, Mindy. And don't bring anyone else to me without proper proof of worth, or you'll summarily be dismissed. I have better things to do than to waste my time."

The maid quaked. "Yes, ma'am."

"I'm sorry," Becca whispered to the maid as they went to the back door. "She must be a fright to work for."

"Good-bye." Despite her harsh tone, something in the maid's eyes told Becca she had guessed right.

Back outdoors, Becca's steps slowed in spite of the fact a light snow fell. Maybe Father's warnings had been true. Maybe she was too worthless to get any type of job. "Lord, what should I do?"

∞

"Don't bother to announce me, Harrod." Hazel's commanding voice floated three floors up to his private study from the front hall. He wished he'd had the foresight to stay in his downstairs study where he met with business associates. But it was too late to change now.

"Nash will see me any time."

Nash cringed at the prospect of seeing her, but he prepared himself by putting away his Bible and making sure his face looked pleasant when she entered. He heard the muffled voice of Harrod, no doubt objecting that Nash shouldn't be disturbed without notice, but he knew no amount of opposition from anyone would deter Hazel. Nash envisioned her tossing her hat, gloves, and wrap to Harrod in a dismissive way. Poor Harrod. He'd be getting a generous bonus for his birthday this year.

Soon Hazel breezed into the study. "Nash, why didn't you send word you're home? I had to hear it from Laurel's upstairs maid who heard it from your chambermaid."

"I'll have to tell my chambermaid not to gossip."

"Truly, Nash, you are such a jester." She flitted her hand in his direction. "Why are you alone up here in this lonely study, popular as you are? Now that your official period of mourning for your father is over, it's time to resume your social life. I hope you're planning a party to celebrate your homecoming."

"I hadn't given the notion much thought."

She stood erect, reminding him of a stern sea captain. "Have you no intention of offering me a seat?"

"Please sit down." He nodded to the only other chair in the room.

She let out a breath, which told Nash she had expected him to rise and escort her to the chair. His mood allowed for no such nicety.

"Now, as for the party," she said as she seated herself, "I must consult your cook to be sure we have a proper menu. We wouldn't want anyone to think I'm engaged to marry a poor man, now, would we?"

Marriage to Hazel. The thought made him shiver.

"Cold, dear?" Hazel asked. "No wonder, with how you never allow the servants to keep a decent fire going. It's winter, you know, and you have plenty of money to keep the house warm. Why, when I stepped in the hallway just now, I hardly noticed the difference between the outdoors and inside."

"I hadn't asked for a fire in the front rooms today since I wasn't expecting company."

"But what if someone of great power, prestige, and influence comes to call? Surely you wouldn't want an important person to suffer the indignities of cold."

"Anyone dropping in unannounced deserves what he gets." Nash grinned in hopes she would see the spoonful of levity in his remark, but her open mouth showed horror.

"How terrible! Laurel would never stand for such an inhospitable attitude."

"Mitchell Gill is to be commended for earning money faster than the rate at which your sister can spend it."

"She spends it to keep up appearances, and that's what we should do once we're wed." Hazel's nose lifted a bit as she sniffed.

Nash leaned back in his chair. "Keeping up appearances is costly and not good stewardship."

"You sound like the preacher. Wasn't that the topic of his sermon last week? I never said we wouldn't give a little to the church. At least enough to keep up our standing—worthy of our position as occupants of the Abercrombie family pew—and to assure our family proper treatment on each and every baptism, funeral, and wedding," Hazel countered. "And speaking of weddings, when shall we set our date?"

"I suggest that might occur after I make a formal proposal of marriage. And I have no intention of doing so."

Hazel waved her hand as if batting at a gnat. "Ever since we waltzed the night away at the Harris cotillion, everyone knew it was only a matter of time before we'd be wed."

Nash tightened his lips. Indeed, he had been enchanted by Hazel that one night—the night they met when she moved into Providence to live with her sister. She had looked especially beautiful and beguiling, and her charming conversation had kept him entertained all evening. For a few fleeting moments, he thought he might love her one day.

He had no idea that she would become so unpleasant and self-serving overnight.

Or that, desperate for a society match, she would latch on to him and never let go.

Perhaps he had been the one who beguiled her, although he had made no promises nor been anything but a gentleman. He wished he'd never seen her, for no matter how sour a disposition he displayed in her presence or how much he protested he had no plans to marry her, she and her sister seemed bound and determined that Hazel would become Mrs. Nash Abercrombie. Even his absence, during which he never wrote her, hadn't dampened her resolve. He had to stop her plans. But how?

"I must say," she prattled, "Laurel pesters me every hour on the hour about when we will be having our engagement party."

Nash could feel time closing in on him. The situation had become clear. There was no hope in putting her off.

"Everyone is so excited about our wedding. Have you spoken to your groomsmen yet?"

"No." He didn't want to speak to anyone.

"I believe I mentioned twelve groomsmen, but now the number has increased to fourteen. Laurel wants me to include two of our cousins as bridesmaids I hadn't considered since they were in her wedding. I know someone as powerful and popular as you can easily find fourteen groomsmen."

Nash didn't answer. Of course, by asking every woman they knew to be in her wedding, Hazel had eliminated them from considering Nash as a suitor. He suspected Laurel had mapped out the strategy and Hazel hadn't hesitated to go along with it.

"But enough wedding talk. Men are bored to tears with such things. At least that's what my brother-in-law tells me whenever Laurel and I start discussing it."

Nash didn't answer. He knew Gill's protests of boredom signaled to the women they should come to their senses, but they were too stubborn to take the hint. Nash had a feeling he wouldn't be bored listening to the woman he really wanted to marry speak about their wedding.

"About the wedding, Hazel..."

She arched an eyebrow. "Yes?"

"I had hoped by my lack of correspondence with you while I was away that you would have discerned my feelings. However, I can see that I'll have to state my thoughts plainly." He paused. "It pains me that you continue to speak of the wedding. I have tried to tell you many times that I have no intention of going through with it. Why won't you listen?"

"Don't be ridiculous, Nash. Everyone knows we're planning to wed. You're just getting cold feet, that's all."

"I'm afraid it's more than cold feet, Hazel." Feeling pain at having to hurt her, Nash paused. "You are a fine woman in many ways, but I just don't harbor the type of fondness for you I would need to make you my wife. I beg you not to live in your dream world any longer. I cannot play along. I ask your forgiveness for any embarrassment you might feel by calling off the wedding, but it's better to suffer a little embarrassment now than to be miserable for the rest of our lives, isn't it?"

"Oh, pshaw. You'll change your mind by the time I return. Which brings me to my real reason for stopping by today. I must make a trip to Hartford for at least a month, perhaps longer. My friend from finishing school, Joan Dillard, has asked me to visit, and that means of course I must visit all my relations who live in the area or they will be quite offended. You understand."

"Of course."

"And of course I must make a special side trip to see my great-aunt Nora. She has been ill."

"I'm so sorry to hear that. I pray she will recover quickly."

"That's the first thing you've said all day that sounds like you possess the least bit of warmth," Hazel pointed out.

"Blame it on the cold weather," he quipped. "After all, my house is freezing, as you reminded me."

Hazel eyed the fireplace near Nash's desk. "Now that you mention it, it is getting colder in here. You allow the servants to be much too slothful, Nash. Really, you need me to run this household with an iron fist. We can't marry a moment too soon."

If Hazel were the type of woman he could love, Nash would have run into her arms, stroked her hair, and murmured sweet words about the long-awaited day. But he couldn't. Judging from Hazel's frigid look and stiff demeanor, she didn't miss any signs of longing or affection.

He couldn't marry Hazel. Not today, not next month, not ever.

∞

Becca stood on the street and looked at a row of fine homes. She had to keep trying. Maybe people on a different street would be friendlier than the ones she'd seen so far. No one had been helpful except for that nice maid who, for some reason unknown to her, worked for that awful woman. In other circumstances she and the maid might have been friends. Becca kept walking past the John Brown house.

POWER STREET.

"Maybe this is it. Maybe I will find God's power on this street." Her mood lightened by her silly joke, she tried a couple of other houses without success. The afternoon sun would disappear soon. She had to find something.

She watched a fashionable woman depart from the next house. She didn't turn Becca's way, so she couldn't see the woman's face, but Becca had no doubt it bore aristocratic features. The woman boarded a fine conveyance, and she was soon on her way. If she were the mistress of the house, maybe it wasn't a good time to ask about a position. Or maybe the woman was a daughter. Regardless, Becca had no time to waste speculating. She went to the back.

Even in the cold, the kitchen window had been left open a crack. Surely the fire burned hot in this house. Peering into the back-door window, Becca saw a congenial-looking woman with gray hair and plump arms pulling a cake from the hearth. Becca wished she hadn't smelled such a sweet aroma to remind her she had run out of her own house before lunch. A wiry maid with a hooked nose sat at the table, polishing silver forks with a cloth blackened by her work. She knocked, and the maid dropped a fork.

"I'm sorry," Becca called through the door. "I didn't mean to scare ya."

The maid grimaced and picked up the utensil before approaching the back door. "We weren't expecting anybody. Not just yet, anyway. Who are you?"

"I—I'm Becca Hanham. I'm here about a job."

"Already? Harrod worked fast." She saw Becca's satchel. "Set that in the corner. I'll show ya to yer room later."

Becca felt as though she'd been thrown in the middle of a story without reading the first chapters. But since the maid seemed friendly, she didn't ask questions. The cook was in the process of forming dough into a loaf. The yeasty aroma promised the baked bread would taste delectable. Becca hoped if she were hired here, her pay included meals.

"I'm glad to see ya, girlie. I got plenty o' work fer ya," the cook said.

The maid nodded. "Let me tell Harrod you're here."

Becca felt nervous. The cook eyed her with a bit too much happiness.

"But I hadn't sent word yet," she heard a man protest just outside the kitchen door.

"Well, somebody's here."

A man that Becca figured to be Harrod, with a proud carriage and well-kept white hair, entered the kitchen and studied her from head to toe. "Who are you and how did you hear about the position? I haven't sent word yet."

She filled him in on her personal details. "I—I didn't hear about a job, really, but I'm lookin'."

"We're hirin'," Cook said. "Our scullery maid eloped with the neighbor's footman this mornin', and I'm needin' help here. So do ya want the job or not?"

Harrod scowled at the cook. "I am in charge here. You are to remember that."

She shrank from him. "Yes, sir."

Becca tried not to quiver. If Harrod could make a strong woman such as Cook obey without question, he must be influential indeed.

The butler turned his attention to Becca. "She is right. We are in need of a scullery maid, and with so many women working in the factories nearby, household help is short. You will find that young Mr. Abercrombie is quite generous with his servants, and the work here is far less dangerous than many of the positions you'll find in manufacturing. We offer room and board, Thursday afternoons off, and an allowance of two dollars a week."

The offer was a far cry from the good relationship she might have with children, but without any other offers and snow falling with a vengeance just beyond the window, her choices seemed too limited for her to refuse. Besides, the idea of helping a cook appealed to her. Maybe she could learn new dishes to prepare at home. She nodded as she curtsied. "I accept."

"Good. That is a very wise decision, I assure you," Harrod said.

"Now that the master's home, we'll want everythin' to go just so," Cook said. "Even though he breaks me heart when he won't let me cook him a nice lobster." She placed both hands over her heart as though the motion would hold it together.

"Your opinions are not important," Harrod chastised her. "You are here to serve." He looked at Becca without blinking. "And that applies to you, as well, girlie. Don't forget it." Having dispensed his advice, he departed the kitchen.

Cook shook her head. "He likes to look strict, and I reckon he is. But he has a soft heart, that one."

As interesting as Harrod appeared, Becca wondered more about her new employer. "You say the master's home? Home from where?"

Cook handed her a bonnet and apron. "Home from a business trip abroad. Went all over Europe to increase business, he did. He's in charge of the tradin' company he inherited from his father now, and lots of people depend on him."

"He sounds very important." She hoped she would be worthy to work even as a scullery maid for someone so prominent.

"Oh, he is."

"Is he very old?"

Cook guffawed. "No, child. He's a bachelor still, livin' all alone here with just us servants. It's high time he married. Though I wish he warn't marryin' the one that's runnin' after him."

The master seemed more and more interesting. "Oh?"

The older woman shook her head. "I shouldn't have said that much. Now there's no more time for chat. There's work to be done." She escorted Becca to the scullery just off the kitchen and pointed to a mound of pots in need of scrubbing.

With effort she kept her mouth from dropping open upon seeing so much work waiting for her. "If there's just the master, then why so many pots?"

Cook shook her head. "You don't expect the servants to starve, do ya? We have to fix them their meals, too. And speakin' of servants, I come from a long line of servants. I'm a McIntire."

"Oh, I know some of yer clan, then. Patrick and Joseph play with me brothers."

"Yea, them's me nephews. I know who ya are." Pity filled her eyes. She clucked her tongue, and Becca realized the cook was aware of her father's reputation as a drunk.

"Seems like ever'body knows ever'body." Impoverishment was no shame. She could have held her head up, if only Father with his drinking and slovenly ways hadn't besmirched their name.

"Now, now, girlie. What yer father does or don't do ain't yer fault. Besides, ye're startin' yer own life now." Her voice became brisk. "As soon as ye're done there, ye'll be helpin' me with the master's dinner."

"What's fer dinner?" Images of food she had never eaten but only heard about—oyster stew, tender roast pork drenched with brown gravy, vegetables swimming in a sauce of butter and cream, and the cake that had just come out of the oven—popped into her mind.

"The master asked fer vegetable soup, bread, and cheese. I declare, sometimes my talents are wasted here." She glanced at the cooling cake on the counter. "He'll usually take dessert if I have it, though. That's why I made it."

"Oh!" Becca couldn't help but eye the fluffy-looking treat as though she were an ant at a picnic. She inhaled to allow its sweet scent to fill her nostrils.

Cook chuckled. "There'll be enough fer ya to have a thin slice. The master don't mind. He can't eat a whole cake anyway."

"But what about the rest of dinner?" If she had enough money to live in a fine home and pay servants well, she'd eat like a queen every night. "If he's eatin' that poor, are we servants on bread and water?" Eager for information, she had blurted the term "servant" for the first time in reference to herself. The idea sounded so strange she wondered if she could ever become accustomed to it.

Cook let out a hearty laugh. "We'll be havin' the same. I know that sounds odd, and in most fine homes, I'd venture it would be odd. But he lives simply. All that'll change when Miss Caldwell becomes his wife. Mark my words. Now off to the scullery with ya. Ye've got work to do."

Scrubbing pots wasn't easy, but she already knew that from her chores at home. Throwing herself into the task, she relished the chance to prove her worth. If she failed at this job, an unwanted match with Micah awaited.

Soon she heard Cook's exasperation. "I've got soup to prepare. Why must she leave the silver in the way?"

Becca rushed to the main part of the kitchen and saw Cook with her hands on her hips, shaking her head at silver implements on the table. "Shall I move those, Cook?"

Cook thought for a moment, then looked at the kitchen door. "No tellin' where she went. Oh, all right, girlie." She picked up a set of silver candlesticks with marble orbs in the center and matching marble platforms on the ends. "I think she's gettin' ready for Miss Caldwell to visit. She demands that all the silver stay shiny whether or not it's bein' used at the moment. She looks in the drawers, ya know." Cook scrunched her nose. "Here. Put these in the sidebar in the dinin' room."

Becca took them and found herself surprised by their substantial weight. "Yes, ma'am."

One candlestick in each hand, she pushed open the door that was already ajar and entered the formal dining room. She'd prepared herself to see luxurious furnishings, but when she saw the extent of the room, she stopped and took a breath. The space seemed more immense than her entire home. A mahogany dining table with twelve matching seats beckoned guests to a party. Carved corner cabinets displayed dishes too pretty to use for eating—even for formal dining. Oil paintings of floral arrangements added beauty to the room, as did a table runner with intricate embroidery. Brass candlesticks with tapered, cream-colored beeswax candles adorned the table.

Gawking too long wouldn't be advisable, since Cook was sure to call her back into the scullery if she lingered. She looked for the sidebar and found a heavy piece of furniture with a mirror. It had two rows of drawers she suspected held utensils and table linens. On the bottom, two doors looked as though they concealed spaces tall enough for the candlesticks to be stored standing. She decided to try one of those. As she shifted both candlesticks to one hand so she could open the door, one dropped. The *thud* it made against the floor made the chime in the floor clock across the room vibrate.

"Oh!" She gasped. Bending down to retrieve the fallen stick, she realized her hands shook, and her heart beat with such fear her body felt like one big pulse.

Cook ran into the room. "Girlie! What happened?"

"I–I'm sorry. I dropped one. I didn't mean for that to happen."

Harrod entered. "What is all the commotion?"

Cook pointed at Becca. "She dropped a candlestick. She didn't mean no harm."

"Give that to me." Harrod extended his hand and took the candlestick. Becca watched, still shaking, as he inspected it. "No harm done. Amazing." He looked at the floor. Bending toward it, he squinted and pointed. "What is that I see? A dent?" He pursed his lips.

"She didn't mean it," Cook protested.

"No, I didn't."

Harrod looked her in the eye. "You have done irreparable damage to the master's residence. Such clumsiness will not be tolerated. Miss Hanham, pack your belongings and prepare to leave at once. You are dismissed."

Chapter 3

From his upstairs study, Nash heard voices in the dining room. The butler sounded upset, a condition unlike his usual composed self. Nash ventured into the room to assess the situation.

He saw Harrod, silver-and-marble candlestick in hand, along with Cook and a servant he'd never before seen. He studied the girl and was struck by how familiar she seemed. Who was she? "I say, what's happening here?"

Taken by surprise, Harrod straightened, then answered, "Mr. Abercrombie, sir. I beg your forgiveness. I was quite distracted by an incident here, and I didn't hear you come in."

Judging from her mode of dress, Nash discerned the girl was the new scullery maid. Try as he might, he couldn't keep from staring at the brunette beauty.

The girl surveyed him, fear lighting her eyes. She blushed and averted her gaze to her feet.

"The girl will be gone within a quarter hour. You have my word," Harrod said.

Nash shook his head and held up his palm. "Wait."

The girl looked back up with crystal blue eyes peeking at him from under midnight black eyelashes. Her pale, heart-shaped face stirred a memory; suddenly he knew. Before him stood the girl who sold him that box of lucifers so many years ago. Except now she was a woman. An extraordinary-looking young woman. The light in her eyes told him she recognized him, too. Her lips parted, and her fear seemed to diminish. If only he could paint a portrait to capture such loveliness!

"Where is she going?" he asked Harrod without looking at him.

"Sir?" he responded. "Why, I suppose she shall be returning to her home."

Nash kept looking at her. Just seeing her brought to his heart emotions he'd never felt, emotions far beyond compassion and pity. He was drawn to her in a way he had never been drawn to a woman. The feelings took him by surprise in their existence—and their intensity. He could hardly speak. "Whatever for?"

Harrod touched his arm. "Sir, this, this—girl, dropped one of your dearly departed mother's candlesticks and caused a dent in the dining room floor that I do not believe can ever be repaired. If you will inspect the damage, sir." He pointed to a small nick in the floor, causing Nash finally to take his gaze from the new maid.

"Oh, that. Well." He searched for a defense. "That could have been made by my boot this very morning. And as for those candlesticks, I never liked them."

"But, sir!" Harrod protested.

Nash focused on the girl. "What is your name, miss?"

She curtsied. "Becca. Becca Hanham, sir."

Seeing her legs shake in fear, he felt pity.

"I—I'm sorry for my mistake, sir. I pray you will forgive me."

"That's all I needed to hear. Becca, you shall remain in my employ if that should please you."

She blushed a most flattering shade of rose. "I couldn't ask for a better answer to my prayers, sir."

"You were actually praying that I could keep you on as my scullery maid?" Nash couldn't imagine anyone wanting a job of low station so much.

She looked him in the eye. "Yes, sir. I've seen the Lord answer prayer before, and He sure did this time."

"Indeed." Nash smiled at her, and her face softened.

Harrod cleared his throat. "Of course your decision is final, Mr. Abercrombie. She will continue to function as your scullery maid. However, I assure you, never will she touch a piece of valuable silver again." He eyed the tiny nick. "If I may say so, Miss Caldwell will be very upset to spy such a spot in a dining room where she will be entertaining once she is your wife."

Nash tried not to shudder. Though Hazel would never entertain in his home, he wanted to avoid unpleasantness with her all the same. "Please have it filled in, then, if possible."

"I'll do my best. Restoring it now would certainly be wise."

"She's going on a trip to Hartford. There should be time to have it repaired before she returns."

"Yes, sir." Harrod examined the nick once more. "The cost could be considerable. May I suggest we subtract the amount from the girl's pay to compensate for the damage? She should not have been so careless with that candlestick."

Harrod had his full attention. "No, I shall cover the expense. She admitted her mistake, and that is enough for me."

"Very well. You are too kind."

"Yes, sir," the girl agreed. "Thank you, sir."

Seeing her straight on, he knew for certain the match girl stood before him. He remembered the encounter well. He wasn't supposed to be out that night except he had forgotten his father's birthday—a lapse that still made him cringe to remember—and he needed to purchase a last-minute gift. He hadn't planned to stumble upon a destitute girl begging any passerby to purchase her wares. Papa's prosperity and the Abercrombie position had shielded him from the realities of child labor and deep poverty. When the Abercrombies bestowed Christian charity—and those occasions happened often—Papa made the decision. Before that evening, no one beseeched Nash for help. The girl's pitiful clothing and the way she shivered against the cold had brought him to such sorrow he felt led to buy enough lucifers to last a year and then pay more than they were worth. His generosity was his first step as a Christian man, young though he was.

Because it was the first time he'd acted on his own to give charity to another person, remembrance of the brief event stayed with him. From time to time he recalled her cherubic face and wondered what had happened to her. The unmistakable wide blue eyes, soft pink cheeks, and dark hair falling in curls spoke of her as a young woman. What a beauty she had become!

He couldn't believe it. So the girl had grown up and become his scullery maid. His heart lurched, almost stopping with happiness at finding her once more. His stomach quivered with an unfamiliar, disconcerting, and strange type of excitement. He wanted to experience it again.

Without notice or beckoning, an idea popped into his mind. An idea that could change his life forever.

∽

Of all the houses in Providence, she had somehow stumbled on Nash Abercrombie's—the boy she had been praying for all these years. How did that happen? Was it the Lord's doing?

The master's authoritative voice resonated in the room, and Becca recognized its beauty. The tone sounded as comforting as it had the night she first met him, but the pitch had grown deeper, more mature. Hearing him made her skin prickle in delight, much like listening to a sentimental song.

And to look at him! His very presence affected her. She hadn't expected to see him again, looking so comely with lustrous hair that rippled like the bay waters at midnight and eyes as brown as a luxurious cup of coffee. His glance left her weak to the core. Becca felt her face warm. Her breathing became rapid, and her knees felt as though they could no longer hold her weight.

"Off with you, now," Harrod said, though not in too harsh a tone.

Cook nodded and gave Becca a gentle shove to prod her into the kitchen. Becca wanted to look back at the master one last time, but she knew better.

The kitchen, with its cooking aromas and warm fire, seemed like a place of sanctuary. As soon as the door shut behind them, Becca headed toward the table, pulled out a chair, and plopped into it. She couldn't resist allowing her gaze to fall toward the door. "So that was the master," she whispered.

"'Tis he." Cook made her way to Becca and placed her hand on her new charge's shoulder. "Ya had quite a scare, almost bein' fired. Good thing Mr. Abercrombie showed up when he did."

She nodded.

"Ya seem flushed." Cook touched Becca's cheek with the back of her hand. "What's the matter? Are ya ill?"

"N–no." She may have seemed ill but felt far from it. If her feelings were illness, she wished she could be sick all the time. To demonstrate Cook need not worry that Becca couldn't work, she forced herself to stand.

"But I wouldn't imagine ye'd be expectin' to see the master yet. And ya won't be seein' him any more tonight, either." Cook shooed her new scullery maid with a swoop of her hand. "He'll be with us tomorrow mornin' at prayer time. But ye're to speak to him only if ye're spoken to, ya hear?"

"Oh." He would never remember her. She felt her hopes that she could ever thank him melt.

"Ya do understand." Cook's voice sounded sterner than Becca had heard from her. "Harrod hired ya to do yer work invisible-like. Ya ain't allowed to take liberties in talkin' to anybody who'd employ ya, or you'll be turned out on yer ear in no time."

So she was no longer a person. "I understand."

"I have a feelin' ya ain't used to bein' a scullery maid, are ya?"

She shook her head.

"Haven't ya ever worked a day in yer life?"

"Of course. At home."

Cook waved her hand at Becca. "No wonder ye're so sheltered. Ye're a pretty girlie. I imagine ye'll be movin' on to better things shortly. But for now, do yer best at the job before ya, and all will work out. Especially if ya take my advice and behave as ye're expected. Ya see, us downstairs servants ain't allowed to be visible to the master. If he sees ya, look down at the floor and stay still till he passes."

This advice came as a shock. "That don't seem polite. Not so much as a greetin'?"

"Never. Speakin' to the master's very impolite. And you most assuredly don't want ta speak to his new wife once he marries." While Becca hid her thoughts, Cook rattled on. "Just between you and me and the fence post, I don't much like that woman what's been chasin' him. But I'm just a cook, so I got no say in the matter." Cook leaned close enough to whisper. "Her name's Hazel. We servants call her Witch Hazel." She laughed so that her chest bobbed up and down, but she clapped her hand over her lips to stifle herself.

How horrible this Hazel woman must be. Yet no matter how awful she was, no one in Becca's station stood a chance with an Abercrombie. Discouraged, she retreated to the scullery and busied herself with the pots. She scrubbed through the dinner hour, wondering when she would be able to eat her portion of delicious-smelling soup, but it stood to reason that the servants would eat after the master and then the upstairs servants.

"Cook?"

The older woman stopped kneading dough long enough to answer. "Yea?"

"Do you think I could go home long enough to tell my parents where I am?

I'm afraid Mother might worry."

Cook glanced outside and nodded toward the black night and newly fallen snow. "She'd worry more if she knew ya was walkin' the streets this late. No, ye'd best go to bed. Ya can have a bit o' leisure before ya shut yer eyes. Six thirty comes mighty early in the mornin'."

"Six thirty?"

"If I was you, I'd rise at six. Ye're lucky ya don't work for a large household with lots of servants. If ya did, the pile of dishes ye'd be lookin' at t'would be three times as high." She glanced around the kitchen and grinned. "Ah, this is an easy life."

Becca doubted "easy" was the word, but gratitude for any mercy the Lord showed filled her heart. Thursday would arrive in a day. Then she'd go home and tell her parents what transpired.

Harrod entered.

"Yer cocoa's up soon." Cook's voice betrayed her impatience.

"I am not here for that." Harrod regarded Becca. "Girlie, Mr. Abercrombie wishes to speak with you."

Using her peripheral vision, Becca could see Cook's eyes widen. Becca pointed to herself. "Me? Have I done somethin' else wrong already?"

"He says not. I do not know what his business is with you. Come with me."

Becca looked down at her clothing, splattered with grease, water, and soap. "May I freshen meself?"

"There is no time. He awaits."

Though Harrod lingered at the kitchen door, Becca had to speak to Cook. "Ya—ya didn't say I did a poor job, did ya?"

"Oh no. Ya did a fine job, especially for one not used to such work. Why, I'd tell the master meself, if I wasn't so busy."

Becca nodded. She believed Cook hadn't complained about her. She had no reason since Becca had been careful to be obedient and industrious. She wasn't as sure Cook wanted to face the master to defend Becca.

"Come along, girlie," Harrod prodded. "You won't find out what Mr. Abercrombie wants as long as you keep standing here."

Trying to hide shaking hands by keeping them clasped, Becca followed Harrod through the house. While the furnishings and decor told the story of a wealthy man, the setting didn't strike her to be as ostentatious as the house where she was interviewed by the aloof woman. She hoped her meeting with the master would go better than that.

When they arrived at the study on the third floor, Harrod announced her. She entered, and Harrod shut the door behind her. Nash sat in a leather chair behind his desk. She held back a gasp with wonder at being so close to him once again. Nash's face looked even more handsome and kind than she remembered. To be working for a man who exuded such generosity of spirit was nothing less than a gift from God. Yet she could only be a servant to him. And if she'd done something wrong to cause her dismissal, she'd lose even that status.

Avoiding his gaze so as not to appear bold, she observed her surroundings. To her surprise, his study was small and dark with nautical touches. The room contrasted to Mrs. Gill's spacious and light sitting room enhanced by floral wallpaper. Two hurricane lamps on Mr. Abercrombie's desk provided him light. She withheld a smile. Perhaps a man felt more at ease in an atmosphere akin to a ship's cabin rather than a rose-colored loft flooded with sun. She also noticed a fixed ladder left of the doorway and a hatch above. This must have been the access to the widow's walk on his home. A small fire glowed in the hearth. However, his presence made the room seem as warm as the most appealing early summer day. Still, she approached him with trepidation, not looking him in the face. She felt uncomfortable talking to the master alone in defiance of her earlier instructions to do everything possible to stay invisible to him. She hoped she wouldn't make a fool of herself. She said a prayer for wisdom.

He stood to greet her, revealing a fine figure of a young man. The gesture gave her the impression that he could treat her as a person of high station—an experience unknown to her. "Sit down, please." He motioned to the chair in front of his desk. The fact he offered her a seat surprised her.

He returned to the leather chair behind his desk. She noticed it held papers stacked in neat piles that weren't too large. No doubt he paid every paper bill on time, maybe even before it was due. "No doubt you already know that I am Nash Abercrombie."

"Y—yes, sir." She stole a glance of his face and held her breath.

"Do you know why I summoned you?"

She clasped her hands more tightly. "No, sir. I hope my work is satisfactory. If it ain't, I can learn. I promise. My mother says I always catch on real good." Realizing she rambled and had repeated an unfortunate phrase that brought her unspoken insult before, she bit her lip.

He smiled with warmth. "I have no doubt you are smart. Very smart. And as for your work, I've heard no complaints. I have another reason for summoning you. I wanted to see if you are who I think you are. Did you perchance ever sell lucifers on Meeting Street?"

"I did." So maybe that's what this was all about. "So ya remember the night ya saved my life." Her voice sounded more hopeful than she meant, and her smile felt too wide.

"Yes, I do recall that bitter night. But you say I saved your life? I hardly think I can credit myself with such a noble deed."

"Oh, but ya did! If ya hadn't come along when ya did, I'd of stayed out in that cold, dark night till I froze to death. Cook told me I'm supposed to be invisible and not talk to ya none, so I hope ya don't mind if I take this chance to tell ya thank ya, sir. Ya have my eternal gratitude, and I promise to work hard while I'm in yer employ to show just how grateful I am."

"You need not work harder than you must. An honest day's work is all I expect from anyone in my employ." He leaned forward. "I admit, I was drawn to you when I saw you here, just as I was drawn to you when you were selling lucifers all those years ago. I never could explain why something in your eyes caught my attention, but I never forgot you."

Though his eyes held nothing but kindness, a fleeting thought unsettled her. She'd heard stories of unscrupulous masters, and she wasn't about to relinquish her virtue to him or any man. Perhaps she shouldn't have mentioned just how grateful she was. "Thank ya, sir." She looked at her cotton-covered knees.

To her relief, she heard him shift back in his chair, so she summoned the courage to return her gaze to him.

"I was only out that night to run an important errand. It was not my habit to wander the streets in the dark, but I'm glad I had the chance to buy lucifers from you." He paused. "Tell me about yourself."

She flinched. What could she tell him? That her family lived in poverty? That her father insisted she wed an oaf or get a job because of yet another new baby on the way? After taking a deep breath, she told him about her life. The version she recounted softened the harsh reality without engaging in a fib.

His eyes showed compassion. "I don't find your situation surprising. I understand you had no chance to return home since you were just hired. Does your mother know where you are?"

"No, sir."

He glanced at a small clock on his desk. "It's far too late for you to wander the streets alone. I'll have a messenger send word to your family."

"Thank ya, sir." She thought for a moment and asked, "Are ya always so kind to yer servants?"

"I hope they all think me kind, although I have set my attention on you in particular for a reason. I have a question for you. You have nothing to lose by answering, even if your response is to decline." He let out a breath, as if bolstering himself to ask.

What could make him nervous, such a powerful man asking a favor of a mere scullery maid?

"Go ahead," she prodded, hoping he didn't mind.

"My request is unorthodox. . ."

There was that word again. Apparently it was quite popular with the upper classes. She resolved to find out what it meant.

". . .and I pray you won't be offended, but you see, I'm in quite a pinch, and I really need your help."

"My help? But I ain't nothin' but a maid, and the lowest maid at that. What could I possibly do for ya?"

"Something I hope you will find easy." He took in another breath. "Miss Hanham, will you marry me?"

Chapter 4

Becca felt too astounded to answer. From a scullery maid to a fiancée in a matter of hours? No, he couldn't be proposing marriage.

"I can see from the expression on your face that you're shocked. Of course you are," he said matter-of-factly. "I didn't ask you in the proper manner." To Becca's further surprise, he rose and made his way toward her. "Would you stand, please?"

Too amazed to do anything but obey, she did.

He bent down on one knee and took her hands in his. "Becca Hanham, will you marry me?"

She wished she could sit in a chair nearby, for the feeling of weakness in her knees once again made its presence known. Instead she summoned her strength and answered, "Sir, this must be a joke."

His face turned serious. "I assure you, it is not."

"You want me to marry you?" She felt dizzy with emotion.

"Yes. I know you weren't expecting me to propose, but since I noticed you, I have given the prospect thought and prayer. Please, think and pray on it overnight if you like." Still he remained on his knee.

"I don't need that much time. I—I'm flattered. More than flattered." Never would she have imagined a man of such importance bending his knee before her. A vision of Micah entered her head. His future wife would be lucky if he demanded marriage before belching and then insisting that she pour him a portion of ale. Becca wished her position in society would permit her to wed the man before her. "Please, you don't have to stay on yer knee."

With the agility of a sportsman, he arose. The thought occurred to Becca that other than seeing his house and learning about his servants, she knew almost nothing about this man. But that wasn't the only reason she hesitated. "I can't accept. I don't know why ya took leave of yer senses, but once ya wake up, ye'll see yer family wouldn't allow us to wed."

Deep sadness filled his countenance, and she wished she hadn't caused it. "I was the only child of my parents, may the Lord rest their souls, and I have no other family. At least, not any family close enough in relationship with me to care or to be affected in any significant way by our marriage."

Thinking of her large family, the idea of such solitude made her sad. Yet Nash didn't live outside of the world like a monk. He knew people. "But yer friends. . ."

"Any friends of mine who wouldn't accept my choice of a wife are not my friends."

She felt too touched for words, but she had to respond. If he spoke the truth—and his conviction made him seem as though he did—she still worried about the consequences of the match. "Why me? And why now? I ain't nothin' but a match girl ya remember from years ago, and ye're a young man that bought me wares so I could take refuge from the bitter night. But as much as I am grateful to ya—and I am, I can promise ya that—that ain't no reason to marry me or fer me to marry ya, either."

"Do I not have enough to offer you?"

She gasped. "How could ya ask such a thing? Ya have so much to offer any woman. I know ye're a Christian. I see a Bible on your desk, and Cook told me ya lead the servants in prayers each mornin'. I want a Christian man."

"That doesn't surprise me. Your spirit is so sweet."

She felt herself blush, and she looked downward. "But I want even more than that. Mebbe I'm expectin' too much, but I want to love—really love—the man I marry one day."

His expression softened. "Your response shows me how right I was to ask."

"Come again?"

"You obviously have no idea how many women would jump at the chance to seize me for my fortune regardless of their personal feelings for me one way or another. I realize you might not know exactly who I am, but anyone can see from my home that God has rained financial blessings on my family. And your first thought? That my marriage to you would adversely affect me. And that you don't love me. At least not yet." Becca would have sworn she almost saw mist in his eyes. "To be with someone so unaffected is refreshing. You have no idea."

She couldn't imagine any woman wanting such a compassionate and handsome man only for his fortune, but thought saying so would be much too bold. "Love is very important to me. Some might say too important. But I don't agree with 'em."

"And neither do I."

Preparing herself to say one of the hardest things she imagined she'd ever have to say in her life, Becca inhaled and steeled herself. "Then ya understand why I gotta say no."

"Please don't answer me yet. I know my question comes as a surprise. A shock, even." He glanced at the empty chair. "Please. Take a seat and hear me out."

She nodded and obeyed.

He returned to his seat behind his desk, crossing his arms as he settled into position. "I know it sounds harsh, but I have a reason for my proposal. You see, I wish to discourage a woman named Hazel Caldwell. She's a member of my set and has many family connections, but I have every reason to believe that her family fortune is dwindling and she's looking for security. She sees my money as her security."

"How awful!" Becca blurted before she could stop herself. Embarrassed, she looked at her lap. "I'm sorry. I should never have said that."

Nash's mouth twisted into a rueful curve. "Truth be told, I can hardly expect any woman not to consider my fortune when thinking of marriage to me. But I want my future wife to consider me as a person, just as I would consider her—as I consider you—a person. You and I are alike, you see. I don't believe it's right for me to marry a woman I don't love and who doesn't love me."

So Cook had been right! Mr. Abercrombie was in a terrible romantic mess with a frightful woman.

Nash continued. "I realize we don't know each other well enough to discern love or not. We need not wed right away. Could we use our engagement as a time to get to know one another? I vow to you that if you decide not to go through with the wedding, I will set you free with no further obligation whatsoever."

Thinking through his offer, Becca didn't answer right away.

"Perhaps I do sound foolish." He leaned toward her, and his eyes looked imploring. "Do you think me ridiculous to want to marry for love?"

"No, sir."

His smile was bittersweet. "You are so lucky, Miss Hanham. You don't have to consider society and position when you wed. You are free to marry whomever you like."

"That ain't so, sir."

He startled. "Oh?"

"Ya see, I'm only here 'cause me father said I had to find a job or marry somebody I don't love."

"Really?" Surprise registered on his expression, and his eyes held a questioning look.

Becca could only imagine that he wondered, without fortunes and connections to consider, why there would be a need for her father to suggest a loveless match. Sheltered from poverty as Nash was, Becca doubted he could comprehend deep desire to improve one's lot in whatever way, however miniscule. She might explain that to him. One day, but not now.

"You left the marriage out of the story you told me before," he pointed out, choosing discretion.

"I didn't think ye'd care about it, to tell the truth."

He smiled. "I suppose if I were an ordinary employer, I wouldn't. But I'm glad you told me. The fact that you might be able to understand my predicament gives me some consolation."

"Yes, I do." If only Becca could agree to his solution, but she was still unsure. "There must be a lot of grand ladies who'd want to marry ya, Mr. Abercrombie, if ya don't mind me sayin' so. What about one o' them?"

"They consider me unavailable because Miss Caldwell is a force with whom to be reckoned." He shrugged. "I may have the power to change the right woman's mind, but I don't feel drawn to them enough to pursue anything beyond an acquaintanceship."

Becca felt pity for the master, a surprising emotion considering that by all appearances, he sat on top of the world. His servants knew him as a captain of commerce in Providence. "I—I don't know what to say."

"Don't say anything. Let me summon my driver, Jack, to take you home tonight. I don't think he's gone to the pub yet. Take the morning off, and give me your answer during afternoon tea tomorrow."

Later, Nash escorted Becca to his carriage and helped her embark. With amusement and pleasure, he noted how she observed the conveyance with wide eyes, much as she had noticed the house. So in awe was she that she seemed to be walking in glass slippers, reminding him of the little cinder girl in the old fairy tale. He hoped he could be Becca's prince.

Returning to his study to tidy up the last bit of remaining correspondence, Nash found himself daydreaming about Becca. When he told her he had prayed about whether or not to ask her hand in marriage, he had not exaggerated. The open Bible he had left on the table beside his chair told a tale of how he had consulted scripture as he prayed. The fact Becca was not the expected choice for him would indeed cause consternation in certain quarters, but his heart told him the fair young lady was worth getting to know. Being with her as a potential wife would never be possible if she were to remain his servant, but his daring proposal put her in a new position. If Becca agreed to give him a chance, he felt certain the feelings she had already stirred in his heart would grow. If only time spent together would cause love to pour into her heart as well. He hoped he could make her life a better one, not with riches but with a lifetime of love.

Lord, Thy will be done in this matter.

Mother was in her room tending to the babies, Father was out, and her other brothers and sisters occupied themselves with their own concerns and were not impressed by her comings and goings, so Becca managed to sneak through the front room without being noticed. A lingering scent of porridge didn't tempt her, even though she never had partaken of soup at the Abercrombie house. Excitement had overcome hunger.

She headed for the room in back she shared with many sisters. She hoped to find clean water in the plain white pitcher to wash her face so she wouldn't have to fetch it herself. Eyeing the small oak vanity, she didn't assess the rest of the room as she walked toward the corner.

"What are ya doin' here?" Naomi's voice pierced the air.

Becca jumped and clutched her hand to her chest. "Ya scared me to death!"

"I'm sorry," a nightshift-clad Naomi apologized, hairbrush in hand. "Ya scared me to death, too!" Recovering in a flash, Naomi looked into a small mirror that had been her Christmas gift. She studied herself before nodding and placing the hairbrush they all shared on the vanity beside the pitcher. "So did ya get a job?"

"Yea, in a fine home for a wonderful master. He lives all alone except for his servants. A devoted lot, they are, but no family." She sighed. "Much has changed since this morning."

"Oh?"

Becca hesitated, wondering if she should take her sister into her confidence. But she and Naomi had always been close in age and spirit, and the urge to tell someone hounded her. She decided to trust her sister. "The young master asked me to marry him."

Naomi plopped onto the nearest mattress. "What? He asked you to marry him? The master of a fine house? I don't believe it."

"I can hardly believe it myself."

"Ya think he meant it?"

"I—I do."

Naomi gasped. "Oh, Becca! What are ya goin' to do?"

Becca placed her forefinger on puckered lips. "Shh! Not so loud. I ain't said nothin' to nobody but you."

"And it's a good thing, too. We don't know nothin' about livin' like society people." She beamed. "But you'll find out soon."

Becca sat by Naomi. "I ain't accepted yet. And I ain't sure I'm gonna."

"Why not?" Naomi clasped her hands to her chest and looked upward. Becca could see from the faraway look on her face that she saw not the cracked ceiling, but a vision from a different world in another part of Providence. "Just think. Ye'll never have to work again. Ya can wear dresses that make ya look like ya came out of a store window. Ya can eat rich food and sleep till noon. Mebbe I can visit and we can have tea on a fancy silver service and those little sandwiches that my friend May says she has to fix for her mistress." She gasped and clutched Becca's knee. "You'll be the first person we know who'll be the mistress of a manor instead of just a servant girl." As her excitement increased, her voice grew louder.

"Shh! I told ya I ain't sure I'm gonna accept. The more ya talk, the more I think mebbe I shouldn't. He don't know nothin' about our family, how we live." Becca couldn't help but compare her current surroundings to the Abercrombie residence. What would Nash think once he set foot in such a place?

Naomi eyed their room and sighed. When she spoke, her discouraged tone of voice told of her agreement. "When do ya have to tell him one way or the other?"

"I promised I'd show up for afternoon tea tomorrow." The thought made her nervous. She had little idea what to do at a formal tea, even alone with the man who would be her fiancé. "I might not consider it at all," she said, omitting how his mere presence made her feel light as a butterfly living in fairyland. "But I'm grateful to him fer savin' my life that night—the night I told ya about."

Naomi didn't have to think long. Becca had told the story often. "Ya mean that's the same young man what paid ya so much fer that box of lucifers?"

Becca nodded.

"That's gotta be the Lord's doin'. Why else would ya land in his house of all places?"

The notion had occurred to Becca. "I know it. Especially after I knocked on so many doors before that." She sighed. "And now I feel sorry fer him. He's got this awful woman chasin' him."

"How do ya know she's awful? Have ya met her?"

"No. But he don't paint a flatterin' picture of her. Her name is Hazel, and the servants call her Witch Hazel behind her back."

Naomi giggled. She tilted her nose upward and took on an affected accent. "I suppose she talks very snooty."

Becca grinned in spite of herself but then turned serious. "I ain't never met her, but I don't imagine I'll sound too educated against someone like her."

"True." Naomi looked worried. "I don't mean to hurt yer feelin's, but ya ain't no fine lady, and anybody breathin' can tell soon as ya open yer mouth."

"Only me own sister could get away with an insult like that." Becca scrunched her nose and rubbed her knuckles on Naomi's back in a playful manner, a gesture the sisters had always shared.

"Ya know I speak the truth." Naomi slapped at Becca's knee with a strike that didn't sting. "And I worry. You ain't got no decent dresses, neither. He's gonna be expectin' ya to be a hostess sooner or later. How are ya plannin' to fit in with all those society women?"

Having concentrated on Nash, Becca hadn't thought about his friends. Anxiety gripped her midsection. "I don't know. Mebbe I'm not supposed to fit in but be meself."

"Ye'll be laughed out o' Providence."

"Mebbe not. The Lord can perform miracles." A feeling of nervousness struck, and Becca felt she needed consolation and comfort. "How's about we ask now?" Becca took her sister's hands, and they prayed.

Father entered. "What you two girls prayin' about?" As usual, he hadn't bothered to knock.

"Nothin'." Naomi dropped her sister's hands, crossed her arms, and narrowed her eyes at her father.

"Becca will tell me. Won't ya, girl?" His voice took on a tone that told her she'd feel the sting of his belt on her legs if she didn't.

She swallowed. "I got a job."

"What is it? A nanny like ya planned?"

"No, sir. A maid."

"Oh." His voice deflated. "How much they payin' you?"

Temptation to tell him a dollar fifty knocked on her brain, but she shook it aside. "Two dollars a week plus room and board."

"Humph." He wagged his finger at her. "You be sure to bring me that money every week."

A realization occurred to Becca. "I might not be able to."

"And why not?" His voice held a challenge.

Naomi shook her head, warning her not to reveal everything yet. But considering Father's determination to squeeze her salary from her, telling all seemed to be the only option. "I might not be a maid long. I—I might not even be a maid now. The master—Nash Abercrombie—said he wants to marry me."

Father's laughter filled the room so much the thin walls seemed to shake. "You? You, girl? What are they feedin' ya up on top of that hill? Whiskey? If they are, must be mighty good. Bring me some next time ya come home, eh?"

Becca's face warmed in humiliation, but she couldn't deny the story sounded preposterous. "I'm doin' him a favor, he says. He wants to get rid of a fortune seeker."

Father's mouth slackened before he let out a boisterous chortle. "Does he now? Is he outta his head? Ye're nothin' but a Hanham. What makes him think ya don't want his fortune, too?"

Becca thought for a moment. How did he know, indeed? Perhaps because she never dreamed of any fortune and he realized that. Besides, he asked her to marry him when such a proposal never entered her mind. She remembered his references to her spirit. "He knows I'm a woman of faith."

"That may be, but I'll wager he'll drop ya like a hot potato as soon as he gets rid of this fortune seeker he's talkin' about." He nodded, rubbing his chin. "At least ya can take advantage of the situation. Collect as many trinkets as ya can before he gets tired o' ya. Tell him ya want big diamonds and rubies."

Diamonds and rubies? The thought hadn't entered her head. She never ventured where people expected women to wear fine jewels. On the contrary, in her part of town sparkling stones would only attract thieves and thugs.

Disgust filled her being. Leave it to Father to suggest she collect as many diamonds and rubies as possible to secure her future—and his supply of ale. Still, his admonitions made her feel uneasy. Father was a man of the world and knew the ways of men. What if his warnings were true? What if Nash Abercrombie left her high and dry as soon as Hazel Caldwell was out of sight? The idea of trinkets didn't comfort her, but made her feel like a woman for hire. "I don't think I'll accept his proposal."

"That might be a good idea," Naomi said.

"Mind yer own business, Naomi." Scowling, Father crossed his arms and planted his feet on the floor. "I've heard of that Abercrombie family. They got plenty o' money. Ya better accept that offer if ya know what's good fer ya."

Becca didn't have to ask what that meant. If she didn't obey, Father was sure to throw her out of the house for good. And though the noisy, crowded rooms weren't much, her home did offer shelter and the love of her mother and siblings. God commanded her to honor her parents, so she had to do as her father insisted. Too bad the Bible never promised all parents would look out for the best interests of their children above their own.

She prayed for the courage to face whatever her future held.

Chapter 5

The following day Nash returned home early from the office for afternoon tea. Not that he had accomplished much at work anyway. All he could think about was his proposal of marriage and what answer Becca might give him.

Sitting fitfully in the chair in his study, he tried to read the paper, but a story on another bank robbery didn't hold his interest. His thoughts wandered to matters of immediate concern.

Nash never envisioned that God would send the match girl from all those years before who had touched his heart. Perhaps he'd be a laughingstock for pursuing a poverty-stricken woman of low station. But simple clothing couldn't hide a sweet spirit. To Nash, that was much more valuable than an important family name. A verse from the twenty-seventh chapter of Proverbs popped into his head. "A continual dropping in a very rainy day and a contentious woman are alike." Of course the author didn't speak of Hazel, but the verse described her. He smiled in spite of himself.

Ah, Becca. Such a contrast. He prayed she would trust him enough to move forward with his proposal. If she did, he was determined she would never be sorry.

Harrod entered. "I am confirming that you still desire high tea for two to be served at five in the front parlor, sir."

"Yes."

"Thank you, sir." He cleared his throat but didn't look Nash in the face. "I am reluctant to mention this, but the new scullery maid did not report for work this morning. Under ordinary conditions, I would not make mention of this, but in light of her clumsiness yesterday, I felt I must. Perhaps she is embarrassed by your generosity of spirit and didn't feel worthy to continue working here. I can only speculate."

Since he'd never thought of Becca as a scullery maid, Nash had forgotten to let Harrod know about the previous night's events. "I'm so sorry, Harrod. I should have told you." He paused and studied his butler. Harrod stood erect with an expression of anticipation before Nash. "I have asked someone to marry me."

Harrod didn't smile. "Have you confirmed your engagement to Miss Caldwell?"

"No. I have proposed marriage to someone else."

"Indeed?" Harrod's voice rose with happiness. "If I may be so bold, do tell me about this lucky woman. I assume you met her during your trip abroad. Was it a shipboard romance, perhaps?" His eyes took on a worried light. "Those can be tricky, but if she's from a prestigious family, you may have been right to throw caution to the wind."

"Oh, I threw caution to the wind. But not aboard ship."

Harrod let a breath escape. "I must say, I am relieved you did not lose your head while crossing the Atlantic. Miss Caldwell is digging for gold, but at least we know she comes from a good family. I have heard too many stories about the riffraff who travel on ships and trains to pose as perfectly respectable people in hopes of catching a prize such as yourself. A man in your position cannot be too cautious."

"Your words are wise, and so I'm sure you'll be disappointed by my choice." He paused. "You see, there is a reason why Becca Hanham did not report for work today. Instead she is my guest for afternoon tea."

"Oh." The unflappable Harrod seemed disconcerted. "I see. Then I must make haste to find another scullery maid."

"Not yet. She has a question to answer for me first." He paused. "You see, I asked Becca Hanham to marry me."

Harrod couldn't have looked any more shocked if a tempest had struck without warning and scuttled him. "But, she is a—a scullery maid."

"Yes, I realize it's shocking. I'm a bit shocked myself. But I don't regret asking her." His voice grew stronger with determination.

"Sir, I am loath to discourage you, but. . ." He let out a slight cough. "Would you feel at ease with her in the company of your friends? Or would she?"

"I've thought of that. Certainly I don't want to subject her to ridicule. That's why, if she does accept my proposal, I'll work with her to be sure she looks and acts highborn before I open my home for a dinner party."

"If I may say so, you have much work ahead of you."

"You mean to say *we* have much work ahead of *us*. I expect you to help, you know."

Harrod sighed in the manner of an adult indulging a child. "Why did I sense you might say that? But for you, I shall comply. Anything to rid us of the prospect of Miss Caldwell."

"How many of the other servants know we hired Miss Hanham as a scullery maid?"

Harrod thought for a moment. "Other than myself, Cook and the downstairs maid. I don't believe she had time to meet anyone else."

"Good. I need all the servants to support me and not make issue of Miss Hanham's humble origins. While I will never deny her background if asked, there is no need to subject her to more gossip than necessary."

"I don't believe you'll be able to shield her forever. People will find out one way or another."

"I don't doubt it. But once they grow to love Miss Hanham for her sweet spirit, her station won't matter."

Harrod's mouth twisted, a sure sign he didn't agree. Nash ignored the gesture. He only wanted to think of how good he could make life for Becca.

∞

Becca entered the Abercrombie residence through the back door. The appetizing scent of baking bread greeted her.

Cook spied her and stopped whisking a small green bowl containing raw eggs. "I see ya finally decided to show up fer work. Harrod told me the master knows all about it and you had the mornin' off."

"Yes, ma'am." Becca regarded dirty pots and pans that awaited washing.

"Ye're lookin' pretty today." She sniffed the air, her nostrils flailing in and out. "And I do believe I smell perfume." She eyed her charge. "Ye're lookin' and smellin' much too fancy fer a scullery maid."

Becca had dressed her best—meaning in the same dress she wore yesterday. Mother had allowed her to borrow a few precious drops of lavender-scented toilette water that Becca and her siblings saved up to buy for her as a Christmas gift just a month ago. Mother had also arranged Becca's dark hair in a flattering uplifted fashion with ringlets framing both sides of her cheeks. Before she left, Mother kissed her good-bye and gave her a tight hug. Despite the mountains of work brought about by so many siblings, Becca would miss being with her family every day.

For the first time since her birthday the previous autumn, she felt lovely. Lovely enough to face Nash and give him her answer.

Cook persisted. "Why'd ya fix yer hair up like that?"

"Mother styled it," she responded, stalling for time. Cook stared at her, so she could see there was no way out of offering a direct response. "I—I don't reckon you'd know. Mr. Abercrombie proposed marriage to me, and I'm here to give him an answer."

She dropped her fork in the bowl. "Marriage! No!" A hearty laugh filled the kitchen. "I didn't take ya for a lazy daydreamer, but that's what ya are, sure enough."

Becca paused as she tried not to be offended. Perhaps to Cook's eyes she did seem lazy and a dreamer. "No, ma'am. I'm not lazy, and I'm not a daydreamer. I can't believe it, either. But it's true." Becca filled her in on the details.

"That is a surprise, girlie. I didn't think ye'd ever be the master's match." She regarded her with a discerning eye. "Ye're mighty pretty, though, and I think ye'd be even prettier once he gets ye into better clothes."

Becca tried not to cringe.

"Any plan to get rid of Witch Hazel is a good plan in my book. She'd be a misery to work fer, she would. She tries to take over whenever she comes here as it is. But ye—now ye would understand the trials of a servant 'cause ye're a hard worker from what I seen." Cook lifted both hands in surrender. "Ah, but work! Just look at what ya done to me. Just one day out and already I'm stuck without a scullery maid."

"I'm sorry." She realized she meant it.

Cook laughed once more. "Ye'd be crazy to be sorry." She resumed whisking the eggs, her face brightening. "I'll have to ask me brother's daughter. Didn't think o' her till now."

Harrod entered. "Cook, must you speak at the top of your lungs?" He spotted Becca, and his demeanor changed. "Oh, Miss Hanham. What are you doing here in the kitchen?"

"I–I'm still a scullery maid until I speak with Mr. Abercrombie, ain't I?"

He looked taken aback. "I don't suppose you have been dismissed." He cut his glance to Cook.

"She told me about the proposal. Since she works in the kitchen with me, I have a right to know." She set down the bowl and placed her hands on her hips. "Now I ain't got a scullery maid."

"We'll discuss that later. Come along, please, Miss Hanham, and if you plan to accept Mr. Abercrombie's proposal, remember that you are not to enter through the back door, but the front." He studied her. "Not that I ever expect you to enter alone again in any event."

The front door! She thought about the first door she had knocked on and how rude the butler had been. She'd love to knock on that front door today. Just as quickly, she put away such an indulgent thought. More important matters—and a much more important man—awaited.

"Mr. Abercrombie said he will meet you in the front parlor." Harrod led her to a room warm in temperature and inviting in atmosphere. Even a cursory examination told her that even though the decor all over the house seemed grand, the finest pieces had been saved for the best room. Chairs fashioned of carved wood and a stuffed sofa draped in silk seemed so luxurious, she feared she shouldn't sit at all, though the foot-and-claw leg designs seemed substantial.

Before she chose a seat, her gaze caught a set of portraits above the sofa. The man and woman portrayed must have been Nash's parents. If so, Nash looked just like his father, with big brown eyes and a kind but manly face. His slim-figured mother was portrayed in the high style of her time, but the expression on her lovely face didn't show the least bit of arrogance or entitlement. They must have passed on their graciousness of spirit to their son so that he didn't mind taking a chance on her, a mere servant girl.

Nash's voice sounded from behind her, catching her off guard. "Do you like those portraits?"

She jumped a bit and turned toward him.

"I'm sorry. Did I startle you? Forgive me."

Seeing him again brought back feelings of high excitement. Glad for a topic other than the answer she had to give him, she pounced upon it. "Yea, they're beautiful. I got lost lookin' at 'em."

"Those are my favorite depictions of my parents." He joined her in viewing the portraits.

"You mean there's more?" The thought of spending a great sum of money to have one portrait painted was beyond her imagination, much less commissioning several.

"Yes," he responded. "There's a set in the bedchamber they shared, painted later in their lives. And in the library is yet another portrait of the three of us when I was but a tiny babe. But this set is my favorite because the likenesses capture their happiness during the time they were a courting couple." He took them in as though seeing them for the first time. "I can stare at these paintings and forget time, too. I wish you could have known my parents. I think they would have liked you very much."

The idea warmed her spirit. "Really? How come?" The question made her sound like a small child instead of the dignified woman she wanted to be. She tried not to wince at her own embarrassment.

He didn't seem to notice her discomfiture. "They wanted a Christian woman for me, and from the way you speak of your prayer life, I know you love our Savior. And you are beautiful in appearance."

Becca felt herself blush. She averted her gaze, taking sudden interest in the arrival of the promised afternoon tea. The maid set it on the low table that looked to be created for the purpose. As Becca and Nash sat in opposite chairs around the table, the maid poured rich, reddish-brown liquid into china cups. Becca inhaled the scent of the hot beverage, spiced as it was, with the luxury of a cinnamon stick protruding from each cup.

Nash dismissed the maid and offered Becca a small plate of finger sandwiches, the kind Naomi said her friend May had to prepare for her mistress. Dizzy in the realization that she occupied such a position, Becca took one that looked pleasing while Nash took two.

"My father especially would have loved your spirit of adventure," he noted. "Who else would knock on doors until she found the lowest form of work? And if you agree to marry me, that will be an adventure indeed."

Holding her sandwich, she tried to speak in the manner of a highborn woman. "Indeed."

"So do you have an answer for me?"

She thought they might sit and talk a bit first, but she could see by the way his leg moved up and down with nervous energy that Nash was as anxious as she.

The moment she'd been awaiting had arrived. Now that it had, she felt her heart beat all the way up to her throat. Her voice didn't want to cooperate, but she willed herself to speak from the depths of her soul. "Oh. Yes. Yes, I do. I accept your proposal." She took in a breath, not believing the words as they fell from her lips. Was she really herself—Becca Hanham, impoverished servant girl— or had she stepped into someone else's life? At the moment she didn't care, as long as she could hold on to the dream. Never had she been so happy—and so scared—at once.

Nash's eyes shone like her brother Samuel's when the big kids let him in on their games. "That is the news I wanted to hear." He took her hand in his and brushed his lips just above her knuckles. "I am honored by your acceptance."

Such words left her feeling light-headed and unable to say anything gracious. Or anything at all, really. How could someone of such stature be honored by her acceptance?

If he noticed her puny state, he hid it well. "This calls for a celebration." He summoned Harrod, who appeared in an instant. "Send Jack to the Providence Arcade for lobster."

Harrod sent Nash a knowing look that Becca didn't quite understand. "Yes, sir. If I can find him."

Nash's lips tightened. "See that you do. Miss Hanham deserves a fine meal, the first she will partake as my fiancée."

Heart still beating beyond measure, but with happiness rather than anxiety, she felt her own eyes sparkle. "I don't care if we have boiled water. I'm just happy."

"As am I. But of course, I want to make sure I have your father's blessing."

She tried not to laugh. "Father's blessin'? He'd bless a frog if he'd take me outta the house. He's tired o' feedin' me. Ya know that's why I took that job as a scullery maid to start with."

The fact she had to broach the subject of her father brought his admonitions to mind, spoiling her moment. Nash claimed happiness, but did their impending wedding please him, or just the chance to rid himself of Miss Caldwell?

When she looked back into Nash's face, she saw pity. No matter what her feelings for her father, she saw no good in turning Nash against him. "Oh, Father ain't so bad. With a brood to feed, he's gotta think about what's best fer ever'body. Accordin' to age, I'm next in line to marry. And there's a new baby on the way sometime this summer."

"A happy event indeed," Nash observed. "Even though I can't pretend to understand what it must be like to live with so many brothers and sisters, I can speculate on the difficulties your father must face. Under normal circumstances, I would have approached him before even asking you to marry me. However, these are not the usual circumstances. I would feel more assured if I could confirm from him that he is agreeable to my request for your hand. I hope you understand."

"Of course." She more than understood. His concern made her feel special.

Nash eyed a small black marble statue of a pyramid on an occasional table. "But let's talk about other things while we wait for dinner to be prepared. Would you be interested in learning a bit about the trinkets I have on display in this room? Each one holds meaning for me."

Becca agreed without hesitation. Time moved at a rapid clip as he pointed out *objets d'art* and souvenirs, talking about worlds near and far, all unknown to Becca. At first she felt nervous, realizing she had no idea about the exotic places he described. She relaxed after she could see that Nash enjoyed sharing his interests with her, even though she often felt some of her questions would sound silly to sophisticated ears. She appreciated his patience and reveled in his joy as they talked.

As the room grew dark from twilight's falling, the maid, without interrupting them, lit candles so they could see. Becca wished time would never move forward, but soon they were called to dinner. Panic and anticipation visited her when she realized that for the first time she'd be taking her meal in a real dining room, not an overcrowded area at home with too many people and too few chairs.

When they entered, they found a long table set with fine linens and dinnerware. She had never dined on a surface covered with cloth of any description. With so many people in her house, the most practical solution was for her sister to wipe bare wood with a wet rag after each meal. She doubted Father would have let Mother indulge in the purchase of linens even if they'd had the money. And cloth napkins! The men in her house, regardless of the fact the older ones knew better, were fond of wiping their mouths on their shirtsleeves. The women tried not to smear their faces so they wouldn't need napkins.

The silver looked heavy and patterned with so many flowers that Becca imagined each utensil held enough to populate a garden. Crystal glasses appeared delicate. She hoped she wouldn't break hers before the night ended. She reached for a carved chair, but Nash took it by the other side and pulled it out, nodding for her to take a seat. No man had ever pulled a seat out for her. The attention felt exciting but strange.

Nash said a blessing over the meal, a pleasant start that made her feel more comfortable with him. His words sounded so natural she could discern he wasn't putting on a show for her, a fact that relieved her. Then, following his example, she set her napkin in her lap and realized her dress was nowhere near fine enough. She needed clothing—and fast. But how could she think of a new wardrobe for herself when her family couldn't even pay for enough food? She prayed her sparse wardrobe wouldn't cause Nash embarrassment.

The hook-nosed maid Becca once thought of befriending had become her servant, presenting her with a bowl of soup. The appetizer, floating in a rose-embellished bowl, proved rich and creamy. She felt full after she ate it and, out of habit, pushed back her chair to take the dish into the kitchen until the maid rushed over to retrieve it. She looked fearful of being reprimanded, giving Nash a sheepish look. But his benign expression told them all that no chastisement was forthcoming.

Being waited on made Becca feel odd and undeserving. At least the maid didn't make eye contact, in effect pretending she'd never seen Becca in the scullery. She would have to restrain herself so she could sit through a meal without rising to help.

Considerate as usual, Nash asked Becca about her brothers and sisters. The conversation lasted throughout the dinner, well past the promised lobster.

"How did you like your meal?" Nash asked after a dessert of cake drizzled with fig icing.

"Wonderful. I've never been so full. And I've never seen so much in the way of cream and butter in my life."

Nash chuckled. "Cook did her best to please, as you can see. Do you wish to eat meals this rich every night?"

The lavish meal had indeed been a treat, but she wasn't accustomed to so much food, and it felt heavy on her stomach. How could she tell him the truth without seeming ungrateful? She answered without looking up. "Uh, well. . .it was delicious, but I ain't sure I could."

"Good. I don't want to overindulge at every meal, either. We can eat more simply and save an abundance of cream and butter for holidays. I happen to like johnnycakes, for one." He smiled.

"Johnnycakes!" Becca restrained herself from jumping up and down like a toddler. The corn cakes, popular in Rhode Island, were a special treat at her house. "They're my favorite, too."

Nash chuckled. "I think you and I will get along just fine. Now, if you will, I'd like to escort you to the parlor for coffee. It's a little luxury I enjoy."

"Of course." She found the custom strange, but pleasurable, since it gave her more time with Nash. The next hour flew by for Becca as the clock chimed on the quarter hour.

"It's getting late, and I hate to see the evening end," Nash said as they lingered over the last drops. "I'll have Jack take you home."

"Home? But I thought I'd stay here with you."

"Oh. I hadn't considered you might think that." His eyes filled with regret. "If you were still my scullery maid, such an arrangement would be fine and good. But now that we plan to wed, I'm afraid tongues will wag if we share the same residence before our wedding day, the presence of servants notwithstanding."

"You didn't seem to care much about waggin' tongues when you talked about our match." Her disappointment made her tone seem more argumentative than she liked.

"I realize I might seem contradictory. Such is not my intent. It is important to me to protect your reputation." He turned even more serious. "I won't deceive you, Becca. Because we are worlds apart in rank, even with both of us conducting ourselves with the utmost propriety, there will be talk. You are taking a courageous step to agree to marry me, and I appreciate you for it. I hope you're not too afraid."

"No. Not with you beside me."

"Good. Go home now, and sleep well tonight. I'll send Jack over to collect you in the morning, and we shall continue our adventure."

∞

Later that night after she had shared the remaining food from the Abercrombie kitchen with her astonished family and told them about the evening, Becca tossed and turned on the mattress stuffed with straw. Fashioned for one, she nevertheless had to share it with her sister. Every once in a while Sissy, slumbering beside her, would tap her to discourage so much movement, but sleeping proved difficult as she relived the evening's events in her mind. Nash's advice to sleep well seemed impossible to follow. She couldn't remember the last night she went to bed with a satisfied belly. Conscious that the younger children should have enough, the older siblings and Mother had always eaten last, dividing between them the portions left after the youngsters had partaken. Never had she eaten until she couldn't eat more. Filled with food far richer and in greater quantity than she was accustomed, she could hardly breathe. She reminded herself that she couldn't eat as much in the future. But how could she waste a drop of such fine food? To do so seemed sinful. Maybe she could ask Cook to send out small portions for her.

Excitement didn't help. She could only think of her new life. Being overworked and the pressure Father put on her to provide money kept her from being completely happy all her life, but poverty never worried her. She had become accustomed to a meager diet and her mother's embarrassment of being unable to pay bills on occasion. Winter meant shivering in rags against the cold, even indoors. But in this neighborhood, most families lived the same—maybe a bit better off on occasion, but often worse. Not until Becca peeked into the homes of Providence's well-to-do did she see the gap for herself.

Nash came with his money, and she wasn't sure if she'd ever be comfortable in riches. Yet if he loved her as much as she now believed she could love him—indeed, already she had started growing fond of the kind and dashing gentleman—she'd do her best.

The next morning she rose, still tired but too excited about going back to Nash's to care. Donning her same dress, she hoped he wouldn't mind seeing her in it yet again. Surely the women with whom he grew up owned many ensembles. One of their everyday dresses must look better than her best frock. She tried not to think about it because there was nothing to be done.

She left the bedroom and found her father and brothers waiting for breakfast. Mother and Naomi scurried to prepare them a modest meal.

"What are ya doin' here among us?" Father asked as soon as he spotted her. "I thought ye'd moved in with that fancy feller o' your'n." His voice grew menacing. "Ya didn't spoil things, did ya?"

"Oh no, Father. It's only proper fer me to come home ever' night now that I ain't a servant."

Father nodded. "I hadn't thought of it that way. Ye're right."

"We had a good evenin'," Becca said. "We talked and even had coffee after dinner."

"That's why ya couldn't sleep last night," Naomi said. "Ya kept me awake."

"She kept me awake, too," Sissy added.

The other sisters murmured in agreement.

"I'm sorry." Becca looked at each of them in apology.

"What possessed ya to drink coffee at night?" Mother asked. "If we're lucky enough to have any, I drink it in the mornin' to stay awake."

"I hadn't thought about that. I'll try not to drink it so late anymore. Oh, but I was so excited I don't think warm milk could have put me to sleep last night."

"Ya did have an excitin' evenin'," Naomi admitted.

"Hey, wait a minute." Father grabbed her left hand. "Where's yer ring? Don't rich people give rings when they say they're gonna get married?"

Becca looked at her bare hand. Father squeezed it so tightly it hurt. "I—I don't know. He didn't give me one." She pulled her hand out of his grasp.

"Ya better do as I say and start collectin' those trinkets. This'll end soon enough." He nodded in a knowing way.

Mother changed the subject. "When are ya supposed to go back?"

"I think he mentioned somethin' 'bout pickin' me up today. I guess he'll send Jack."

"Who's that?" Willie asked.

"His driver."

The sound of horses' hooves could be heard just outside the door.

"Mebbe that's him now." Becca rushed to the front door and opened it. The Abercrombie carriage was parked outside. "Yea, that's Jack. I'll get ready to go now." She hurried into the bedroom to retrieve her coat and bonnet.

When she returned to the front room, Becca was shocked to see Nash. "Mr. Abercrombie!" She wanted to embrace him, but with her family watching in shock, suspicion, and awe, she thought better of it.

Nash, clad in a fashionable morning suit, stood on their doorstep. Though he dressed less ostentatiously than many in his social set, his suit showed him to be a man knowledgeable of the latest style and possessing the ability to afford an expert tailor. Wide-eyed stares from children and adults on the street trying not to look his way told her how out of place he appeared in the neighborhood. Waves of embarrassment swept over Becca, emotions that made her feel ashamed. Shaking off the feeling, she reminded herself that poverty defined her but was no sin. "Won't you come in?"

Instead of recoiling, Nash acted with the utmost politeness—as though he were one of them—as she made introductions. To her shock, he even presented each of her siblings a small gift—toys for the younger set and scented toiletries for the older ones. Though he had only spent his pocket change, Becca surmised he had no idea how much the day seemed like Christmas to all of them.

"I hope I might take this opportunity to speak with you, Mr. Hanham," he said after pleasantries had been exchanged.

Greed glinted in his eyes. "Clear out!"

His family scattered. Even Becca had to leave. She prayed her father wouldn't say anything to embarrass her.

Chapter 6

Nash sat across the rough-hewn table from Mr. Hanham. Never had he dreamed that a man wearing tatters and appearing on the verge of drunkenness before the noon hour would be his potential father-in-law. But his fondness for Becca had grown in a short time, and he knew deep love for her could develop without effort. Gossip and ridicule were sure to follow when people discovered her background, but he'd meet the challenge. A loveless marriage would be a worse fate. And with Becca beside him, he feared nothing.

Mr. Hanham eyed a younger man who seemed to be near in age to Becca. "Stop combin' yer hair here in the kitchen, Elias. What's the matter wif ya? Fergot yer manners?"

Elias's puzzled expression told Nash that his father didn't usually reprimand him for grooming in the same area where the family ate.

"Run along now." Mr. Hanham's tone said he meant business.

Elias nodded. He was the last sibling to exit, so Nash and Mr. Hanham were left in relative privacy. Studying the older man, Nash could see that he must have been handsome not so long ago. Traces of Becca could be seen in his face, aged beyond its years thanks to poverty and hard drink.

"So"—Mr. Hanham eyed him and took a swig of ale—"I understand ya want ta marry me daughter."

"Yes, I would. I beg your pardon for not consulting with you first, Mr. Hanham. I'm afraid my proposal was a bit impromptu."

"Imprompt—what?"

Nash searched for a definition. "Uh, unplanned."

"Oh. So how do ya make all yer money?"

Though the query was appropriate from a future father-in-law, Nash nevertheless tried not to reveal his surprise at the blunt way Mr. Hanham expressed himself—and so early during their interview. He cleared his throat. "I am in charge of the trading company I inherited from my father. My business is stable, and I believe your daughter will have a comfortable life."

Mr. Hanham indulged in a fresh drink of ale, looking at Nash over the mug. "So ye're really goin' through with it?"

"That is my honest intention, yes, sir."

The older man set the mug on the table. "Not that I blame ya. She's a mighty pretty thing." He wiped his mouth with his shirtsleeve, prompting Nash to notice a lack of table linens.

"Yes, she is," he answered with genuine cheerfulness. "But her spirit inside is what attracted me to her."

"Really?" Mr. Hanham picked up his mug.

"Yes. One fact that impressed me most about her was how important her family is to her. So you can see especially why I pray you can support and bless our union."

Mr. Hanham downed the rest of his ale, set the mug on the table with a *thump*, and looked Nash in the eye. "I know she's pretty, but so are those high-society ladies. What do ya want with a girl outta my brood? I may be poor, but I ain't stupid. I know what some of you wealthy types think you can get away with."

Nash held back a retort at such an insult, forcing himself to remember this man didn't know him as a person, but from rumors he'd heard from others about a world strange to him. If Nash were honest with himself, he'd have to admit some of the rumors about his cohorts were true. "I understand your concern, Mr. Hanham. I admire you for wanting to protect Becca. Yet if my intentions were less than honorable, I wouldn't take the time and effort to approach you to ask you for her hand in marriage. In fact, I'd be more likely not to mention marriage at all."

"True," he conceded. "She told me ya asked. You're a rich man, and my daughter don't got no dowry to offer. How do I know ya don't plan to break off the engagement as soon as that woman nobody likes goes back to wherever she came from?" He crossed his arms and scowled at Nash.

So Becca had filled her family in on all the details about Hazel. He hadn't forbidden her to share, but the truth embarrassed him. Perhaps he should have asked her not to mention Hazel. He tried not to wince. "I realize why you might be suspicious, but let me assure you again that I am entering this engagement period with full intention of marrying her. If she'll have me, of course."

He laughed. "If she'll have ya? I'd think she'd be on her knees thankin' heavenly Providence fer lettin' her get the attention of a man as rich as you."

Nash was taken aback by the man's brash statement. The crude reference to his fortune reminded him of Hazel at her worst. He resisted the urge to retort, considering the family's sad surroundings. He kept his tone even. "I do hope I have more to offer her than riches. I have gotten to know her a bit, and we seem congenial. I have no reason to think that will change."

"Ye can't live on talkin'."

"True. I will provide for her and do my best to increase your comfort as well. Perhaps I might see my way clear to find a modest house for you. A house near mine so Becca can see her family every day."

His eyes widened. "Ye'd do that? Fer us?"

"Yes, I would."

"I'm not so sure I'd want to live in a fancy neighborhood. We're simple folk. We won't fit in."

"With the right education and changes in appearance, you could. I can help your children move up in the world."

For the first time, the older man sobered, and his expression softened. "I didn't expect quite that much. Truth be told, I was just hopin' fer a hundred dollars. Guess that makes you a fool."

"I'm no fool."

"Fool or no, I'd say this calls for a drink." He summoned for his wife to bring Nash a portion of ale and to pour himself another.

She rushed in and hurried to obey. As Nash watched in awe of her speed, she placed an empty cup on the table.

"None for me, thank you," Nash said.

Mrs. Hanham stopped in midmotion, her expression taking on a resigned look. "Warn't there good news?"

"Yea, there was," her husband answered. "I told him we'd let him have our Becca."

The older woman's face lit, her cheeks growing to the size of small apples as she smiled. "Then I'd say this does call for a round of ale, Mr. Abercrombie. Don't ya want ta celebrate?"

"I don't need to drink spirits. My light heart and the prospect of marriage to your daughter are celebration enough for me." Making such a declaration aloud made Nash realize how strong his feelings for her had become.

☙

Though winter chill bit, Becca waited out front in pale sunshine while the two most important men in her life decided her future. Sissy and Naomi stood nearby, talking to each other since Becca hadn't entered their conversation. Their presence heartened her. Younger than Becca yet closest to her in age, they sensed when she needed them nearby even if few words were exchanged.

Familiar sights and sounds of her neighborhood floated overhead. One benefit colder weather provided was a lessening of the stench of horse manure and rotting garbage, though such odors proved inescapable in the best of weather. Most adults—and some children—worked in the factories or elsewhere during the day, so the streets weren't filled with whoops and hollers of happy games. The ragman pulled his cart, shouting about his wares, but Becca shook her head when he made eye contact with her.

What was taking them so long? "Father in heaven, Thy will be done."

As time passed, the chill made itself known through her coat. Shivering, she reached for the door just as it opened and Nash strode through it. His relaxed facial expression indicated he hadn't been too shaken by the encounter with her father. Becca caught a glimpse of her two sisters out of the corner of her eye.

Naomi and Sissy pretended to watch a passing merchant hocking pots and pans, but Becca knew their ears were tuned to whatever news Nash had to share.

Nash glanced at the sisters and seemed to understand. "Are you ready to go home with me?"

Home with me. The words sent a satisfied shiver down her spine. The idea that her home would forever be with him still seemed unreal—like a fantasy she had entered and would soon be asked to exit. But she didn't want to leave the fantasy. Not ever. Glancing at her front door, she wanted to point out he could stay for lunch, but with the Hanhams' finances in a pinch, she didn't want to put him in the position of pretending he liked the porridge Mother served.

"Yea, I'm ready." She turned to her sisters and bid them farewell for the day. They giggled and curtsied to Nash, a gesture Becca found both embarrassing and amusing. Ever poised, Nash tipped his hat to them and bid them an elegant farewell before helping Becca into the conveyance.

As soon as Jack shut the door behind them, Becca felt relieved to be in semi-privacy with Nash. Or at least away from her sisters' curiosity. Yet a little feeling of insecurity visited her, making her almost afraid to ask. "So ya asked Father fer his blessin'?"

"Of course. I said I would, didn't I?" His smile suggested teasing.

A relieved breath escaped her in spite of her best efforts to remain calm. "And give ya his blessin' he did, no doubt."

Nash settled into his seat. "Yes. He agreed after much questioning that we can marry."

"Questionin'?" She felt her face flush red. "How dare he ask anything of a fine man such as yerself. I'm sorry."

He leaned toward her and took her hands in his. Even in her distress, she couldn't help but notice they were the hands of a gentleman. Strong and manly, yet smooth. Looking at his fingers, she observed they were well tended, not rough and calloused like the hands of the men of her acquaintance. His fingernails were healthy and clean with no half-moon-shaped lines of dirt. "You have no need to ask my forgiveness. Your father's questions helped him earn my respect. If my intentions had been anything but honorable, he would have seen it, because his queries would have been hard for a man with ill intentions to answer truthfully. I know he's rough on the edges, but I think in his own way he cares about you." He gave her hands a quick reassuring squeeze and let them go. She wished he'd hold them forever.

Becca thought her father's real motives were caring about himself, but she decided not to argue. She lowered her voice and stared at the carriage floor. "He—he didn't ask for money, did he?"

"No."

"Good." She let out a relieved breath. The sigh filled the carriage, surprising her with its intensity.

"I want you to know I did offer your family a modest home."

She looked up and gasped. "A house? He asked fer a house?" Without thinking, she glimpsed outside and observed the homes they passed and wondered if he planned to buy one of those. Since the most insignificant residence in his neighborhood would far surpass their present accommodations, no doubt Mother would be grateful.

"No, he didn't ask for a house," Nash assured. "I offered it willingly. I hope you aren't too distressed about that."

"Distressed? No, but I'm not for sale."

"I know. I'm being a bit selfish, I must admit. I think having your family nearby will make you happy, and your happiness in turn makes me happy. You see, after we're married, I want you to see your family any time you like. I can see how much they mean to you."

This man thought of everything. She felt her throat closing as her emotions increased. "They—they do," she somehow managed.

"Your dedication to them increases your stature in my eyes. I've seen more of the world than you have, and you'd be surprised by how many people forget their families once something good happens to them or they gain access to a little money. It's as though they're ashamed of their relatives. I don't see you as having such thoughts."

"Never." She didn't have to pretend her strong conviction.

"Even better, I think the offer put aside any reservations your father might have had about my sincerity."

Becca didn't want to admit that his report of the interview eased her mind, too. With each passing gesture, Nash convinced her he was a man of his word. If it had been proper, she would have embraced him on the spot.

He changed the topic. "I told Cook we'd be content with vegetable soup and bread for luncheon. You'll find soup is my favorite dish during the winter months. I hope you don't mind that."

Though being in the carriage had dulled the winter chill, a bowl of steaming liquid to warm her inside and out sounded delectable. "I don't mind in the least."

"Good. I'm sure she'll have roast for dinner and no doubt fruit jam tarts as a treat for dessert."

"Everything sounds wonderful." Her mouth watered in agreement, though she felt guilty since her family wouldn't be eating so well.

"I want you to stay fortified. We have a lot of work to do."

"A lot of work?" She tried to envision what he meant.

He peered outside. "It seems we have arrived at our destination. If you'll follow me to the parlor, we'll sit and talk."

A nervous feeling hit, but the prospect of spending time with him in what had become her favorite room in the house cheered her. He helped her disembark, and they went to the formal room without delay. Becca took the chair she liked best and watched his movements as he sat across from her. No matter what his task—even something as mundane as seating himself in a chair—he moved with fluidity and grace, yet in a manner unmistakably masculine.

He tried to assure her right away. "As for the work I mentioned, I promise it's not as gloomy as spending your waking hours in the scullery."

She leaned forward. "What, then?"

For the first time since they left the Hanhams', he seemed uncertain about what to say next. He leaned forward and rubbed his thumbs together before looking her in the eyes. "Becca, may I be honest with you?"

As long as she could keep looking into his mahogany eyes, she didn't care what he had to say. She'd listen all day. "I hope ye'll never be anything else."

"Yes, but I don't want to hurt your feelings. Please try not to take offense at what I am about to explain to you, but it has to be said." He paused and took a breath. "I'm sure you realize you haven't been trained to be a lady accustomed to living a life filled with the finer things and mannerisms with which I am familiar."

"Oh." She looked downward. "I know it."

"The work I mentioned isn't work, really. In fact, I hope you can find pleasure in what I have in mind for you. It involves training you to be at ease among my friends and acquaintances."

"Trainin' me? Ya mean I have ta go to school?" Recalling repetitive ciphering, she scrunched her nose.

He chuckled. "Not exactly. I just want to show you how to conduct yourself in your new world, that's all. You can trust me when I say I am doing this for you more than for myself. I want you to be comfortable in my world and able to present yourself as a refined woman. We will start with your wardrobe and your manner of speech."

"I don't mind the idea of wearin' pretty dresses, but I don't know much about talkin' like a society person."

This time he didn't chuckle, but laughed outright. The musical sound broke the tension, and he relaxed in his chair. "You're smart. You'll get the idea soon enough. For one, be careful never to refer to riches or wealth. You must not appear to be self-conscious about having funds at your disposal. Doing so in our social setting is considered quite tactless and impolite."

"I—I think I can remember that." Her lips curled in a rueful manner. "We don't hardly ever talk about money where I come from either 'cause there ain't none to talk about."

He flinched but recovered with good grace. Becca wondered if his embarrassment stemmed from her sorry financial state or the way she spoke. Maybe both. "I'm glad we understand each other. Now, Harrod and I will be instructing you on how to form your words properly and how to speak with an expanded vocabulary."

Her stomach lurched with anxiety. "That sounds hard."

"It might seem strange at first, but you'll soon become accustomed to speaking as a lady should, and before you realize it, you'll sound as though you attended a fine finishing school. Proper speech will become a habit. A habit you'll be so proud of you'll never want to break it." The warmth in his gaze seemed convincing.

"I guess."

"Better to say, 'I suppose.'"

"Oh." She clapped her hand over her lips. "I suppose."

"I have also engaged a voice teacher for you. Mrs. James will be by this afternoon to evaluate your singing ability and let us know how she feels about your talent. Hopefully she can teach you at least one or two songs so you can sing in front of a small group of friends. Informally, of course."

"Sing? In front of a group?" The idea left her with nervous queasiness. "But how come?"

"Being a lady means speaking and dressing well, of course, but knowing how to entertain at home is important as well. Fine ladies develop skills such as playing the pianoforte or singing. Sometimes both."

Her stomach jumped. "I just sing hymns with the rest of the congregation in our little church, and sometimes we sing old folk songs at home. I ain't never sung in front of anybody who really cared much what I sounded like."

"Hymns and folk songs are fine. She can judge the range of your voice based on those. Remember, she's there to work with you, not to be unduly critical or harsh."

"I ain't so sure. . . ."

"Oh, please do try. I think you'll enjoy singing greatly once you have a few lessons," he said. "I would have suggested the pianoforte, but I don't think it will be possible to have you proficient in any song on such a complicated instrument in time to entertain our friends."

Our friends. That sounded divine. Divine enough for her to decide to overcome her fears. "Then I'll sing as good as I can."

"As *well* as I can."

"Oh." She didn't care for the fact he had to correct her grammar, but at least he was kind and it was part of the lessons she had to learn. She wasn't sure she could have abided someone less compassionate. "As well as I can."

"Very well." He surveyed her appearance from the top of her head to the ends of her scuffed shoes. His gaze didn't seem critical, nor was it without sympathy. Still, she knew her mode of dress and manners had a long way to go to be considered adequate. Remembering that both of her soles sported holes, with a self-conscious motion she planted both feet on the floor so he wouldn't see. "We must address the fact of your appearance."

"Yea," she responded.

"Yes."

Couldn't she say a word that was right? "Yes." She suppressed an impatient sigh.

"As for your appearance, of course you already realize you cannot wear the same simple frock every day." His voice sounded kind, and his eyes told her he wished he didn't have to be so critical. "I thought you might enjoy an outing, so we'll stop by the cobbler's for several pairs of new shoes—"

Several?

"—and the milliner's for new bonnets and hats."

New bonnets and hats? He said more than one? Shoes, too! The shoes she wore were several years old since her feet hadn't grown in a while, and they were her only pair. Owning more than one new pair seemed like something out of a storybook.

"You look pale," he noticed. "Are you quite all right?"

She nodded so fast her head must have looked like a bouncing ball. "I—I only hope I can be worthy to wear such finery."

"You are worthy, no matter what you wear."

"Well, if you'll have me ta look like a lady, I'd better sound like one. I'll work on me speech."

He grinned. "Better to say, 'my speech.'"

She clapped her hand over her lips again. "My speech."

His kind laughter filled the room. "You don't need to put your hands over your mouth when you make a mistake. You have nothing about which to be ashamed. Even the best of us have to learn proper speech."

"E–even you?"

"Even me." He grinned. "My governess, Miss Winters, had quite a time with me, but she made sure I learned."

"Was she as cold as her name?" Becca couldn't resist asking in jest.

He leaned toward her. "Even colder."

Becca shivered in an exaggerated manner, but bolstered him. "Oh, I'm sure ya were a good little boy."

"Not as good as she would have liked, I'm afraid." He changed the topic. "Oh, and I have wonderful news. I took the liberty of asking Harrod to hire a ladies maid for you."

"A ladies maid? Why, indeed? I'm perfectly capable of dressing myself, Mr. Abercrombie."

He looked at her attire with a studied eye. "First and foremost, now that your father has blessed our engagement and we can move forward, you must call me by my Christian name. And as for your toilette—if I may be so indelicate—of course you can adorn yourself in such a simple frock, but you'll soon change your mind when you see the buttons on the dresses I'm having made for you today. I may be a bachelor, but it's hard not to notice how many buttons adorn most ladies' frocks."

Buttons? Dresses? Ladies maid? It was all too much.

She had an idea. "Can't one of me—my—sisters be my ladies maid?"

"The thought did occur to me, but I'm assuming none of your sisters has experience as a ladies maid."

She didn't have to think long. "No."

"Please pardon me, as I mean no offense to you or your sisters, but I feel since you are new to this type of life, you need someone with experience. Someone familiar to this world who can give you compassionate advice," he said. "Harrod has just the woman. I have no doubt you'll like her. In fact, she will become your closest female companion, a friend and confidant to you. She worked for one of Providence's finest families, and the only reason she's available now is because her mistress, sadly, has departed this life."

"Oh, I am so sorry."

"Yes, she will be missed, but I am confident she resides in heaven now. We are blessed that the timing is fortuitous for the maid, since there was no other position for her in the family. Her name is Bernice Knowles. She's due to arrive tomorrow morning."

Remembering how Cook knew her family, Becca felt a bolt of unexpected fear. "Does she know who I am?"

He hesitated. "I did ask Harrod to fill her in only on the details she needs to know. My trusted butler and I would never consider placing you in the hands of anyone, servant or otherwise, who would do you harm. I assure you, she will understand the situation and will treat you with the greatest respect and courtesy. If she doesn't, you can report any infraction to me and she will be dismissed without question."

A different kind of fear visited Becca at this statement. She had never possessed the power to determine anyone's future, including her own. Her father had always decided what she would do and when she would do it, and she never interfered with the affairs of her mother or any of her siblings. The idea that one word from her could cause the loss of a job for anyone scared her. She wasn't sure she wanted that kind of power.

Obviously unaware of her anxiety, Nash continued. "Harrod will be instructing Bernice to help you stay on top of your speech patterns and any other little niceties you need to know. But if she is ever in the least bit impatient or harsh with you, that will not be acceptable and will be cause for her dismissal."

"Oh, I ain't plannin' to dismiss anybody."

"Perhaps it is better to say, 'I have no intention of dismissing anyone.'"

She nodded. "I have no intention of dismissin'—dismissing—anyone." Such elegant speech sounded strange to her ears, coming from her own mouth, but as Nash had pointed out, she'd have to become accustomed to speaking as a well-positioned lady would.

"See, doesn't that sound much more lovely?" he asked.

She nodded. "Yes, it does." Without letting Nash know, she congratulated herself.

"I told you you'd learn quickly." He became more serious. "After we marry, you can dismiss any servant you like."

She gasped. "I ain't—I mean, I'm not sure I want so much responsibility."

"With each feeling you share with me, I become more confident that I made the right decision to ask you to marry me," he said. "Only a person of character would make such a statement. Many other people thrown into your position so suddenly would be almost drunk with the prospect of lording their newfound authority over others. I can see you will be a wonderful wife for me."

Wife. Her heart beat faster at the prospect. Could it be true? She still didn't believe it. "I hope so."

"Not that I think you'll have cause to dismiss anyone, at least not anyone we currently have in our employ. My servants have been faithful to my family for many years, and I have no reason to think you and they won't be congenial."

"I'll do me—my best. I don't wish to cause disruption. My father ain't—I mean, isn't—fond of work, but for the most part, I know how much people depend on their jobs." She swallowed. "So when do we get started on our work?"

"I can see we need to help you develop patience." His tone was indulgent, not reprimanding. He drew a small velvet pouch out of his desk drawer and handed it to her. "This seems to be the right time to present you with a token of my commitment to you."

She waved her palm toward him. "Thank you, but I can't take a gift."

"Of course you can. It's tradition. At least, it's tradition in my family."

Remembering Father's insistence that she gather as many jewels as possible, she felt too uncomfortable to accept anything. "It's not tradition in my family. My mother just has a thin gold band, and she didn't get that until her weddin'—wedding—day. That's all I'll need. Keep whatever it is in that box."

"Then you don't know it's a ring." His rueful grin tempted her.

"What else could it be?"

Nash shrugged. "It may be, and it may not be. Why don't you open it and see?" He handed it to her.

Deciding there was no other option, she took the box from him. Opening it she found a gold ring set with a large ruby flanked by a small diamond on each side. The idea that anyone would give her something so exquisite left her wordless. All she could do was try to fight back tears of happiness. "It's—it's beautiful! I wish I could take this, but I can't." She sniffled.

"Yes you can."

"No." She handed it back to him. "I can't."

He looked puzzled, and then a flicker of realization crossed his features. "You're afraid if you accept it, I'll think you're materialistic, don't you?"

"Materialistic? Do you mean that I only want your money?"

"Yes. That's what it means, and no, I don't think you just want my money. Not for a moment." He paused. "With your permission, may I speak frankly?"

"Yes."

"Let me remind you that already there is a woman desperately wanting to be engaged to me—thinking she is engaged to me even though I never asked her to be my wife—and I have every reason to think she is interested in nothing but my money. But she does offer a pedigree and already knows what's expected of her in our social circle."

Becca winced.

"So think, Becca. Why would I propose to someone else I thought wanted nothing but my money?"

She thought. "I—I suppose you wouldn't."

"That's right." He touched her hand so that it seemed as though a butterfly had lit on it for the briefest of moments, then withdrew it. The gesture was enough to show her his growing feelings, yet assured her he planned to remain a gentleman. Her tension diminished as he continued. "I realize all of this must be overwhelming to you. You have left a world where you had to scrape for a morsel to eat each day and entered a domain where you can enjoy more than enough of everything you could want or need. Of course none of this feels natural to you."

"It don't—doesn't. I'm sorry. I'm such a fool."

"No, I am the one who shouldn't have rushed you by introducing so many changes in the course of a morning." He stared at the ring. "I should have waited before giving you Grandmother's ring."

She gasped. "Your grandmother's ring!"

"Yes. Grandmother Abercrombie wore this all her life. She presented it to me as long as I promised my future wife would wear it."

By now tears coursed down her cheeks. Even when she cried because of happiness, Becca wasn't prone to prettiness. Knowing her face must make her look like a bloated, overripe tomato made her feel worse. "Of course I'll accept it. How could I offend your dear grandmother?"

"I'm sure she's smiling down from heaven now." He took it out of the box. "Will you let me see your left ring finger?"

She extended her hand.

He slipped it on her finger. "How does that feel?"

The ring was a bit loose and the stone made it feel too heavy to bear, but she'd wear it no matter what. She nodded mutely as she stared at the jewelry, not believing it adorned her own hand and not someone else's.

"Wear it for a few days and see how it feels. We can see our family's jeweler to have the fit adjusted if necessary."

Too elated for words, she could do nothing but nod. She tried not to stare at the ring, the first piece of jewelry she had ever owned, as though she were afraid of it. Imagine, a fine man such as Nash Abercrombie trusting her with his grandmother's ring! She remembered her father's glee at the prospect of newfound wealth. He'd be happy to see her sporting such a fine ruby and diamonds, but the ring would always be hers.

Harrod entered the parlor. "Dawn Cobbs has arrived, Mr. Abercrombie."

Nash whipped his head toward the butler, refocusing his attention. "The seamstress?"

Harrod's eyes widened, and for a moment Becca wondered if he feared he had made a mistake. "Yes, sir. The seamstress you asked me to engage."

"Oh. Yes." His distraction told Becca he wished the interruption weren't necessary. She, too, wished she could put off the seamstress and linger with Nash. "Indeed," Nash answered. "Send her to the Blue Room and tell her Miss Hanham will be in shortly." He smiled. "I hope you enjoy choosing patterns and cloth for your new dresses. I think you'll need at least three to start."

"Three? That number seems extravagant."

"Perhaps it is extravagant for where you came from, but not at all for where you are today. We'll start with basic frocks for you to be presentable at home, plus one dress for finer occasions. We'll keep increasing your wardrobe at a quick rate and also as special needs arise. And they will. I promise."

Put that way, she could see why he thought three dresses would barely help her start. Images of parties, summer outings, and fine dinners floated into her head, making her both awed and anxious. She tried to concentrate on her awe rather than her anxiety. Unwilling to seem ungrateful by not responding quickly, she rose, and he followed suit. "I'd better get ready now."

"I shall have Harrod show you to the Gold Room so you can freshen up. Though I still don't think you should stay here overnight until we are wed, that can be your room when you need the occasional nap or to retire for relaxation during the day. If you don't find your bed comfortable, your dresser adequate, or any other accoutrements suitable, don't hesitate to notify the maid."

She studied his expression to see if he was teasing her. Surely he realized any room of her own would be a dream. Did he have any idea how luxurious she felt knowing she had her own bed? What a contrast to sharing a tiny mattress! His serious expression told her he meant what he said. Since he'd had more than enough all his life, maybe he didn't understand the impact moving into such a grand lifestyle had on her. She prayed not to become ungrateful or spoiled.

"And though I hate to rush things for you, try not to take too long, as Mrs. Williams will be here shortly to teach you the fine points of speech and etiquette. In the meantime, the seamstress awaits."

Chapter 7

For the next few days, Becca didn't see much of Nash. Instead she spent her time amid a flurry of ladies employed to wait on her hand and foot and to teach her how to behave in society. Becca felt undeserving, grateful, and overwhelmed. How would she remember everything they told her? The proper way to address important people. How to distinguish one fork from another. The difference between a butter knife and a fish knife. Sizes of spoons according to purpose. They instructed her to pace her eating so she didn't conclude any course before her guests. Dining slowly felt strange after years of chaotic meals at the Hanham house.

And learning new songs to sing! The teacher's method of unrelenting criticism discouraged more than inspired her, but for Nash's sake, she persisted.

Their continued efforts evidenced themselves most in her appearance. Bernice, the ladies maid Nash hired, proved her worth. As soon as they met and Becca saw her sweet, plump face and upturned mouth, she knew she could get along well with such a cheerful soul. Bernice had been born in a Boston slum, so she knew what it was like to come from humble circumstances.

"I started in the scullery and worked myself up to being a ladies maid," she told Becca during her first day on the job. "When I started with my first mistress, Mrs. Devon, my speech was much like yours. There's hope, Miss Hanham."

Bernice's reassurances comforted Becca, though no doubt her new maid thought they had much work ahead of them. Still, she sympathized with Becca and did everything she could to help her transition, which lessened the burden for them both. Not only did Bernice gently correct her grammar and speech, but she also made Becca look the part of the future Mrs. Nash Abercrombie. Though she always made a point of being clean, Becca had never spent so much time on her appearance. Bernice styled and restyled her hair for different times of day, and she promised that once her new dresses were completed, she would help her don the appropriate dress for each time of day. Bernice even sprayed rose-scented toilette water on Becca, a luxury she enjoyed.

As they got to know one another, Becca felt more relaxed in Nash's house. She wasn't sure she'd ever be comfortable as the center of so many servants' attention, but she tried to relax and allow herself to be tended by others.

When she wasn't being served, speech and music lessons occupied her time. Practice was a must, and sometimes repeating the same song over and over bored her, but rehearsing proved less of a chore than she thought it might. As for speech, she tried taking tips from the poetry of the King James Bible. Such inspiration helped.

The outdoors held its distractions. Nash had offered to teach her how to handle a horse, taking her to the country to ride horses he boarded there for hunting and pleasure. Even in the chilly weather, she found she enjoyed the lessons. After she became accustomed to the pretty dapple gray filly he chose for her, she relished the feel of controlling such a large beast, riding along with fresh air delighting her skin. Even better was the chance to spend time in Nash's company. Rarely did they gallop, so they could talk as their horses trotted.

They took meals together and spent time with one another each evening before she went home. Every day confirmed her growing fondness toward him, and though he never played less than the gentleman with her, she could feel his emotions toward her grow as well.

As time passed and her new maid grew familiar with Becca's hair, she experimented with styles until Becca found one she liked in particular. Curls framed her face, and more curls cascaded from the top of her head, touching her shoulders for a lovely effect.

Becca stared at herself in the mirror as she sat in front of the vanity. "Oh, Bernice! For the first time since Mother styled my hair for me to tell Nash I'd marry him, I feel beautiful. Only this time I'm enjoying the experience even better, for I am not as nervous." She couldn't help but pat her curls with a light hand.

"I'm glad I could please you, Miss Hanham. I am eager to see the complete picture once you are in a new dress. The seamstress will be here for your final fitting today, am I right?"

"Yes. I hope the alterations are such that I'll be able to keep them all today."

"Just wait until you see yourself dressed as a lady should. I expect you shall look as a young princess does when she goes to her first ball." Bernice let out a little sigh.

Becca giggled. "It won't be a ball gown. Just a morning dress."

"Just a morning dress? It sounds as though you are already starting to think like an Abercrombie."

Bernice's observations left Becca feeling mixed emotions. To survive in her new environment, she had to think like a woman born to society. But she never wanted to forget her beginnings. "Do I sound like a snob?"

"Oh, I did not mean to say that."

"I know." She patted Bernice's hand. "I don't think you could utter a bad word about anybody if your life depended on it. You know you can be honest with me. So how do you know I haven't let all these blessings I don't deserve go to my head?"

"That statement, for one. And I see you reading your Bible every morning. As long as you cling to the Lord, you'll keep a humble heart. And I know that's what you have because I can see it. I think Mr. Abercrombie can see you have a good spirit, too. You're beautiful on the outside; that's a fact. Yet I believe your spirit is the real reason he chose you."

"Thank you." Bernice's opinion had come to mean something to Becca. Nash had been right. The servants had been respectful of her—more respectful than she deserved—but Bernice had become an advocate and a friend.

Her ladies maid adjusted a curl. "You are improving every day in manners and elegance. It is time for you to look like a lady as well. You have much of which to be proud."

She looked back in the mirror. "But such an elaborate style. I hardly recognize me—myself."

"You will become accustomed to so many new things that sooner or later you will not even think twice about them."

"Do you really think so?"

"I know so. Why, think about the way you eat now. Mr. Abercrombie does not overindulge as they like to in some fine households in Providence, but the food is superior, indeed."

"Yes it is."

Bernice sent her a wry smile. "I daresay you don't miss the meals your mother makes out of what little she has."

"I can't say I do. I've been taking food home at night, so the family's diet has improved greatly."

"I trust Mr. Abercrombie has found a new home for your family, as you were telling me was his plan."

"Oh yes. There is one for sale now only a mile away bordering on our old neighborhood, and I do believe Mr. Abercrombie plans to buy it for 'em—them." Bernice delivered her the kind of soft smile that reminded Becca of her understanding mother. Becca would have to remember to speak with proper enunciation even when they were alone. "I do slip now and again, don't I?"

"You are doing very well. I am impressed by how much progress you have already made in such a short time."

"My most difficult challenge has been learning to sing. At least, that's how Mrs. James makes me feel."

"She's not known for a sweet temperament. However, you should learn much from her since she's an expert vocalist," Bernice assured her. "Many society people have taken lessons from her."

"I can see she's an expert. I just wish she'd be more encouraging." Becca stood and regarded herself in the mirror. "I look forward to wearing a dress that matches the hairstyle you fashioned for me."

"That time will be soon. And with the arrival of more dresses, you shall be changing clothing throughout the day so what you wear is suitable for each activity. In fact, we shall be spending most of our days together getting you dressed and undressed and dressed again."

"That sounds as though dressing consumes a great part of the day."

"That it does."

"I hate to impose on you to spend all your time dressing me."

"You never impose on a servant. That is something you must not forget. You must become accustomed to all of us waiting on you."

"I feel so lazy." Perhaps she shouldn't have blurted such a bold feeling, but with Bernice she felt she could be honest.

"That feeling will pass. And you'll soon become accustomed to heavier garments with some loss of movement," Bernice said.

"Loss of movement?"

"Yes. Ladies' dresses and intimate apparel are heavier and allow for less freedom. After all, menial work is not expected of them. Or of you."

Even though she hadn't lifted a finger in the Abercrombie residence since she had accepted Nash's proposal, she'd always helped Mother, so the idea that she would no longer cook, clean, or tend to others seemed strange. "I think I shall miss working."

Bernice laughed, her bountiful chest moving with each echo. "You won't miss it long, no doubt. Now go on and greet your fiancé for the noon meal. He awaits."

∽

Since he had arrived home from his office a few moments before noon, Nash slipped into his bedchamber to freshen himself. The room, painted a pleasing shade of blue and decorated so anyone entering would know it unmistakably belonged to a man, served as his familiar retreat away from his cares and worries.

Relaxing in posture, he splashed spice-scented water on his face and hands to wash away the grime from the street and ash particles ever present in the city air. A few strokes from his boar bristle brush with a carved ivory back, a cherished past birthday gift from his father, made his hair glisten. The process soothed away the cares of a harried morning at work and prepared him for light supplication to sustain him for the afternoon ahead. The ritual had become a fond one, even fonder now that Becca waited to partake of lunch with him.

Whistling "Saint's Delight" on his way down the hall, he slipped into his study to wait for Becca. A highlight of his day happened when she would emerge from the Gold Room and meet him so he could escort her to the dining room and they could partake of their meal together.

Today the seamstress, Dawn, would bring the three dresses he ordered for Becca to the house so she could see how they fit. He mused upon who was more pleased by the prospect—Becca or himself. If only he could defer his business so he could witness her face light up when she looked in the mirror at the finest dresses of her life. He didn't mind seeing her in the same tired frock day after day, but she'd no doubt feel more settled into her new role while wearing dresses that made an attempt to match her beauty. Not that any garment, even one fashioned from the finest silks and ermine, decorated with gems and pearls, and sewn with gold thread, could compare to her natural glow and the radiance of her spirit that enhanced her physical beauty.

He contemplated how much she appreciated even the slightest favor he showed her. Never did she expect special consideration, acting as though she never left the home in which she had been born. In a way perhaps she hadn't, since she returned to it each night. The discreet arrangement seemed to work. In hopes of quelling gossip, he had warned the servants and teachers against mentioning Becca's presence and progress until they were ready for her to be introduced to the larger society. Since they valued their jobs, Nash felt certain they had honored his request.

When she arrived at his residence each morning, a wide-eyed look still appeared on her face. The fact amused him in a most pleasant way. What a contrast this sweet young woman was to Hazel. To the manor born, Hazel never let go of her sense of entitlement and reminded others with each encounter, in ways both large and small, that she believed they owed her the world. He remained amazed by how Becca conveyed a sense of gratitude toward God for how He had led her to Nash—and Nash was convinced that's what happened. Some less-fortunate women might have taken the attitude of Becca's father—that Nash should shower Becca with gifts so she could cash in and have a small fortune to show for her experience should the situation go awry. He felt certain Mr. Hanham didn't see that Nash discerned his attitude.

But Becca. She was such a gift. An image of her drifted into his mind, much as a placid wave might wash upon white sand on a moonlit night. The picture made him much happier than any beach adventure. He took his seat in the chair behind his desk and closed his eyes.

So immersed in thought was Nash that he didn't hear Becca's soft footfalls as she walked down the hall toward his study. Not that she was easy to hear on the best of days since a thick runner carpeted the floor, but usually she didn't catch him in an utter state of daydreaming.

"Are you ready for lunch?" she asked.

He jumped a bit. "Oh. Yes." Looking at her, he saw she appeared different. He studied her to see if he could figure it out before asking her.

"Nash, you're staring." She averted her eyes.

"I beg your forgiveness. I—you look quite extraordinary today, even more extraordinary than usual. There's something different about you."

"It's my hair. Bernice styled it differently." She touched her fingers to an outer curl and pivoted. "Does it please you?"

His heart beat faster as he noticed her beauty. "Yes. Yes it does. Very much." He moved toward her.

"Do you think this will look nice with my new dresses?" she wondered. "Truth be told, I believe that's why Bernice fixed it this way today."

"Bernice is a very smart woman. I do think the style will do the dresses justice." He took her chin in his hand. "If I may be so bold, I was thinking about how no dress could do your beauty justice."

She looked at the rug and fluttered her eyelashes, but the motion seemed genuine instead of practiced affectation, as he had seen many society ladies perform. "You flatter me."

"No, I don't. It's true." He held back the urge to stroke her stunning mane of curls. Clearly Bernice had worked hard on Becca's hair, and to disturb it would be a shame. He focused on her big, beautiful eyes, the refined shape of her nose, her full, pink lips. She took in the slightest of breaths. Nash stared into her eyes and saw them grow wider. Though not a naive man, never before had he experienced the intense feelings of yearning that Becca's mere presence stirred in his heart. "I can resist you no longer, my darling." He drew her into his arms with more urgency than he intended, but she didn't seem taken aback. Soon he became lost in her warmth and drew his mouth toward hers.

"I don't want you to resist," she murmured.

When their lips met, the sweetness of the moment far surpassed his fantasies. So this is what love felt like! He wanted more. He drew her closer in an embrace and kissed her again, deeper this time. She did not refuse, but returned his passion.

In touch with each other's spirits as they were, they chose the same moment to break away, with ever so much gentleness, from one another. Though he suspected his kiss had been her first, when she looked into his face, her expression bore no shame but revealed only the most pure romantic love.

"I love you, Becca Hanham."

"And I love you, Nash Abercrombie. I have loved you since that first night I met you. Not because you saved my life, but because you were ever so kind to me though I could do you no favor."

"Don't you recall what Jesus said? 'Then said he also to him that bade him, When thou makest a dinner or a supper, call not thy friends, nor thy brethren, neither thy kinsmen, nor thy rich neighbours; lest they also bid thee again, and a recompence be made thee. But when thou makest a feast, call the poor, the maimed, the lame, the blind: And thou shalt be blessed; for they cannot recompense thee: for thou shalt be recompensed at the resurrection of the just.'"

"Yes, I remember that passage from the Gospel of Saint Luke, although never could I recite the verses with such eloquence as you possess."

"Father required me to commit the passage to memory, saying that our family must live by it. He was a great adherent of a concept that in recent years has been termed as the French language phrase *noblesse oblige*."

"Noblesse oblige?"

"Yes. Those of high rank or birth are obligated to treat those who are not as blessed with great honor, respect, and consideration. So for me to buy lucifers from you that night was no sacrifice."

She took a moment to absorb what he told her. A lump formed in her throat. "I'm grateful your father taught you to be so thoughtful of others."

"As am I. And of course you know that compassion toward others is a part of our history here in Providence. Who better to demonstrate the concept than Roger Williams?"

"Yes, the founder of Rhode Island Colony and our fair city of Providence." Wishing to impress Nash, Becca reached back into her memory to recall long-ago history lessons learned at her mother's knee. "He thought people should have freedom of conscience. But freedom also means responsibility."

"I see you have been taught well," Nash observed. "Oh, and that reminds me. We must find some volunteer work for you to do. What are your interests?"

She'd been so busy helping her mother and adding to her family's lean income that unpaid work had never been a consideration. "I'd like to volunteer, but I don't know where. There are so many people who need help."

"True. Too many people need help." Regret colored his voice before he brightened with a suggestion. "You have a heart for children. Might I suggest that you put your domestic skills to use making blankets for orphans?"

She brightened. "That sounds wonderful. I'll do it."

"We'll have you involved in my church soon as well. Come now; we must make our appearance in the dining room or Harrod is sure to investigate."

Chapter 8

Becca gasped with excitement when she saw the results of her new seamstress's work. "Oh, Dawn, this dress is absolutely stunning!" She stood still in her bedchamber as Bernice fastened the last of eighteen silk-covered buttons on the back of her new floral-patterned dress using a long hook made for the purpose. For the first time she understood why society ladies needed personal maids. She never could have donned such an elaborate garment by herself.

Recalling the costume Mrs. Gill wore during their interview, Becca considered in amazement her own attire even prettier. She lifted the skirt to examine the pattern and feel the texture of such elaborate fabric. "Are you sure this is a morning dress? It's much too fine to wear around the house."

"Even the Abercrombie house, Miss Hanham?" Dawn's sharp features softened at the compliment.

"Maybe even the Abercrombie house," Becca said, only half in jest.

Bernice eyed a gown made of a green silk reminiscent of fresh mint sprigs. "I cannot wait to see you try on the evening frock."

"With your delicate figure and refined features, you're sure to look like a princess," Dawn agreed.

"I believe I want to save the most luxurious for last. I'd prefer to try on the blue afternoon frock next." She took in the loveliness of the colorful wardrobe. "I'm glad you already had such beautiful fabrics on hand so I wouldn't have to wait."

"Yes, ma'am." Dawn beamed.

Bernice spent considerable moments undressing Becca down to her new undergarments and then replacing the morning frock with the blue outfit. As Bernice fastened more buttons, Becca could see she would be spending more time in her toilette than she had previously spent diapering the babes at home.

As everyone predicted and Becca hoped, the afternoon dress looked just as good on her as the morning dress. She tried to imagine changing into a special garment for no other reason than the fact it was after lunch. Now that the dresses had arrived, such a ritual would be a reality of each day.

Bernice picked up a pair of kid leather shoes with slight heels. "Please be seated, Miss Hanham, so that we might change your shoes."

Becca complied and gave over her feet to the maid. As Bernice removed the first kid leather shoe she already wore, Becca couldn't help but think it was much too good for daytime. Yet the cobbler had insisted they had been fashioned for that purpose. "I don't want to take these off."

Dawn and Bernice laughed as Bernice slipped heeled shoes onto Becca's dainty feet. After they had been delivered the previous day, she'd tried them on several times to practice walking in them. They looked better than they felt.

Her efforts to learn how to walk in dressy shoes were rewarded when she saw how well they complimented the elaborate evening dress Dawn had sewn for her. Noting the dress, she couldn't help but be pleased. The color was striking, and the neckline accentuated her frame and complexion and complemented her figure while maintaining a perfect degree of modesty. She looked the seamstress's way. "I love how you followed my instructions and wishes exactly."

"Thank you, Miss Hanham." Dawn glanced at her lap and back to Becca for approval. "Since you seem pleased with my work, would you see your way clear to ordering the other three dresses Mr. Abercrombie mentioned at our last appointment? If so, I would be ever so pleased."

Becca didn't hesitate. "Yes, I would. When shall we meet next?"

"If I am not imposing on your busy schedule, I can stay as long as you please. I set aside all afternoon, and I brought enough patterns and fabric samples to keep us occupied the rest of the day."

Becca smiled. "I can think of few better ways to spend an afternoon."

∞

Later, as the dinner hour neared, Becca realized for the first time since she'd set foot in Nash's home that she felt as though she belonged. Though clothes didn't indicate one's character, her new hairstyle and dress gave her a feeling of confidence, the likes of which she had never before felt.

Preparing to greet Nash after his long day of work, Becca felt nervous somehow, though she didn't know why. Of course he would love to see her in the dress. She only hoped the reality of her appearance now that she had transformed into a lady would live up to his fantasy.

Soon Becca entered the study so Nash could escort her to dinner. He sighed when he saw her. She looked into his eyes, noting how he studied her with an awed expression. "I never thought it would be possible for me to say this, since you have always been lovely, but I've never seen you more beautiful. You flatter that dress."

She felt herself blush. "You mentioned you like the color blue, so when Dawn showed me the fabric this color she had on hand, I thought you might like to see me in it."

He smiled. "The other ladies will be envious of how good you look."

Other ladies. Nash meant to compliment her, but instead his words produced an anxious queasiness, reminding her of how she felt the first time Nash suggested she would sing in front of his friends. If she could put off meeting his friends forever, she would. She knew the day she'd be introduced to them would arrive, but she'd kept her mind from it. She'd been enjoying the dream of being in Nash's world, alone with him and his doting servants. Training, purchasing of dresses, horseback riding, and other ideas he had for her were for one purpose: to make sure she could survive in his world. A world filled with others certain to judge her.

Waking up from her semidaydream state, she saw Nash staring at her, eyes widened with concern. She had to say something. "I—uh—I don't want anyone to be envious." The words she spoke were true. And truer still was her next utterance. "I just want to make you happy."

"You make me happy, my dear. Happier than I have ever been."

∽

Each night, unwilling to remain in clothes that would make her seem too regal for the humble circumstances of her birth, Becca put on her old dress and returned home. Though she'd worn similar dresses all her life, not until she had donned herself in luxurious clothes did she realize how scratchy the mean fabric felt against her skin, or the drab and worn condition of her attire. Bernice always looked sad when she helped Becca transform from lady to impoverished girl, but Becca held her head up and resolved to remember she had not always been so fortunate. She would never be ashamed of or forget from whence she came.

Her efforts to fit in with her old surroundings didn't keep her family and friends from noticing the difference in her manners and the way she carried herself. Fresh confidence radiated from her, and she knew it even as she embarked from Nash's carriage. One night in particular, a night saturated with the false promise of early spring that encouraged all to be out and about, she felt more stares than usual aimed her way.

"She always did ride a high horse," she heard one of her old rivals whisper, thinking she wouldn't overhear.

Becca clutched the handle of her basket containing food, focused on the front entrance of her home, and walked in a dignified manner straight toward it.

"I heard Micah's courtin' Susanna now," another hissed in a voice loud enough to be heard a block away.

She wished Sissy or Naomi were nearby so she could say, "Poor Susanna," with enough vigor to dispel any myth that she cared what Micah did. Instead, she smiled in a most unaffected manner and nodded toward them. Narrowed eyes were her reward. She stepped through her front door before the catty women could make new observations.

"Becca!" Several of her siblings ran to greet her. Though they shared a deep love that could never be broken, the food she carried held its own appeal. The amount of leftovers didn't fool Becca. It was an open secret at the Abercrombie residence that Cook had been told by Nash to prepare more food than needed so Becca's family could enjoy plenty.

Mother greeted her with a kiss on the cheek. "We sure been eatin' good since ya hooked up with that man o' your'n."

Becca had to concentrate on her speech when among her family. Listening to them made it all too easy for her to fall back into old patterns. "I am glad you enjoy the food I present to you, Mother. Cook is quite generous to prepare extra provisions for us."

Father entered from the back bedroom. "I thought I heard me a hoity-toity miss out here. Who do ya think ya are, talkin' like that? Think ye're better'n us? Yer own family?"

Such questioning would have left her quaking in the past, but Nash's love gave her strength. "No, sir. Please realize that I must speak in this manner if I am to please Nash. I thought you wanted me to please him."

Father's gaze shot, unashamed, to the ruby ring on Becca's left ring finger. "Any more trinkets?"

"No, sir. He has been spending considerable resources and effort training me to become a lady."

"Time and resources? Ya can tell me all about it while we eat. That food ya brung smells mighty good."

∞

"The morning mail has arrived, sir." Harrod entered the study carrying several letters. "This is a certain indication your friends have discovered you're home."

Nash swallowed. He'd relished his time alone with Becca. Never had he rushed home from his office every day at lunch and each evening with such determination, but since she spent each day there, he was eager to return to his residence. Becca's poise and polish deemed her ready to meet his friends, but he wasn't ready to share her with anyone, no matter how innocent the capacity. He'd told Becca the ladies would be jealous of her, omitting that men would envy him. If only he and Becca could stay in their dream world, untouched by outsiders forever.

Harrod's voice broke into his musings. "It is past time you resumed 'at home' hours, in my view. You have been devoting entirely too much time to business, and since your engagement, you have almost become a recluse. A popular man such as yourself needs to socialize with his friends."

"I'll get out and about soon enough. Winter is a good time to keep to oneself. Furthermore, I haven't been encouraging visitors yet for Becca's sake."

"The moment of truth is upon us. I hope she is ready."

"I think she is. Haven't you noticed her progress?"

"Yes. She has done very well. But is she ready to face Miss Caldwell and Mrs. Gill?"

"Let's hope so. For all our sakes."

Without further observation, Harrod excused himself. His mention of Hazel and her sister was not a good sign.

Nash shuffled through the mail, looking for any missive appearing to be from Hazel. His body slumped when he saw his reward—a note written in a fine hand on cream-colored stationery. Hazel's hand. The note he dreaded.

He broke the seal of gold wax embossed with the letter *C* so he could read the message:

> *Nash,*
>
> *I trust you are well. I am in hopes your entire house has not come to ruin in my absence with no one to help you oversee the staff.*
>
> *My visit with my aunt here in Hartford is drawing to a close. I shall arrive in Providence on Tuesday and expect to see you promptly at seven in the evening. Laurel says we must move forward with great haste to prepare for our wedding day. She believes an autumn wedding would be lovely, as do I.*
>
> *Have Cook prepare lobster for our dinner, to be served promptly at eight thirty.*
>
> *Yours,*
Hazel

He set the letter aside and let out a heavy sigh. "Lord, I pray Becca will be ready."

∞

Becca sliced her fork into the last bit of white cake with fig icing. She had filled out a tad since arriving at Nash's, but not too much. Her assurance and ease at the dinner table made meals much more enjoyable than they had been when she first dined with him. Nash could relax, too, since he didn't have to correct her. Now their conversations focused on matters of importance. Nash told her most men didn't think women should bother themselves with business or politics, but he interspersed some tidbits about the world along with talk about interesting items appealing to the sensibilities of the fairer sex. She looked forward to their nightly chats.

After pleasant dinner talk, he turned serious. "Becca, I have something to tell you."

She stiffened. "Yes?"

"You will be going home later tomorrow night than usual. Be sure to let your family know."

A thread of excitement went through her. Perhaps he had something interesting planned. "Of course. You will be needing me here?"

"Yes." He cleared his throat and patted his mouth with his napkin. "Miss Hazel Caldwell will be arriving. I think it's time the two of you met."

Miss Hazel Caldwell. *Witch Hazel.* Becca shivered.

"You have nothing to fear," Nash consoled her.

"You could tell what I was thinking. I must be an open book to you."

"Your reaction is natural, considering our circumstances. I want you to know how proud I am of you. Your level of accomplishment is extraordinary. You are not the same person who knocked on my back door seeking a job."

Becca contemplated what he said. True, she didn't feel the same. Her speech sounded strange to her ears as she listened to well-formed words leave her lips, yet it sounded so much prettier and more refined. No one would ever hear her complain about her new wardrobe. The dresses had taken her from a sad gray mourning dove to a bright bird of paradise. She enjoyed wearing colors—colors that pleased her eye. Judging by the way Nash looked at her whenever she entered a room, she could see he found her new dresses pleasant to view as well. Then again, the kiss had changed so much. The new light in his eyes told her his expressed feelings remained true.

Time and time again, she relived his kiss in her mind, and the memory became fonder with each reliving. He'd made no move to kiss her again. The fact might have made her feel insecure except he radiated love for her each time they spoke or shared any achievement, big or small. While she yearned for him, she appreciated that he treated her with respect.

He took her hand in a brief motion of comfort, then let it go. "Go home tonight and sleep as well as you can. I'll send Jack for you at three in the afternoon. When you arrive here, please have Bernice help you into your blue dress."

"I know that's your favorite. But. . ." She hesitated.

"What is it?"

"I don't mean to sound ungrateful, but if we are to start seeing your friends now, won't I need more dresses? Not that I mind wearing the same ones every day, but you said—"

"Yes, I know. And considering how I've spoken to you so often about wearing a variety of dresses, you don't sound ungrateful—you sound right. I'll contact Dawn and ask her to move faster on our latest order."

"Thank you." That matter settled, a sudden panic filled her about a different concern. "I won't have to sing, will I?"

He laughed, though in a kind rather than mocking manner. "Of course not. This isn't an evening soiree, but a dinner with an acquaintance." He leaned toward her and lowered his voice to just above a whisper. "If it makes you feel better, she won't be singing for you, either. You'll be missing a poor performance delivered with much more confidence than warranted, I assure you."

Whether he exaggerated to make her feel better or if he spoke the truth didn't matter; his levity encouraged her. She giggled, then turned serious. "I'm really not ready to sing for your friends."

"I don't expect you to be ready yet. But sometimes I arrive home early enough from the office to hear the very end of your lesson. I must say, you sound identical to a songbird." He nodded to the maid, granting her permission to pour him a cup of coffee.

Under normal circumstances Becca would have protested his use of such hyperbole, but her embarrassment superseded modest objections. "You hear me sing?" She gasped, chagrined at the thought of entertaining an unseen but important audience.

"I don't mean to eavesdrop. It's just that when I hear you, I can't help but stop and listen. Neither can the servants. Even Harrod has complimented your voice to me."

"Even Harrod? Oh my, I must be putting on quite a show for the entire household." Becca felt a mixture of discomfiture and satisfaction in learning she had earned such high praise but hid her emotions as she shook her head at the maid to decline the caffeinated beverage.

"Mrs. James is pleased by your progress." He stirred two lumps of sugar into his coffee.

"She is?" Her voice reflected her genuine shock.

He poured cream into his drink, transforming the liquid to a mellow brown. "That's what she tells me."

Becca recalled her teacher's chilly instructions, never laced with approval. "I wish that's what she would tell me."

"Oh, she's a bit taciturn. The fact she praised you without my prodding is remarkable indeed." He drank from his coffee cup.

"Indeed."

"Yes." He set down the cup. "My dream is that we can perform together sometime soon."

The idea sounded like a fantasy. To sing a duet with him? No love song written could express how she felt about him. "Together? So you're a vocalist?"

"I wish I had such talent. No, I merely strum an occasional guitar."

"I learn something new about you every day. Perhaps after this visit with Miss Caldwell"—she shuddered—"you can play a few songs for me?"

"If she doesn't depart too late." A mischievous light glowed in his eyes. "I have a feeling she won't be staying too long once she sees us together. So please try not to worry about tomorrow. I'll be here as your biggest aficionado."

She'd learned many new words in recent days, but "aficionado" stumped her. His teasing grin told her he wanted her to guess its meaning. Asking what words meant could give away her humble background, and for Nash's sake she wanted to put on a flawless performance for Hazel. She made her best effort. "I'm glad you'll be there to support me, Nash."

"Perfect!" His smile grew wider. "See? I told you that you have no reason to fear Hazel."

She could only hope tomorrow would prove him right.

Chapter 9

The next day Becca noticed the appealing scent of beef roasting over the hearth. In anticipation of Hazel's arrival, Cook had placed the meat in a pot with assorted vegetables. The aroma filled the house, making the place seem cozy and inviting despite cold spring rain falling outdoors. Any other time, Becca would have relished the thought of such a delectable treat and anticipated taking leftovers to her grateful family. But the arrival of the unwanted guest left her with no appetite, even this close to the dinner hour. Perhaps a lack of hunger would serve her well. Eating large portions would make her seem unladylike and subject her to possible ridicule from her rival.

Rival. That's what Hazel symbolized to Becca, even though Nash had no interest in her. Still, she had a feeling Hazel would put up the fight of her life to keep Nash once she discovered Becca's presence.

She said a silent prayer. *Lord, please be with me. I wish Hazel no harm. Indeed, I want her to find a man who really loves her. And Nash doesn't love her. Guide me. In the name of Jesus Christ, Amen.*

Becca summoned her courage before she entered the study where Nash awaited. His glance touched her from the top of her head to the tips of her new shoes and back to her face. "I see Bernice styled your hair in the way I prefer. And your dress is perfect. I'm glad I spied you before the gentlemen of my acquaintance, or I would have risked losing you to a wave of competition."

"Never."

A knock on the front door rang all the way to the study.

"That's her." Nash confirmed Becca's worst fears. "Now please don't worry." He rose, and Becca followed suit. Nash stopped her. "Please wait here until Harrod or the maid sends for you. I want to see Hazel by myself first."

"Oh." As much as she'd feared and dreaded this moment, now that Hazel waited for them in the parlor, she wished she could go with Nash and get the initial meeting out of the way.

"I won't tarry. I promise."

⸻

"What took you so long, Nash? I was just getting ready to go upstairs to find you," Hazel said as soon as his feet hit the bottom of the steps.

"Greetings to you, too, Hazel." He couldn't help but think about his lack of emotion. No yearning to touch her prodded him. Even wearing a stunning dress with not a hair out of place framing a face everyone in Providence considered beautiful, she held no appeal for him. Instead, the feeling of a cannonball in his gut made him realize all the more how right he had been to choose Becca.

Eyeing Laurel sitting beside Hazel on the sofa, Nash held back a sigh. He might have known Hazel would bring her financier to hurry along the nuptials that no one but they were planning. Out of courtesy, he nodded. "Laurel."

"Nash," she volleyed with the spirit of a catapulted rapier.

"I wasn't expecting you. I'll have the maid set an extra place." He seated himself in the chair next to the fireplace.

"I thought I mentioned Laurel would be joining us," Hazel said without any remorse coloring her voice. "There is enough food, isn't there?" She turned to her sister. "I wouldn't be so bold in front of society, but since we are alone, I'll speak freely, Laurel. You know our Nash. Never wants to risk wasting so much as a drop of gravy. At least for once he has a decent fire lit."

"You can't expect a man to run a house properly," Laurel said. "You know ours would fall apart overnight if Mitchell were forced to tend to the staff and other household affairs himself. Poor Nash. He needs you, Hazel, dear."

"Indeed." She crossed her arms.

Spotting Harrod from the corner of his eye, Nash sent him a quick nod, indicating he should retrieve Becca from the study.

Hazel sniffed. "What's that I smell? Is that beef?"

"I do believe it is," Laurel answered.

Hazel twisted her mouth in a way that irritated Nash. "I distinctly told you to have Cook prepare lobster for us tonight. What is wrong with your incompetent staff? The first thing I'll do after we're wed is fire the lot of them."

Laurel placed a restraining hand on her sister's arm. "Now, now, Hazel. I'm sure there was simply a misunderstanding." She looked up at Nash. "Isn't that true?"

"No, it is not true. I know you wanted lobster, Hazel, but I asked Cook for roast beef. And it's a good thing, too," he continued over her outraged gasp. "If I had ordered lobster, we would have been short because I wouldn't have ordered extra for unexpected and uninvited guests."

"Well!" Laurel, in usual circumstances the epitome of icy civility, appeared flummoxed.

"Nash, apologize this instant!" Hazel demanded.

"Since you have been frank in your speech about my wisdom, or lack thereof, in handling my household affairs, I thought I should show you the same measure of respect."

"That's all right, Hazel," Laurel said. "He's clearly overwrought from the prospect of your impending nuptials. Grooms can get nervous just as brides become jittery. But you are the perfect couple, so a little tiff over an informal dinner that will be forgotten by tomorrow is no reason to remain angry. When there is a dinner to be hosted here that will count, Hazel will see to it that nothing is omitted. So for now, let's forget our harsh words and enjoy our meal."

"Wise counsel, I must say," Nash agreed. "However, there is another guest who will be joining us."

"Another guest?" The pitch of Hazel's voice reminded Nash of a girl languishing in toddlerhood. "But I thought we would be planning our ceremony tonight. No stranger needs to be privy to our personal affairs."

"Oh, but she is not a stranger. At least not to me."

"She?" Hazel's voice betrayed a mixture of horror and suspicion. Laurel's eyes widened.

"Yes," Nash answered. "Would you care to meet her now? She's waiting upstairs in the study."

Hazel froze, then tried and failed to put a pleasant expression on her face. "I suppose I have no choice."

"Of course we would be glad to meet any relative you hold in high esteem," Laurel managed with a bit more civility.

Harrod, displaying his uncanny knack for perfect timing, entered. "Miss Hanham, sir."

∞

Becca panicked when she spied a familiar figure sitting on the sofa beside a woman she didn't know. Mrs. Gill! What was she doing there?

There was no time to give him the courtesy of an explanation. "I can't go in there," she whispered to Harrod. "Please don't make me."

"But you must. He has already asked for you."

"Make an excuse. Please," she hissed.

Nash spotted Becca and called to them. "Is something the matter?"

"Not at all, sir." Harrod gave Becca a puzzled look but without further ado escorted her in, and Nash, looking not the least bit vexed, introduced her to the two women. His identification of Mrs. Gill as Hazel's sister cleared up the mystery. Still, Becca wondered why Mrs. Gill joined them. Nash hadn't mentioned anyone but Hazel. Becca kept her composure, looking with reluctance at Mrs. Gill. Though the woman looked her up and down in the same manner she had during their interview, no flicker of recognition flashed over her features. She didn't wonder why. Her hair and mode of dress rendered her almost unrecognizable. Becca breathed a sigh of relief and took a seat in the chair across from the women. Nash sat in the chair beside her with only a side table separating them. She could feel the comfort of his presence and was grateful for it.

"Pleased to meet you, Miss Hanham." Hazel's voice sounded as though she felt anything but pleased. "And how is it that you are related to Nash?"

She searched for a truthful answer. "Uh. . .uh—we met many years ago, but have recently become reacquainted."

"So it would appear." Mrs. Gill looked down her nose at Becca, reminding her of their recent interview. "We know all the prominent families in Providence. Indeed, even in most of New England. How did your acquaintance escape us, I wonder? I would have thought we would have met you at one event or another."

Harrod reentered. "Dinner is served."

"Very well, Harrod," Nash answered with the verve of a man who enjoyed hosting. "Ladies, shall we retire to the dining room?"

The sisters exchanged glances, hesitating. Their reticence signaled a small victory for Becca, but the battle was far from over.

Silence ensued until they were seated and Nash offered grace. Soon the first course of a clear soup was set before them. As they ate they spoke of people, places, and events unfamiliar to Becca. Nash tried to steer conversational topics to those of a more general nature, but working together, the sisters ignored his cues. Becca had no idea how the women managed such a feat, but they seemed to have reached silent agreement that they would do everything they could to keep Becca from contributing to the conversation. She sat silently through the first two courses. By the time the roast beef arrived, her misery had peaked.

Hazel scrunched her nose to express her distaste. "I had really been anticipating the lobster I requested. Beef is such a disappointment, especially since we just had cold roast for luncheon today."

"I'm sorry we couldn't please you tonight." Nash's voice held not a shade of regret.

"This looks delicious nonetheless," Mrs. Gill noted. "I'll have my cook steam some lobster tomorrow night for you, Hazel." She cut into her roast, the knife sliding through easily thanks to Cook's skill in meal preparation. Before taking a bite, she looked at Becca. "Did you hear about Janette Jones?"

Becca didn't look at her, focusing on the food on her own plate. "I'm afraid not."

"Whatever the news is, I doubt I'm current on anything concerning Miss Jones," Nash quipped. "And I doubt any such news would be of interest to my guest."

"So you don't know Janette Jones?" Hazel's gaze bore into Becca. "Why, I thought everyone in Providence knew her."

"Oh, but surely you know the Danforths," Mrs. Gill prodded Becca. "Elizabeth is in a family way again. This will be her fifth child. Which reminds me, how many brothers and sisters do you have, Miss Hanham? Perhaps I have had the pleasure of making acquaintance with one of them."

"I'm in no mood for idle chitchat," Nash interrupted.

"Then you shouldn't have hosted a dinner party," Hazel retorted.

"But this gathering is much less intimate than I anticipated," Nash shot back.

"Hazel, I would prefer to hear about your trip to Hartford. Do indulge me."

"Oh yes." For the first time, Hazel seemed disappointed that the topic had been directed to her.

"Everyone was asking after Nash," Mrs. Gill pointed out. "That is what you told me, wasn't it, Hazel?"

"Oh, yes indeed. I could tell my cousins in particular wondered why they haven't received wedding announcements." She looked sideways at Becca.

"Did you tell them they haven't received announcements because I never proposed?" Nash's tone revealed his impatience.

"But of course we have an understanding. We have ever since that night at the Harris's."

A hint of sadness shadowed Nash's face, and Becca could feel his embarrassment at having to hurt someone's feelings. As obnoxious as Hazel had proven herself to be, she deserved the respect of others as a fellow person if for no other reason. The fact that Nash felt that way about a woman who had made herself the bane of his existence heightened Becca's love for him.

"Of course you have an understanding." Mrs. Gill looked in a pointed manner at Becca.

"I'm sorry to disappoint you, but we do not," Nash said.

The sisters gasped, but Mrs. Gill recovered first. "Surely you don't mean that, Nash. Why, to break off the engagement would cause considerable embarrassment to you and everyone else."

Nash ignored Mrs. Gill and turned his face toward Hazel. "I'm sorry. I never wanted to hurt you or anyone else. But as I must repeat, a little embarrassment now is much preferred over a miserable marriage that will last the rest of our lives. Don't you agree?"

"Miserable marriage! How dare you!" Hazel rose from her seat with such a rapid motion that the back of her chair struck the mahogany sidebar behind her. She didn't even look to assess the damage, choosing instead to throw her pristine white cloth napkin on top of gravy-laden roast beef. Becca cringed. Her family didn't enjoy the luxury of cloth napkins, but she was no stranger to laundry. The Abercrombie laundress would not be happy when she discovered a greasy stain covering the linen.

Mrs. Gill laid a consoling hand on her sister's arm. "Now, now. Nash is just nervous since the wedding is upon us. There's no need to vex him or yourself."

Hazel didn't seem to hear anything Mrs. Gill had to say. An accusing finger pointed Becca's way. "It's you, isn't it?"

Unsure how to react, Becca let out an uncomfortable gasp in response to the accusation.

Hazel's eyes narrowed. "I'm right! It *is* you!" As she spoke, her voice rose in timbre. "You're the reason why Nash is backing out of our wedding. Why, I knew it was you from the moment I first laid eyes on you—you—you—trollop!"

Nash stood. "I realize you are overwrought, Hazel, but I will not tolerate my dear Becca being called such a despicable term by anyone and especially not in my home. She is nothing but the finest of women, and you would do well to follow her example."

"Follow her example? Why, I don't even know the woman. And I never wish to." Her gaze set itself on Becca's ruby ring, and her face turned red. "Nash, is that your grandmother's ring?"

"It is indeed."

"Then—then. . ."

"Yes, it's true, Hazel. Your guess is correct. It is time for you to reconcile yourself to facts." Nash's voice sounded colder than Becca had ever heard. An unpleasant shiver visited her spine. At that moment she wouldn't have considered changing places with Hazel. "Becca Hanham is my fiancée. We plan to marry this autumn."

Becca's heart beat at a rapid pace. Because of the other women's vexation, she suppressed a smile.

"Oh, so you think you want to marry her?" Hazel's features wrenched in anger, and she turned her wrath to Becca. "Regardless of what Nash tries to tell us, I don't believe for a moment that you're one of us. I'll find out who you really are, Becca Hanham, and when I do, I have a strange feeling that Nash won't be so proud to have you on his arm. Society won't stand for one of its own making a poor match. You will never be accepted, and Nash will no longer be welcome among the elite of Providence. Do you really want that? Do you really want him to lose everything—his prestige, his friends, his influence, and ultimately his business? Will you still want him when he can no longer afford to buy you this kind of life?" She swept her hand over the room to remind Becca of the finely appointed house. "Come along, Laurel. I have nothing more to say." With a lift of her skirts, she turned to exit.

Though Mrs. Gill seemed the stronger of the two women, she rose to obey. "Don't worry about us. We have been guests in your home many times and can see ourselves to the door."

As the women left, Nash remained silent, and Becca stared at what was left of her roast beef. Any other time she would have relished such an appealing repast, but the women had made the entire meal a nightmare. She clasped her hands together, hoping to conceal their quaking.

Nash covered her hands with his. "Don't let anything she has to say worry you."

"How can I not? We can't keep my identity a secret forever. And even if we could, I couldn't live a lie. Not even for you."

"Of course not. And I would never ask you to."

"But she said she'll ruin you."

"She may try, but she will not succeed. My positions in both my personal and professional life are secure. My family has run our business for decades, and while your background is humble, your behavior is impeccable and your character above reproach. I don't believe good businessmen would abandon their dealings with me because of you, and if any do, I am confident the Lord will send other provision. As for my friends, well, we may find out who they really are. . .together."

His words warmed her spirit, yet fear lingered. "But the embarrassment. . ."

He took her hands in his. "I won't promise there won't be talk and whispers, especially with Hazel fueling the fire, but it will pass and they will see that not to accept you would be wrong. Remember, we are Rhode Islanders and have a fine tradition of fighting for those whom others spurn. True, Hazel has shown by her wretched attitude toward you that some of us can be dreadful snobs. However, I believe once you start to mingle with people whom I hold in high regard, you will learn that most of us are not." A sad light entered his eyes. "Oh, I'm sorry this has turned into quite a bit more of an ordeal than even I imagined."

"I don't mind for myself, but this is only the beginning. I know you are a gentleman and you want to keep your word, but I think I should leave now. Let me go back to my home where I won't be a bother or threat to you. Hazel must have gotten the message by now. She's angry, but surely she sees she can't have you for herself. You don't have to keep your promise to marry me. I won't burden you." She meant every heartbreaking word. She'd anticipated meeting Hazel to be a dreadful event, but even the servants' nickname for the woman hadn't prepared her for such appalling behavior.

He took her hands in his and squeezed them. Their warmth consoled her. "Oh no, my dear. You are never a burden. If anyone is a burden, it's Hazel and her sister."

"I must admit, I can see why you are reluctant to wed her."

"*Reluctant* isn't a strong enough word. Being with you only confirmed what a mistake it would be to take her as my wife. Even if you walked out the door this instant and never looked back, I still wouldn't marry Hazel."

"Really?"

He nodded. "You have brought me more joy in these few weeks than I have felt in my entire life. The more I see how well you conduct yourself, the more I respect you. Certainly tonight was a great test of how you behave when others are rude. You have earned a place at the Abercrombie table not because of your birth, but because of who you are. Why, I can even say I'm proud of who you are."

"Proud?" She could hardly believe she was hearing such words.

"Yes. Please say you'll still marry me. Together we will face Hazel and all her cohorts."

"Oh, Nash. With you I feel I can face anyone."

He smiled. "And now for our next step, in which I'll prove how proud I am of you. It's past time for your family to take part in our life together."

"My family?"

"Of course. Would they be agreeable to taking dinner with me next week?"

She didn't know what to say. Did Nash not realize that no one in her family owned clothing fit to eat at the Abercrombie servants' table, much less with Nash himself? She couldn't imagine them feeling anything but uncomfortable.

"What's the matter, Becca? Are you quite ashamed of me?"

"Ashamed of you? Of course not. I'm not ashamed of my family, either. It's just that I'm not sure how they'll feel about supping in such a fine home."

"They will be related to me by this time next year. I'm afraid they'll have to become accustomed to dining with us." He smiled. "Would you like me to send several seamstresses to your house to sew them some dinner clothes? Perhaps being dressed for dinner will make them feel more at ease."

Becca held back her thought that her father would rather have a pitcher of ale from the tavern than a new suit from the haberdasher. But Mother—she would enjoy such a dinner. And for her sisters, the occasion would be nothing less than the fulfillment of a fantasy. Her brothers—well, they would enjoy a feast of plenty. "That is very kind of you. I'll mention it tonight when I go home."

Chapter 10

Back at her house later that night and donned once again in her plain housedress, Becca felt nervous as she served her father and the oldest boys at the Hanham table. Hazel's visit had set their dinner hour quite late. Still, her family didn't complain. Becca and her mother plus the girls and small boys would eat in two more shifts after the men. At least now that she knew Nash, their main meals no longer consisted of thin gruel and ale. With better quality food from the Abercrombie kitchen, mealtimes had become a source of enjoyment rather than dull routine. She couldn't help but contrast their present way of life to Nash's and felt grateful to him for the fact they would soon be moving to better quarters.

Becca made sure to give Father an extra portion of ale to put him in a good mood. She waited until her older brothers threw dinner down their gullets and hastened out to whatever mischief awaited them on the darkened streets and her sisters occupied themselves with chatter and chores. Tired after another long day, complicated by the burdens of an advancing pregnancy, Mother plopped back into her seat at the table.

Becca sat in the chair across from Father as he enjoyed robust swigs of alcohol. "Father?"

He gave her a sidelong glance. "What is it, girl?"

"My fiancé has asked if I can bring my family to dinner at his house next week."

Father set down his mug. "Did he, now? If the leftovers you've been bringin' are any clue, we'll be eatin' high on the hog that night, eh?"

Mother's expression revealed her discomfort and slight alarm as she touched the sleeve of her dress. "But what will we wear?"

"Nash has already thought of that. He'll have new clothes made for all of you."

Mother gasped. "New clothes! Why, with the number of us here that will cost a fortune. Are ya sure he wants to do such a kind thing?"

Becca embraced her mother. "Yes, I am. That's the thoughtful type of man he is, Mother. Always wanting to do the compassionate thing. You'll love your new dinner clothes."

"Dinner clothes?" Father spat out the words. "So he's sayin' our regular clothes ain't good enough fer 'im."

"They aren't." Becca tried not to sound grumpy.

"I don't care who he is. He can take us just the way we are. I ain't wearin' no dress-up clothes fer nobody."

"Ya wanted the riches and new house he promised," Mother argued. "Ya got to take the bitter with the sweet, as they say. A suit won't hurt ya none. Not fer one night."

"It's a waste, I tell ya. I won't wear it again." Father snorted and took a swig of his drink.

"You can wear it to the wedding," Becca suggested. "Oh, please, Father, let him buy everyone new clothes. You'll feel much more comfortable in a nice new suit sitting at his dining table. Really you will."

"Kinda like you feel more comfortable in all them fancy dresses he bought ya."

"No. . ."

"I've seen how ya show off to all yer sisters. All of ya squeal like little girls at the sight of blue silk." Father took another swig of ale and scowled. "He thinks he's too good fer us, but since ye've hit a pot o' gold, I'll swallow me pride and put up with it."

She wished her parent could have been more gracious, but his ungrateful attitude was the best for which she could hope from him. "Thank you, Father. Nash and I will speak with the seamstresses tomorrow and schedule a time for you to be fitted. We think it's best if you go to her. He'll send a carriage tomorrow to pick up you and the boys. The next day, Mother and the girls will go."

"I just don't like it," Father argued. "Sounds to me like he's tryin' to make us some society types. We ain't. And I don't want to be. Why can't he just give us the house and let us live like we want? Did ya ask him fer money like I asked ya to?"

Becca swallowed. Though standing up to her father would never be easy, knowing Nash had made her stronger. "I don't mean to disobey, but I shouldn't ask for money. I just don't feel right about it. Don't you know he wants to discourage a society woman who wants his money? Besides, I'd marry him even if he lived right next door and didn't have a dime."

∽

"Are you quite ready to go to the milliner's, my darling?" Nash asked the following day.

Becca looked forward to seeing what type of hats Miss Dawkins had created for her. "Yes, I am."

He peered out the window. "Well, we have a glorious, sunny day for our errand. Life can't get much better, can it?"

Becca had to agree.

He turned and made his way toward her, the motion stirring the appealing scent of bay rum spice he always wore. "Only, my life will be at a climax on the day we wed."

"As will mine," she agreed. "And I hope each day afterward I can only make your life better and better."

Taking both of her hands in his, he answered, "I anticipate you shall, my darling." He kissed the back of each hand and squeezed them before letting go. "Come, let us take the carriage now."

"Now?"

"Yes, is that quite all right?"

"Of course. I just wasn't expecting to leave so soon. Shall I don my coat?"

"A fine idea. A nip of winter still permeates this fine spring air." He inhaled deeply. "But speaking of your outer wrap, I've been negligent in taking care of you. It's past time for you to have outer garments sewn. Two, in fact. One for spring and one for winter."

She nodded. The standing wardrobe in the Gold Room was becoming full.

The ride to the milliner's allowed her enough time to catch Nash up on the news. "Oh, and I did speak with my family about the dinner. They'll be happy to see Dawn and the other seamstresses about clothing. Or perhaps I should say, Mother and my sisters are happy. I can't promise my male relatives are just as eager."

He chuckled. "Women's clothing is lovely and colorful, while we men are forced into dull colors and starched collars. No wonder they're not eager."

She smiled. "Thank you for understanding. So much has happened to me—to all of us—in such a short time."

"I know. With God's grace, we'll soon understand each other completely." The carriage stopped in front of the shop.

"I'll take this opportunity to go to the dry-goods store for Harrod, sir." Jack jumped off the conveyance.

"Very good. But do be back in due time. Don't keep me waiting as you did last week."

"Yes, sir." Jack sent him a sheepish look before he vanished.

"He seems to be in a hurry to run that errand," Becca couldn't help but notice good-naturedly.

Nash's lips thinned. "I do believe he has his eye on the shop girl. He's a good driver for the most part, but sometimes he gets too distracted by his personal affairs to pay proper attention to his work. Years ago my father promised his mother we'd take of him, so I hate to let him go."

"It's hard to control a love-struck man. I've seen that look in my brother's eyes. You might have a wedding in your household soon."

"Another one? Indeed." Nash smiled and jumped out, then extended his hand to help her disembark.

Caught up in her world with Nash, she took his hand, grateful for the excuse to make the slightest contact, and smiled at him. He looked into her eyes. Getting lost in his gaze, she almost missed her step, but managed to retain her composure. She could look in his eyes forever. . . .

The tip of her toe had no sooner hit the street than she heard the horrifying scream of a woman from the direction of a nearby bank. She remembered Nash and Mother mentioning a rash of robberies. Surely they hadn't stumbled onto the scene of a crime!

A man ran out of the bank and looked in both directions. Despite Becca's unspoken prayer that he wouldn't head in their direction, he did. Gunshots followed, gashing the air.

"Get back in the carriage. Now!" Nash insisted.

She turned to jump back in but moved too late. Without warning, a hand gripped her arm, ripping her from Nash's hold. Another scream followed amidst more gunfire. One bullet flew so close, Becca heard it whiz by. She let out her own scream.

The robber's grip wasn't the comforting hold of Nash, but a rough vise.

"Unhand her!" Nash demanded.

Ascertaining that Becca's escort was unarmed, the robber ignored Nash's demand. Instead, he kept her in front of him to discourage more gunshots from being fired in his direction. Before she could shout again, he forced her to mount the horse with a rude motion, then whipped up behind her.

"No!" Nash cried.

The robber responded by shooting once in Nash's direction. Nash ducked to avoid being hit. Becca screamed and reached for the gun to take it away from the criminal.

He wrestled his arm away from her while keeping hold of the bridle. "Try that again and I'll shoot ta kill."

Looking back well into the distance, she saw Nash pursuing them on foot. Even as strong as he was, Becca knew he had no hope of catching them. She loved him all the more for trying. The evil look on the robber's face told her he would stop at nothing to escape. At that moment she resolved not to interfere with her captor's intent, fearful that he would keep his word and Nash would be shot and fall dead before her. The idea brought a storm of tears to her eyes. Unencumbered, trails of hot, salty water streamed down her cheeks.

Winded, Nash stopped and waved. "I'll find you, Becca! I love you!" he shouted as the horse galloped into the unknown.

∽

Watching the horse rush away with his Becca, Nash felt embarrassed and helpless. If only he could have caught up with them! Why did he have to lose his head and run instead of jumping into his carriage and giving chase with the horse?

His fiancée had endured the dangers of poverty and its accompanying hardships all her life, yet with money and position behind him, he couldn't even protect her during a routine trip to the milliner's. Then again, despite being aware that robbers were about in town, he still hadn't expected to meet one—and be shot at, no less.

At that moment Jack pulled up in the carriage. "Shall we give chase, sir?"

Nash nodded. "We can try." He jumped aboard and held on as the conveyance made haste. Though Jack ran the horses as fast as he could, they were no match for the unencumbered horse they pursued.

"We lost him, sir," Jack admitted after several miles.

Upset, Nash had to agree. "I suppose if I hadn't lost my head and tried to run after the horse on foot, we might have had a chance. Go back to town. We must notify the police."

"Yes, sir." Jack urged the horses on, quickening the pace. Once they returned to the scene of the crime, they found police questioning witnesses.

An older woman pointed at Nash. "They run off with a lady what was with him."

A detective looked Nash up and down. "Is this true?"

" 'Course it's true," the woman protested. "I saw the whole thing."

Nash nodded. "I wish it weren't true, but he took my fiancée, Miss Becca Hanham, hostage and made off with her. Officer, you must do something. You've got to save her. She's everything to me." Though he had professed his love to Becca with every bit of sincerity he possessed, the fact that she could be lost to him forever made him realize the depth of emotion he had developed for her. He recalled her sweet kiss on his lips. What he would give to have her close once more!

"Slow down, sir," the officer urged. "What's your name?"

"Nash Abercrombie."

He blanched. "Oh. I'm sorry, Mr. Abercrombie. I didn't know. Of course we'll do anything we can to assist you. . . ."

"I don't ask for any more consideration than you'd give any other citizen. I just ask that you do everything you can to find her. He—he used my Becca as a hostage." Nash choked on the words. Not one to show emotion and never one to blather, Nash felt tears threaten. He couldn't let anyone see him like this. They might think him less of a man. "My driver and I pursued him to the outskirts of town before we lost him."

"Tell me as best as you can, sir. I know you must be shaken. They said the robber shot at you."

"Yes." Trying not to think about that part of the adventure, Nash related the horrible events and described the robber as a bulky man with dark hair.

The officer made notes. "Yes, that matches the description of one of the bandits. Lately they've been working solo. We'll find them all and bring them to justice. That's a promise, Mr. Abercrombie."

Wishing he could do more, Nash boarded the carriage and went home. All the while, he wallowed in self-doubt. If he hadn't brought Becca into his world, she would have avoided being snatched. He, not she, should be with the kidnappers.

"Lord, deliver her safely into my arms. I don't know what I would do without her."

A repulsive laugh bellowed from the lips of the robber who had taken Becca hostage as he looked over his shoulder. "We lost 'em."

Becca's heart plummeted. Why didn't someone—anyone—from town catch up to them? She prayed all hope for her release wasn't lost. Fright seized her and wouldn't let go. Father's worst temper tantrums and outbursts didn't compare to feeling so alone. At least at her house her mother would try to protect her. She had no such ally on a galloping horse ridden by a stranger, heading out of Providence to who knew where. Never had she seen this part of the country, so trying to remember where she went seemed impossible. All she caught sight of was a marker for Meeting Street. Perhaps that tidbit would help in the future.

She couldn't help but wonder if Hazel, or someone connected to her, hired the man to kidnap her, but since she didn't know their comings and goings, misfortune seemed more probable. The man brought the horse to a trot. She sat in front of him with his arms around her, but they didn't comfort her. Being near such a man left her sick. "You've gotten what you want from me. I protected you from getting shot. Will you let me go now? I'll walk back into town myself."

"Let ya go? But I'm not finished with ya yet."

Her stomach lurched. What could he mean? She whispered, "Lord, I pray Thee will keep me safe."

"Shut up with prayin'," he hissed. "It's enough to give a man a headache."

Surprised that he heard her, she swallowed. Fear kept her from disobeying, but no one could keep her from petitioning the Lord silently. She prayed.

Soon she eyed a small log cabin near a churchyard at the end of a lonely country path. That must be where he was taking her. She couldn't help but note the cemetery. Would they kill her and bury her there in an unmarked grave? Or throw her unprotected corpse on top of some other poor soul's and cover them both with dirt? Anxiety clutched at her midsection.

Lord, I pray this isn't the last time I see the outdoors.

With a rough motion, the heavyset man pulled her off the horse and set her on the ground. Taking her by the hand without ado, he escorted her to the house, opened the thick wood door, and pushed her into a small room with tiny windows, lit only by two anemic candles. Becca's eyes adjusted quickly, and she saw two women and a man.

The first woman, a brunette with few wrinkles on her face but telltale grays in her hair, rose from her seat. "What took so long?"

The man had a question, too. "Did ya get a good take?"

A younger woman with a plump figure and ash blond hair jumped and ran to him, throwing her arms around him. "Dolph, I thought you'd never come back. I—I thought you might have been killed."

For a flash of an instant, Becca felt sorry for the blond. How would she feel if she were waiting for Nash, worried that something terrible happened to him? But then, Nash was neither a bank robber nor a kidnapper. . . .

Becca expected Dolph to console his female companion, but instead he grunted and made his way to the nearest wooden chair.

"What have we got here?" The brunette had noticed Becca and stared at her. Becca cut her glance to the blond, whose slitted eyes and folded arms revealed she considered Becca a threat. Becca looked at the floor in hopes of showing her that Dolph was safe from her affections.

"What does it look like I've got here?" Dolph sneered.

"We weren't supposed to bring a woman in the picture," the brunette said. "Have you gone mad?"

"Maybe I have, and maybe I haven't." As Dolph shrugged, the angle of his face in the light revealed he needed to shave his dark whiskers. "I grabbed her without thinkin' since she was the only woman around. Then, at first, I thought she was from the poor side of town, what with that old coat. But look underneath at this dress." He gave Becca's sleeve a tug that threatened to ruin Dawn's expert sewing. She tried not to flinch or pull away, fearful of inciting an unwelcome reaction from her captor. "She's got money, this one has. Isn't that right, Mac?" he asked the man.

"Yea," agreed Mac, nondescript except for an acute slimness of frame.

"You should of seen the man she was with. He was wearin' clothes good enough to see President Polk."

"So she was with someone?" the blond asked, looking into Dolph's face.

"Who cares?" the brunette asked. "We don't need her here."

"We needed her when they was shootin' bullets at me," Dolph said. "If it hadn't been for her, I might be dead sure enough." He looked Becca over as though she were a prize.

"Somebody will pay dearly to get this girl back. Don't ya think?"

The elder woman nodded. "Mebbe so."

"Who are ye?" Dolph asked.

The brunette woman surveyed her. "She looks mighty familiar. Like I should know her."

"Quiet. Ya don't know no high-society women." Dolph turned to Becca. "Now who are ye?"

Praying she didn't put Nash in danger by telling the truth, she put on a braver front than she felt.

She tilted her head high. "I am the fiancée of Nash Abercrombie."

Chapter 11

Distraught beyond expression, Nash returned to his house to wait for news. He shared the story with Harrod, who soon brought tea to Nash in his study as comfort. Nash let the tea grow cold as he paced back and forth. He debated sending Jack to let Becca's family know what happened, but thought better of it. Such terrible news would best be delivered by himself in person. After all, he'd gotten her into the situation by bringing her into his world. Losing Becca would devastate her family, particularly her mother and her sisters Naomi and Sissy. Perhaps Becca would have been better off had he left her alone. But he could not imagine life without her.

"I'll wait two hours, and if there's no word, I'll venture out to tell them," he muttered. "Lord, I know we are to wait for Thy time, but I pray that in this instance, Thy time is mine."

Harrod knocked. "Forgive me for the interruption, but the newspaper published an extra today, sir. I thought you would want to see it." He handed the paper to Nash.

"Thank you, Harrod. You are dismissed." He sat at his desk and devoured the account of the daring escape and kidnapping. His name and Becca's appeared, along with the details. He groaned, thinking about the gossip sure to ensue. Of course no reporter would write an account of a robbery gone wrong, along with gunshots and an impromptu kidnapping, without publishing their names.

Once again, Harrod knocked. "Otto Blevins to see you, sir."

Nash was in no mood to see anyone. Already the police had been by to question him about receiving a ransom note. So far, he had not. "With my apologies, tell him I am indisposed at present and will see him another time."

Harrod's mouth tightened, but otherwise he remained unruffled. "Shall I tell everyone else the same?"

"Yes." He rubbed his chin. "Just how many people are there?"

Harrod placed several calling cards on the corner of Nash's desk. "As you can see, because of the newspaper's extra, many of your friends have stopped by inquiring about your health. They are concerned. Of course, I gave them no further details."

"If any more stop by, tell them I am well and will see them soon."

"I'll do my best to keep them at bay, sir." Harrod shook his head and left the study.

His exit left Nash alone with his thoughts. He stared out the window to a cloudy day. When would the kidnapper return Becca, or at the very least, send a ransom note? Why didn't God answer his prayers and grant her return?

Again, Harrod knocked.

"I told you I don't want to see anyone," Nash snapped.

"Yes, sir. However, I would not interrupt if I didn't feel, in my judgment, it wasn't necessary."

"Of course. I'm sorry. I don't mean to be harsh. I'm in a foul mood."

"You have every right to be," Harrod agreed. "Again, I would not have dared interrupt, only I feel certain you will want to see Miss Hazel Caldwell."

"Hazel? Did she say what she wanted?" He knew she was angry, but he didn't expect her to show up at that moment.

"She said she has a letter you will want to read."

"A letter?" His curiosity was piqued, especially since he knew Hazel wouldn't bother unless the matter really was of the utmost urgency. "Very well. Escort her to the parlor, and have the maid send in tea."

Soon he entered the parlor. They wasted little time in exchanging pleasantries. Hazel carried a copy of the extra edition with her. She folded it to reveal the article about the events. "This is a disgrace! Being seen in public with this woman." Her nostrils flared with anger. "I have many friends in this town, and it didn't take me long to find out the real identity of your so-called fiancée. Imagine, trying to pass her off as a respectable woman. Really, Nash, have you taken leave of your senses?"

"I have not. Hazel, I am in no mood to discuss your opinion about my fiancée. As you can see for yourself in the newspaper account, she has been kidnapped. I am frantic with worry, and I await word from her kidnapper. I fully expect to be asked for a ransom. A ransom I will gladly pay to have her safe in my arms again."

"You—you really have become—fond of her, haven't you?" Her mouth slackened, and hurt evidenced itself in Hazel's voice. For a moment Nash could almost feel sorry for her. Almost.

"I love her," he proclaimed without wavering.

"You love her?" she sneered. "The idea of you even thinking of marrying her is a disgrace to everyone in Providence." She threw the paper on the tea table, almost hitting the pot full of hot beverage. Ignoring the near mishap, she folded her arms and faced him. "Now, I'm aware that you men sometimes indulge in, shall we say, little indiscretions. We women understand, and I can forgive you—"

"How dare you!" If Hazel had been a man, he would have been tempted to say something stronger.

She winced but did not apologize.

He stood his ground. "I assure you, I have no intention of conducting myself in such a way. While of course I am not perfect, I do try to live by God's commandments."

"Really?" she huffed. "Surely you have no intention of wedding that little back-alley girl. Why, how can you even look twice at someone who not so many years ago sold matches on the street corner? I understand she was even your scullery maid. You must think this is a joke, although it's not in the least bit funny."

"It's no joke, Hazel. Unlike you, I look at the person's heart. Of course, the fact she's beautiful to behold is a blessing." He smiled at the thought of his Becca. "And she wasn't a scullery maid for even a day."

Her voice hardened, lowering in pitch. "Ten minutes or ten years—it doesn't matter. How can you betray everyone you know by associating with a servant? It's nothing short of disgusting, if you ask me."

"And I'm sure plenty of your friends have sought your opinion."

"Indeed, and they don't think too highly of you." She crossed her arms with even more resignation.

"I will have to live with their poor opinion. Once Becca is returned safely to me, I am determined we shall wed as early as this spring."

Hazel wagged her finger. "You are making a fool of yourself, Nash Abercrombie." She let her voice linger on his last name, reminding him of its significance in society.

Nash was eager to move on to more important matters. "Did you say you have a missive for me?"

"I do. It contains a demand. A demand I think you will find distressing." She drew a letter out of her pocket. "You'll see it's a ransom note, asking the sum of three thousand for my return. But as you can see, I have not been kidnapped."

"Here. Give me that." Nash didn't intend rudeness, but he snatched the letter from her in a bold manner and read it.

Mr. Gill:

I no yur responsybal for Nash Abercomby's intinded, Hazel Calwell. We hav her hear saf and sownd and now we want the sume of $3,000 for her return. Met me at the Baptist Metin Howse at 8 oclok tonit with the mony or else. Do not bring anybody else or yu wil regret it.

"These demands are terrible," Nash murmured.

"Indeed." Hazel watched him read, regarding him with a hint of satisfaction. "I wonder what they'll think when they find out they have a little match girl instead of a woman of substance?"

Nash rolled the letter in his hands without concentrating. "I doubt they'll care, as long as they get their money."

"Funny how they didn't recognize the little Hanham girl. You'd think they'd live right next door to each other."

"Just because her family is poor doesn't make them criminals. I resent that implication."

"I didn't mean such an implication," Hazel assured him, although Nash knew better than to believe her.

"At least this note means she's alive. My poor, gentle little Becca. I hope they are treating you well," he muttered, then looked heavenward. "I thank Thee, Lord, for such favor."

"Why I do believe you mean that," Hazel observed. "No one will ever understand how you can love a little match girl when you could have married me, one of the most well-connected women in all of Providence. I'll certainly never comprehend how you could release me. When you first introduced me to your little maid, I was willing to fight for you. In fact, I had every intention of doing everything I could to ruin you. But no more. My sister and brother-in-law tried to convince me that you are worthy only of my pity and certainly unworthy of my time. Now that we have had this little meeting, I can see they are right."

Such a proclamation didn't surprise him. Mitchell's business dealings were aligned with his, so Nash's ruination—assuming Hazel possessed such power—wouldn't benefit their family. "I'm sorry to lose your good opinion of me," he said and meant it. "However, I deserve no less. Perhaps we can be on better terms in the future."

"Of course I will always be civil to you in polite society, Mr. Abercrombie, but my interests will lie elsewhere. I assure you, suitors will stand in line at my door as soon as they find I am free."

Not sure how to respond, he smiled. "I wish you well."

A slight pout visited her lips, a gesture she always used when upset and one he would not miss. He couldn't recall ever seeing Becca pout. "My relatives will not pay the ransom, so this problem is yours now." Triumph colored Hazel's voice. "By the by, according to the note, you have exactly five hours from now to pay. You'd better hurry."

"Five hours?" His stomach lurched. "Then I suppose I should thank you for bringing this letter to my attention."

"Of course. I wish you the best of luck. I don't approve of your taste, but it is not my wish to see even that little fortune seeker die at the hands of a kidnapper."

"Becca is not a fortune seeker, and if you insult her ever again, I shall never forgive you."

"Perhaps not." She gave Nash a sly look. "Although, I must speak now for your own good. For even though you have thrown me aside, I will always harbor a certain regard for you. Have you ever considered that she might know her captor?"

"No! I must protest—"

"Hear me out. Did you ever consider that, if not Becca herself, perhaps someone in her family might be setting up a ruse to collect money from you?"

He felt himself pale. "I—I hadn't considered such a thing."

"Perhaps you'd better consider it. Good day."

As Hazel left, Nash tried to put her suggestion out of his mind. Surely no one in Becca's family would stage such an event to extort money. Becca's observations about how her father treated her—treated all of their family—cluttered his mind. A drunk looking for his own benefit. But what would he have to gain? Wouldn't his future father-in-law be much better off allowing his daughter to marry him, affording her lifelong wealth instead of a one-time windfall? The story of the goose that laid the golden egg came to mind.

Nash couldn't help but focus on the note scrawled in a childish hand. "Lord, please forgive me for putting Becca in danger, even though that was never my intent. Guide me now, please."

He almost wished Becca's family had set up the kidnapping. Then he would know for certain she'd be safe. But if they hadn't, then the love of his life faced real trouble. If harm did befall her, he could never forgive himself. If only they'd chosen another day to go to the milliner's, Becca would be sitting beside him now, perhaps chattering about her new hats or making plans for the wedding.

Plans. God has a plan for everything, even if it's beyond human comprehension. He had to remember that. In the meantime, gathering the money to pay the ransom took precedence over everything else.

At that moment, he decided to refuse to consider the possibility of Mr. Hanham's involvement in the kidnapping. Nash would treat him as a worried father. He resolved to let his future father-in-law know about Becca's whereabouts. Perhaps Mr. Hanham would accompany Nash on the drive, although, fearing for his future in-law's safety, he would not allow him to meet the robber.

Glancing at the floor clock visible from its position in the dining room, he realized he had just enough time to go by the bank to collect his money, then see Mr. Hanham before he contacted the robber at the historic meetinghouse. He imagined the founder of the congregation, Roger Williams, would be none too pleased if he knew the site had been chosen for such a transaction.

∞

Sitting alone in a small, sparse room, Becca prayed for help, recited the Lord's Prayer many times, and brought to her mind many Bible verses that gave her comfort. When would help come? " 'The Lord is my shepherd; I shall not want. He maketh me to lie down in green pastures: he leadeth me beside the still waters. He restoreth my soul: he leadeth me in the paths of righteousness for his name's sake. Yea, though I walk through the valley of the shadow of death, I will fear no evil: for thou art with me; thy rod and thy staff they comfort me.' "

The blond, whom Becca had learned went by the name of Maizie, entered without knocking. "Here's your dinner."

Becca's head snapped toward Maizie in surprise. Thinking of escape, she hadn't considered a meal. As much as she hated to admit it, the broth with carrots and corn preserved from the summer crop emitted an aroma that promised a delicious respite. A thin slice of coarse bread without benefit of fruit preserves accompanied the soup, along with a small cup of water. "Thank you."

She set the meal on the only table in the room and studied her charge. "What were you mumblin' to yourself?"

"A psalm."

"Oh." She shrugged. "Do you really believe all that rubbish they talk about in church?"

"Rubbish?" The idea of her Lord's Word being called "rubbish" offended Becca, but she didn't want to bristle lest she set off Maizie's temper and diminish her circumstances. "I—I believe in the Lord, yes."

"Lots of good that's doin' you now."

Becca paused. "The Bible didn't promise things would always be perfect, but He sustains me through hard times. I can tell you that."

"Is that so?" Maizie's mouth twisted in doubt.

Becca studied her captor, noting her unenergetic demeanor and sour expression. Against her will, she blurted a thought. "Are you happy?"

Maizie's mouth dropped open. "Happy? Why, I'd never thought much about it."

Becca didn't see how anybody could be happy living with criminals and taking part in their crooked way of making a living, but she decided that wasn't the time to pass judgment. "Well, I'm happy most of the time, even though life for me isn't perfect. My faith helps me."

"Then you must be the only person in church who's not a hypocrite."

Becca noticed the hurt in the woman's eyes. "I'm sorry someone disappointed you. But not everyone will. May I pray for you?"

She gasped, and for the first time since Becca saw her, a hint of a smile shone on Maizie's face. "For me? You'd pray for me? You don't have reason to do that." She paused and narrowed her eyes. "Wait. This is a trick. You want me to help you escape, don't you?"

"I'd like that," Becca admitted, "but that has nothing to do with my prayers for you. I'll pray for you right now. We can pray together."

She startled. "Y–you're the first person what ever offered to do that for me."

"Then let's pray now—"

"Maizie!" her companion called from the next room. "What's the matter?" She entered the room. "Is the girl givin' you trouble?"

"No. No." She shook her head in quick motions, then turned her face to Becca. "I'll be back to pick up your dishes shortly."

Though the opportunity to pray with Maizie alone was lost, Becca said a prayer that the Lord would keep her in His care and guide her to a better life walking with Him. She petitioned that another opportunity to pray with Maizie would present itself and that in the future God would put more sincere Christians in Maizie's path. Then, in a soft voice, she said a blessing and ate the meal in silence. The delay meant lukewarm soup, but the broth comforted her even as anxiety never left. At least since she had shown compliance, they had chosen to trust her enough not to bind her or stuff her mouth to keep her quiet. For those kindnesses, she was thankful. Yet she longed to see the one sure to be her rescuer.

Nash, where are you?

∞

Calculating that he had just enough time, Nash went about his business quickly, deciding to be driven in his carriage rather than riding on horseback in case Mr. Hanham did agree to accompany him to rescue his daughter. Nash first stopped by the bank. The institution's president scratched his head and looked at Nash with doubting eyes when he withdrew such a large sum. Though innocent, Nash felt guilty. Thankfully no one questioned him. With the money in his pocket, he instructed Jack to drive him to Mr. Hanham's.

"Stay here and wait, Jack," Nash instructed as he disembarked.

"Yes, sir."

Nash hoped the driver would obey. Jack had become even more careless of late. Glancing at the sidewalk, Nash noticed stares coming his way and wondered if Becca felt odd when she arrived in such style each evening.

Becca. He prayed he'd see her soon.

Nash remembered the day he asked Mr. Hanham for Becca's hand and had spent considerable time with the family. Would he ever become accustomed to such poverty? The conditions still shocked him. Looking around, Nash tried not to show his disdain. The homes had never been fine, but neglect hadn't helped. Nash realized that in most cases, lack of money rather than sloth resulted in their unkempt appearance.

Children wearing rags walked about with no shoes. Their image reminded him of Becca that long-ago night when her eyes beckoned him to help her. He'd never regret that, no matter what happened in the future.

He knocked on the door.

"Who is it?" yelled Mrs. Hanham.

"Nash Abercrombie."

"Nash! Nash!" some of the children cried before opening the door. Becca's two-year-old brother and three-year-old sister ran to him and hugged his legs. He greeted them and smiled for the first time since Becca was kidnapped. The older girls, hovering in the background, looked at him with awe as though he were some kind of angel.

Their mother turned to them. "Girls, be on yer way."

"But, Mother—"

"Be on yer way." At the sound of her raised voice, the small child she held started yelping, and she rocked him on her hip. "Mr. Abercrombie, nice to see ya. To what do I owe this pleasure?"

He doffed his hat. "I wish this were a social call. The matter I have on my mind is quite urgent. May I speak with your husband?"

Her mouth dropped. "I'm sorry. I ain't got no idea where he is. Is everythin' fine?"

He wished he could console her, but to do so would be to lie. "If I may ask, you have no idea when he might return?"

"No, sir."

Nash couldn't help but wonder if Becca's father was with the criminals, just waiting for him to appear at the meetinghouse with the money. Anger flared at the thought, and he prayed it wasn't so. "And you have no idea where he's gone?"

She shook her head. "I don't have fine tea, but ya can come inside for a spot of ale. I'm sure my husband wouldn't mind if I give ya some under the circumstances."

"Forgive me for being unable to accept your hospitality, but I must take leave of you."

"Is—is everythin' all right?" she asked again.

Nash searched for something comforting to say but could offer little. "I pray it will be in due time. I'll be back."

Without time to search every tavern in town for Becca's father, Nash found Jack waiting for him. He sighed with relief and instructed him to drive to the meetinghouse. As Nash rode, his nerves jangled, but he had to face his enemy. Unwilling to put his driver in danger, he disembarked two blocks before the meetinghouse.

"If I don't return in half an hour, summon the police."

"I don't think it's right for me to let you go alone, sir. Let me come with you."

"I can honestly say I wish I could, but the letter said I am to bring no one. I wouldn't dare put you in danger by doing so."

Jack nodded slowly. "Yes, sir. I'll be right here."

Twilight was falling, so the trees cast ominous shadows. He set his chin high and walked like a brave man to the meetinghouse.

"Stop right there," a voice commanded from the shadows. "Don't get smart. Remember the gun? I still have it, and if I have to shoot, this time I won't miss."

Chapter 12

Nash walked toward the sound of the harsh voice coming from behind the meetinghouse. "I won't try anything. I'm unarmed."

A man emerged, holding a gun on Nash.

Nash recognized him as the robber he saw earlier. He displayed his hands, fingers spread, to show he spoke the truth. "Please, put your weapon away. I don't seek to harm you. I only want Miss Hanham back." He put his arms down but kept his hands in full view of the robber as he looked for Becca. "Where is she? I won't give you any money until I see her."

"That's yer mistake. I'll give ya the girl when I'm ready." Still holding the gun, the robber studied him. "Say, ye're the man what was with Miss Caldwell when this whole thing started."

"That's right. Only you don't have Miss Caldwell in captivity. You have Miss Becca Hanham. My fiancée. I am Nash Abercrombie."

His eyes squinted in confusion. "I don't know what ye're talkin' about." He scowled. "This better not be a dirty trick."

"It is not." Nash lifted his hands another inch for emphasis.

"Well, I don't guess I care who ya are, as long as you got my money. Do ya?"

"Yes, I do." He patted his suit coat to indicate its location.

The robber nodded and inspected the horizon. "Are ya alone?"

"Yes. I would never endanger anyone about whom I care." *At least not intentionally*. He swallowed. "So where is she?"

"You'll see her. For now, I want the money. Hand it over." He shook the gun at Nash to show he meant business.

"All right then." Nash withdrew a roll of large bills and threw it near the man's feet. Even in the darkness, he could see the greed in the kidnapper's eyes as he hurried to retrieve the money.

For the first time, the man's gun wasn't pointed at Nash. Taking advantage of his distracted condition, Nash charged him. With a quick chop of his wrist, he knocked the weapon from the man's hand. He followed the movement with a knee to his soft belly. The man fell to the ground. Nash recalled his boyhood days of playing cricket and with agility retrieved the weapon lying nearby before his adversary could beat him. Though the criminal weighed more than Nash, he was strong enough to hold him in a vise grip with his hands and knees. He put the Colt revolver's barrel to his temple.

"No! Don't shoot me!" The kidnapper's arms shook as he held them upward on the ground to signify surrender.

"Where is she?" Nash's voice sounded threatening even to his own ears. "I demand to know."

He shook his head. "I don't know. My partner said he'll send word where to meet her tomorrow."

"That's not good enough." Seeking to fortify his advantage, Nash retrieved the money from the ground, then pressed his knees deep into the man's inner thigh. "And you are in no position to tell a falsehood."

Sweat beaded on his brow, and he grimaced. "I said I don't know."

Nash exerted so much pressure on the man's leg that he could feel sinewy muscle under layers of fat. He could smell the stench of nervous perspiration. "I'm the one with the gun now."

The man grunted, and his face became even sweatier. "All right. I'll take you to her, but only if you give me half the money now."

Nash tried to conceal his anger at the man's gall. "I won't even consider giving you anything until I see her."

He cut his gaze sideways in the direction of the gun and scowled. "Fine. Come with me."

"Don't try to escape." Nash rose to his feet. He never allowed the gun's barrel to point away from the man's head.

Huffing, the man used considerable effort to steady himself. He rubbed his thigh where Nash's knee had bruised it and scowled at his captor.

"It's not as amusing to be the one held with a gun to your head, now is it?" Nash couldn't resist asking without an ounce of levity.

His frown deepened.

"I'm concealing this gun in my coat pocket, but it will continue to be pointed at you at all times," Nash warned. "Do not even think about making a false or sudden move."

The man nodded.

"I'm going to lead you to my carriage now." Jack would be waiting since nowhere near a half hour had passed. The idea that Jack would help him keep the robber under control relieved Nash. He swished the gun eastward. "Take the path. My driver is waiting."

"I told you not to bring anybody," he growled.

"That is neither here nor there now. Go."

Nash could feel anger emanating from his captive, but he obeyed. After all, only a fool would argue with a revolver.

They kept walking along the path, well past where Nash had been certain he'd left Jack waiting.

"How much longer?" the robber asked. "My leg hurts."

Nash tightened his lips. How could he admit to this criminal that he couldn't depend on his own driver? Normally Nash wouldn't employ someone so unreliable. Often he wished his father had never promised Jack's mother they'd take care of her boy. To leave Nash alone in the dark, knowing he was to meet an armed man—the thought upset him. Still, Nash had to maintain his composure.

"We'll keep walking," Nash ordered. "Lead me to her."

"I don't know if I can with this bum leg," he protested.

Nash drew the gun from his pocket so its full force would come into view. "You can and you will."

"Oh, all right," the man growled.

Nash put the gun back in his pocket. They walked toward Brown University on College Hill. He feared an accomplice might pounce on him, but no such event occurred. Instead, well before they reached the school, the robber ducked into a brick house. A lone light shone through a front window.

Nash's heart beat wildly as they stepped over the threshold. Joy at the prospect of seeing Becca battled with sickening images of his beloved bound and gagged. He listened for muffled cries of distress coming from anywhere in the house.

Nash was surprised when a woman greeted them rather than another man. Surely this plain and plump member of the fairer sex wasn't a criminal. But anyone who held his beloved Becca for ransom couldn't be held blameless.

"Is this Mr. Gill?" Though not a conceited man, Nash caught a flirtatious inflection in her voice.

"No, it's Mr. Abercrombie. The girl's fiancé."

"Oh." Disappointment colored her voice. "So, what—what did you bring him fer?"

The robber's eyes narrowed. "Shut up, woman. That's not yer concern."

Another woman, a blond, entered. "What's going on in here?"

"Where is Miss Hanham?" Nash tilted his head toward the door from which the blond had appeared. "Is she in there?" He restrained himself from pushing past her and finding out for himself.

The woman ignored Nash and addressed her comrade. "Did he give ya the money?"

"I will give you the money when I see Miss Hanham," Nash snapped. "Where is she?"

"Miss Hanham? Who is that? I've got Miss Caldwell with me." The plump woman looked to the robber for guidance. "Dolph, what is the meaning of this?"

"Quiet. I'll explain later. Show him to the room."

She looked puzzled but obeyed. "Come with me."

Nash watched as the woman unlocked the door of a back room. With only one candle for light, Becca sat in a chair. To his relief, they hadn't placed her in restraints. Nash pushed past the woman and ran to his beloved. "Becca!"

She gasped, jumped up, and ran into his arms. "Nash! I've never been happier to see you!"

"Nor I, you." He squeezed her in the way of a fond protector before breaking their embrace. He looked into her eyes. "Did they treat you well?"

Becca's glance went to her captors and back. "As well as a kidnapping victim can be, I suppose."

"You've retained your sense of humor, I see." He smiled at her. He wanted to cover her face with kisses, but since others were present, he refrained.

Dolph's rough voice interrupted his dream state. "Well, ain't that nice?"

Nash turned his head to see him holding a gun on them. He felt himself flush with embarrassment. How could he have been so careless? Allowing himself to become distracted, he had put them in danger. He reached in his pocket for the weapon he had confiscated from his opponent.

"Don't even think about it," he said. "Put your hands up and come along with me."

"I'm sorry, Becca," he muttered into her hair.

"God is with us." Her courageous assurance defied the fear he saw in her eyes.

"Is that what you think?" Dolph sneered. "Then ya'd better say yer prayers since ya ain't got much time left. Now hand over the gun and the money, or I'll take both of 'em from ya."

Seeing no alternative, Nash surrendered to his demands.

Dolph took the roll of bills and handed it to his companion. "Put this under the bed." She nodded with quick jerking motions.

"Don't you worry none," he assured his companion. "I'll be back for you."

∽

Becca couldn't remember when a walk through town took so long. Under cloak of darkness, the kidnappers had changed locations from the cottage in the woods just in case someone tipped off the law. She could feel her pulse in her throat. She could tell by the strained look on Nash's face—which she could see since her eyes had adjusted to the lack of light—that he was hatching a plan for escape. She prayed he would be successful.

"Stop." The man's abrupt command forced them to obey. Becca nearly ran into Nash as both of them came to a halt.

A buggy awaited them on Olive Street. In such a conveyance, commonplace all over town, no one would ever guess its passengers were being held captive. The criminals had thought of every way to keep from being discovered, as far as Becca could see. What would happen to Nash and her now? Her heart beat fast as her fear increased. Was this the night she would die? Though confident she would see the loving face of Jesus when the Lord called her home, Becca nevertheless wanted to live long enough to marry Nash and give him a family. Such prospects seemed more and more slim as their time with the robber increased.

Holding a silver flask, the thin man they called Mac jumped from the driver's seat. "What took so long?" he snarled, revealing a missing front tooth.

"Don't worry. Everything went just as planned."

Nash stared at him.

"Well, almost. I got the man—well, the man what cared enough to pay the ransom. And I got the girl and the money, just as we said. What more do ya want?"

Becca wanted to cry out, to do something, anything, to get out of the situation. What did Nash want her to do? She sent him an imploring look, but he shook his head almost indiscernibly, signaling her to remain calm. Standing with his usual perfect posture, she wondered how he could retain such composure.

If the kidnappers had any idea what Becca was thinking, they didn't let on. Dolph curled his fingers at his partner, asking for the flask. He extended a fleshy hand. "Here, give me a swig o' that. It's been a long night, and I need a snout full."

"There ain't much left." Mac relinquished the refreshment.

Dolph drank deeply and then wiped his mouth with his sleeve. He tilted the open flask toward Nash. Becca smelled the bitter odor of whiskey but didn't flinch since she was accustomed to the stench, thanks to her father's habits.

"I don't care for any, thank you," Nash responded with more politeness than the situation warranted.

"I wouldn't be so picky if I was ye," Dolph said. "Ya might not like the plain old corn liquor I got. Ye're used to fancy French wine, I'll wager."

Despite his goading, Nash stood erect, and his expression didn't waver.

"Whatever you take now will be your last." He waved the flask in front of Nash's nose.

"That's right." Mac laughed. He eyed Becca, his thin face reminding her of a scarecrow. "I notice the girl didn't even bat an eye when she smelled our liquor. I thought society women turned up their noses at our humble beverages. Mebbe she drinks in secret. Mebbe she'd like a swallow." He leaned toward her. "How's about it, girl?"

Dolph protested. "What? I wouldn't waste my liquor on any woman. Well, mebbe one or two o' the wenches I know at the tavern, when I wants to put 'em in a good mood." He winked, and Becca shuddered. She felt Nash's body tense even though they weren't close enough to touch one another.

The men pushed them into the buggy, which was soon on its way. She didn't wonder why they didn't bother to blindfold Nash and her. They had no plans for them to see the light of day again. To Becca, each second in time seemed to be an hour. Finally they came to a stop.

Dolph got out but held his body near the exit. "Get out."

She obeyed and surveyed the location. The place Dolph had forced them to halt was so remote and forested that Becca knew screams would never be heard. She envisioned Dolph digging a shallow grave for their dead bodies and running off with Nash's money. She studied the revolver. At least if he shot them, their deaths would be quick.

"Heavenly Father, save us!" Becca prayed aloud as her foot sank into muddy ground.

Dolph and Mac laughed in tipsy mirth. "She thinks God will help her now. I get tired of hearin' her pray. Don't ye?" Dolph nudged Nash with a force that made Becca jump.

"Never." Nash pursed his lips, but the glint in his eyes gave Becca courage.

"Turn around," Mac demanded.

"So you're going to shoot us in the back. I might know men such as yourselves wouldn't have the courage to face us in our moment of death." Nash's voice sounded harsh.

Moment of death? How could he be so calm? Yet he was every bit the man. The strong man she loved. The man with whom she wanted to spend the rest of her life.

If we die tonight, I will have gotten that wish. I will have spent the rest of my life with him.

Becca's breathing had become pronounced. Couldn't he take this chance to grab the gun? What did they have to lose? Death was certain if he didn't do anything, but a bit less certain if he did. "Nash, please!"

The men chortled. "There's nothin' he can do fer ya now," Mac insisted.

"That's right," Dolph agreed. "Men like him, they look down on people like us. For once, we got the upper hand."

"And if ya want ta know the truth, I'm havin' me a bit o' fun with it all," Mac admitted.

The smile on Dolph's face looked nothing short of evil. "Ya were brave before, knockin' the gun out o' me hand, but I was alone then. Ya wouldn't dare try anything like that, with it bein' both of us. And if ya do, things will be worse for yer girl here."

Too fearful to be ashamed by making a pleading gesture, Becca sent Nash the most puppy-eyed look she could muster, begging him to do something, anything. His glance went back and forth between the two men. Surely he was thinking. . . .

Without warning, Nash let out a whoop that could have awakened the dead and gave Mac a swift kick. In a flash he followed suit with Dolph. "Run, Becca!"

Becca wanted to remain and kick and punch the criminals as well, but she imagined her little blows wouldn't accomplish much. Besides, if she ran fast enough, perhaps she could find help.

She wished she didn't have to run from the scene in spite of realizing that was her best course of action. Desperately she wanted to know Nash would survive, yet to sacrifice her life when he had just done so much to save her would dishonor him. She rushed into the darkness. "Lord, I beg Thee to help us!"

The sound of a horse's hooves beating on the path shocked her. Who could be out this time of night and in such a remote place? She stopped and looked at the path, then back at Nash. Dolph punched him in the gut while Mac held him.

Tears streaming down her face, Becca's stomach churned, but as soon as the criminals heard the horse, they stopped beating Nash. Widened eyes told her they didn't know how to react. They hadn't expected anyone to ruin their plans. Becca was sure the horseman must have witnessed what he interrupted. Anticipating the stranger would keep her safe, Becca ran back toward the scene.

The rider drew close enough to be heard. "Stop! Stop right this instant!"

Becca's hand clutched her throat when she recognized the sharp baritone. So uncertain was she that her voice quivered. "Father? Father, is that you?" How could it be, when they didn't own a horse?

As soon as she uttered the words, the criminals panicked. One fired a shot at the horseman.

Becca's hands shook as she sent them skyward. She screamed, "Father!"

Having escaped injury, Father jumped off the animal and ran toward the group. Dolph lifted his gun to shoot, but Nash charged him. Grabbing his opponent's wrist, Nash was able to keep the gun from hitting its mark. Meanwhile, Father subdued a hapless and drunken Mac.

Becca feared they wouldn't be able to keep the men under control long. In answer to silent prayer, she heard the sound of approaching horses.

"That's the police," Father told Dolph. "After me wife told me you stopped by, I summoned 'em before I came here."

Nash and her father kept the criminals confined long enough for the police to arrive and take charge. After the police expressed their gratitude to Nash and her father for their bravery, they departed.

Becca hugged her father. "Thank you, Father! Thank you from the bottom of my heart."

His mouth twisted in an unusual show of modesty.

"Father, I never guessed you would be my rescuer. Why, you were shot at, all for me. I can't believe you would make such a sacrifice."

Nash agreed. "Thank you, Mr. Hanham. If you hadn't appeared the moment you did, I'm not sure what the outcome would have been. I don't think I exaggerate when I say I owe you my life. I cannot express my gratefulness enough."

"You can express it by takin' care o' me daughter."

"Father!"

Nash laughed. "That's quite all right, Becca. I intend to take care of you anyway. I can only hope our next trip to the milliner's won't prove so dramatic."

Becca sent him a rueful smile. "Perhaps next time she can deliver the hats to our house."

∽

"There you are!" Mother's face relaxed with relief as Nash, Becca, and Father entered the noisy front room. "I was so worried. What happened?"

"Tell us! Tell us!" Naomi added amid the siblings' pleas to hear about the adventure.

Father filled them in on the evening's events. To Becca's surprise, he didn't exaggerate. Then again, they had such a close call that stretching the truth hardly seemed necessary.

"How terrible! Let me look at ya." Mother did just that. "Oh, I'm so relieved ye're safe and sound!"

"As am I," Nash agreed. "But tell me, how did your husband know where we were?"

"Let me tell it," Father said. "Yer driver, Jack, was at the pub. I could tell by the way he was braggin' in front o' me that he didn't recognize me. But I sure recognized him. He was sayin' that he was comin' into some big money soon."

"Wait, you say Jack was at the pub? Tonight?" Nash's voice registered his surprise, then his disappointment.

Mr. Hanham nodded. "He said he had a couple o' men collectin' money fer him, but he'd be a rich man in a matter of hours."

"Then no wonder he wasn't there when I needed him," Nash muttered, hurt evident in his voice. "He abandoned me deliberately."

Father didn't seem to hear Nash. "Bein' a man o' the world as I am, I decided I'd better figger out what Jack meant. I figgered he wouldn't talk without a few drinks, so I engaged him in talkin', tellin' him he must be smart, and by plyin' him with ale. It took awhile, but I finally got him to the place where he said he had a girl out in the woods near the old cemetery who was mighty valuable. I didn't understand exactly what he meant, but I knew somebody was in danger. Then he said luck was with him and his friends. Without plannin' it, they kidnapped his employer's fiancée, and that gave 'em the chance to ask for a ransom. When he said that, I knew I had to do somethin' fast."

Becca held back a gasp.

"I ran home, not even finishin' me ale, mind ya. I went to the smithy and gave him the promise of a dollar to let me borrow his horse so I could follow you, Mr. Abercrombie. He wouldn't a let me have it, 'cept I told him ye're a rich man and ye'd make good on it." He paused and stared at Nash. "Ya will, won't ya?"

Nash smiled. "Considering I came out of our adventure with the full amount of money and my life—plus the life of the only woman I've ever loved. . ." The look he sent Becca said it all. "I'd say I'd be happy to give the smithy ten times as much."

"A dollar's enough." Father lifted his index finger to hold their attention. "I don't pray much, but I did ask God fer some help tonight. I suspect I should give Him credit fer me spyin' a buggy makin' its way down a road out of town. 'Mighty odd time fer anybody to be headin' out o' town,' I thought to meself. So I follered it. But I was thinkin' with me brain, I was." He tapped his temple. "Before I left town completely I thought to ask a little boy sellin' lucifers on a street corner to tell the police to go in the same direction the buggy was goin', 'cause there might be trouble brewin'. I paid him a penny. He seemed happy enough."

Nash nodded. "I'm glad they took the boy seriously. But then again, they've been desperate to capture this band of thieves, so no doubt they were following up on any clue."

"Thank goodness they were finally successful," Becca noted. "I was going to run as fast as I could to find help, but I was so afraid I would never see Nash alive again." She placed a hand on his arm. "Oh, Nash, you were so brave!"

"With the Lord as my guide." Nash looked at Becca's father. "I'm thankful for your quick thinking, Mr. Hanham. My driver has some explaining to do. To the police."

Becca felt sorry for Jack, but he had brought his punishment on himself.

Nash's expression turned wistful. "The Lord used another unlikely person to help us. If I'm to be honest, I must say that I have Hazel to thank as well."

"Hazel?" Becca asked. "That is strange."

"Yes. She's the one who showed me the ransom note sent to her brother-in-law. That told me right away I needed to act quickly." He sighed. "That was before I let the criminals know I am engaged to you, not Hazel."

Becca smiled, blushing.

"I propose a big celebration, a formal party for all our friends. At that time we shall announce our engagement and wedding date."

"Are you sure?" Becca asked.

"More sure than ever." The conviction in his voice did more than enough to convince her.

"But Miss Caldwell. . ."

"I assure you, she has no reason to hope for our match any longer."

"Oh." Becca faced him straight on and looked him in the eyes. Eyes she wanted to see every day for the rest of her life. "You kept up your end of the bargain. I don't remember a time I've been happier. But I know I was not born to your world. To marry me will be a sacrifice for you. I want you to know that from this moment, I release you of any obligation you feel toward me. I want you to feel free to marry a woman of your own station. That's what my dream is for you—acceptance by your friends and your happiness."

"If you really mean that, then you'll marry me tomorrow. Your spirit touched me that night long ago when I first bought lucifers from you, but when I saw you again as a beautiful young woman, my heart was captured. The time we've spent together since then has only confirmed my initial feelings for you. Now I can't imagine life without you." He sent her a boyish grin. "If you'll marry me, I promise you'll never have to touch another dirty dish." He lifted her left hand in his and regarded the ruby ring. "Grandmother instructed me to give her ring to my future wife. When I presented it to you, I meant to keep my promise. I don't want a society maiden. I want you, Becca Hanham. If you'll have me."

"If I'll have you? Why, I'd marry you even if you lived right here on this street."

Laughing, Nash took her in his arms. They kissed, knowing their time together had bonded them forevermore.

Epilogue

Nash and Becca stood under an ivy-covered archway leading to the gardens of the Abercrombie country estate a few miles from Providence. The delicate scent of flowers gave the air the feel of a wedding. A four-tiered cake Cook took two days to bake and frost graced the center of a buffet table.

Becca looked up into Nash's eyes. "I have married the man I love today."

"You only love me today?" Nash teased, holding his arm around her waist. "But I will love you today, tomorrow, and every tomorrow God sees fit to grant us, my darling."

"As it shall be. My love for you will never die."

Becca wouldn't have cared if they'd married in a barn, but the wedding itself had been everything she could have imagined and more. She looked out among their guests as they indulged in the wedding feast held outdoors under a lovely New England summer day. They had all wished her well as Mrs. Nash Abercrombie. Even Hazel, now being courted by a wealthy older man, didn't seem to begrudge her such happiness.

She couldn't help but notice Father looking stiff in formal wear and her brothers pulling now and again on their collars, but her male relatives had all done her proud by displaying their best behavior. Even the smaller siblings, acting as ring bearer and flower girls, shone. Mother and Becca's sisters blossomed in the environment, reminding Becca of the rose petals their guests had placed along the garden path for Nash and her.

During the engagement period, Becca had come to know his intimate friends and had even drummed up the courage to perform for them. After she sang her initial song, the others joined in and had great fun showing off their respective talents to one another. Many such a pleasant night of music and parlor games bonded them, so her fears that they would never accept her had long since faded. Clearly their high regard for Nash superseded any urge toward snobbery. Then again, Nash had trained her well, and she felt more and more comfortable among his set as time progressed. The idea of socializing with them for the rest of her life no longer seemed formidable. Nash did confess that his friends had quieted a few snippets of gossip, but that only proved their loyalty. Two of Nash's customers dropped their accounts with him to protest his match with Becca, but the Lord quickly sent more to replace them. Truly, the Savior had answered their prayers in every respect.

Nash surveyed the buzzing reception along with her. "I understand we have one of the largest wedding parties reported in Providence."

Becca laughed. "When one has so many siblings, that's likely to happen. And look at Mother and Father. They are absolutely beaming."

"I hope they'll enjoy their new home. There should be more room for all your siblings now. Granted, they will still share bedchambers with one another."

"Yes, but in quarters not nearly as cramped," Becca was quick to point out. "I'm so grateful to you. For the first time in my memory, Father has stopped drinking, and my brothers and sisters aren't spending their time daydreaming about how to leave home as quickly as they can. I'm so glad they'll be living near us, too. I couldn't ask for more."

"I wouldn't have it any other way."

"What a dream." Becca sighed. "To have everyone I love near me always—especially you, Nash. I never considered being well-off or powerful, and certainly I never envisioned that I would be a member of your society. I never thought I'd wear anything but rags, and here I am in the finest garments I can imagine. Yet none of those things matter to me." She looked into his face, marveling once again at how handsome he looked. "The dream you have made come true for me is one of undying love. The love of a compassionate man of God was all I ever wanted. Thank you for giving me that."

"The gift of your love has made all my dreams come true, Becca. I'll love you forever."

Unashamed of their love, they shared a kiss, the first of the many more they were assured of sharing for the rest of their lives.

 **Tamela Hancock Murray** is an award-winning, bestselling author living in northern Virginia. She and her husband of twenty-five years are blessed with two daughters. When not spending time with friends and family, Tamela enjoys writing stories of faith, hope, and love. Tamela also loves hearing from her fans! Check out her Web site at www.tamelahancockmurray.com

ALL THAT GLITTERS

LYNETTE SOWELL

Dedication

To the ladies at Five Hills Assembly with love: The three Debbies, Lisa, Diane, Bonnie, Dottie, Nancy, Faye, Elfi, Pauline, Nam Sun, Katrina, Tiffany, Christine, Ruby, Marcy, Doris, and Chichi. May you always find great books to read, good coffee (or tea) to drink, and priceless friends to share them with. To my wonderful husband, CJ. Thank you, as always, for your love and constant support. I could not do this without you!

Chapter 1

Miss, I simply cannot do this." Francesca Wallingford's maid frowned at her hands, clad in Francesca's second pair of silk gloves. "All will know I am not—"

"Nonsense." Francesca glanced out the carriage window at the Paris evening. The gaslights beckoned them, and the party awaited. Stuffy, pretentious, and thoroughly uninteresting. Until they arrived, of course. "Elizabeth, you shall remember your lessons and be the pride of my heart this evening. Imagine, they will wonder who this most *charmante mademoiselle* is who appeared suddenly this season along with Miss Francesca Wallingford. And we shall laugh at them all later."

"If I am discovered. . ." Elizabeth touched her throat.

"That will not happen. I assure you that your natural grace will be evident; and not everyone speaks French, so your limitations there should only prove the more engaging." At last, the carriage drew near to the grand house where the latest in a series of balls would keep them dancing and frolicking like so many peacocks until dawn peeked through the tall windows of the ballroom. But tonight, Francesca would find a measure of interest in watching Elizabeth's venture into society.

Elizabeth's hair had never known the heat of an iron, much as the young woman had spent hours helping curl Francesca's own tresses. And Francesca had no skill in curling hair, yet somehow she had managed to curl Elizabeth's hair into a passable style. Although Francesca's robin's egg blue gown—of last season—had been too long for Elizabeth's more diminutive frame, the two of them had managed to shorten the gown and transform it into this year's fashion. No one would be the wiser, especially since Mother remained at home with yet another headache.

"Your mother will not approve," Elizabeth said as if in response to Francesca's pondering.

"Ah, but she knows my brother and his wife will be present this evening, and it is not scandalous in the least for me to travel with my maid." She tried not to wince at the mention of Elizabeth's true station in the Wallingford household.

And it was best not to think of what James and Victoria would say, should they recognize Elizabeth. She hadn't considered that. Of course James might tell Mother, and then. . .

"You look worried, miss."

"I am not the least bit concerned." Francesca patted Elizabeth's hand. "Tonight we shall both lose ourselves in the music, and you will remember this evening always."

The carriage stopped, and Francesca wouldn't allow herself the childish luxury of ducking her head out the carriage window to see the line of carriages ahead of them. *Sit up straight, Francesca.* The impish voice that belonged to her mother hissed in her ear, almost as if Mother sat next to Francesca.

Francesca braced herself as the carriage rocked. The driver appeared at the door a moment later.

"Follow me." Francesca smiled at Elizabeth, who looked as though her hands had frozen to her lap. "No one will bite you. I promise."

The door swung open, and Francesca waited for the driver to move the steps into place. Her heart gave a curious flutter, and she touched the top of her bodice. She stepped cautiously, taking care not to duck her head when leaving the carriage. A perfect exit, as she'd always been taught.

Once exited from the carriage, she turned to face Elizabeth. The poor girl's face had turned pasty white.

"I. . .I. . ." Her shoe with its slippery sole touched the top step. Then it skidded.

"Steady now, miss." The driver's hand on Elizabeth's elbow steadied her.

"Thank you kindly." Elizabeth bobbed her head.

"Elizabeth!" Francesca's throat caught. "Are you quite all right?" Her maid tumbling down to the pavement in front of the main doors wasn't the entrance Francesca wanted them to make. Had that occurred in Mother's presence, Mother would have glided away into the grand house and left the poor young woman in a humiliated pile of silk and not spoken to her the remainder of the night. Francesca knew this from experience. But she wouldn't desert poor Elizabeth, who gently shook her skirt as Francesca had instructed her.

"Yes, miss." Elizabeth stood tall. "Um, I mean, Francesca." Her cheeks bloomed a shade of rose.

"Good. Perhaps we're in time for the first dance, although we missed the early supper." Francesca had wanted to add, *because Mother took forever deciding if she could bear the bright lights and music,* but she thought better of it. The timing had been perfect to launch Elizabeth, as it were. They'd barely gotten away when Mother was on the brink of not permitting Francesca to attend at all. Except for the fact that Count Philippe de la Croix would be hosting the event, Francesca would have remained behind at the Wallingfords' accommodations and attended to Mother.

She took a few steps and nodded to the doorman, who swung the great doors open for them. Now, where was Elizabeth?

Francesca glanced over her shoulder. "Elizabeth, are you coming?"

"Yes, um, Francesca." She trotted two steps until she drew even with Francesca's right shoulder. The music of an orchestra swallowed them up as they entered the foyer.

"Now remember." Francesca leaned closer to whisper. "You must not follow behind me. Walk beside me. Tonight, you are not. . ."

"I know." Elizabeth nodded. "And thank you for letting me have this chance. I have always wanted to attend one of these fancy parties."

"I hope the evening does not disappoint you." Or get them both into trouble. Francesca hadn't considered that possibility. James liked to remind her about considering consequences presently to avoid a future grief. If they were discovered, Mother surely wouldn't dismiss Elizabeth, whose family had served the Wallingfords for longer than Francesca had counted birthdays.

Francesca sponged gloomy thoughts from her mind and instead nodded at several acquaintances she'd encountered at other parties that season, but didn't stop to introduce Elizabeth. Just as well, since Elizabeth's upturned lips seemed frozen in place. They needed to find the ballroom and the source of the music, as well as greet their host and hostess.

"*Meece* Wallingford." The accented voice speaking her name made Francesca pause.

The voice's owner had dark eyes, dark hair, a wide smile. *Oh, Lord, I never thought a man could be so handsome.* Count Philippe de la Croix stood before her. Francesca's knees wobbled.

"Yes." Her hand was caught up in a strong one, and the man's lips lingered a bit longer than exactly proper. She didn't want to let this hand go. "You—you must be the count." She remembered herself and gave a slight curtsy with a nod of her head.

"Only at court, Meece Wallingford." The count, still holding her hand, tucked it under his arm. "Here, in this grand place, I am but Philippe and you must call me such, as my mama does."

"But, we haven't been properly introduced." Francesca bit her lip. She'd sounded just like her mother. The count's presence addled her head. No wonder Mother had wished for her to attend tonight. A scheme involving Francesca and the count, no doubt.

"Ah, but our mothers have spoken, and it is as if I know you already." He drew her along with him toward the sound of music.

"But. . ." She normally didn't repeat herself like a chatting bird. The elegantly carved doors to the ballroom swung open—the count must have quite the influence at this home—and Francesca held her breath as they entered.

No one announced their arrival, yet it seemed as if the room collectively paused. It was not on Francesca's account, she knew that much. The man next to her held the room in his gaze.

"See, Mademoiselle Francesca, they are as enchanted with you as I am. Now, you will do me the honor of first dance?"

Francesca's muddled mind fumbled. Elizabeth. She cast a glance over her shoulder. Her maid followed on mincing steps.

"Go," Elizabeth mouthed. "I will manage."

With that, Francesca was swept into the whirl of silken skirts and fine waistcoats. Peacocks on parade, all of them. Wasn't that what she'd imagined? And poor Elizabeth. What if she became entangled in an unwelcome conversation and Francesca was nowhere near to rescue her?

"I understand you are quite the artiste, *n'est-ce pas?*" The count's voice sounded lower in this crowd.

"*Oui*, but I prefer to think I merely dabble in paints."

"Your mama believes otherwise. Although," and here Count Philippe gave a soft chuckle, "I think she holds your talent in far less esteem that she would like that I believe."

"That is probably true." Francesca smiled at him, and his own smile increased in return. An ally? If he saw through Mother's scheming, perhaps tonight would not be so bad.

A glimpse of dark red hair caught Francesca's eye. The last time she'd seen hair that color was a painful memory. Barely out of childhood, a tearful departure. Promises of letters that never came. Whispers of scandal. A friendship she'd mourned and buried.

"Are you all right, Mademoiselle Francesca?" Count Philippe's brow furrowed.

"I am fine. The room is rather full tonight, and I had to catch my breath." Now she'd sounded rude, as if the dancing had caused her discomfort.

The music ended, and the dancers surrounding them applauded. Francesca did the same.

"Talented, are they not?" The count applauded as well.

She nodded. The man with the dark red hair wouldn't turn around. Perhaps it was just as well. Her mother had simply informed a then-devastated Francesca "that Finley boy" would be going away, and none of them would ever see him again.

"You are looking for someone?"

Francesca glanced at Philippe, who also scanned the room. "Yes. No. I am unsure. I thought it might be. . .an old friend. But never mind." Undoubtedly Mother had instigated her and Philippe's meeting tonight, and she mustn't disappoint her. Not that she would find the task of becoming better acquainted with the count a horrible one.

The orchestra at the end of the gilded ballroom struck up another tune, this time a waltz.

"Shall we, then?" Philippe offered his hand.

Francesca smiled up at him. No memories would mar this evening.

After three songs, Francesca's feet throbbed in her new dancing slippers. She thought of Elizabeth's feet, probably comfortably tucked into her old pair, with a wad of cotton in the toe to make up the difference.

Elizabeth! She'd nearly forgotten her maid. No sight of Elizabeth in the elegant blue dress she'd traded for her day uniform of dove gray.

"You do that again, searching for someone."

"My friend, Elizabeth. We arrived together, and I wanted to see how she fared thus far."

Philippe drew her off the dance floor and toward a pair of empty chairs beside the wall. "Forgive me. I should have thought. . .I should have introduced her to someone."

"No, it's all right. I am sure she is fine." Well, she hoped, anyway.

A familiar face emerged from a cluster of chatting women. But not Elizabeth. Rather, Francesca's cousin, Lillian. With her demeanor, she could have been Francesca's mother's daughter. The young woman swept up to them, her skirts swishing with each stride.

"Francesca." Lillian trilled her *r*, and that set Francesca into a coughing fit. She'd heard Mother affect the same pronunciation in the past. "It is good to see you this evening."

Francesca wouldn't allow herself to lie and express pleasure at seeing Lillian. "Thank you. Mother is home with a headache, but she insisted I attend anyway. And so I have."

"*Un*-accompanied?" Lillian sounded as if Francesca had decided to spend the evening running barefoot and clad in her dressing gown through the Paris streets.

"No, of course not." Francesca bit her lip. If there were one person who would prance into their drawing room on the morrow and reveal everything to Mother, that would be Lillian. Francesca ought never to have allowed Elizabeth one evening, like the Cinder-girl in the fairy tale.

"And you." Lillian blinked at the count and wiggled one shoulder. "You must be the Count de la Croix."

"Oui." Philippe inclined his head in the slightest of nods. "I don't believe I've had the pleasure—"

"Lillian Chalmers." Up went her hand.

Francesca watched the introduction. She could hear Mother now, exclaiming over Lillian "wresting" the count's attentions away from Francesca, especially after Mother's obvious attempts to make an excellent connection.

A trickle of perspiration wound its way down Francesca's back. Her nose itched at the scent of Lillian's perfume.

"Why, yes, of course," Lillian was saying.

Francesca missed the rest of the exchange. She had the urge to stick out her foot, just a teensy bit, enough to send Lillian headfirst onto the ballroom floor. But she kept her feet tucked beneath the hem of her gown.

"The next quadrille, Count?" Francesca's cousin asked.

"Oui, Mademoiselle Chalmers." Then Philippe bowed to Francesca. "Mademoiselle Wallingford, may I sit beside you when next we dine?"

"Yes, of course." She smiled at him and then at Lillian, whose lips sealed into a thin line. They joined the other couples for the dance, and Francesca sank onto the empty chair at last.

She almost felt her feet sigh with relief, but her heart pounded. Where was Elizabeth? She tried to spot the shade of robin's egg blue amid the silk and taffeta that spangled the already opulent room.

Despite Count Philippe's request to dine next to her, Francesca wanted to stomp from the room. Her orchestrated plan had crumbled. She'd lost Elizabeth, her feet had been sorely abused, and Lillian's watchful eyes glared at her from the dance. Someone's giggle made Francesca grit her teeth.

But then she smiled. There was Elizabeth at the opposite end of the ballroom, her hands clasped in front of her as she stood before a vivid mural. Nary a hair had escaped its proper place, and her face glowed as she spoke with someone. Francesca couldn't see the speaker because of a woman's elaborate feather headpiece that blocked her view.

Elizabeth chatted as if she'd found an old friend. This did not bode well. Had her maid forgotten their carefully constructed plan, which involved Elizabeth trying to remain inconspicuous? Francesca didn't know whether to dash across the room at once, or pray for help. Or do both at once. She could find an excuse to whisk Elizabeth out the nearby glass door that led to what she assumed was a balcony. The air in here was full of perfume, and warmth radiated from silk-covered figures promenading around the ballroom.

Then, the wearer of the fabulous feathers moved. A figure with hair the color of dark copper and wearing an elegantly cut waistcoat bowed to Elizabeth, then walked toward the large glass double doors that Francesca had selected as an escape route.

Francesca stood. She needed air. She also needed to find out how Elizabeth fared and get a glimpse of this mystery man.

"Elizabeth, are you all right?"

"Yes, miss." Elizabeth's glance darted to either side. She placed one of her gloved hands over her mouth.

"No matter. I don't think anyone heard you, with all the music." Francesca moved closer. "Has anyone discovered you?"

"I don't believe so. Two women who addressed me only spoke French, and another pair, well, I wasn't sure if I answered their questions correctly." A line appeared between her eyebrows.

"What did they ask you?"

"How long I was staying in Paris, and if I'd been to any recent parties." She wrung her hands. "I'm afraid I sounded rather dull. I don't even know whose home we are at."

"This is the home of Count de la Croix and his mother. I thought I had told you. But you did well. Except. . ." Francesca frowned. "Who was that man you were speaking with just now?"

"A Mr. Finley, I believe. Most friendly. But somehow, he seemed to know I don't belong here."

∽

The night air greeted Alfred Finley as he exited the stuffy ballroom. He shouldn't have come, but Mother had insisted, and when she insisted on something, only God could stand in her way, and she wouldn't argue with Him. So Alfred humored her and brought her to the ball. Last he knew, she sat comfortably, chatting with Countess de la Croix.

Mother, the sweet woman, was trying to marry him off before she left this life. She'd even said so. The thought made him smile even as the thought of losing the one person in this world who loved him most made his throat hurt. Not that her health was a real concern, although she seemed to get out of breath easily and likely would not dance tonight.

He had danced but one dance, then waited beside a painted wall. A number of dances passed, and he found himself speaking with a young woman who reminded him of a young filly, ready to bolt from the room. She nearly tripped over her hem of her blue dress more than once.

After a hesitant introduction, he discovered she did not speak French, and she spoke quite plainly. What made him pay even closer attention was the fact that the Miss Elizabeth McGovern had accompanied a Miss Francesca Wallingford that evening.

He also knew that the name McGovern was the name of the family who served the Wallingfords, and Miss McGovern had calloused fingers that clasped and twisted a worn pair of gloves. What had Fran gone and done?

The young girl Francesca had moods as unpredictable as the wind, and both Alfred and her brother James had enjoyed taunting her when they were children. But the idea of bringing a maid to the ball? Nothing good could come of the escapade. And poor Miss McGovern would return to her mundane life on the morrow.

A light breeze lifted Alfred's wonderful auburn hair as Francesca approached him. She felt thirteen again, all legs and arms and feet, and well aware of the childish infatuation she'd had with her one-time family friend. His dark eyes seemed to know her and sense her slightly improper thoughts about his hair. And the scar on the left eyebrow marring an otherwise appealing countenance? *She'd* been responsible for that scar once upon a time.

"Mr. . .Mr. Finley?" Her first impulse had been to shriek the man's first name and embrace him as if he were James. Mother would be proud of her self-control tonight, if perplexed at her letting the count speak to any woman but her.

Alfred reached for her gloved hand, and raised it to his lips, barely brushing them on the back of her glove. "You are well?"

"Yes, yes, I am quite well, thank you." Unspoken questions battled in her mind until they silenced each other. She clutched her hands in front of her.

"Fran—"

"Alfred—"

They both spoke at once then laughed. The noise made a man and woman walking along the balcony turn and stride the other way.

"I never thought I'd see. . ." Francesca started. But the man before her was now a stranger. His smile disappeared, and he appeared to assess her.

"What brings you here tonight?" he asked.

"My parents know the de la Croix family, and wanted to make sure the family was adequately represented this evening." That was all the explanation she would give him before she knew the intent of his question.

"So you have come on your own?"

"No. My. . .Miss Elizabeth McGovern has accompanied me. And my brother and his wife are here, somewhere." She should be the one asking questions. Not this pointless quizzing.

"Interesting, Miss Elizabeth's last name."

"Why is that?" Francesca's pulse hammered in her throat. He knew. Would he tell James? This had been a bad idea, a very bad idea indeed, borne from idleness and dissatisfaction, and the consequences would be entirely her fault.

"Is her family still in your family's employ? I seem to remember her mother was wont to spoil the fun of the Wallingford children." He glanced over her shoulder toward the glass door behind her. "But the fact Miss McGovern is here tonight. Is it customary for—"

"The *help* to dress like one of the family?" The cool night air teased Francesca's hot cheeks. "No, it is not. And her presence here tonight is truly none of your concern."

Alfred let out what sounded like something between a cough and a snort. "Really, you almost sounded like your mother. Did she scheme to make sure you were introduced to the count?"

Francesca clutched her skirt. No wonder he'd gotten that scar as a young man. Served him right, taunting her that she was too inexperienced a rider to take the fence. Of course he followed her and landed up in a bush with some nasty cuts, but no one had ordered him to chase her on horseback.

"I'm not privy to my mother's schemes. If you must know, I am eighteen now and am capable of making my own decisions."

He shook his head. "So says the lovely bird in the gilded cage. And I am sorry for ruffling your feathers. I shouldn't have spoken in that manner, after not seeing you for so long. My memories of our childhood are pleasant."

"As are mine." Francesca could not think of what else to say, but unclenched her hands and smoothed her skirt.

"When will you return to New York?" The moonlight showed his sheepish look. "Your family still has a city residence, don't they?"

Francesca took a deep breath. A gilded cage, indeed. "We will be departing Paris soon and travel to London; then we depart from London next week for New York. But this summer we'll be in Newport. My father has overseen the building of our new summer cottage, Seaside, and the home is finished at last."

"My plans are nearly the same as yours. Construction on Tranquility is nearly completed, and it needs decorating and my mother's attentions. So I am sure we shall see each other often." With this, Alfred smiled, and she glimpsed the boy on the brink of manhood who'd teased her years ago.

"I'm certain we shall." She let Alfred take her hand. But then there was the count, probably still dancing a quadrille with Lillian.

"There you are, my dear!" Victoria's voice rang out across the balcony. "Mother said you would be coming tonight as well. And where is Elizabeth?"

Alfred gave Francesca a pointed look, the corners of his mouth twitching.

Now Francesca's feet really hurt, and she couldn't even run from her sister-in-law's question.

She turned to face her sister-in-law in time to see Elizabeth emerge from the ballroom, with James on her heels. Alfred was probably enjoying this spectacle.

Francesca squared her shoulders and said, "James, I can explain," just as she had many times in the past.

Chapter 2

Newport, Rhode Island
June 1895

Rain pounded the windows of Seaside's library, and Francesca frowned as she stared through the drops streaming down the panes. She'd barely had a chance to see the new gardens or discover the path to the sea walk—a path that Father said he'd ordered constructed with her in mind. Her paints she'd brought from Paris still lay untouched in their case, a gift from Count Philippe.

His attentions in Paris had made her head spin, but before her return to America, she'd seen a glance or two he exchanged with Lillian Chalmers. Probably after whispers that Francesca had brought her *maid* to his party. She wasn't quite sure about the whispers, but the sound of Mother's outrage no doubt carried for miles.

Now Francesca's head hurt at remembering seeing Alfred's transformation from the image of a young man she'd carried in her memory. Propriety insisted that she not inquire about exactly what had sent him away so long ago. But their conversation suggested he wouldn't have minded her asking. Yet his demeanor at the ball also made her feel like a spoiled child.

Alfred's words came back to her. A *lovely bird in a gilded cage*. Francesca moved from the cushioned bench upon which she'd reclined and paced the gallery's balcony. Someone had lit a fire in the massive granite fireplace at the opposite end of the library's lower level. Francesca preferred the seclusion, especially since the family's return from Europe.

"Father above, I thank You that Elizabeth has kept her position. Forgive my selfishness. I did not think about what would happen, should Elizabeth be discovered. She only wanted some fun, and I wanted to see the night through someone else's eyes." Francesca sighed. James had gone straightaway to Mother after the ball, and it was only due to Father's intervention that Elizabeth's entire family was not dismissed.

"Nonsense. Good help is hard to find, and this is all because of Francesca's high-spiritedness," Father had said.

Francesca had not seen Elizabeth in the week since the family had moved to Newport for the summer. All her mother would reveal was that Elizabeth would be assisting in caring for the family's laundering "until further notice."

According to Mother, Francesca's idleness was to blame for the whole fiasco, to be sure. Mother insisted on filling Francesca's time with tennis lessons, luncheons, sailing, horsemanship, and art classes. The art classes and riding she didn't mind so much, but although she enjoyed her various gowns and riding habits, the idea of changing her wardrobe several times a day made her want to don a bathing suit and run screaming down to the edge of the ocean.

"Consuelo Vanderbilt will not outstrip you in your pursuits," Mother had insisted. "Despite your deplorable behavior in Paris, we shall make sure you find an acceptable match."

But then Consuelo was a Vanderbilt, and even Francesca knew the Wallingfords' bank account couldn't outstrip the Vanderbilts'.

"Yes, Alfred, you're right." Francesca stopped at the gallery's railing and clutched the polished wood. She could still smell the oil worked into the grain, and the brass fittings that held the railing together gleamed. "My cage is gilded."

Eighteen and introduced to society meant her parents, especially Mother, had plans.

"What am I to do?" Her voice echoed off the bookshelves and was only answered by the crackling in the fireplace. Perhaps if Mother's intentions bore fruit, Francesca would wed the count. She would live in Paris, of course, and gain a title by their marriage. But what if the count's enchanting manners made a polished cover for a dark heart?

Francesca touched her throat as if a hangman's noose had tightened its grip. The curious fluttering in her chest occurred again.

She should appreciate her station in life. At church on Sunday, the minister spoke about remembering "the least of these." Surely, she could help someone less fortunate than herself. But look how she'd tried to help Elizabeth. Now *that* had turned out to be a disaster. Perhaps the Lord had something else in mind, something more practical.

The main door of the library opened, and men's voices filled the room. Francesca had no way to exit, save the small, narrow staircase that led to the upper gallery. She took refuge again at her little cushioned bench. Perhaps during a lull in conversation she might sneak down the stairs and beg her leave discreetly.

"So tell me, young Mr. Finley, what is so important that you would brave the weather to discuss with me today?" said Father. "You could have sent word and come another time."

Alfred! Now Francesca dared not leave, even discreetly. The memory of her humiliation in Paris made her cheeks burn even now.

"As you know, we in this room have received many blessings from God because of our hard work." This older Alfred sounded confident, as if he were addressing an equal. "It's my determination to seek ways that we can benefit humanity."

"You're quite right," Father responded. "Although I like to think I had more to do with my success than the Almighty. Many men do not rise to a state such as ours, though they labor their entire lives. If labor must always lead to God-given success, then all who labor should live as kings. Yet one man still rises higher than another, and I feel it is more due to human effort than Providence."

"I am sorry you feel that way, as if financial numbers trump success. I know I have been gone these last several years, but in my travels I have met a number of people whose lot in life is not as ours, but all the same they have contentment befitting royalty."

"Shall we sit down? You, too, James. Victoria will keep, my son." Father chuckled.

Footsteps fell softly on the woven carpet that covered the parquet floor of the library, and Francesca guessed that the three men had taken their seats on the upholstered chairs, a pair that faced each other and the third that faced the fire.

"Cigar?" Father asked.

"No, sir."

"Very well."

"Alfred, my old friend," James said. "Tell us what has become of you all this time, and what has compelled you to return to our circle."

"A long story. You know why I left." At this, Alfred hesitated, and Francesca heard only the pop of a burning log. "I thought it best to save my mother the shame, and spare her the ever-present reminders of the past by my very presence. Then word came to me just over a year ago that she had become ill, and I knew I could stay away no longer."

Mrs. Finley, ill? Francesca recalled the sweet woman who used to frequent the Wallingford home along with her son. After Alfred's sudden departure, those visits stopped as well.

Francesca crept to the balcony railing, where it met a corner of a bookshelf, and settled herself in the nook to watch. Unless one of them looked directly up to where she stood, they would not see her.

"The people I spoke of, with success beyond that which is measured in dollars, lived simply. Reverend Stone and his wife first knew me as Alfred Wadsworth. Upon my arrival in Colorado, I used my mother's name before her marriage. I did not wish to reveal my identity as Alfred Finley until I realized that no one in Colorado cared whether I was Finley or Wadsworth. I rented a room from the Stones, and all the while I remained under their roof, I observed that they lived richly."

The smell of cigar smoke made Francesca's throat tickle. She swallowed. Alfred, renting a room and working as a laborer? But then he always cared for his own horse, and never thought himself above cleaning a stall, not like so many of those who never lifted a finger to care for their own mounts. Francesca's own father had demanded she know the skills of horse care, in the event she was out riding and a mishap should occur. But the Finleys had fewer staff than most large households. She forced her attention back to the conversation and tried to clear her throat without making a sound.

". . .assumed control of my father's affairs once his death had been confirmed, and I merely stepped into the position upon my return to New York."

"There are some who question your legal right to that position and its—shall we say, assets?" A tendril of smoke rose from Father's lit cigar; Father's right arm casually draped on the armrest, his figure hidden from view by the high-backed chair.

"I would appear in any court of law if anyone dared contest that right," said Alfred. He leaned forward in his chair, the fire making his dark hair glow. Francesca smiled.

"Now, now"—Father gestured with his cigar—"no reason to be testy. I was simply making an observation, and you've no doubt considered that possibility with returning to New York. So, tell us about what you envision."

"I would like to use some of my resources to begin a foundation to help send young men, and even young women, from such families as the one with whom I lived, for university training."

A foundation, intended even to help young women go to the university? Francesca wanted to be leaning against the back of Father's chair and asking questions herself.

"You don't say. I suppose you've come to me to ask for my support as well." Francesca could see smoke ring drift toward the ceiling and fade away.

"Yes, actually. There are hundreds, probably thousands of young people who deserve a chance to have an education." Alfred stood and moved to stand closer to the fire. He reached for a poker and jabbed at a wayward burning log.

"I admit your idea sounds intriguing," said James. "But how would we select who is deserving? And how would we know they would succeed and not merely be taking advantage of an opportunity for their own selfish reasons and not for the greater good?"

"My son is right." Father stood and faced the fire. "We would need to develop criteria for screening. They must be excellent scholars already, and must not be ruffians or rabble-rousers. They must be willing to work, as well."

"So you're in favor of supporting this idea?" Alfred asked. He stared at Father, who glanced at the chair where James still sat.

Francesca wanted to say, "Help him, Father! Say yes!" But she kept silent. The earlier tickle in her throat came back, and she fought back the urge to clear her throat. Would that she had access to her financial assets, she would ask the banker to send some of it to Alfred to help him begin his new venture.

As it was, her throat rebelled and let out something between a squeak and a small grunt. Alfred's gaze flicked to the balcony, and Francesca froze when his eyes locked with hers. He turned his attention back to her father.

"Mr. Finley, I'll have to say I would like to give this matter serious consideration." Obviously Father hadn't heard the noise. Francesca let out her breath.

Alfred gave Francesca another glance, and this time she smiled at him and nodded. He looked down at the hearth. "Thank you, sir. It's good to know you will consider joining me. I have seen both sides of the world. Like the Apostle Paul, I have been abased, and I have known abundance. And through those good people, I learned contentment."

James rose from his chair. "I'm glad you've returned, my friend. I regret we didn't get to speak more until now. We'll have to discuss this foundation in more detail. Perhaps others will join us."

Francesca realized Alfred wasn't going to look up toward her again, so she moved back to her bench. The men chatted more about the sailboat James wanted to purchase, and Father remarked about the rain letting up soon and invited Alfred to stay for a cup of tea and join the ladies in the parlor. The library door opened, and the men's voices drifted into the hallway; then the door shut again. Francesca made her way downstairs and tiptoed from the library.

She nearly collided with Mother in the great hallway paved in marble. "Mother, you gave me a start."

"There you are, young lady. The seamstress is arriving soon for your fitting. I told her no matter what the weather, I wanted her here." Mother's sunshine yellow gown fit her mood. "We have less than two weeks until our first party in our new home, and I will not be outdone by Mrs. Astor. Your father ordered tea in the parlor, but I told him we would otherwise be occupied. Besides, that Finley fellow is here, and I don't feel like entertaining him."

Francesca ignored the barb about Alfred and tried not to grit her teeth. "About the guest list. How many are coming?" Francesca knew Mother had been in a tizzy, preparing for a grand party to welcome the local residents of Newport to the Wallingfords' new home, but the sting of her summer schedule had preoccupied her thoughts.

"No less than one hundred. It's about all we can prepare for on short notice, but I didn't want to have too small of a guest list. Mrs. McGovern is contacting a florist, and I must give her a count for the caterer."

They passed the portrait of her parents, now hung on the wall where anyone could see it upon entering Seaside. The recently finished painting had taken most of the winter to complete, and Francesca had savored every moment of watching the artist work. Her mother considered painting a worthy avocation, but not to be pursued, as the career of an artist itself was equal to that of an actor or a musician.

"Thank you, but I must be going." Alfred and James entered the hallway from the parlor. Alfred shook James's hand. "Perhaps I can return the favor and invite your family to join me for an outing."

An outing! Francesca wanted to clap like a little girl, but she felt Mother's glare radiate across the hall and strike Alfred. But her old friend didn't flinch.

Father emerged as well and clapped Alfred on the back. "I understand you need to leave. The rain should be over soon."

"Mr. Wallingford, I require your assistance in the drawing room," Mother said and nudged Father's elbow. "Francesca?"

"I'll be right along, Mother."

"Very well. Don't dally." With that, her parents continued along the hall.

James eyed her curiously, and he shot a glance at Alfred. "I'll see you again soon." He strode toward the grand staircase in the entry hall.

"Miss Wallingford." Alfred gave a slight bow and extended his arm for Francesca. She cast a look toward her parents at the other end of the hall. Mother's arms moved like a windmill, and Father kept up a steady nod as they headed the other way.

"Mr. Finley. I apologize for listening to your conversation earlier, in the library."

"I believe we had you trapped."

"That you did." Her face burned. "Well, I should like to say that I like your idea very much. If I had access to my funds, I would help immediately."

"How generous of you." He smiled at her. "So, how have you been occupied since your arrival here?"

"Mother has planned my summer for me, nearly every waking moment." Francesca sighed. "You were right about the gilded cage, though."

"Gilded cage?" Alfred frowned.

"In Paris. You spoke of me as a bird in a gilded cage." They paused at the foot of the staircase.

"Oh. So I did. I am very sorry. I shouldn't have done that." A slant of pale sunlight reached through the stained glass that graced the top of the main doorway and touched Alfred's hair.

"At first I was taken aback by the statement, but I understand what you meant." She withdrew her hand from the crook of his arm, and her fingers felt cold. "So, Mr. Finley, how have you come to acquire the means to start a foundation?" Francesca dared not mention that the rumors said he'd left their circle with nary a penny.

"Good investments put in place by my late father, which I then reinvested in shipping. Steamships have led to speedier imports and such." He smiled at her. "I'm thankful I had something to come home to." He looked as though he wished to say more and instead thought better of it.

"Your mother is ill, I understand?"

"She had a hard winter, but her health improved enough so that she wanted to spend spring in Paris. And this summer, I expect that her health will improve all the more now that she will be moving into Tranquility. She is in good spirits."

"I shall be sure to remember her in my prayer time." Francesca placed her hand on Alfred's arm, and he covered it with one of his own.

"Thank you. I am glad to hear it."

"Francesca!" Mother's shrill voice echoed down the hallway.

Holmes, the doorman, appeared with Alfred's hat. "Mr. Finley."

"Until next time," said Alfred. Holmes opened the front door for him, leaving Francesca to gather her skirt and see what Mother wanted. Her pulse pounded at the feeling of Alfred's hand on her own. Completely improper, but oh so nice. She hoped her cheeks weren't too flushed as she dashed along the hallway.

Chapter 3

Enrico, you are a master artist and undiscovered genius." Alfred leaned back to get a better view of the artist working on the large mural in the dining room of Tranquility. The scene, a sweeping view of a Western plain with the Rocky Mountains rising in the distance, wasn't typical of the murals seen in other homes. Alfred had wanted a dramatic reminder of God's natural artistry, and all he had brought with him was a dull photograph. Yet Enrico had brought the West to life on Tranquility's dining room wall.

"*Grazie*, Signore Finley. The colors are correct, yes?" The man, barely five years older than Alfred, looked down from the scaffolding that rose to the tall ceiling.

"They're just as I remember them." The memory of the West's grandeur resonated inside Alfred, and nothing matched it save the ocean that roared but a hundred yards or so from his home.

"I will finish soon. I promise. But I might need more paint." Enrico turned back to face the wall and picked up his brush.

"I'll make sure you have the supplies you need." Alfred moved along the scaffolding to study the lower part of the painting. "Have you ever thought of selling your paintings anywhere besides in New York? Many people would pay you well for a portrait."

Truly, just as elegant as anything he'd seen in Italy. While some of his associates commissioned artists in Europe, Alfred had found Enrico selling his small oil paintings on a New York City curb. He immediately recognized the man's talent, and asked him to come to Newport to paint the murals for Tranquility. Alfred spared himself the expense of "importing" talent, and he hoped that Enrico's display of ability would bring money and recognition to the artist and his family—a small way that Alfred could make a difference and money well spent.

"*Sì*, once or twice. But my English is not so good and I do not know how much to ask. I knock on a door, they will turn me away, thinking I beg." Enrico's voice echoed in the nearly empty room.

"If you would like to paint portraits, I would be glad to help you find families who seek a good artist."

Footsteps in the hallway outside grew louder. O'Neal, Alfred's assistant, appeared with a folded piece of paper. O'Neal's father had been in the employ of Alfred's father, and upon Alfred's return to New York, he'd found the younger O'Neal in need of a position.

"Yes, O'Neal?" Never Jonathan. Just O'Neal. Alfred had addressed him by his first name only once. The poor fellow had practically grabbed the nearest chair and mopped his brow with a handkerchief.

O'Neal gave Alfred a nod and handed him the paper. "From Mr. James Wallingford."

"Thank you very much." Alfred popped open the seal as O'Neal vanished from the room. Tennis and lunch on Friday. He considered that for a moment. He was due to travel back to New York on Friday, but he supposed he could leave on Saturday instead.

He'd never wanted to play the games of the society in which he traveled. But if he were to gain any support for the Finley Humanitarian Foundation, he didn't know what else to do. And James was his friend, so he knew his friend's motives. The idea that he might see Francesca poked his mind.

"Enrico?"

The sound of a paintbrush being dabbed on a wall ceased. "Sì, Signore Finley?"

"We'll be leaving for New York on Saturday morning."

"My mama will be happy to see me."

"As will mine." Alfred had promised once the furniture arrived, he would move his mother from their Manhattan home to Tranquility. He had French doors installed along the seaside view of Tranquility, on both the first and second levels of the house. He could picture Mother taking her breakfast in this room—or her own private sitting room on the next floor above—and then sitting outside to enjoy the morning sun and fresh air with a cup of tea.

Alfred stepped onto the patio and stopped to recheck a door handle before he focused on the view before him. One of the workers could tighten this, or Alfred could just do it himself. He might forget to add the loose handle to the list of items to do before he proclaimed Tranquility complete. But then he had no tools. Alfred studied the patio paved with blocks of gray granite. They'd hold up well to the elements and still look elegant.

Mother could scarcely wait to see the home, just as he could scarcely wait to move to Tranquility for the remainder of the season. New York City was still close enough to take a train if the relaxed atmosphere of Newport slowed him down too much. He could work here on occasion, and most of the gentlemen with whom he needed to do business were at their Newport "cottages."

The very name attached to the grand homes that lined the coast at Newport made the corners of Alfred's lips twitch. Most people thought of a cottage as a simple home by the beach, sometimes no more than one small room with a makeshift kitchen and simple sleeping area. Alfred shook his head.

The sea breeze wiggled the edge of the invitation in Alfred's hand and caught his attention. The Wallingfords had known the Finleys longer than he had been alive, and he considered James the brother he never had. While James had corresponded with Alfred during his years of absence, his friend's mother, along with some of the set with whom both families associated, deemed Alfred a pariah.

Shortly before Alfred finished at boys' school, a Mr. Cromwell, Mother's family friend from Boston, made an appearance. His hair had the same curious tinge of red as Alfred's. Alfred was never sure when the whispers started, and Mother refused to tell him why. And while Father was still alive, he had refuted what claims he could.

The old feelings swirled inside Alfred. He squeezed his hands into fists, and the paper in his right hand crumpled. No one had listened then, and the rage of youth had done nothing to help him. In fact, it only drew more attention to his hair. No one seemed to care that Mother's hair, though golden, had a reddish cast in the sun. Alfred realized Mother was right to tell him some battles were not his to fight, and Father helped him pack carefully for the trip west.

"The space will do you good, son. There will be time enough one day for you to take the reins of what I have set up for you."

Now after Alfred's return, James had turned into an ally. If James had tennis and lunch in mind, then tennis and lunch it would be. Alfred's thoughts drifted to Francesca. Always in her brother's shadow when they were younger, she'd been heartbroken when the two young men went to Yale, and then Alfred left for Colorado. Francesca's blithe spirit hadn't changed over time.

But what had caused Francesca to put a ball gown on her maid and whisk her to a Paris party? Cruelty, it was, to tempt a young woman with a life she would likely never have. Alfred had seen it often enough, the wistful glances of some of the "help," as they were called, right alongside the resigned expressions of those who "knew their place."

Was Francesca's escapade an attempt to demonstrate the superficiality of their station? Her words on that rainy day had touched his heart, that if she had a means to give toward the Finley Foundation, she would do so.

Alfred wondered, too, if her escapade was just that—a young woman's silly trifling. Francesca had always been prone to impulsivity. He touched the scar on his eyebrow, recalling the fateful day when she'd baited him when they were much younger. He'd seen some of that same spirit that evening in Paris.

In matters of the heart, however, Alfred didn't care to trifle. Nor did he see it as business, as some of his associates were wont to do.

The sound of a throat clearing behind him made Alfred turn to see O'Neal in the doorway.

"Sir, have you decided on a response to Mr. Wallingford's request?"

"Yes, O'Neal. Please send word to James Wallingford that I shall be glad to attend tennis and lunch on Friday."

"Straightaway, Mr. Finley." O'Neal inclined his head slightly and turned on his heel.

Business on Friday. It may be a light sport and a luncheon, but Alfred knew the game. And he would most certainly play.

∞

The midmorning sun had edged higher over the tennis court at the Newport Casino, and Francesca missed the ball. Again. Today's match would not be won by her. Victoria, her sister-in-law, grinned in triumph at Francesca across the net.

Despite the fact she had pictured Alfred's face on the ball, she still missed. The one time her racquet did connect, she'd blasted the ball over to where the men sat, discussing the boring things that men often did.

She wished she didn't want to join them to sit at Alfred's side. Thoroughly improper.

Now Victoria prepared to serve one last time. "Here it comes."

Francesca gritted her teeth. Perhaps she had a chance to save the match and her dignity. She watched the ball. Swung.

The racquet sent the ball directly into the net.

"I win!" Victoria dropped her racquet and clapped her hands.

"Next time, I promise I will not make it so easy for you." Francesca moved to the net and picked up the wayward ball from the court.

"My dear Francesca." Mother's voice echoed across the court. "You are certainly off your game this morning. Are you unwell?"

"I am well, but it has been a warm morning." She dabbed at her forehead.

"Here." Victoria joined her at the net and reached across for the ball. "I will put our equipment away. You look a mite peaked."

"Come sit in the shade." Mother patted the empty seat beside her. "You are overexerting yourself and will doubtless get freckles."

Francesca might as well have been a seven-year-old wearing long braids as she trudged to the area cloaked in shade. She tried to sit on the empty chair without using an unladylike posture.

"Elizabeth, we require your assistance." Mother's voice made the men glance in the women's direction.

"Yes, ma'am." Elizabeth, now clad in her customary maid's garb, emerged to stand by their table. Her gaze darted to Francesca, who gave her a nod and a smile. At least Elizabeth's mother, Mrs. McGovern, hadn't attended with them. Mother's "second in command" at Seaside liked to run the house while Mother spent the money.

"Lemonade for Francesca and Victoria." Mother waved as if Elizabeth were a stray fly.

"Straightaway, ma'am." Elizabeth gave a little curtsy and turned away from them.

Memories of Paris jabbed like barbs at Francesca. Elizabeth's excitement at seeing a real party and wearing a fine gown. Her smile as she spoke about her conversation with Alfred. A night when Elizabeth almost seemed like another young woman attending a grand ball with a friend.

"Thank you, Mother, for removing Elizabeth from working in the laundry. I have missed her working in the house."

"So long as you remember what her true place is in our home, and that you remember yours."

"I promise never to do anything like I did in Paris again. It was unkind to Elizabeth." Other words wanted to form themselves on Francesca's lips, but she restrained herself. Ladies must *always* restrain themselves.

"Very well." Mother fanned her face. "Perhaps a luncheon outdoors was unwise. You are right; it is warm."

Francesca allowed her gaze to travel to the table where the men sat. James and Alfred chuckled over something, much as they had when they were younger. She hadn't seen James laugh like that in a long time. Francesca found her own smile creeping across her face. Then Alfred glanced her way, and she felt like she'd been playing tennis nonstop for an hour.

"Your lemonades. The lunch you ordered will be served soon." Elizabeth placed a tray on the table and presented Francesca and Victoria with their drinks. Then she disappeared again before Francesca could express her thanks.

Victoria sat at the empty chair with a glass of lemonade on the table in front of it. She took a sip. "Delicious."

Francesca picked up her own glass and enjoyed the sweet tartness. Another look toward Alfred with her traitorous eyes. Mother noticed everything, and doubtless she would see Francesca's wandering gaze.

"I know what you are thinking, my dear." Mother laid a gloved hand on one of Francesca's.

"You do?" Francesca sipped her lemonade.

"You are thinking of the count, I am sure."

Francesca's throat caught, and she coughed. The lemonade stung as it hit the inside of her nose. She snatched the napkin from her lap and pressed it to her mouth.

"Fran, are you all right?" Victoria rose from her chair.

Francesca nodded. Now her eyes burned with a few tears from the shock of choking on her drink.

"Oh, my dramatic daughter." Mother shook her head. "Please, be careful. I did not intend for my keen observation to distress you."

"I'm. . ." Francesca coughed and glanced toward the men. Alfred's brow furrowed ever so slightly as he regarded her. "I'm all right."

Mother followed Francesca's glance, and then she made something like a grunting noise. "I know that you made quite an impression on him that night, despite your unwise actions. In fact, I received a letter from Count de la Croix's mother just this morning." The volume of her voice rose with each phrase.

The fifth commandment flickered through Francesca's mind, although honoring her mother was not the urge she possessed at that moment. She lowered the napkin from her mouth and folded it neatly.

She found her voice again. "Are they well?"

"Yes, yes, and they are coming to New York shortly, and then likely will tour Newport." Mother leaned closer. "And you will *not* entertain any thoughts of resuming your friendship with that. . .that Mr. Finley. The count must believe you have suitable prospects, and that will raise his interest."

"But. . ." Francesca wanted to say she and Alfred had not even found much of an opportunity to speak with each other, not as much as she'd like. But the possibilities. The possibilities lingered between her and Alfred even now, from his unspoken concern for her current discomfort, back to the shared glances in the library. Times like this, she would cast off propriety but for the scandal it would cause.

"Mother Wallingford," Victoria started to say. "Surely there is no harm—"

"There is no harm now," Mother interjected. "Of course not. I realize they've barely seen each other. However, Francesca has been launched, and her father and I want what is best for her, and that is not to follow childish whims."

At the word *launched*, Francesca felt as if she were rigged with sails instead of wearing her new tennis dress. Fortunately, she hadn't had a bottle cracked over her stern.

"I think that we would make a good match," Francesca ventured. "While it is true that I find Philippe most agreeable, and he seems like a kind man—"

"*Philippe*? You are calling him by his first name?" Mother fanned herself more rapidly. "Did he ask you this?"

"Yes, yes. He did so the night of the party."

"Well, we shall be sure to invite him and his mother to Newport. Surely they will be in attendance at other events this summer season." She sounded almost triumphant.

"Lillian did manage to secure the count's attentions that night also, you should know."

Mother brushed away Francesca's comment with her free hand. "That is of no consequence. Your cousin's family has nothing to offer him. I have the utmost affection for my sister, but I cannot see her current station helping her to gain a count for a son-in-law."

Their luncheon arrived, cucumber soup and tiny sandwiches and sherbet to cool off the warm noon hour. Instead of responding to her mother's comment about Lillian's family, Francesca ate her soup, hoping the cold concoction would reduce the heat inside her.

Victoria began a conversation concerning other parties of the season, and while Francesca knew Victoria liked to dance as much as any young woman did, parties had never been her favorite diversion. She excused herself.

"Where are you going?" Mother asked.

"I shall be but a few moments." Francesca walked the path from the tennis court to the side entryway of the building. She found Elizabeth in the hall.

"Elizabeth."

The maid froze and turned to face her. "Miss Francesca." She inclined her head slightly and smiled.

"Thank you for getting us the lemonade. I wanted to tell you so earlier, but you left the tableside quickly."

"I am doing my job, miss. And, honestly, your mother gives me a fright sometimes and makes me afraid I might drop something." Elizabeth bit her lip.

"About Paris. . ." Francesca felt as if a chasm opened in the marble floor between them.

"I had the prettiest night of my life, and I will always remember it." She moved as if to turn back toward the kitchen area, then paused.

"What is it, Elizabeth?"

"The young man with the coppery hair at the table today. He was there that night in Paris, and spoke to me."

"Yes. He is a family friend."

"I hope you don't mind me saying, miss, but he has a good heart. He treated me as if I belonged, even when I wasn't well spoken as a grand lady. I know your family has plans for you, but I thought I'd let you know."

"I know. He does have a good heart. At least, I believe so." Francesca smiled. Perhaps the chasm between them wasn't so wide after all.

A clatter from the kitchen at the end of the hallway made them both look.

"I must go. But I will help you prepare for your nap this afternoon."

"No, please. I'll be fine." Francesca tried to reassure the young woman. They couldn't return to the way things were before Paris and Francesca's crazy scheme.

"Very well, miss. I'll see you before supper." Elizabeth turned and headed toward where the sound of the noise had come.

Francesca had wanted to apologize about Elizabeth's punishment, but some things she just couldn't atone for. She sighed. She might as well return to the group outside before Mother came to find her.

She turned the corner and nearly ran into Alfred.

⚭

The sherbet had done little to cool Alfred's mood. What had begun as a leisurely late morning business conversation with James and the elder Mr. Wallingford had ended with a distraction.

And that distraction had nearly collided with him in the hallway as he went to retrieve his hat.

Francesca, her cheeks flushed, skidded to a halt. Her tennis skirt swirled around her ankles. "Al—Mr. Finley. I beg your pardon. I was in a hurry."

"And I should have been paying closer attention to where I was headed."

"You are leaving already?" Her pretty face sank into a frown.

"I must prepare for my return tomorrow to New York for business."

"How. . .how did your business fare this morning? With James and Father?"

"Quite well, quite well. I see that the young woman who accompanied you in Paris is in her place once again."

Francesca's face darkened. "Yes. She is. I am thankful she didn't lose her position."

"Please promise me you will never do anything like that again."

"You sound almost like my mother." She placed her hands on her hips.

"But my motivation for asking such a promise is different."

"How so?"

"That young woman likely is taunted every day by a life she will never have, and it was not right of you to fill her head with dreams." Truly, he didn't understand why he must explain to her.

"She told me it was the prettiest night of her life and she would always remember it."

"When I found her she was nearly in tears from the rudeness of two women who made fun of her extremely poor French. And you were gallivanting about the ballroom—"

"I was not gallivanting." She touched his sleeve. "And I have already asked forgiveness for my actions. If you must know, Elizabeth and I were only having a bit of fun. I was rather tired of the pretentiousness around me and wanted to view the room through fresh eyes—Elizabeth's."

He stared at her hand on his sleeve. "And in the morning, she had to return to her regular position of serving and being invisible until she was needed."

"I. . .I don't know why I feel I must explain my actions to you, of all people."

"And now *you* are the one who sounds like her mother."

Francesca, her face red, darted to the side and passed him. The grand door to the outside opened, letting a glare of light into the cool hallway.

Alfred turned and watched the door close behind her. That dratted temper of his. If only he hadn't overheard snatches of conversation about the count. Did Francesca mean she'd thought she and the count would make a good match? Or him? He used quick strides to find the man who would both obtain his hat and call for his horse.

A large gilded mirror hung in yet another hallway, and Alfred paused. His own cheeks were flushed red. All that talk of the count that had drifted over from the ladies' table, and Alfred had fallen into Mrs. Wallingford's trap without warning. Demonstrations of jealousy would never win Francesca's heart, nor could Alfred's bank account win the Wallingfords' approval. And the last remark about Francesca sounding like her mother? Unconscionable. Somehow he must make amends and prove his worthiness, or his plans for his foundation might be threatened as well.

Chapter 4

S ailing. He's taking us sailing." Francesca danced around her bedroom and tried to remind herself that she was still miffed at Alfred Finley. She had changed her shirtwaist three times and a fourth hung ready on its hanger in the wardrobe. Any of them would go well with her dark blue walking skirt, but today she wanted to look extra special. She flopped onto her elegantly carved bed. The sky blue walls, edged with white molding, lent a peaceful air to the room despite the fact the bed was littered with clothing.

No matter that she couldn't seem to make Alfred understand she'd meant no harm and truly regretted her actions with Elizabeth in Paris. Then there was always the unspoken disapproval from Mother whenever James mentioned his friend. The two had been cooking up something for Alfred's foundation while working in New York, and this weekend Alfred was taking James out on his sailboat. Of course James would pine for Victoria if he left her behind, and so he wanted her to come along also, and of course that meant Victoria wanted Francesca for some feminine company. Mother frowned, but gave her permission to accompany the group.

A knock sounded at her door. "Fran, are you nearly ready? James is having the carriage brought 'round. Mr. Finley has asked us to meet him at the boat slip at nine o'clock."

"One moment, Victoria." Francesca rolled to her feet in a most unladylike manner, but no one else was present to witness the action. She groaned and put on the original shirtwaist of white muslin with dark blue embroidery on the high neck. Her calfskin boots with their high heels must do, as she had nothing else that might be appropriate on the sailboat's deck.

She left the other garments in their disarray and joined Victoria in the hallway. She wore a black skirt with narrow white stripes, and a white frilly shirtwaist. A gauzy bow from her hat was tied under her chin. Sweet and calm, Victoria always managed to make Francesca feel as though her hems were too long and her feet too large. "I'm ready."

Victoria studied her face. "Have you applied rouge or some such nonsense to your cheeks? They look quite rosy."

"Of course not." Francesca stopped short and touched her hair. "Oh, I've forgotten my hat. Pardon me, and I shall fetch it straightaway."

"I will head downstairs." Victoria laughed. "My dear, we're not running from a fire. We'll wait for you. I daresay your anticipation of today's activities has your head spinning."

Francesca skittered back to her room and tried to slow her feet and her racing heart. There. The simple straw hat with its dark blue ribbon would be ideal to ward off freckles, sunburn, and headaches from the sun. She settled it on her head and looked in her mirror as she tied the ribbon. Yes, her cheeks bloomed red, but not from rouge.

This would be a long period of time spent with Alfred, the most since she'd seen him in Paris and knew for certain he had returned. Of course, James and Victoria would be along, as well as the sailors operating the boat. But still.

Perhaps James would even speak to Father, if he saw how well she and Alfred got along. Mother couldn't stand against all of them. Because she knew if Mother had anything to say about it, Alfred would never be a match for Francesca.

She ambled down the grand staircase and joined Victoria. "I'm ready, and calm now, thank you very much. I can scarcely wait to be out on the sea, though."

Victoria linked her arm through Francesca's as they stepped out the front door, held open by Holmes, the doorman. "And I am so glad you will be accompanying me. The men will talk of their stuffy business dealings, and I'm afraid James is still rather the newlywed, as I am."

The family's carriage drew up to the porte cochere and stopped. James hopped out and held the door for them. "A beautiful morning, and off we go, ladies."

Less than twenty minutes later, Francesca found her pulse racing again as they drew up to the Newport marina where Alfred's elegant little sailboat, the *Grey Gull*, waited. Father never had much of an interest in sailing, and James had been too preoccupied with Victoria to get a sailboat.

"You're here." Alfred greeted them with a wide smile as he stepped up onto the pier. "I've brought lunch for us." Several men in white shirts and pants were raising the sail and tying and untying ropes.

Francesca looked up as the sail rose and the *Gull* bobbed where it was tied. She accepted Alfred's offer of his hand to assist her as she stepped down onto the boat. One foot nearly slipped on the deck, but she caught herself in time. Had she lost her footing, she'd likely have ended up in Alfred's arms, and nearly regretted not letting her feet go where they may.

"Miss Fran."

"Mr. Finley." She smiled at him, and he indicated some built-in seating on the sailboat where passengers could enjoy the voyage out of the sailors' way.

"Al, good to see you," James said. "I don't know how you feel, but if I could make my office here instead of New York, I'm afraid I'd want to be sailing or riding instead of at my desk."

"I feel the same way. Which is why I've returned to New York so I can accomplish something with my time." Alfred inclined his head to Victoria. "Mrs. Wallingford."

Francesca glanced at her sister-in-law as she boarded the vessel. It still sounded strange, sometimes, to hear someone besides her mother addressed as Mrs. Wallingford.

They settled into their seats and cast off from the dock. Francesca leaned back on the cushioned seat and loved the sound of the water rushing past, the snap of the breeze hitting the sail.

"Miss Francesca." Alfred took the seat beside her.

Francesca cast a glance at James and Victoria, lost in their own conversation. "Mr. Finley."

"I was happy when I learned you would be permitted to accompany us today." The light wind ruffled his hair, shining dark copper in the sunlight.

"And I can't tell you how happy I was to be allowed to come. The time has never seemed right when we saw each other, and we always seemed to be unable to finish our conversation. That is, I meant to say. . ." Francesca stumbled over her words. "I am sorry you have had the wrong impression. We seem to have started out badly."

"And I am sorry for my assumptions and my earlier words about your actions." Alfred's tone softened. "While there are many years between us, I do know you have a kind heart. You were not maliciously trying to hurt your maid's feelings."

"I was not, truly. But you were correct. I was thoughtless, and for that I am sorry. Elizabeth is doing well, though, and no longer working in the laundry. If I could take back my actions, I would." A gust tugged at her hat, and she gripped it with one free hand.

"I shouldn't have demonstrated my disapproval as I did. Try as I might, I don't always hold my temper. Bad for business, and bad for friendships, my wise mother tells me." Alfred fiddled with his tie, reminding Francesca of a young boy.

"So long as the sun does not go down on your anger." Francesca nodded. "I understand. Oftentimes when I am vexed, my mouth wants to run of its own accord. And I find myself asking God and others for forgiveness later."

They sailed along in silence, and right then Francesca wanted Alfred to take her hand. But he was an honorable man, and likely would not have done so even if James and Victoria weren't there. And they would never be allowed to spend time alone. Unthinkable. She had so many questions to ask him, especially about when he left years ago.

Alfred rose then and headed to the tiller where he addressed the head sailor. "Clement, thank you. I'll take the tiller for a time." He grinned at Francesca, then called out, "Come, stand with me if you wish. I will let you steer."

As the boat skimmed along, Francesca found her feet. How could she resist the invitation? Victoria shot her a sly look.

Sitting on a sailboat was one thing. Trying to stand and then walk was yet another, Francesca discovered. Her stylish boots did not provide secure footing, but somehow she managed her way to where Alfred stood. She hung onto the wood trim on the railing.

"This is a beautiful boat." She clamped her hand onto her hat.

"It was my father's, and I had no idea he owned it until this past winter." He squinted over the water. "So I've been waiting for this chance to take her out. Of course, I let Clement sail her until we get out of the bay. Always best to let an expert take charge."

"I was sorry to hear of your father's passing. Did you get to see him. . ." Francesca bit her lip.

"I was at his side, as was Mother, when he left this life. Mother telegraphed me in Colorado, and I arrived in New York in time."

"For that, I am glad." Francesca recalled Mother's description of the funeral procession on a rainy March day over a year ago, but Mother did not speak of Alfred. "I wanted to ask you some questions, but I'm not sure it's entirely proper."

"If it is one thing I remember best about you, dear Fran, is that you were never quite good at being proper. Although I daresay today even your mother would approve of your behavior." He leaned a bit closer, as if to be conspiratorial. "But ask away."

"When you left, no one would really explain why. And I. . .I missed you." The admission burned her cheeks. "James was finished at university, and he was too busy learning the family business. I also have a suspicion that Mother, Father, or both forbade him to speak about you. All I knew was it had something to do with your father."

Alfred let out a sigh that made him sound like a much older man, with the weight of years pressing upon him. "Rumors and suspicion have a way of gaining a life of their own. Jacob Cromwell is my mother's friend and his hair has a reddish tint. So does my mother's hair. Years ago, they were to be married. Something went awry, and my mother married my father. I knew him always as Uncle Jake. Someone—I still don't know who—made a simple remark about their friendship. Perhaps someone also said Uncle Jake and I have a similar shaped nose."

"How horrible. I am so sorry that you had to leave."

"When Mother explained why I no longer received invitations to the clubhouse activities, I wanted to storm into their lounge and explain the truth to them, that I was always Charles Finley's son and how dare they." Alfred's jaw pulsed.

"I could understand that. How many of them have family members with less than perfect pasts? And your circumstances were based on hearsay." Between hearing the sordid tale and the movement of the sailboat, Francesca felt like her insides had been put in a butter churn. "Sometimes I almost hate this wealth.

I love the clothes and the parties and the baubles, I must admit. But where do we start thinking we are better than others and put on airs because we possess more?"

"Dear Fran, I've upset you, and for that I wish I hadn't told you what little I've confessed to you. Do not hold it against them. Another scandal always has a way of rolling in like a thunderstorm, and the old ones are forgotten by most."

"Except my mother." Francesca frowned. "I wish I could make her see. . ." She stopped before her words betrayed her heart. The whole situation was truly impossible.

"As do I," Alfred said softly. "But do not forget. There is One who far surpasses your mother in authority, and it is He to whom I commit my future."

"I see no other path for me, and I fear my mother especially has already mapped out my future." She didn't want to think about Mother's schemes, not now on this most perfect of days.

"Here, take the tiller. You cannot help but smile when steering a sailboat. The men will do their jobs, but you can command." Alfred placed a hand on Francesca's shoulder, and guided her to stand at the tiller.

Francesca grasped the handle. The boat felt as if it were very much alive under her touch, and wanted to pull its own way. "The current is strong."

"But the wind is stronger, and we will use it to guide the boat where we wish. Hold tight. The *Gull* is a kind sailboat, but even she gets frisky at times."

Alfred was right. Despite her earlier gloomy thoughts, a smile stretched across her face. She glanced toward her brother and sister-in-law. James rose from where he sat and applauded.

"Well done, little sister. And I promise I will not tell Mother." He gave her a wink, and Alfred a nod. "We wouldn't want her to forbid you from attending the Vanderbilts' upcoming ball."

Francesca wished they didn't have to go back to shore. The thought of leaving such freedom behind her felt like a weight. But at least they would all have a picnic together.

∽

Alfred saw the wistful look on Francesca's face in spite of the fact she stood at the *Gull*'s tiller. Perhaps he had said too much, but he at least had wanted to give Francesca some answers.

He'd intended to invite James to join him today, James alone, for an outing to remind them of their childhood antics. That, and to firm up more plans for the foundation. To be sure, the senior Mr. Wallingford had shown a tepid reaction to Alfred's idea. But Alfred knew that James had given him his full support, and one day the reins of the Wallingford shipping and banking empire would be in his hands.

Yet James had wanted to include Victoria, who in turn asked to include Francesca. A natural occurrence, but Francesca's presence distracted him. He didn't know if he'd told her too much about his reasons for leaving their society years ago, but she deserved to know.

Francesca now bit her lip as she clutched the handle of the tiller. "Am I doing this right?"

"Of course not." James popped up from where he sat. "You're likely going to run us aground, and then where will we be?" He moved to Francesca's other side and plucked at her elbow.

"You must find yourself quite amusing, dear brother." Francesca stuck her tongue out at him. "I've done nothing of the sort, and I'm sure Alfred will take charge, or any of his fine crew, should we run into trouble."

Alfred chuckled. "Don't pay him any mind, Fran. He's no more a sailor than you are."

"Very well then." She grinned at him, then released the tiller and took a step back. "I shall go join Victoria."

The boat shuddered, and Alfred grabbed the handles. "Silly girl." He shook his head. The *Gull* resumed its normal happy course along the coast. Instead of turning back for lunch, he decided to find a good spot and drop anchor, and they could eat and bob safely on the quiet waves.

"Careful, Al." James's voice held a low tone.

"To what are you referring?" Alfred had his suspicions.

"Fran has always been a high-spirited girl, and I expect the woman Francesca will be the same. I don't want her heart broken because of disappointment."

"She was practically a child when I left."

"Of course. But now she's out in society and there are other forces at work. Namely, my mother."

"I do not aim to break her heart." Alfred's palm hurt from gripping the tiller. In a moment, he would call for one of his boatmen to help him slow the boat and drop anchor. "In fact, once I am more established as head of my father's business dealings and people are accustomed to my presence, I am going to speak to your father."

James sighed and leaned on the rigging. "It's not that simple, you should know."

"I realize your mother and other individuals will see me as little more than the questionably legitimate heir to the Finley holdings, but I am sure your father is a reasonable man."

"Of course you're right. But I'm afraid my parents—my mother, especially—have their sights set higher than the Finley name. Quite frankly, you're our financial equal or perhaps even a bit better. Your father was a shrewd businessman and built his empire from practically nothing. As did mine."

"Who do you think your parents are focusing on?"

"A title—and old money." James shook his head. "I despise it, really. Mother's airs are intolerable. Not a day goes by that she's not sniping at Victoria about some sort of faux pas, imagined or otherwise."

"A title and old money, you say." Alfred reminded himself about self-control, and holding his temper. The narrow-mindedness of some folks set him off nearly every time he came across it.

"Which is why I said to be careful. Francesca may be harboring dreams that will be dashed like a ship on those rocks lining the coast, should her dreams not come true."

Chapter 5

Francesca tried not to clutch Victoria's hand too tightly. The entry hall of the Vanderbilts' cottage, Marble House, glowed in all its resplendence and made Seaside look pretentious in comparison. In the glow of the Tiffany glass, the marble seemed more like liquid stone than that of a hard surface. The sun had at long last gone down, and a breeze blew from the bay. Dances did not start until well after sundown, and Francesca knew their driver would return to the Vanderbilts' residence shortly after daybreak and an early breakfast.

"Ladies, I shall rejoin you when the dancing begins." James took Victoria's free hand and kissed it. "We men have business to tend to, but you can be sure we will arrive promptly at supper."

"Of course, my love, you always do." Victoria smiled at him, and the women continued their walk to the ballroom, following the crowd.

"You really love my brother, don't you?" Francesca asked.

"That I do, although I didn't at first." She glanced at Francesca. "Does that surprise you?"

"No, I can't say that it does. In our position, we have few choices of whom to marry. Those of us who have a choice, that is." Francesca glimpsed another pair of young women, who, like herself, were experiencing their first summer out in society.

"You needn't worry, I'm sure." Victoria nodded to another acquaintance of the family's. "Your parents have your best interests in mind. Was that Mrs. Copley or Mrs. Hamilton? I can never remember. The one whose husband owns the steel company."

"I don't know. I am good with faces, but names sometimes escape me." Francesca pondered Victoria's words. "But what you said about my parents. Do you know of anything that they have planned?"

Victoria drew her toward the wall of the great gilded ballroom they'd just entered. She leaned closer. "I dare not say, because I have heard nothing certain. Now, mind you, I despise eavesdropping."

"As do I, but sometimes it can't be helped."

"One morning, I was in the library, searching for a book of poetry I'd left on the window seat in the gallery. Your mother and father were there. They only passed through. I don't know if your father was searching for his cigars or his glasses, but they were only present for a brief moment."

Francesca wanted to drag the words out of her sister-in-law one by one. "All right. So what you are telling me is only part of the story. I understand."

Victoria took a deep breath and said, "I heard your father say something like, 'Unlike you, I believe the idea has merit. Financially *we* shall not gain anything by the connection. But our daughter will be happy.'

"And then your mother said, 'If her future is secure, then I know she will be happy. Our grandchildren will have more than she even has now. Thankfully she does not remember those early days of hardship.'

"Then your father roared and said something like, 'What he owns far exceeds money and stature. I will not bend to this idea of yours.'

"And then the two of them thundered from the room, and I heard nothing more of the conversation. You know this can only mean one thing."

"They were trying to select a husband for me, worthy of my trust fund." Francesca's heart pounded. "I can only guess who they argued about, but I'd rather not say."

"You should make your own intentions known now, if you prefer someone, before it is too late," Victoria said. "I did so about James. He was as kind and intelligent and handsome as any I'd seen. While I did not love him at first, I knew love would come. And it has. Oh, it surely has."

"Do you mean—?" Francesca grasped Victoria's hand.

Her sister-in-law whispered in her ear. "By this time next summer, you shall be an aunt."

Francesca clamped her hand over her mouth, then calmed herself before anyone else noticed her delighted reaction. No, they were too busy examining Mrs. Vanderbilt's embellishments to the room. Not that it needed any embellishing.

"I am so happy for both of you."

"Thank you. We plan to announce it at family supper, tomorrow night." Victoria glowed as if happy to share her secret with someone.

Another friend wearing a sparkling tiara glided up to them. "Victoria, how are you this evening? Is James here?"

"I'm quite well, Millicent," Victoria replied. "James is here, too."

"We need your opinion over there about a particular matter, if you don't mind joining us for a moment."

"Of course not. Fran, I'll be back shortly." Victoria nodded at Francesca.

"I'll see you then." The orchestra members were assembling at their seats for the first dancing to begin. Supper would not be until midnight, but Francesca's stomach already growled. A familiar figure in a gown of sapphire blue approached her and stopped. Her cousin, Lillian.

"You've heard the news, haven't you?" Lillian asked. "Consuelo and Winthrop Rutherford had a *secret* engagement. And her mother learned of it. They *locked* her in her room."

"Why? Did she threaten to run away?"

"I'm not quite certain, but it is a known fact that he is *not* the one her family considers suitable for her to marry."

"How awful for her." Francesca scanned the room for the diminutive young woman with large, dark eyes. And how devastating, to be denied one's true love. And how sad that she felt she must be engaged secretly to someone not of her mother's choosing. "Have you seen her tonight?"

"Not yet." Lillian nudged her. "Look. There is your Mr. Finley."

Alfred was shaking James's hand, and gesturing to another gentleman in a fine suit nearby. "He's not *my* Mr. Finley."

"Ah, but I hear he is yet unattached, and he has known our family for years." She leaned closer. "Do you think your mother will hear of a union between the two of you?"

"I. . .I think that is doubtful, as you know quite well."

"Well, I also have heard that the Duke of Marlborough has been seen about. *He* is deemed to be an acceptable match for Consuelo. She is worth twenty million, after all."

"Mrs. Vanderbilt probably wants her daughter to be a duchess." Francesca shook her head. "A title."

Lillian's eyes took on a curious light. "Yes, with a title there is not just money. But influence. Could you imagine? The respect one would have with a title."

"I have to admit, when I first met the count in Paris, he quite turned my head." Francesca glanced toward Victoria, who had greeted one of her friends and was no doubt catching up on news.

"He turns *every* woman's head. I wonder how much he's worth?" Lillian linked her arm through Francesca's.

The sisterly gesture made Francesca pause. The younger of the two by six months, Lillian should have been the kind of cousin to have for a friend while growing up, but for some curious reason her cousin always wanted to compete with Francesca. When Francesca had received a pony when she turned eight years old, Lillian had demanded one, too. Painting lessons, which Lillian promptly gave up but where Francesca excelled. Although, Lillian could sing, and no doubt if someone played the pianoforte tonight, Lillian would somehow manage a turn to stand and sing beside the instrument.

"I certainly have no idea. He does seem wealthy enough."

"A New York estate, and a place in London, besides his Paris residence." Lillian nodded and smiled at another young woman passing by them.

"You seem to know quite a lot about the man," Francesca observed.

"Dear cousin, we must know as much as we can about the people in our circle. It will only be to our advantage. Surely you understand that."

"I am tired of the posturing I see and the pretentiousness."

"Surely it is but a phase of melancholy you are going through. Perhaps your mother should send for a doctor. There must be a remedy." Lillian paused, and Francesca had to stop short.

"Beatrice, darling, how *are* you?" Lillian said to a young woman they encountered in the ballroom.

Francesca took in the sight of the golden room. What a birthday present from Mr. Vanderbilt to his wife, but even Francesca had heard the murmuring that their marriage had troubles. The gilded mirrors and marble walls glowed in the light of the chandeliers. And the fireplace, imported from Italy with its bronze sculpted figures. The ceiling, too, reminded everyone that *this* was no ordinary ballroom.

The orchestra in the corner was tuning up, the sound a pleasant cacophony. The others in attendance clustered around the perimeter of the dance floor.

"You *will* save me at least one dance, won't you?"

Francesca did not have to turn to know the owner of the voice. Since that day of sailing, she had longed for the chance to see Alfred again. Aside from glimpsing him at church one Sunday in town, she had not had the pleasure. Could he glimpse the eagerness in her face?

"But of course. And more than one, even." Practically brazen, Mother would say, but Francesca did not care at the moment. "Have you been busy? I haven't seen you since that day we went out on the *Gull*."

"Yes, I have been busy. One of the reasons I am here tonight is because William Vanderbilt has learned of my plans for the foundation. As he is engaged in philanthropy himself, I know there is much that I can learn from him. We are planning to meet and confer more in New York, but as his wife wanted a balanced list for the ball, my name was added."

"Imagine. I'll have to tell Mother that. Surely that should raise you in her estimation." She laughed.

☙

Alfred could listen to Francesca's laughter all evening. She no longer possessed the giggle of a young girl, but the warm, rich laugh of a woman. He ought to have retreated with the small group of men heading to Mr. Vanderbilt's study, but as the evening went on, he realized he would regret not spending as much time with Francesca as he could.

The orchestra then struck up a lively tune, and dancers paired up. Alfred offered his arm to Francesca. "First dance? Then we will not be disappointed if the opportunity does not come our way again."

"Of course."

She was light on her feet, and her smile remained bright. Alfred didn't care if he never had the chance to speak with Mr. Vanderbilt that evening.

"Please forgive my mother. She's been unconscionable this summer," Francesca said halfway through the dance.

"I understand. She is not the first." He led her to the turn, released her hand, and then took her other one. "I am well aware of how the game is played."

"But our parents were friends, and I don't see how she can put on airs like she has." Her brow furrowed.

"It happens. We feel we must put forth an image, be the example. God's chosen elite." He caught her around the waist.

"Well, I am tired of the image," Francesca admitted. "Surely you are not serious about being the elite?"

"Of course not." He loved seeing the pretty frown on her face. "I only say what I see in the philosophy of some."

"But I see that what only makes us different from those without is our money, and perhaps our education. Look at the ball in Paris. My sweet maid Elizabeth wore an old gown of mine, and I passed her off—if not completely—as one who moved in society's upper circles." The music ended, and the couples applauded as they headed to the edges of the ballroom.

"It was quite convincing at first. Small details clued me in, but those were superficial," Alfred said over the noise of clapping hands.

"My point exactly." Francesca remained by his side, and they watched another group of dancers take the floor. "Deep down, we are all alike. We want security, love, and we want to belong. God Himself is no respecter of persons, as the Bible says."

"My, my. Serious thoughts for a beautiful evening." What Alfred wouldn't give so that Francesca could be by his side always. Her compassionate nature and not just her beauty appealed to him. Which meant he needed to speak to Mr. Wallingford. James's cautionary words came back to him. He had no idea if any plans had been set in motion, but if Alfred could prevent heartbreak for Francesca, he would.

"I'm sorry." The worry left her face with a smile. "Just seeing the grandeur of this house amazes me, and it makes me wonder why we must all have so. . .much. What we spend on dinner could feed families for months. It almost makes me want to move to a simple house and bake bread."

"But you enjoy the parties and such?"

She nodded. "Part of me does, and I feel guilty sometimes about that. I know I'd probably be miserable were I to exchange places with Elizabeth for a time. I *like* being comfortable and doted upon."

"You want a happy medium."

"I do. And I also want to make a difference." Francesca placed one of her gloved hands on his arm. "This is why you must succeed. To make a difference. And to encourage the others in this room tonight to do the same with what God has given them."

He saw another gentleman nod at him, one of Mr. Vanderbilt's associates with whom he wished to speak. Time for the retreat before supper. "For your sake, and those who will one day benefit, I'll do my best." He gave a slight bow. "I must go for now, but I hope to see you at supper."

"I hope so, too."

Alfred straightened his tie and tugged on his cuffs as he left the ballroom. The sounds of male laughter drifted from an open door. He had never entered William Vanderbilt's lounge at Marble House and felt as if he were going to appear before royalty. But like Francesca said, people were alike, deep down.

He believed that most in the room would want to make a difference. Perhaps he should start a discussion about educational reform and increased accessibility.

Instead, the first person he spoke to brought up the subject of his unmarried state. Reginald Avery with his graying handlebar moustache had but one wife, yet the portly man was known to have dalliances on the side with much younger women. Alfred wasn't sure the man would want to lend his support to Alfred's idea. But he saw no harm in speaking to Reginald.

"You're wound up tighter than piano string, young Finley." Reginald clapped him on the back. "You either didn't sow enough wild oats out on that frontier, or you need to get married. Or both." He punctuated the air with throaty laughter that made a few heads turn in their direction.

"I'm actually starting a philanthropic foundation."

"Foundation, shmoundation, m'boy." He blew a puff on his cigar. "What do you plan to do?"

Alfred explained about the foundation and the need for educational reform as a means to better all young people, not a select few, and thus improve the quality of life for everyone. "And that's why I'm determined to use my assets for the common good."

"With a speech like that, you ought to run for office and not be holed up knocking elbows with us stuffed shirts." The man had a glint in his eye. "Tell you what. You start finding some of those young people who need a hand, and I'll talk to my banker about a contribution."

"You will?" Alfred hadn't expected this. His original target had been Octavius Millstone, a manufacturing giant who was now debating something with Mr. Vanderbilt by the fireplace—judging by the way he gestured, nearly striking someone's head with his waving arms.

"'Course I will." Reginald's face took on a more serious expression. "I had a hardworking father who brought us here when we were wee ones. He always wanted us to do better than what he did. I was the only one who did. Don't want you giving money to any slackers, though."

"You can be sure these students will be hard workers and ambitious." Alfred shook Reginald's hand. "You'll hear from me again about this matter. Thank you, thank you very much."

∽

The supper hour arrived at last, and to Francesca's delight she had a seat across from Alfred. The gentleman to his left kept him engaged in conversation, but Alfred would glance in her direction from time to time. The woman to his right wore a resplendent headdress that made her look quite like rooster's plumes sprung from the crown of her head. The sight must have amused Alfred as well, for his eyes danced with merriment.

The empty seat beside her became occupied, but Francesca merely sensed someone settling onto the large chair. She wondered if they'd required assistance, as she had, to push the massive piece of furniture up to the table.

The man wore a fine suit, and Francesca appreciated that as her gaze moved from his arm to his face.

Count Philippe de la Croix.

"Mademoiselle Wallingford, I was hoping to see you this evening." The rich tones of his voice made her want to lean closer to listen, but she stopped herself.

"It is good to see you, Count de la Croix. And thank you again, for the kind gift of the paint set. I'm afraid I haven't had the opportunity to use them yet." Francesca remembered how she'd exclaimed over the store that carried artists' supplies while strolling Paris streets with the count. Was it barely two months ago? It seemed a lot longer than two months. But then, she hadn't become quite as reacquainted with Alfred as she had now. Much more than reacquainted. Alfred was talking to the gentleman beside him, but she caught his eye, and he smiled at her.

Then Alfred's gaze traveled to the count, and his smile faded almost imperceptibly.

The count was laughing at something someone had said, and Francesca tried to see who occupied the seat on the other side of him. She caught a flash of sapphire blue silk and glimpsed ebony curls against alabaster skin.

"Francesca, dear cousin." Lillian leaned forward in her chair. "It appears we have the best two seats at supper tonight." She looked up at Philippe through her long eyelashes.

Before Francesca could reply, Philippe said, "No, it is I who occupy a coveted chair. The two most beautiful debutantes in the room, and both from the same family."

A trilling giggle from Lillian.

"Thank you, Count de la Croix." Francesca refused to further contribute to the man losing his hearing, as Lillian just had.

"Please, it is Philippe. As it was in Paris, Francesca."

Somehow his hand had grown closer in proximity to Francesca's left hand that rested on the table beside her salad fork. His little finger touched hers, and she wanted to draw her hand to her lap.

"Very well. Philippe it is."

"*Pardon*, Francesca. *Un moment*." He turned to listen to something Lillian had said.

When Francesca glanced toward Alfred, his chair was vacant.

"Mr. Finley was called away," said the woman wearing the rooster plume headdress.

"Oh, I hope nothing is wrong." Francesca thought he might have let her know he was leaving, and not departed like this, without a word. But they had not come together, and he was not bound to inform her of his actions. Had he noticed Philippe's attentions? She did not return them, and she chided herself on being a silly girl to think that Alfred cared at all. In that manner, anyway.

Chapter 6

Francesca had no way to send word to Alfred to inquire about how he fared, so she asked James about him after the ball, as they rode home in the carriage and yawned all the way back to Seaside.

"I am not sure," James said. "He did not speak to me before he left. He did, however, look like a thundercloud as he passed by us where we sat."

"It's the count, I'm sure of it." Victoria echoed Francesca's yawn. "On the way to supper, he did admit that he hoped the man was seated as far from you as possible. I think he's a little jealous."

"Jealous?" Francesca echoed. "But I did nothing. . ."

"It's not you. It's the count, of course. He is clearly interested in you. Remember those paints he gave you in Paris, and even the night of that ball. You know which one, when you brought Elizabeth—"

"Don't remind me." She still regretted the foolish action.

"You made some sort of impression on him."

"Well, I'm not trying to. Really. A count?"

"I warned Alfred that day we went sailing," James said. "Mother is plotting something, but neither she nor Father will be specific."

"That's what I'm afraid of." Francesca bit her lip.

∞

"With Mr. Finley opening his home, we must have a larger gala," Mother said one morning later as she looked up from her writing desk in the parlor. "And we will make sure *not* to invite Mrs. Alva Vanderbilt."

"Why aren't we inviting Mrs. Vanderbilt?" As soon as Francesca asked, she knew the answer. Mother had learned the social dance well.

"She has not come to call yet this season. While it is true our family was included in her gala activities two weeks ago, I want to show her that we are to be reckoned with."

Francesca focused on the envelope in front of her. If she wasn't careful, she'd pen the wrong spelling of the street name. Her hand ached, and she set down her pen and rubbed the muscle around her thumb.

She should send up a prayer for thanks that she was born to such a family, to such a hardworking father and loving mother and brother. But ever since her father's ship—or ships—had literally come in, Mother had transformed somehow.

A long time ago, Mother would sew and cook and bake. But now other people saw to such tasks that Mother deemed mundane. Francesca wasn't sure she cared much for the change.

"Will you be inviting Alfred and his mother?"

"Of course." Mother's pen moved efficiently over the paper in front of her. "We want them to recognize that Seaside is the latest jewel of Newport. But that does pose a quandary for me."

Francesca finished writing the address on one envelope, then blew on it as she'd been taught. "How so?"

"There will be enough unattached women at the fete as well, but I would not dare insult any of the other fine families by insinuating that Alfred would be suitable for their daughters."

"You don't mean that, do you?"

"Well, he certainly is not invited for *your* benefit."

"I am sorry. I was not assuming—"

"However, if I invite less than the best families of Newport, word will circulate that we Wallingfords are substandard." Mother lifted her letter to the light. "Mr. Finley, how I wish you hadn't come to town."

Francesca held her tongue. Directly confronting Mother never worked. She started on the next address. "You are inviting Mr. and Mrs. Wrentham, and their daughter and son?"

"Yes. I suppose they are in New York at the moment, so we must use their city address."

Francesca nodded and scanned Mother's address book for the correct entry.

"I know! We shall, of course, invite my sister, and her daughter Lillian. Perhaps she will be suitable for Mr. Finley. As best I know, my sister has not found a match for Lillian."

"I. . .I can't say as I see that Lillian and Alfred would make a good match." Francesca detested the tone of her voice and how it betrayed her. She tried to keep her pen even on the paper.

Mother made a most unladylike grunt. "*Romance* has nothing to do with a good match. In our circle, we cannot think of such superficialities. Our choices are few. But Lillian has a tidy trust. Not to the caliber of yours, I am sure, but she would bring a fine contribution to any union."

Francesca fought to remain in her seat. She didn't know what was wrong with her. Ever since Paris and Count Philippe's ball, either she felt happy or vexed, and very little in between. Instead of giving in to the urge to run from the room, she imagined walking along the sea walk. Father's promised path to the sea had given her many happy hours. She pictured herself watching the waves, the wind lifting her hair. She would look up and see someone walking toward her on the sand, the sun illuminating the red in his hair. . .

Mother's sigh made her look up.

"Are you all right, Mother?"

"I. . .I. . .This gala is for you as well." Mother reached for a handkerchief and discreetly dabbed her eyes.

"This makes you cry?"

"Only for happiness, dear daughter." Mother rose from her chair and moved to where Francesca sat with her lap desk. "Please, stand so I can hug you."

A hug? Francesca stood and placed the lap desk on her chair, then received her mother's embrace. It was not her birthday, nor Christmas. She could not remember the last time her mother had hugged her.

"Francesca, your father and I have done everything for you and your brother's sake. One day, James will run Wallingford Shipping. As you know, we have a trust laid up for you, that you will carry to your marriage one day. I know it is merely money, but it symbolizes our love for you." Mother returned to her chair and sat down at the desk.

"I do appreciate what you and Father have done."

"You know that your life has been far, far different than my and my sister's lives. My mother was a seamstress, and she wanted me to be a schoolteacher. My father was a tradesman. And your father was from obscure beginnings as well. But God has smiled on us, and we never want you to worry for your future."

"Mother, I know I shall be well taken care of." The now-familiar feeling of a noose surrounded Francesca's neck. She picked up her lap desk and took her seat. What was Mother trying to say, exactly?

"All the same, I trust that this upcoming fete will ensure that." Mother smiled now. "But I'll say nothing further. This fete will outshine anything we've done yet here at Seaside."

∽

Francesca stood on the balcony of her bedroom, which overlooked the lush green lawn. A stream of carriages led to the front porte cochere of Seaside. Somehow Mother had arranged for new uniforms for the stable hands, so they looked like livery men wearing white powdered wigs from long ago.

Here came the stream of peacocks. Few of these people probably cared for her, and most of them she barely knew. But most had come to see the latest jewel on Newport's Bellevue Avenue so they could repeat the story to others who had not been on the privileged list. One man, his suit rather plain yet neat, alighted from a carriage and paid the driver. He stood on the driveway and craned his neck to look at the magnificent structure.

Francesca recalled her own first reaction to seeing the fine summer home her father had commissioned construction on not quite two years before. This man pulled a notebook from his pocket and a stump of pencil, and scribbled something down. A reporter. Mother had mentioned a special guest. But a reporter had never attended any of the Wallingford social functions before. Not that Francesca knew, anyway. She left the balcony. She might as well submit to the rest of her beauty regime before she made her appearance to the guests.

"Miss Fran, the iron is hot." Elizabeth stood by the vanity and its empty chair. "Are you ready?"

"Whether I want to be, or not." She tried to give Elizabeth a confident smile, moved to the chair, and sat down. She stared at her reflection, framed by the gilded wood of the looking glass. Alfred's phrase echoed again in her mind. *Bird in a gilded cage.*

"Miss, you've been outside often of late, and your hair feels dry," Elizabeth said as she brushed Francesca's hair, which tumbled past her shoulders. "We must use a treatment for it one quiet evening."

"If. . .if you would like to do so as well, I would not prevent it."

"Ah, but I have too many duties in the evening, and my mother and father require my assistance in our quarters. I would not have the time to sit and wait for my hair to dry afterward." But Elizabeth's smile was wistful.

Francesca thought of Alfred's proposed foundation. "Elizabeth, have you ever wanted to attend a university?"

Elizabeth wound a lock of Francesca's hair tightly around the hot iron. Her cheeks flushed pink. "No, miss. To me it is no use to want something I cannot have. I don't believe I am much good at book learning, although one time I might have wanted to be a teacher. I love children."

"I see." She didn't bother to mention Alfred's foundation. Elizabeth was a realist and "knew her place," as Mother would say. She had no more freedom than Francesca did.

Soon, Elizabeth had created a series of curls that she brushed out, and pulled Francesca's hair into a high pompadour. Tears came to Francesca's eyes, much as they had when her hair had been styled as a little girl. She had learned long ago that such tears did not hasten the end of the torture. But tonight's tears came because, although Francesca had means and wealth that her maid did not, the means and wealth meant nothing to her freedom.

Once Elizabeth had ceased from securing Francesca's hair with combs, Francesca reached for her bottle of favorite perfume. A knock sounded at Francesca's door, and then it opened.

Mother breezed in, her newest silk gown fitting her form well, and nary a hair out of place. "You are nearly ready?" She clutched a flat velvet box. "All of the guests are seated, and you must make your entrance for our early supper before the orchestra begins."

"I'm ready. But Mother, I don't understand. I have already been presented to society. And I noticed a reporter outside the door earlier. What is happening tonight? This party isn't just a grand opening for Seaside."

ALL THAT GLITTERS

Elizabeth stepped back a few discreet paces as Mother joined Francesca at the vanity.

"Please, sit down, my dear." Mother gestured to the cushioned chair.

Francesca took her seat and noticed the frown line between her eyebrows. She smoothed it. But her nerves jangled.

"Here. Jewels for our jewel." Mother opened the box, and Francesca sucked in a breath. A necklace of topaz that matched the blue of her eyes, each topaz edged with winking diamonds.

"Oh. Mother." Francesca touched the necklace. "So beautiful." The part of Francesca that adored comforts and baubles won out. Money brought beauty, she'd learned. And oh, what beauty in that velvet box. She willed herself to enjoy the beauty of the gemstones for a few moments.

"Here." Mother fastened the necklace, which lay perfectly against Francesca's neck. "He's right. The color is perfect."

Francesca turned to look at Mother instead of her reflection. "Who's right?"

Mother's touch on Francesca's hair was softer than the brush of a butterfly's wing. "The necklace is not from your father and me."

And should Alfred venture to give her something so grand, Francesca knew her mother would never allow it. She guessed at who had given her the necklace, and forced a smile. But her body went numb.

∞

"Are you comfortable, Mother?" Alfred asked as he took his own seat at the long dining table that filled the length of the room at Seaside. He estimated it seated about thirty guests, and he knew for sure that others would arrive for the after-supper dancing.

"Yes, yes." She waved off his attention and touched the comb tucked into her graying hair. Diamonds caught the light from the chandelier. "The Wallingfords have outdone themselves with this elegant home. Methinks they tried to best you, my boy."

"Perhaps they have." He studied the massive mirrors that lined one wall of the dining room, the other side of the room lined with doors that opened to face the sea, much like the dining room at Tranquility. A frescoed ceiling—imported from Italy and reinstalled here at Seaside, he'd been told—glowed in the lights from below. Alfred glanced at the faces nearest him.

The Wallingfords had seated him and Mother close to the head of the table, where three place settings remained empty. Probably for Mr. and Mrs. Wallingford and Francesca. Alfred nodded at James across the table and a few seats closer to the empty chairs. Mother turned to speak with someone next to her, a family member of the Wallingfords, Alfred guessed.

A lone chair waited at the end of the table next to Count de la Croix. So he'd been given one of the coveted spots closest to the family, with Alfred near enough to see all that would be said and done. After the day of sailing and the picnic with James, Victoria, and Francesca, Mrs. Wallingford's message was clear: he was still not good enough for her daughter.

"Mr. Finley, isn't it?" A young woman seated across from Alfred asked. Her hair, dark as ink, had been caught up in the latest style, and her lavender dress contrasted with her green eyes. The tip of her nose formed a point that almost made it seem as if she smelled something disagreeable. But her smile was pretty enough.

"Yes, it is. Forgive me, I know I have seen you before, and if we have met, I regret that I don't recall your name."

"Lillian Chalmers. Francesca is my cousin." She blinked, her long lashes fluttering.

"Oh, yes. I believe we have met before."

"Paris, this spring. We attended some of the same functions."

"Mother loves to be out and about, and I, of course, must see to accompanying her."

Lillian gave a soft giggle, and her earrings wiggled. "Surely that is not the only reason you attend balls."

"Miss Chalmers, you are quite right. I do enjoy speaking with charming young ladies as yourself, especially after being confined in stuffy meetings most of the week."

She flicked a gaze toward the head of the table. "It is fortunate that our hosts are not present to hear you speak in such a manner. I'm surprised you are here at all, actually."

He appreciated her candor. "I am well aware of at least one of their opinions about me. But I am not deterred. So, have you seen much of this grand home?"

"Nearly every inch. Auntie Wallingford made certain that Mother and I saw it all, before we returned to our summer residence in town." Again her gaze traveled in the direction of the empty seats.

Count de la Croix inclined his head toward them both, and Lillian turned scarlet. A secret affection for the man, or merely a response to acknowledgment from one so well bred? Alfred couldn't guess.

The man seemed amicable enough when they had spoken in Paris and had even seemed interested in the foundation Alfred had determined to launch, although the count was not sure if he would be able to contribute.

Motion at the dining room entrance made the diners look in that direction and rise. Francesca stood with her parents in the doorway. Her dress looked opalescent in the gaslights and candles. Something brilliant and blue flashed at her neck. She appeared as if she were going to be sick, but smiled at the roomful of people.

The three of them walked to the head of the table. Mrs. Wallingford extended her hand to the empty chair next to the count, and Francesca moved to stand behind it. The count pulled Francesca's chair away from the table. As she sat, she looked down the table of guests, and her gaze settled on Alfred.

He remembered his first hunting trip with his father, and the doe they had seen in the woods. The creature froze when they happened upon it, and it wore an expression much like the one Francesca wore now, before it disappeared. Francesca looked down at the place setting before her.

Mr. Wallingford remained standing, as did his wife, while the dinner guests sat down. "Thank you, guests, for gracing our home with your presence this evening. Please enjoy all that we have to offer you. Before supper begins, my wife and I would like to share some news with you." He glanced at Mrs. Wallingford, resplendent in a purple gown and wearing a headdress that reminded Alfred of a peacock's tail. Her face glowed like the sun in the August heat.

"God has blessed our family, to be sure. And we in turn are happily including you this evening. Seaside was built to be a place of cool respite for us during the warm summer months, and we plan to entertain on a scale such as this for many summers to come.

"As you know, our daughter, Francesca Genevieve Wallingford, has joined the ranks of society this spring, and we have carefully considered her future."

She paused, and with the pause, cast the beam of her smile at Francesca, whose fingers curled around a salad fork. Her lips sealed into a thin line, and her chest moved almost imperceptibly as if she struggled to breathe. Francesca glanced at Alfred, then away again.

The glance tore at his heart, and his pulse roared in his ears.

"We are proud to announce that by this time next year, we shall have a son-in-law, Count Philippe de la Croix."

Alfred's pulse was drowned out by the smatter of applause that echoed off the dining room ceiling. His hands clapped as if he were a puppet, and someone else forced them together and apart again.

Francesca and the count rose. He took one of her hands in his, and she looked up at him and smiled. But the fork remained tight within her grip.

Chapter 7

Francesca lost track of how many days she had wept. Her eyes hurt, her eyelids swelled and rimmed with red. While it was true the count had turned her head in Paris, she didn't want to *marry* him. She rolled over on her bed and stared at the wall covered in hand-painted fabric. The blue normally soothed her, but even it could not put a salve on her aching heart. The food on the tray that rested on her vanity chair remained untouched.

"A more ungrateful daughter never lived." Mother's earlier words still hung in midair, like a banner gracing Francesca's bedroom.

True. She ought to be thankful. The count was not an ogre, nor did he seem cruel. Had her heart been unclaimed, the sweet kindnesses that Philippe had shown her the night of the Parisian ball would have made her his forever. She remembered how he'd made her feel in Paris, taking her breath away.

Worse, the lovely jeweled necklace that matched her eyes so perfectly had not been an indulgence of her parents. That exquisite treasure had been selected by Philippe in New York, before he traveled to Newport. And undoubtedly the sight of her wearing the necklace had told him what he wanted to know. Even now it winked at her, from its castoff place on her bureau. The ring that had been passed through generations of Philippe's family lay next to the sparkling necklace.

"I tried. Dear Lord, I tried. But how can I force myself to accept these plans?" The words fought past her parched lips. She had not prayed much of late, when it seemed like so much was out of her hands. Everything, in fact.

Even her wardrobe. Mother wouldn't let her select even a simple gown, now that she was pledged to be married to a count. Why, that was European nobility, and one must look the part.

Francesca had mentioned at the time that one could put a dress on a cat and that wouldn't make the feline a countess. She'd simply been scolded for impertinence and reminded of her earlier unwise actions regarding Elizabeth.

If she couldn't even select her own apparel, she didn't know how God could move upon her behalf. In the fairy tales, the prince would ride in and save the day. But now, because of her wealth and apparent status, her life had been scheduled and planned, and she was expected to go along with the whole thing.

"It's good business, Fran," was all Father would say. "The count has strong holdings throughout Europe, and this will only help expand our shipping business."

He could not give her an adequate answer when she asked why she had to marry in order for such an alliance to occur.

A knock sounded at her bedroom door.

"Go away." Francesca hated the tone in her voice, but there it was.

"It's James." The door swung open, and he entered the room. Once he closed it behind him, he moved the tray from the vanity's chair and set it on top of the vanity's top.

"Have you come to drag me back to my senses?"

"No, I'm not strong enough. Victoria's worried about you."

"I know, and I'm sorry." Francesca pulled her dressing gown more tightly around her and sat up on the bed. "I know what Mother and Father did, they did out of love. It certainly explains her odd actions while we were addressing invitations. But there's. . .there's someone else I can't forget. Or. . .I don't know how."

"Yes, I'm aware of that. And so is he."

Francesca's pulse jumped. "And he was there that night at supper, and saw it all up close. I'm sure Mother saw to that with the seating arrangement. I couldn't even look at—at *him*. What he must think of me."

"Fran, Alfred knows that none of this was your doing."

"But surely, I didn't try to win anyone's affections, let alone the count's. While it's true I enjoyed getting to know Philippe in Paris, I returned here. . .unsure. And we made no promises to each other. I had no expectations." She sighed. "That also explains why what Elizabeth and I did was such a disaster. Mother was especially angry because she didn't want her plan to unravel."

"I'm sure you've thought everything over a hundred times in the past three days." James rose and walked to the door that led to the balcony, and threw it open. "Do you see? The day is beautiful, and your beloved ocean waits but footsteps away. Take a walk, pray, and paint. You love to do both."

"You're right. And life is going on without me whether I want it to or not." Francesca joined James at the open door and inhaled the fresh air. She'd missed it, lying here in her luxurious blue cave.

"Have a little faith. You are not wed yet." James tugged a strand of her hair like he had done when she was small. "The best thing you can do for all of us, and yourself, is to pick up and keep going."

Francesca nodded. Part of her wanted to seek the solace of the bed, but part of her knew James made sense. She could change nothing by her weeping except perhaps give herself a worse headache and make her eyes look redder, not to mention her complexion.

"Could you send for Elizabeth, please? I need to get ready."

"That's my Fran. I'll ask her to come straightaway." James planted a kiss on her forehead before leaving.

She smiled at her brother and went out onto her balcony. The noon hour had come and gone, so the heat of the day would soon be past. She would find her new paints, and the wooden box that held her supplies, and head along the path to the sea walk.

By the time Elizabeth arrived, Francesca had pulled together an outfit—not one of Mother's preferences, in all likelihood, but at least she was dressed. Now to see about her snarled hair.

"You haven't brushed your hair in days, have you?" Elizabeth frowned and tried to get the brush through Francesca's hair.

"No, I'm afraid I haven't." She looked at her reflection in the mirror. "I honestly didn't care. Please, do what you can."

"I'll do my best." Elizabeth worked in silence after that, and Francesca felt like her hair was being yanked out by the roots.

Francesca reached back and touched the brush. "The kinks won't come out. If you could just help me put it up, I think that'll be fine. I am just going for a beach walk."

Elizabeth nodded and reached for some hairpins. Normally they would keep up a pleasant chatter, but ever since the ball, words would not come. At least on Francesca's part.

She might as well speak up before the chance was lost yet again. "Do you think I'm foolish, Elizabeth?"

"Whatever for?" Elizabeth's hands made quick work of restraining Francesca's hair.

"My engagement. I shouldn't have been so upset. Perhaps any other unattached woman in the world would have been happy at my sudden change in circumstances."

"But, Miss Fran, you are not any other unattached woman in the world."

Francesca pondered that for a moment before continuing. "What if you had the chance to wed a count? What would your family say? Would they be happy for you? Or mourn the day?"

Elizabeth looked wistful. "Every woman has happy dreams, I think. But I would not venture to dream to wed a count."

"If you were, though. If you knew your family would be well cared for, your future secure. If every night of your life could be as grand as that ball we attended?"

"Part of me would think myself foolish to squander a chance like that. My parents have worked hard all their lives, and if I should have the means to make life easier, I might try." Then Elizabeth frowned. "But money can come, and it can go. It's the people behind the money that we're left with."

"True, very true." The thought made her miss Alfred all the more, to hear his voice and engage in lively conversation. "Thank you for being so honest with me."

"You are welcome, Miss Fran. There. I think this will be passable." Elizabeth stepped back. "Are you going to walk alone?"

"Yes. I'll take Father's beach path and stroll for a while and paint. If anyone asks, I shall be back by suppertime."

"Of course. Did you require anything else, miss?"

Francesca studied her face in the mirror. "A wet cloth, perhaps, or something to put on my eyes to help the swelling. They are still quite puffy, and I shouldn't want anyone to notice if I encounter anyone on my walk."

"I'll bring something back right away."

After Elizabeth had returned with a cool, wet cloth, and Francesca was satisfied her eyes no longer looked quite as red, she put on the hat she'd worn sailing. Such a happy day seemed a lifetime ago, not a mere two weeks.

She descended the staircase and prayed all the while that no one would see her leave or pester her with more questions. The solitude of a walk appealed to her, and the family should be grateful that she at least decided to don fresh clothing, put up her hair, and make herself presentable. Although Mother would probably question the presentable part.

Francesca made it out the side door, and to the wide expanse of green lawn she called freedom. She found the path with its flat stone pavers that led over the ridge and down toward the edge of the beach. What a lovely clambake they'd had on the Fourth of July. Father had come from New York for the day, and it seemed as if the clock's hands had spun backward, to a time when she wore her hair in braids and James wore knickers.

The handle on her paint box dug into her fingers, and she shifted it to the other hand. The small easel she toted under her arm cut into her side. Maybe she should have asked someone else to come with her. She turned to face Seaside, which loomed across the lawn behind her. Its commanding presence could be seen clearly from the ocean. She turned her back on the spectacle of architecture and, instead, continued along with God's creation before her.

She reached the sand and would have been tempted to shed her boots but thought better of it. Light danced on the waves, and a boat bobbed on the surface of the water, looking much like a toy boat might from this distance.

Francesca perched on a rock low enough for her to sit on and drank in the salty freshness of the air. Smart brother, her James. While her situation hadn't changed, it seemed smaller under the wide expanse of blue sky with silky, white clouds painted across it. The sky touched the ocean, its deep greenish blue swirled with dark gray and occasional spots of white from breaking waves.

She needed to paint this and capture the atmosphere. On a rainy day, or even days darker than the few she'd just lived through, just seeing the colors reproduced in paint would do her good. Or perhaps someone else would derive enjoyment from the painting.

SEASIDE ROMANCE

The Master Artist had created beautiful surroundings with His palette. But Francesca didn't much care for the colors used to paint her life at the moment, despite their golden cast. Francesca assembled her easel and set her paint box on the nearest rock. She might as well create something where the colors were of her own choosing.

Gulls cried as they flew overhead, darting over the waves and then swooping closer as if to see what Francesca was doing. Fortunate birds. They had no knowledge of where their next meal would come from, but they soared without a care. Francesca wished she could sprout wings, too, and join them.

Enough. Her gloomy thoughts made the very idea of painting a chore, when normally she could lose herself in painting and forget where she was. Francesca took up her brush and covered the top portion of her board in blue paint. Now to mimic the ever-changing clouds.

She bit her lip and concentrated. Of all the settings she'd painted, she had never painted her beloved ocean before. Now it appeared on the board in front of her. Then came the sand, and the rocky shoreline. A few figures walked along the beach. She didn't know whether to paint them in, or leave the seascape empty of people. She paused, her brush inches from the board.

A shadow slanted over her right shoulder.

∞

"Francesca." Alfred's throat hurt, just saying her name. He had walked longer than he'd planned. Mostly he started walking to see if Mother would be able to make the journey to the sea walk once he moved her to Tranquility.

Francesca turned and looked up at him, shading her eyes from the sunlight with one hand. "Alfred." A kiss of blue paint smudged one cheek, and the fingers of her hand that held the paintbrush bore a variety of paint colors. The expression in her eyes tore at his heart.

"You're looking well."

"I. . .I had to get out and paint." She glanced at the picture on the small easel. "I've remained in the house ever since the other night."

Alfred looked out at the waves keeping up their incessant beat on the shoreline. "This is a good place to be. I'm looking forward to getting Mother moved to Newport."

"How is she?"

"She's had a good summer, and I know the air here will do her good."

"I think I should like to live here all the time." Francesca smiled, but not the full smile Alfred knew so well. "I would never tire of the view."

"Nor I. But I know you will have new responsibilities, as I do."

She nodded, and a few strands of her hair escaped their pins. "I didn't expect this, Alfred. Please don't think I knew when we went sailing, or even the night of Consuelo's ball when the count sat beside me at supper. I knew Mother was scheming, but I never dreamed her schemes would bear fruit. Not like this."

"That never entered my mind for a moment. Not at all. When I saw you the other night, at supper, I saw the shock on your face." He didn't mention the sensation that surged through him of wanting to clear the table of its finery in a fell swoop, take Francesca by the hand, and whisk her away from Seaside and the confinement she must feel.

"I don't know that I shall like winters or summers in Paris."

"Perhaps the count will purchase a home here, or build one for you, so you can be close to your beloved ocean." The words tasted sour on his tongue as he spoke them. The very idea of Francesca married to someone else and living nearby...

"I suppose." The wind whipped her soft words away from her. "I am not aware of all the plans."

"But you enjoy Paris. Think of all the painting you can do, the museums, the concerts." Somehow Francesca being an ocean away appealed to him more, given the future plans.

Francesca glanced up and down the beach. "I don't know if we should be talking. What if someone sees us, and they make a wrong assumption?"

"I am taking a walk. You are painting. We have known each other for many years. You have just become engaged to a count, and I am congratulating you and we now speak of your future." *Liar.* Alfred had no thoughts of congratulation. Perhaps commiseration.

Francesca wrapped up her paints. "I hear no congratulations in your voice. And if anyone sees us, they will not know what we discuss unless they hear us. But anyone can see that I. . ." Her voice cracked, and she swallowed hard. She jammed her paint tray, still damp, inside the wooden box nearby.

"What is it?" He now stood close enough to see a few freckles on her cheeks.

She clutched his coat sleeve. "Please. Take me away, to the west, to Colorado. We can make plans and go by train. Show me those mountains you love and buy me a ranch. We can find your minister friend, and he can marry us."

Alfred looked down at her, saw the pleading in her eyes. He had nearly dreamed the same thing, of disappearing again like he had years ago to quiet the rumors and burn off his anger before he truly disgraced his family.

Little made him speechless, but the fact that she'd begged him to marry her made his head spin. "You. . .you don't know what you're asking."

"Surely you can travel to New York when you must. Or what about mining?" She released his arm and started to pace. "Oh, and your mother. I know she's been ill, and you don't want to leave her. We can manage something."

"We have obligations, Fran. We cannot just disappear and do as we please."

"That's very convenient for you to say." She faced him, hands on her hips. "You've done that before. Why not now?"

"Because I can't run anymore. The rumors may try to resurface, but I've learned.

I can't leave because I encounter opposition." He wanted to catch hold of one of her hands, but thought better of the idea.

"Men." She shook her head. "It is always the same. If I were a man—"

"You would still have difficult choices." Alfred raked a hand through his hair. "Do you think the other night was easy for me?"

"What are you saying?"

"Part of me would love nothing more than to escape with you, to take you away from all this." Somehow the distance had lessened between them. "But no good would come of it, not after a while."

"So because of duty and honor, you would stand by to see me wed another?"

"It's not that simple."

"Have you even tried to speak to my father about anything besides your foundation?"

"I must tread carefully, and truthfully, I was planning to talk to your father before the. . .the other night."

"I really. . .I really wish you had, Alfred."

"I know. But all is not lost. Not yet. Circumstances can change. You must have a little faith."

"I want to, but there is nothing I can do." Francesca sank back onto the rock she'd been sitting on. "And I am tired of doing nothing."

"Dear, sweet Fran. . ."

"Please." She spoke to the sand at the tips of her boots. "Please, call me Miss Wallingford. It would be better if we. . .get used to the way things are. And the way things will not be."

"Very well." Alfred nodded. "But have faith."

She glared at the painting in front of her. "I don't know if I can. But we can never speak like this again."

Chapter 8

The gardens of Kingscote soothed Francesca's spirits as she prayed and walked among the lovely greenery a week after seeing Alfred at the seashore. Was it only a week ago she had begged him to take her away and marry her? Oh, but her tongue had run off on her again. What must Alfred think of her now that she'd spoken so impulsively?

But after resigning herself to only think of Alfred as a friend, Francesca could finally sleep again. Mother remarked that Francesca was a lot more tolerable now that she was no longer experiencing "hysterics."

Francesca felt so, too. Somehow if she pushed away the thought that she was to marry Philippe, a measure of peace came. But she could not deny that her life would change in unimaginable ways after she became the Countess de la Croix. She still, though, felt like the prayers she'd offered had struck the sky above her and drifted down again like lost feathers.

At least she hadn't seen Philippe recently. He had disappeared after the ball her mother had given that fateful night.

She thought of his last words to her. *"I should have thought that you would be happier."* Talking to her almost as if she were a spoiled child, indeed. The idea made her frown.

Elizabeth's footsteps sounded on the path behind her. Francesca closed her leather-bound sketchbook and turned back to face her maid.

Elizabeth pointed to the darkening sky. "Miss, I believe we're in for some rain showers."

"I believe you're right." The afternoon heat had given way to clouds that rolled in from the sea. "Perhaps we should start home before we are caught in the rain."

Elizabeth quickened her steps and joined Francesca at her side. Her maid had been a constant shadow since Francesca had deigned to go out in public after her engagement. If she was not with Victoria and James, Elizabeth would accompany her wherever she went. Had Mother guessed at her secret desire to flee? But she had not been locked in her room like Consuelo Vanderbilt.

The urge to flee did not assail her normally, but only during weaker moments, such as when the family's carriage passed by the nearly completed cottage, Tranquility. Mother had mentioned at breakfast that she believed her old friend, Mrs. Finley, had arrived in town to see the home.

She'd said, "Imagine that, to consider occupying a home before it is properly finished and decorated. Almost vulgar, although I would hate to use the word to describe Mrs. Finley. I have known her too long. Although, considering past circumstances, it is not surprising."

Francesca's tongue was becoming sore, as much as she'd been required to bite on it during recent days. Which is why she'd ended up at Kingscote, strolling the grounds. Mrs. King had given them permission to visit, once she'd learned of Francesca's artistic bent from her daughter, Gwendolyn. Now Francesca's sketch pad had several pages of ideas for future paintings.

A few drops fell, and Francesca hugged her notebook to her chest. She and Elizabeth had a long walk home. Perhaps they should have asked for a carriage to be sent at a certain time, but it was too late to ask for one now. The breeze turned into a gust that pulled at Francesca's skirts.

"Miss, I am sorry. Mother told me it might rain today. I should have listened to her and urged you to stay home."

"No apology necessary." More raindrops beat on Francesca's shoulders and arms where her hat did not provide coverage. Poor Elizabeth wore a much narrower hat.

"Perhaps we should run?"

"Then if one of us slips and hurts herself, we would be far worse than we are now." Francesca shivered. "And no one is home at Kingscote, or I should have sent you to the house to see if we could have assistance."

Another gust of wind, and the beating rain was like needles. A carriage, far ahead of them, was traveling in the same direction. Francesca wanted to wave for assistance but doubted she'd been seen. Whoever was inside likely counted themselves fortunate to be sheltered from the downpour.

Puddles formed on the side of the road. Francesca wasn't going to ruin her boots by tromping through muddy grass, although she guessed by their current state that a little mud would not make them worse.

A splashing sound made both of them turn around. Another carriage approached, its roof and trunk stacked with suitcases and satchels. It was pulled by a familiar-looking pair of matched sturdy bays. Francesca nearly sighed with relief, but her heart fluttered. Her poor nerves.

She and Elizabeth stepped to the side as the carriage drew even with them and stopped. Alfred looked out the window.

"Ladies, please come inside at once."

"Your carriage—the seats—we can walk." Francesca didn't realize how cold she was until she began to speak.

"Inside, *now*." He swung the door open, and both Francesca and Elizabeth climbed inside, water streaming from their skirts.

An older woman sat next to Alfred on the seat. "My dear son, do you *know* these women?"

"Ma'am, I am Francesca Wallingford, and this is Elizabeth." Francesca glanced at her wet hand. "I would shake your hand, but I'm afraid I'm not in the best state at the moment, for which I apologize. We were at Kingscote and got caught in the rain on our return home."

"That is quite obvious, my dear." She leaned forward, her dark skirt billowing around her. "Hmmm. You have your mother's grace, but your father's coloration and I daresay his demeanor."

Francesca didn't know if she ought to thank the woman, or not, so she kept silent.

"You, of course, probably don't remember me, and I daresay I haven't seen you since you wore your hair down. Of course, I'll excuse the fact that you appear more like a drowned waif at the moment."

A smile tugged at Francesca's mouth. She liked the woman's honest unpretentiousness. "You're quite right, Mrs. Finley." Her only memories of Mrs. Finley were that the woman was opinionated and had a loud voice but a kind heart. "I should say that your son has built a lovely home so far. Judging by what I've seen on the outside, that is."

Mrs. Finley looked at Alfred. "You haven't had company yet? It seems to me as if you are dragging your feet at getting this house finished." Did Alfred wince, or was it Francesca's imagination?

"No, Mother. The furniture has arrived, and I've had it set up. But I wanted you to oversee where you wanted everything placed."

"Quite right, quite right." She sighed. "I'm just thankful I've lived long enough to see the home built, praise be to God. I think I shall live to see another year."

"Of course you will." Alfred took his mother's hand. "I've already seen to fires being lit to make sure you are warm enough."

"Well, then." Mrs. Finley patted Alfred's hand. "We must take these two young ladies by our home to ensure they are warm and dry as well. It would not do, would not do for us to leave them off at their home, dripping and soggy."

In the space of ten minutes, they had arrived at Tranquility and entered its great entry hall. A fire roared in the main fireplace. Though the house was large, it seemed to welcome Francesca and Elizabeth.

Alfred had used few words as they entered the house, and he directed a few of his servants to bring blankets and prepare hot tea. His mother gave orders as well, for her bags to be brought to her suite of rooms. In the end, she sighed and followed the maids and carried two of her own satchels upstairs herself.

"I shall return," she announced to them. "I must make sure the bags are in their proper order. Otherwise I know I'll never find anything."

Francesca smiled at her retreating form. She joined Elizabeth at the fireplace. The young woman shivered inside the blanket.

"Elizabeth, are you all right?" She touched her face. Not hot. Just damp, like her own.

"It's just the cold, miss. That cold rain and wind. Once I'm dry, I shall be fine. And a cup of hot tea will help, too."

Francesca tried to keep her own teeth from chattering as Alfred tucked a blanket around her shoulders. The tender gesture made her throat catch, and she wanted to take one of his hands that held her shoulders so gently. Worse, she wanted Alfred to take her in his arms, to warm her and keep her close. *Oh dear.*

Philippe. She must think of Philippe. Were it not for the rain and her concern for Elizabeth, she'd have run off right then. She forced herself to take in the architectural details of the home.

"Alfred, this is truly wonderful." Francesca touched the carved stone of the fireplace. "This isn't marble?"

He shook his head. "Limestone, from Texas. The main structure is built of New Hampshire granite."

"Your mother must be very proud of you."

"I suppose she is."

"She is a vivid woman and speaks her mind."

"Oh, kind words about her. I've heard much worse." He smiled at her, and then the expression faded. "Please excuse me. I'll go see about those cups of tea for you both." He nodded at Elizabeth before he turned on his heel and left them.

Elizabeth left the warmth of the fire and looked out one of the tall windows that ran the length of the entry hall. The bank of windows opened onto a lawn that faced the sea. "The rain is still coming down hard."

Francesca nodded and shivered. "I wish it weren't. Then we could leave."

Footsteps from one of the hallways made them both look toward the sound. A young man, barely older than Alfred, came into view. He carried a tray with two cups. Steam rose from the tops and swirled above the man's head.

"Miss Francesca, Miss Elizabeth, I have tea from Mr. Finley." He nodded and smiled as he placed the tray on the long, low table in front of the fireplace. "Will you be needing sugar?"

"No, I will not." Francesca picked up one the cups and let its warmth sink into her fingers and palms.

"Sir, I'll be taking some sugar, but I can do it myself." Elizabeth joined them, and as she picked up her cup, the man went to reach for it as well. Their fingertips brushed.

"I beg your pardon, miss." The man's neck bloomed red, and so did the tips of his ears. He stepped back as if he'd touched a hot fire poker.

Elizabeth's face resembled the shade of a rose petal, and Francesca suppressed a chuckle. She'd have to ask Alfred about the young man. Then she reminded herself that the last time she and Alfred had talked, it was as if she'd cut off any familiarity with her friend. To be faithful to Philippe, she must.

"So how long has this been going on?" Alfred's mother eyed herself in the looking glass, then remarked as if to no one in particular, "I'd have worn the blue dress, had I known we'd have company."

Alfred leaned against the doorframe. "How long has what been going on?"

"You and the smart young miss downstairs. I may not be as young as I once was, but even I know what those looks mean."

"Mother, honestly." Alfred wished he'd never told Mother he'd pick her up himself from the train station, had never agreed to move her into the house this week. They would never have encountered Francesca and her maid on the road. The two would have arrived home, drenched like the rats Mother had spoken of and little worse for the experience. A twinge of guilt at their discomfort nagged at him, but Alfred stayed strong. He'd done well to keep Francesca out of mind, if not entirely out of sight, since they'd last seen each other. He had enough business in New York to keep him occupied, but here he was, playing the part of reluctant rescuer.

"Well, do I need to inquire about town, or call on the Wallingfords?" She turned and looked at him, her green eyes sharp. She was still a beautiful woman, even with her graying reddish hair.

"I would have liked to have married her, it's true." The admission, spoken aloud, had scratched at the wound on his heart. "But she has become engaged to someone else."

"Someone else?" Mother shook her head. "How could you have let this happen, if you care for her so much? She is from a good family, with excellent prospects. And you two have a like faith. That, in our small circle, is nothing short of a miracle. Plus, she's not hard on the eyes. She'd give you beautiful children."

"*Mother!*" Alfred's voice squeaked like it did when he was thirteen, and he felt about the same age. "You know it's not that simple. Her intended is a French count, and the whole agreement was sealed up neater than a business transaction."

"But he hasn't won her heart, evidently."

"I am not about to ruin my reputation, or hers, or what we've worked for, by overstepping my bounds." He wanted to be honorable, but that day by the sea, he'd nearly agreed to whisking Francesca away.

"All is not lost. How long have they been engaged? I know you would not seek an illicit tryst or anything of the sort with her, so it can't have been for long. I take it the engagement is more of a family arrangement, if she returns your feelings."

"The announcement was made nearly two weeks ago. Didn't you read it in the *New York Times*?" He'd burned his copy as soon as he saw the announcement.

"I suppose I read it, but I didn't make the connection with us. Plus all that news about the Vanderbilts. We must make sure we are invited to the next ball, if possible." She fingered her pearls. "My dear, where are our guests, and who is tending to them?"

"I sent O'Neal to fetch their tea from the kitchen and serve it to them."

"But that's *my* job! I'm the lady of the house. That man's as nervous as a cat, and he's probably spilt both cups over the poor girls—not that being wetter will harm their situation any—and he's likely broken at least one of my china cups." She pushed past Alfred and left the room. "You need to find him a wife."

Alfred had a headache, but he followed Mother down the hall and to the main staircase. He had installed an elevator, but it wasn't operational yet. As Mother didn't quite seem to be ready for the wheelchair she claimed she needed, he didn't see the urgent need just yet.

They found the two young women still before the fireplace in the great room, with O'Neal engaged in conversation with Elizabeth. Her easy manner had made him stop that incessant tugging at his collar. Extraordinary.

Francesca was seated on one of the large chairs that faced the fire and sipped her tea with a bemused expression on her face. Then, she rose from her chair when she saw them enter the room.

Mother bustled over to the chair next to Francesca. "Don't get up on account of me. Last I knew, I wasn't the queen. How are you feeling?"

"Much warmer, and drier, thank you." She smiled at Mother, then looked up at Alfred. He moved to stand by Mother's chair.

"No thanks to my son. I'm sorry we kept you waiting, or I would have seen to your tea myself. Poor manners." She reached over and patted Francesca's arm. "The rain still continues, and here we are. Alfie?" she called over her shoulder in a tone that nearly shattered his eardrum. "Oh, here you are. Sneaking up on us, are you? Well, you must give us ladies the grand tour. I haven't seen this since it was a granite box, waiting for refinement."

Alfred wanted to tell Mother that she was exaggerating, but thought the better of it. "Of course. I apologize for the lack of curtains. The seamstresses aren't quite finished."

Mother rose and tucked her arm through his. "So long as the fabrics are the same as the ones I chose in the spring, no matter. It wouldn't do to have the wrong ones hung, now would it? Ladies, please join us, and bring your blankets if you need them."

Elizabeth said, "Ma'am, if it's all the same to you, I can remain here by the fire." She looked down at her teacup, as if she realized her place once again.

Francesca joined them, and Alfred wished he could tuck her arm through his as well. She pulled the blanket around her shoulders as they started along the first hallway to the left.

Alfred led them into a room with a fireplace taller than him and wide enough to drive a carriage into. "This is the dining room."

"Oh, how beautiful," Francesca said. She stopped and stared at the now-completed mural. "Are those. . ."

"The Rocky Mountains, yes." Alfred led Mother to one of the newly arrived chairs. "Here, Mother. You can try out one of the chairs while you look at the room."

"You've outdone yourself, son. I feel like I can walk into that painting and climb that mountain. If it weren't for my bad back, that is." She settled onto the chair he'd pulled out for her with much display of groaning and not a little creaking. She scanned the room. "Service for sixteen. That's enough for me, you, and your wife. Plus thirteen guests. Adequate."

"Yes, I thought the service for twenty-four you had asked for at the beginning a little excessive." He headed over to the fireplace. The stunning carved wood mantel was his favorite part of the room, besides the mural.

"My dear, this is a Newport cottage, and we are hardly excessive." She waved him off, while Francesca's beautiful laugh filled the room.

"Pardon me." Francesca looked at Mother. "It is refreshing to hear someone speak their mind about how we conduct ourselves."

"The truth can never be gilded. At least not for long." Mother shot him a sharp glance, then flicked a look back at Francesca. "So, tell me about this man you are to marry."

Alfred confirmed in his own mind that the house tour was a bad idea. In a private moment, he'd admitted to himself that he dreamed of having Francesca run this household. She and Mother got along splendidly, and Mother didn't particularly care for most young women of their group and had even chased off a few by her demeanor.

"Well. . .what would you like to know?" Francesca moved closer to the dining table.

"What does he do? Is he here for the summer? I understand the engagement happened recently."

"His name is Count Philippe de la Croix and—"

"Oooh, French, and a count to boot. Divine. Do go on."

"I'm not sure exactly what sort of business he conducts, but he divides his time between Paris, London, and New York. He enjoys entertaining, where many men seem to have an aversion to it, and he is an accomplished horseman and a patron of the arts." Francesca's voice fell flat, and she looked over to where Alfred stood.

"A fine list of accomplishments, to be sure. Isn't it, Alfred?"

"Yes, Mother. I have met the man on a previous occasion and find him most agreeable. Men consider him a formidable negotiator in business, and the women all adore him, and duly so." The old anger bubbled inside him like the sea churning before a storm. "But he can only marry one."

"Yes. How fortunate my parents made him an offer he could not refuse." Francesca stood up straighter, her cheeks shot with red. A strand of honey-colored hair, now drying, stuck to her face. She pushed the offending strand away. Alfred understood more clearly her desire to disappear with him, especially when she looked at him like that.

Mother patted Francesca's hand. "Child, they love you."

"If they loved me, they would listen to me and not their bank account. Forgive my directness, Mrs. Finley. It is difficult to marry the rest of me away when my heart belongs to another." Francesca bit her lip, and Mother squeezed her hand.

Alfred crossed the room and stopped himself before he pulled Francesca close and. . .he struck down the idea. She was engaged, he reminded himself.

Mother looked thoughtful, which may or may not mean a good thing. "My son, you say this count is adored by all the women."

"I suppose he is. I have been too busy to notice his affairs, no pun intended." He gripped the tall leather back of the chair in front of him.

"I don't really know, either." Francesca's face paled. The look she gave Alfred reminded him of the expression she'd worn when her parents announced her engagement.

"Interesting," Mother said. "I wonder if the man has any secrets."

She wore that ponderous expression again, and Alfred wondered what thoughts spun inside his mother's head.

Chapter 9

For the rest of the week, Francesca moved through her tasks mindlessly. Tennis at the Newport Casino. Another clambake given by the Williamses. Piano lessons. French lessons (a new endeavor). And all the while escaping Mother's insistence that she start planning her trousseau. Mother had insisted that Francesca write the count a letter, which Francesca did; but she promptly tore the missive up and threw it away and went to study French some more.

Now on Sunday morning, she squirmed on the pew and tried to pay attention to the sermon. It didn't help that someone's hat blocked her view of the minister, who usually was as interesting to watch as he was to listen to. He didn't merely read verses of scripture, but made them sound as if they were being spoken for the first time.

"Riches. . ." He drew out the *s* at the end of the word. "Riches are fleeting, temporary. One man may find himself king of the world one day, and the next day, possessing little more than a pauper's inheritance. Yet the man remains the same. . . ." He let the words echo off the walls with their stained glass windows. "Or does he?"

Wealth had not changed Alfred, at least in Francesca's estimation. She let her wandering thoughts drift back to the rainy day earlier in the week.

The experience at Alfred's house had left her exhilarated yet troubled. She had not spent much time with Mrs. Finley and was greatly surprised to see that the woman fared so well for one supposedly so ill. Francesca had found herself decorating his home in her imagination—one long hall filled with landscape paintings, the other hall filled with family portraits. The dining room was already perfect, even though the chandeliers had yet to be hung.

But Mrs. Finley's questions about Philippe bothered her the most. To be sure, she had not seen him for nearly three weeks, and here it was Sunday again. Not that she had any strong feelings for him anymore, but he certainly hadn't seemed to act like an engaged gentleman. However, her own words came back to her, about her parents making him an offer. If he merely gained a wife through a business transaction, so be it.

What if Philippe had someone else in mind? What would make a man forsake someone he loved to marry another? Money, of course. A good connection.

She bowed her head as the rest of the congregation did so, but her prayer was likely unique to her. *Father above, give me grace to do what I must. I do not wish to disgrace my family or Philippe, but it is so difficult. Show me the way. Because what I really want to do is run for those beautiful mountains that are painted in Alfred's dining room. How can I love a man and honor a man who does not care for me?*

"Fran, are you ready?" Victoria plucked at her elbow, and Francesca raised her head. "Guess who will be dining with us today? None other than Alfred Finley and his mother."

"How did that happen?"

"James invited them. I think he's trying to solidify the old family alliance."

Her mother and Mrs. Finley in the same room again. She would have to see this. And try not to think too much about Alfred.

As Mother would have it, Francesca could not see Alfred at the noon meal, nor could she hear him very well. They were seated on the same side of the table, with Mrs. Finley and Mother between them.

James never wanted a quiet meal and therefore tossed out a question, not to Francesca's surprise. "So, what did you think of the Reverend's message this morning? About the deceitfulness of riches and the fleeting nature thereof?"

"James, are you addressing anyone in particular?" Mother asked.

"No, Mother. I am simply making conversation. Since it is the Lord's Day, I think it bodes us well to consider the words we heard earlier, and if we might somehow apply them to our lives." He stabbed his slice of meat, and his fork squeaked against the plate.

"Well," Father said, "I am reminded every day that riches are fleeting by the manner in which your mother spends my money."

Francesca ducked her head to the side and stifled a laugh. Father seldom spoke in such a manner, and she couldn't tell if he was truly joking or not.

"Mr. Wallingford, we have money to spare, and our lives here require a certain appearance." Mother huffed, and Francesca knew she probably glared at both her husband and her son. "*We* are the examples to the rest of the world of how, by hard work and God's blessing and good fortune, one can live."

James glanced at Francesca and gave her a look that said, *Here, the lecture commences.*

"I, for one, enjoy a well-appointed home," Mrs. Finley interjected, "and yet I do not ever want to forget the life I once had. Many in our world are *not* so fortunate, and I feel I must do what I can, when I can, to help them."

"Humph. I try to forget every single day the life *I* once had," Mother said.

"I didn't find it so bad." Francesca gulped when she realized she'd spoken aloud. "I know I was very young, but I remember our home in Connecticut, not far from the sea. I loved helping you make the bread, and I still remember stitching my first piece."

"Of course. You were but a child then." Mother leaned forward, as if to see around Mrs. Finley, who seemed to be enjoying her roast beef. "The drudgery of chores was fun to you. You did not have to see, day after day, other homes and things you could not have."

She wanted to melt into a puddle underneath the table. Didn't Mother see how ridiculous her posturing appeared?

"This is why I want to start my foundation," Alfred said. "Many families never have opportunities like ours. I want to give enterprising young men, and women, the chance to enroll in universities. The future is bright, and I believe God wants me to make a difference in the world by sharing what I have."

Mother said nothing in response to that, and they finished the meal in silence. The plates and place settings were collected, as always, and Francesca excused herself. If not for Philippe, she would have wanted to take a walk with Alfred. If not for Philippe, Alfred would probably be speaking to Father.

The men went their way, and the women their own directions. Mrs. Finley thanked them for a splendid meal, and left for home, saying she needed a nap. Victoria took her leave as well, saying she felt like resting. Francesca wanted to follow suit but found herself headed with Mother toward the back terrace to catch some of the sea breeze, where Mother planned to commence reading aloud from the book of Proverbs in the book of verses that she carried.

As soon as they left the dining room, Mother began. "Do not ever refer to our meager beginnings in such terms again."

"Mother, it was not my intention—"

"I hated being poor. If you think your tender years were humble, then you do not wish to know about my upbringing as well as your aunt's. You never lived in a neighborhood one level above the poorhouse." The air crackled with Mother's words. "This is why my sister and I are *trying* to ensure your futures—yours and Lillian's both."

"My future will be secure, even without a count."

"I am your mother, and I know best for you." She stopped at the terrace doors, and Francesca nearly ran into her. "Don't think I didn't notice the looks between you and Mr. Finley. It is not going to happen. He is not going to marry you, take you away from here, squander your wealth, or both."

"Marrying Philippe means I must live in Paris part of the year, so in a sense he will also be taking me away from here." She didn't bother to defend Alfred concerning the idea of squandering her wealth. The idea was ludicrous.

Mother yanked open the terrace door. "That is an entirely different matter."

Francesca didn't see how living an ocean away would be different than marrying Alfred—the thought made her dizzy—and living elsewhere, perhaps on his family estate on the Hudson River.

The fresh air outside diluted some of the acid from Mother's words. Francesca sat on the nearest lounge chair, and Mother took the next one.

"Furthermore, if you continue to test me in the matter of Mr. Finley, I guarantee I can make life very, very difficult for him in our circle." She opened her book of verses. "Now, I believe we left off at chapter four last week, so we shall begin there."

Mother's tone changed to one soft as rose petals as she read from Proverbs, and while part of Francesca knew the sacred words would do her good, all she heard was her pulse pounding in her ears and tasted her own angry words, unspoken. But more than the breeze chilled her at recalling Mother's threat. What could she possibly do to Alfred?

A gull cried somewhere, and Mother read on, accentuating particular verses where she likely felt Francesca was lacking. Her words slowed, and then she yawned.

"Forgive me. I may have overindulged at dinner today."

Francesca said nothing, but waited for Mother to continue reading. She glanced to the side. Sure enough, Mother's head bobbed as she studied the page in front of her.

"For the ways of man are before the eyes of the Lord, and he pondereth all his goings. . ." Mother fell silent, and her head leaned back onto the lounge. A tiny snore escaped from her mouth.

The blue sky looked limitless today, as if any bird could fly straight to heaven. Today might be a good day to send another fervent prayer to the heavenly Father's ears.

Please, help, Father God. I see no change in my circumstances, and I am losing hope. Before long, wedding plans will assail me, and for the rest of my life, I feel as if I will be swept along and become voiceless.

Mother's snoring intensified, and Francesca's fidgets took over. She left Mother lying on the lounge chair, her book of verses resting on her lap.

She didn't want to return to the house, but instead headed for the gardens in the side yard. The new plantings had been skillfully nurtured by the gardener. Next summer they'd likely have roses, and Francesca wondered if she would be around to see them, or if she'd be in New York, or in a rental cottage while Philippe had a summer home built for them.

The hollowness inside meant she'd resigned herself to what would happen. She was sure of it. Francesca was never given to tears unless under extreme duress. She thought she'd been drained of every present and future tear when her parents announced her engagement to Philippe. Yet, sitting down on the low stone bench under a young tree, more fresh tears came, the kind accompanied by sobs.

"Please protect Alfred, Lord. He wants to do Your work. I don't know what Mother could possibly do, but her manner frightened me to think of what she might scheme. Even if it means Alfred and I will never be together, protect him.

He's had enough disappointment in his life."

Francesca drew a handkerchief from her pocket. She could not go on like this. One thing she agreed with Mother on—a lady must never let her emotions master her. She prayed again for the strength to do the right thing.

∽

"So the White Star Line has cut down on transatlantic travel time, and I daresay we'll do the same with our shipping operation. Not just from China and here, but between New York and London as well." Alfred shifted on the cushioned wingback chair. "Another market I'm interested in is Western imports."

"You mean from Colorado, Texas, New Mexico?" James asked.

Alfred nodded. "James, it's beautiful country out there. The local crafts and artisans are undiscovered talent. Any gallery in New York would be foolish not to sell their work. Not to mention the mines in Colorado have great potential."

He paused, and the silence was punctuated by a loud snore from Mr. Wallingford, who'd been listening to the younger men talk.

"It's not that Father's uninterested, you know." James looked apologetic.

"Of course not." Alfred rose and stretched. "I don't want to have overstayed my welcome, so I ought to be on my way now. Back to New York. Are you coming as well?"

"Yes, unfortunately. Victoria says she misses me when I'm gone. But I'm here every weekend, and sometimes for a quick overnight during the week."

"Oh, to be carefree boys once again, without responsibilities. Life was simpler, was it not?"

"To be sure it was. But I like the benefits of adulthood." James grinned.

They left Mr. Wallingford dozing in his great chair. The man likely dreamt of a world where his wife wasn't spending his money.

"I'll see myself out," Alfred said in the hallway. "Side door to the stables, isn't it?"

"That's right." James stopped walking for a moment. "And Al, don't worry about Francesca. She's going to be fine. Mother's a bit. . .hard. . .on her. She doesn't want her to have a life of struggle."

"I know that. But life with me would hardly be a struggle." Alfred tired of having to justify his position.

"Mother has this notion of reputation being supreme. And since, in her opinion, yours has a bit of a smudge—"

"I'd say it's more of an ink stain."

"Don't be so hard on yourself."

"I'm not. I am simply a realist where your mother is concerned."

James darted a glance down the hall as they headed to the side entry. "I'll see what I can learn about this count. Surely his reputation isn't completely stellar, despite the title. Perhaps if Mother can be persuaded that you are a better match, although title-less. . ."

"Thanks, James, for those thoughts. But I won't try to undermine him. That would only paint me as more of a villain in your mother's sight."

As Alfred turned to leave, James called after him, "I know you're the best man for my sister. We just need to convince Mother."

Alfred waved and left through the door. Two paths sloped from the magnificent steps. One path led toward the carriage house and stables. The other led to the Wallingfords' young gardens.

A lone figure sat on a bench underneath a small tree. Francesca. Alfred steeled himself on his first impulse to head toward the garden and instead intended to take the path to the carriage house. She looked up, in his direction.

He found his feet turning in the direction of the garden and his legs propelling him there as well. After the fiasco at dinner, no wonder Francesca sought refuge. When he reached her, he noted her red eyes and the rumpled handkerchief in her hand.

"You shouldn't be here," she said.

"You've been crying." He settled next to her on the bench.

With the silence, they could hear the ocean nearby and a bird twittering away in a tree somewhere.

"I shouldn't." She dabbed at her eyes. "It won't solve anything. But you must leave."

"I'll leave when I'm ready."

"We are in full view of the side of the house. Anyone looking out the windows can see us." Her gaze traveled to the great windows of Seaside that overlooked the garden. "Mother asked for a view of the terrace from her bedroom so she could look out on her roses. She may yet see us, instead. Or else one of her spies that work in the house may."

"Very well. Perhaps we should stroll. Walk with me to the carriage house." Alfred stood and offered her his arm, but she simply stared at it.

"I am afraid for you, Alfred." She looked down at the handkerchief in her hands. "Mother made it very clear to me this afternoon that she is prepared to make trouble for you somehow. She wants to ruin everything you have worked for, and I feel as if I am to blame."

"Why would you think that?" He gritted his teeth, not at Francesca, but at the very thought that Mrs. Wallingford would deliberately work against him. It was one thing to use her daughter as a stepping stone in society, but now to attempt to ruin him for good?

"Because try as I might, even though I am engaged to someone else, I cannot forget you." With this, she stood and gripped his arm, and fresh tears streamed down her face.

He was in agony, trying to keep from pulling her into an embrace. "Francesca, you are not entirely to blame. Because I have not been able to forget you."

Alfred allowed himself to use one of his thumbs to wipe a tear. Francesca moved her face ever so slightly and kissed his palm.

Then she stepped back. "Oh. I shouldn't have." With that, she took up her skirt and ran for the house.

Chapter 10

Alfred's palm burned for the next two days, and the memory of Sunday followed him into the week. No matter how much he cared for Francesca, and no matter how much his business dealings brought him into contact with her father and brother, he had no need to spend more time in Newport than necessary. Except for Mother, who declared just before he left that she was sure she'd be "in sore need of a physician's attention" before the summer's end.

"Mother, if you require my presence, you may simply send word," he'd said. But Alfred firmly believed that she didn't want to be alone. Nor did he blame her. He did not want to face years of being alone, either.

With a word from him, Mother would likely begin sorting through her connections to see if one of them had an eligible daughter of marrying age. She would be a lovely, accomplished young woman who undoubtedly would not quibble at the arrangement—that is, if the Finley reputation and Mother's idiosyncrasies did not deter the said woman's family.

He looked at the papers on his desk, then at the city outside his window. Part of him wanted to return to Colorado and take Mother with him. Weren't there springs reported to have healing waters? Not that anything was really wrong with Mother, although she did have pneumonia over the winter and still became short of breath after walking too quickly.

"Your daily post, sir." O'Neal entered his office.

"Anything of significance?" Alfred rose from his desk. He preferred to think of O'Neal as more of his assistant than a mere servant. He didn't need a man to open doors for him and lay out his suits. He did, however, require someone to lend an extra hand and manage his schedule, which O'Neal did well, as had O'Neal's father before him.

"A letter from Colorado may interest you." He handed the envelope to Alfred.

"Thank you."

O'Neal nodded and left the room.

Alfred sat down again and opened the letter.

Dear Mr. Finley,

We hope and pray this letter finds you well. We were sorry to have you leave us and can hardly believe it has been over a year already. But we know your mother needs you, and we think fondly of you often. Perhaps one day Mrs. Stone and I shall take a train east and visit you. The church is doing well, especially with the influx of new residents moving to the area.

We are thankful, too, that you advised us to purchase interest in the Lost River Mine. Even with our small share, we have received much blessing from a wise investment. Because of this, when Benjamin finishes school, we intend to send him to the university, and Betsy as well, who will read any book we give her. For that bit of advice, we are grateful to you.

Mitchell Hamm was wrong, of course, and I think he is merely jealous that his own efforts to mine silver have come up fruitless. We pray for him. The pursuit of instant wealth has consumed him, as it has many of us. The children ask about you often, and we tell them that mayhap we shall see you again, if not here, then on the other side of Glory.

We remain your friends and humble servants,
Herbert and Abigail Stone

Tempting, it was, to rejoin the Stones at their tiny but growing church in a mining town. There, the veneer of wealth was not as apparent as it was here among the people he knew and his father had known before him. But much as he prayed, he did not believe that returning to Colorado was the answer, even after he had sent O'Neal to inquire about the price of railroad tickets to Colorado for all of them—including Francesca.

To leave on impulse would be to destroy all his father had worked to build for him.

He leaned back in his chair until it squeaked. Mitchell Hamm had made trouble for him in Colorado, or had tried to. Alfred had been the greenhorn, wealthy outsider, and while the small community had grown to accept him, Mitchell had seen him as a threat for some reason. Alfred shook his head. He faced the same here. And he could not continue to live his life running.

∞

The ballroom's veranda at Seaside glowed with rectangles of light that shone through open doors. Francesca wanted fresh air. The dozens of partygoers cavorting on the dance floor of the latest cotillion had quickly raised the temperature of the room. All of them clad in the costume theme of the night—Ali Baba's *Arabian Nights*—had filled the room with turbans and flowing cloaks. The late supper was being laid out buffet-style for the guests, so Francesca darted out to the veranda when the count was otherwise engaged in conversation.

It would have been a beautiful night otherwise, with the fresh scent of the sea and the stars spangling the sky above. Francesca's train and robes attached to her white gown flowed around her. She would have liked to walk with Alfred on the pathway that she now took. The veranda had two levels, the upper level close to the ballroom, and the lower level closer to the lawn. The lower level, graced with potted plants, was shrouded in darkness.

Seaside could have an air of peace about it when not full of people as Mother had arranged for tonight. Francesca glanced down at the ring Philippe had given her at their engagement. Not a symbol of love, or even affection really. They barely knew each other. Business, of course. Business with her family. She should accept that.

Part of her knew she should try to think of the positive aspects of marrying Philippe, and if she let herself, she could almost forget Alfred for a few moments. Until a reminder returned, such as now.

Francesca leaned against the embellished granite railing and stared across toward the path that led to the sea. Footsteps on the stairs made her turn.

"There you are," Philippe said. "Someone told me you had come to get some air."

"It was hard to breathe inside, and I knew that no one would miss me for a few minutes."

"Ah, but I did." He moved closer, and she caught the scent of his cologne.

"I would have returned soon." Francesca felt one of his arms encircling her.

"You are *tres enchante* in the moonlight, my Francesca."

She looked at him, and he covered her lips with his. This was a man who knew how to kiss, and he probably had some practice in the activity, whereas she knew nothing except in the part of her imagination where she tried not to visit. Francesca pulled away.

"Did I do something wrong?" Philippe asked.

"I, um. . .I have never been kissed before. So I would not know."

"Ah, I should have asked your permission first. But I could not help myself, with you standing there so beautiful at my side all evening. *Tres enchante,* as I have said." He sounded penitent. "But, I must ask, did you like it?"

"I. . .I suppose part of me did." She couldn't ignore her pounding heart and didn't want to lie to Philippe.

"What is wrong? Are you angry?"

"No, no." Francesca patted his arm, now that she had freed herself of its hold around her. "There's someone else, Philippe. I care for someone else, and I did not know what my parents had planned. Our upcoming marriage, I mean."

He made a noise that sounded almost like a grunt. "I see. So have you told your parents of your wishes, of this other one you care for?"

"They know my feelings."

"I see," Philippe said again. "And this knowledge did not change their minds. Well, then. A formidable opponent I have, unknown though he is. But I have one thing he does not."

"And what is that?" She could scarcely believe the arrogance she heard in his tone.

"I will be the one marrying you, and I shall stay close enough so that you will have no choice but to give me your heart as well. Surely, I enter business with your father, but I am well aware of the benefits before me." He offered her his arm, but as he did so, reached for her hand with his free one and pulled it underneath his arm. "And there is nothing this one you care for can do about it."

"Of all the arrogant—"

"I am a realist, *mon amour*. I see you are angry, even though you say you are not. Do not make a scene in front of your guests as we go inside, *s'il vous plaît*." He kept one hand tightly around hers as they climbed the stairs to head for the ballroom.

"You can be sure I will not make a scene, but if I did, you can be equally sure that all of Newport would talk about it for years to come. But I will do nothing to disgrace my parents." Francesca smiled as they passed another couple seeking fresh air on the terrace. They reentered the ballroom, where a few guests lingered.

Victoria stood near the doorway that led to the hall. "There you are, Francesca. The late supper is ready. Are you all right? Your face looks pale."

"I needed some air." Francesca tried pulling her arm from the crook of Philippe's elbow, but he held her tighter than a crab claw.

"And now, as you say, she is right as rain again." Philippe smiled at Victoria and escorted Francesca from the ballroom.

"You need not hold so tightly," she hissed as they stepped into the hallway. "I am not going to run away." She nodded at the admiral and his wife on the way to Seaside's dining room. At least physically she would not run. But in her imagination, Philippe would be invisible beside her for the rest of the night.

◇

Francesca's eyes were heavy with sleep, but she complied with Mother's request and accompanied her to the sitting room. Her feet ached, and she longed to shed the new boots that had perfectly matched her gown. Their guests had left after consuming an early-morning breakfast, and Francesca planned to slip upstairs to her bedroom as soon as Mother dismissed her.

Mother showed her to a cushioned chair. "Sit down, Francesca." Then she rang a bell, and within a few moments, Mrs. McGovern, Elizabeth's mother, appeared.

"Yes, Mrs. Wallingford." The woman's hair, probably once the color of Elizabeth's, had been scraped into a tight bun. Her eyes looked tired, and she assessed Francesca with an even gaze.

Francesca matched her look and refused to squirm in the chair. She'd done nothing wrong lately that she could think of, and even if she had, this was not a reason to summon the housekeeper, who did Mother's bidding and acted as Mother's eyes and ears everywhere Mother did not go.

"I appreciate loyal employees, especially when they have my family's interests at heart." Mother smiled at Mrs. McGovern. "This is why I was distressed to hear of certain actions one Sunday afternoon, while I napped on the veranda."

"All right. I'm still unsure of why you've brought me here and summoned Mrs. McGovern." Francesca stood, not wanting to feel as if either of the two women had an advantage over her.

"Sit *down*, child." Mother hadn't spoken in that tone since Francesca was much younger, and had broken an antique vase.

Francesca complied.

"Are you prepared to tell me of your indiscretions?"

"I don't know what you mean."

Mother gasped. "Do I need to have you copy from the scriptures as you did when you were small, and select passages about lying?"

If Francesca weren't already feeling the need to go smash a vase just now, she'd have laughed. "Mother. I honestly do *not* know what you are referring to. Please tell me, and if I *have* done something wrong, I will make amends and seek forgiveness."

"Mrs. McGovern. Did you go to my bedroom on a Sunday afternoon but a week ago, to care for the linens?"

"Yes, Mrs. Wallingford, that I did."

"Tell me what you witnessed."

"Well, the room was warm, so I thought I would open a window to let in the breeze." Mrs. McGovern glanced at Francesca. "I saw Miss Francesca in the garden. With Mr. Finley."

Francesca closed her eyes. *Oh no.* She'd warned Alfred, and she'd fled.

"And what did you see?"

"Mr. Finley touched her. . .in a way that wasn't appropriate."

"That's not true." Francesca stood. "In fact, he wasn't the one who was anywhere near inappropriate. I was crying, and he wiped my tears—"

"Thank you, Mrs. McGovern. That will be all." Mother inclined her head, and the housekeeper left.

Once the door had shut behind her, Mother continued. "So you do admit he touched you?"

"Alfred was not inappropriate. As I said, I was crying, and he wiped my tears with his *thumb*, Mother. That was all. If anything, *I* was the one being inappropriate."

"*What?*"

"I kissed his palm. There! I admit it."

Mother closed the space between them until Francesca could see her pupils crackling. "Didn't I warn you? You are an engaged woman. You are spoken for. And yet you carry on like some—some—"

Francesca knew she could fill in some words for her mother, but chose not to. She braced herself.

"From now on, you shall never be alone except to bathe or sleep or tend to your toilette. I will allow you with Elizabeth, and you can be sure her mother will keep me informed of her actions. As the Finleys are family friends and we cannot ignore their connection, we will attend functions where they are present. But you will not be alone with him, and you will not speak to him nor send word to him in any manner."

Francesca sank back onto the chair. "I understand."

"Furthermore, you must focus your attentions on your future husband. At our fete it was clear the count could not take his eyes from you and wanted to be near you at every moment. Yet you treat him as if he were beneath you. Francesca, if you would make an effort, perhaps you would see that your father and I have not consigned you to a prison sentence."

"Will you lock me in my room at night as Consuelo's parents did?" She regretted the words as soon as they'd escaped her mouth.

"That can be arranged, if need be." Mother went to the door and flung it open. "You may go now. And I shall send Elizabeth up to your room directly."

Francesca clenched her teeth and marched from the room. She would not cry, nor would she knock over the grand palm tree Mother had moved into the entry hallway for the ball last night. Breaking something would only temporarily make her feel better, and it would be wasteful.

Her feet throbbed as she pounded up the unforgiving stairs. This house was cold, cold in the summer, and not from the stonework. She burst into her bedroom and tore off her attire. One of the seams protested and threatened to rip.

Francesca moved more slowly. She actually liked this costume, and had a feeling that Philippe had sent bolts of fabric from France for the gowns she now wore. She draped it on her vanity chair.

Then she draped herself on her bed. "Father above, I can't do this. It's wrong. *I* did not agree to this engagement. They never consulted me. I know I'm supposed to honor my mother, but honoring her is the furthest thing from my mind right now. I feel so trapped. I'm sorry I kissed Alfred, if even his hand."

She succumbed to her tears and let them run like a wild river. Better now than at an inopportune time. She could not be like some young women, getting pushed and prodded along paths not of their choosing, without saying a word. Right now, she didn't feel as if God were even listening.

Francesca sat up and sighed, then found a clean handkerchief to wipe her face. Where was Elizabeth? If anything, Mother was always prompt about keeping her word, and a jailer was not to be found.

A soft knock sounded on the door. "Fran, it's me."

"Come in, Victoria."

Her sister-in-law opened the door and crept in, as if half-expecting to enter a monster's lair. "Are you all right?"

"No, I'm not."

"Is it Alfred?"

Francesca nodded. "This entire situation. I see no way out. I cannot forget my feelings for Alfred; and honestly, I really don't wish to. Yet I feel I must honor my parents."

"I've been praying for you, if it helps you to know." Victoria settled onto the bed next to her.

"I hope it is helping. I see no change in my current state. And they have just become far worse. No matter how much I have prayed, I do not see anything happening." Francesca pulled her robe on and tied the belt. She took her earrings off—they matched the necklace Philippe had given her at their engagement—and tossed them onto her vanity tray.

"I believe God works even when we do not see it."

"I would like to think so." Francesca returned to the bed and sat down again. "But I can't help but think, what if I am supposed to forget Alfred? What if that is what God would have me do? And after Philippe's actions tonight. . ."

"Was he. . .improper?"

"He kissed me. But his attitude toward me, that he would *make* me love him one day, bothered me just as much." Francesca took her pillow and threw it across the room.

"Oh, Fran." Victoria touched her shoulder. "I'm so sorry."

"Me too. What would God have me do, Victoria? I try to obey, I do. But when I feel as if I'm being forced. . ."

"Trust Him, Fran. I know that is easy for me to say, but I also think of the three young Hebrew men thrown into the fiery furnace by King Nebuchadnezzar."

"How so?"

"They told the king before he threw them into the fire, 'Our God whom we serve is able to deliver us from the burning fiery furnace, and he will deliver us out of thine hand, O king. But if not, be it known unto thee, O king, that we will not serve thy gods, nor worship the golden image which thou hast set up.' They still trusted Him, even when the situation looked impossible."

"I feel as if I am in the furnace right now, Victoria." She bit her lip. "And I don't see myself being delivered."

Victoria hugged her. "Have faith, Fran. You are not wed yet."

Chapter 11

Two weeks in the city had not faded Alfred's memory of the last time he had seen Francesca. He had thought it best to stay away until Mother had asked that he come out to Newport and escort her home. He opened the morning paper as he sat across from Mother at breakfast in their spacious New York apartment.

"So, how was the grand fete to which I was not invited?" he asked her.

"Outlandish. I wish I'd thought of it. Ali Baba everywhere, with turbans for the men to wear, spangled tiaras for the ladies, and Persian carpets covering the marble floors. Mrs. Wallingford even hired a troupe of dancers and acrobats and trained monkeys. Quite the spectacle." Mother shook her head. "I won't tell her, though, that the lack of an invitation has ruffled your feathers."

"Mother, I don't have feathers, and if I did, they would most certainly not be ruffled." He poured himself some coffee. "I have a meeting this morning and must be off soon."

"Don't you want to know how your young lady fared at the fete?"

"She is not my young lady, and although I would always wish to know how she fared, I do not think it would change anything."

"That count." Mother frowned. "I don't trust him. He seems like he has too much polish. What do you think?"

"I can't say. I haven't had many dealings with the man." Alfred folded up his newspaper. Too much talk of people he did not want to consider. It hurt to think of Francesca, and it hurt even worse to think of how he'd nearly succumbed to his urge to kiss her in the garden and comfort her as well. But she was not his to comfort. Or to kiss.

"You're off, now?"

He nodded. "I will be back this afternoon."

"Give your mother a kiss."

Alfred complied, then went for his hat. The fine New York morning was full of activity as the city woke up, with the rush of carriages and people on foot.

The offices of Finley Shipping and Imports were located blocks away from their apartment and farther than he usually liked to walk, but this unspoiled morning walk would give Alfred time to think, pray, and clear his head. Father used to have an uncanny way of letting nothing trouble him, but he devoted his full attention to the matter at hand.

Perhaps it was because of his youth, but Alfred had yet to master such a task at age twenty-five. He knew, though, to ask daily for wisdom from above. He had yet to be disappointed; however, the matter of what to do about Francesca left him wondering.

Two figures half a block away and across the street made him pause. They stood at the entrance gate to a fine house that likely made up three of Alfred's own New York premises. He'd known that someone of great status lived there, but had never seen the occupants, nor had he ever been curious enough to know the owner.

As he drew closer, Alfred saw that a tall man with dark hair held the hand of a young woman; her ink-black hair tumbled past her shoulders. She looked as though she wanted to step closer to him, but the tall man darted glances along the street at the passersby and shook his head. Alfred wished he could see her face clearly. He drew closer to the gate across the street.

The young woman turned from the tall man, her head down, and pulled a shawl about her shoulders. She looked back and blew him a kiss before scurrying to a waiting cab.

Alfred stopped on the sidewalk, and someone nearly ran into him.

"I beg your pardon." Alfred tipped his hat and stared back at the gate.

Count Philippe stared back at him from across the street, then slammed the gate shut and disappeared.

Without a thought except to watch for carriages criss-crossing on the street, Alfred darted toward the gate.

"Count de la Croix," he called through the bars. "I must speak with you."

Alfred only saw a short expanse of lawn, and a small flowering garden. No sign of the man who'd closed the gate mere seconds before.

"Sir?" he called out but heard only street noise and the bubbling fountain inside the small courtyard. The very idea that Count de la Croix was keeping company with a woman made the blood burn inside his veins. Not that Alfred wanted to think of Francesca eventually married to the man, but the idea that the count's fidelity was questionable?

He waited, and not patiently. At last, the noise of a large door opening met his ears, and a doorman clad in a starched suit left the house and crossed the courtyard.

"*Monsieur*, I am afraid Count de la Croix is not accepting visitors today. You will leave now, n'est-ce pas?" But the man's tone held no question.

"Oui. I understand." Alfred wanted to pound the gate and demand the count admit him to the estate, but truthfully, he didn't know what he'd say to the man if he were granted an audience with him.

He turned away and continued along. If he had ever thought of a morning walk clearing his mind and preparing him to focus on the day, that inclination was lost. Because now he recalled the identity of the young woman. He'd seen that dark hair before, the porcelain skin, the nose that formed a point. He'd also heard her grating laughter as he spoke with her on another occasion.

The woman was none other than Francesca's own cousin, Lillian.

∽

"How beautiful." Francesca stared at the topaz bracelet on her wrist. "But Philippe, you do not have to give me jewelry every time I see you."

"My Francesca, it has been a long week, and I counted the hours until again I saw your face." He reached for her hand and kissed it.

They stood on the front steps of Seaside where an open carriage and driver waited for them. Francesca preferred to walk barefoot on the rocks near the shore, listen to Victoria attempt to play the piano with her faltering fingers, or attend a lecture with Mother on the benefits of prudence in one's daily life. But if Philippe had a driver with him, surely he would not try anything improper. Although a slight nudge on the inside told her that if he did not mind kissing her on a darkened veranda with people nearby, the turned back of a carriage driver would not deter him either.

"I have heard there is a ten-mile Ocean Drive that one must take while here," Philippe said as he helped her onto the seat of the carriage.

"Yes, there is." Francesca adjusted her hat, then felt for the small packet she carried in her pocket. Victoria had advised her to be prepared the next time she saw the count, and so she was. "It begins at The Elms."

Francesca and some friends had driven the ten-mile course once, and naturally, two of the carriages competed to see who could cover the distance in the shortest time. She suspected, though, that Philippe would want to linger.

"Jean, let us go now. To The Elms." Philippe gestured to the driver, who chirruped to the horses. As they pulled away to head along the driveway, Francesca sent up a prayer and fumbled with the gemstone bracelet that might as well have been a shackle. She had prayed every day and sensed no answer.

Worse, Mother remained silent about the matter and had started to focus on wedding plans. The dress, the church, the cake, who should and should not stand with Francesca as attendants.

"Lillian will be at the end of the line," Mother had said. "The girl is simply brazen. It will be a miracle if my sister finds a suitable match willing to accept her. She has not been properly launched yet."

"You are quiet today." Philippe took Francesca's hand as they passed through the gates of Seaside and onto Bellevue Avenue, in the direction of The Elms.

"I have been thinking. Mother is busy already with wedding plans."

"Oh, but that is good, very good. I want no expense spared. Tell me of these plans, or are they meant to be secret?"

"You already know we will be married in New York, at the end of May."

"But yes, after which I will take you all over Europe for a month, or for the entire summer if you desire." He settled his arm on the edge of the carriage, and Francesca felt his arm nudge her shoulders as the carriage moved.

She leaned forward. "Oh, look! I think I see a boat on the bay."

Philippe frowned and shifted on the seat. "And what about our home? I have several, as you know, but my favorite is in Paris. How did you like Paris?"

"Parts of it I liked very much, such as the gardens. And the Louvre, of course." She had to be honest, but didn't want to give the man false hope that she was enthralled with the idea of becoming his wife.

Now they approached Tranquility, and Francesca tried not to stare at the home and will Alfred to come to a window, step onto a terrace—anything.

"Your friend Mr. Finley." Philippe draped his arm on the back of the seat again. "Do you see him much?"

"No. I have not seen him since. . .it has been three weeks." She fought off the sensation of missing Alfred, of wanting to hear his voice and engage in conversation. To not just kiss his palm. The ring she wore winked at her in the sunlight.

"That is good. The less you see him, the better. You do not need any, how do you say, conflicted thoughts?"

"You sound much like my mother," Francesca admitted.

"She is a woman of intelligence. You would do well to listen to her." Philippe touched her chin. "Do not look so sad. We shall have a wonderful life together, and you will learn to love me."

Another lesson for her. Like needlework, or piano, or French, or riding. She would rather practice needlework than learn to love Philippe. The carriage drew even with Tranquility, and Francesca glimpsed a lone figure on one of the second-story terraces. Alfred could see her, she knew, and she stared at her hands instead of allowing herself to look at him.

Once Tranquility began to grow smaller behind them, they followed Bellevue Avenue until they reached The Elms.

"Slow down, Jean," Philippe called ahead to the driver. "We are not racing."

Francesca was trying to enjoy the view, although the sea breeze barely diffused the afternoon heat. She should have brought a fan, or her parasol. The closed parasol would have served as an ideal weapon, if the need arose. This made her want to smile.

"You look rather pleased. I would like to think it has something to do with me, and this drive today." Philippe showed her the charming smile that had turned her head in Paris. "Please, tell me I am not repulsive. Francesca, do you think I would have agreed to this marriage if it were merely a business proposition?"

"I do not find you repulsive when you do not try so hard to woo me. Women do not always require a strong hand."

Philippe tilted his head back and laughed. "My dear Francesca, I *am* sorry. You are quite unlike any woman I have ever known. Please forgive my behavior the other evening. Please. It will not happen again." He gave her a repentant look.

This almost made her forget the darker side she had seen the night of the ball. But not quite. Now, if they would finish the ten-mile Ocean Drive and be done with it.

"Thank you for saying so." She wondered how many other women he had "ever known." The idea niggled at her.

A few other carriages and their occupants were out enjoying the day as well, and Philippe nodded and touched his hat as they passed. Francesca smiled as well. It wouldn't do for someone to report to her parents they'd seen her looking like an August thundercloud. She would only speak to direct the driver along the course.

"Jean, please turn down this path." Philippe pointed to an area that stopped at a lookout over the sea.

"That's not part of the drive." Francesca noted the path led to a tree-covered area.

"There. Stop and set the brake." Philippe waited until Jean stopped the carriage. "You may go stretch the legs while Miss Wallingford and I. . .talk."

Francesca swallowed hard. She should have brought the parasol. Maybe the packet in her skirt pocket would help. If she could reach it when the need arose.

"A beautiful view isn't it?" Francesca could watch the surf pound the rocks all day.

"Oui, the view is very beautiful." Except Philippe's gaze wasn't focused on the scene before them. He licked his lips.

She felt the heat on her neck, and not from the summer day. "Philippe—"

In a flash, he pulled her to him. She couldn't breathe. His breath smelled, and she had never noticed the odor of cigar on his shirt before. But then she hadn't been that close to him before, either.

Her pocket. She managed to get an arm free and fumble in her pocket. There. The contents of the packet stung her fingers. She turned the end around and shoved the needle packet into his trouser leg.

A bellow rose from his throat and he released her. "Bee? Was that a bee?" He hollered a few other words in French that Francesca didn't dare translate in her head because Mother had said those words were improper and she would not need to use them. Ever.

Francesca scrambled to the other side of the carriage seat. "Not a bee. Philippe, what is wrong with you? I just told you earlier that you are not quite repulsive when you stop trying so hard to woo me. And I told you about women not needing a strong hand."

"Why did you come out with me today, then, on this carriage ride?"

"I was trying to give you a chance. But I also remembered the other evening of the ball."

"Jean!" Philippe bellowed again for the driver. "Let us return Miss Wallingford to her parents."

"Thank you, Philippe." Francesca fanned herself with one hand. "It *is* rather warm today."

"Do not ever do anything like that again, after we are wed."

"Do not ever give me a reason to." Francesca gave him the heat of her glare. "We could have talked and enjoyed ourselves on this drive."

"Talk, talk. Why talk?"

"To get to know one another better." She didn't know why she tried. After the ball the other evening, she should have locked herself in her room and saved herself the trouble.

Soon enough, they were heading along the driveway to Seaside, and Francesca had never been so glad to see her home.

"I will come in with you and see your parents, no?" Except Philippe wasn't asking. He tucked her hand inside his arm, but didn't clamp tightly like the other evening.

They scaled the granite steps together and entered the house.

"Miss Wallingford, Count de la Croix." Mrs. McGovern greeted them as they stood in the main hallway. "You have returned. Mr. and Mrs. Wallingford are on the terrace."

Francesca wondered what fresh troubles the woman was going to cause her. Poor woman, seeing a life she could never have played out before her every day. Francesca only hoped Elizabeth would not learn the same bitterness.

Francesca walked with Philippe along the grand hall, straight for the rear terrace where her parents sat, enjoying the breeze.

"You are back so soon," Mother said as she rose.

"Yes, we are." Francesca glanced at Philippe, who somehow had gained a limp since leaving the carriage.

"What a charmante town Newport is," Philippe said. "And thank you for allowing your daughter to ride with me. It has been most. . .enlightening."

"I am very glad you have had the time to spend together." Mother beamed.

"Oui, I have discovered one thing today." Philippe nodded. "Francesca and I do not see the need to wait nearly a full year before we wed. We should like to marry in January, after the New Year."

Mother started fanning herself. "But the preparations. . .I don't know if there's enough time to do everything in that short amount of time."

"Mother, we don't have to marry in January." *Or anytime, for that matter.* "This was *not* my idea."

Mother gasped. "You would call the man you are to marry, a count, a liar?"

"It is more his idea than mine."

Philippe merely stared at her with the darkened expression she'd seen at the ball.

"Anyway, since when has anyone considered what *I* want in this entire agreement? Marrying in May was unacceptable. January? Unthinkable. Anytime? Unimaginable." Francesca ground the words out. "If you would please excuse me, I think the heat and sun have gotten to me. I must go lie down."

She nodded at Mother and bowed at Philippe, then scurried to her room before she said anything worse.

Chapter 12

Welcome, ladies of Newport society, welcome one and all!" Mrs. Finley's voice could be heard above the crashing waves as she stood on the lawn of Tranquility. "I am so glad each of you could attend today. We gather, not just for ourselves, but for women everywhere."

Francesca stood beside Victoria among a group of nearly two dozen women. She wore Philippe's family ring out in public today after Mother's chiding that she needed to show her engaged status.

After the fiasco of the Sunday drive several days ago, Francesca had not seen nor heard from Philippe. Just as well. Mother had hit a frenzy of wedding planning now that they'd lost months in which to see to details. Francesca told her mother to choose whatever she wanted on such short notice.

"Hello, cousin." Lillian sidled up to her. "I wonder what the old windbag speaks of today."

"Lillian, hush. She means well, and I for one want to hear her." Francesca shot her cousin a glare and adjusted the silk sash that hung over her shoulder. Mrs. Finley had given each woman such a sash upon her arrival that said Votes For Women in large letters.

Mrs. Finley continued, "I have asked you to come today, not merely for a day of ladies' diversions, but also to consider our rights as women, namely the right to vote.

"God has given us minds to reason. While we are considered the weaker sex, weak does not mean weak in our minds. My body is failing, I know. There may come a day very soon when I shall not be able to move around as I wish. But my mind is strong. And I realize that we have a voice, that we women can make a difference, not just in our homes, which we run more efficiently than our men could—"

At this, a few of the women tittered. Someone said, "That's for certain."

"We have been blessed like few women have been in our era. We also have the power to influence generations to come and change the world. But to do so, we must learn that we have a voice, and with God's help, we must use that power." Mrs. Finley paused. Waves crashed on the beach. No one spoke.

Francesca nudged Victoria, then started to clap. Her sister-in-law followed suit, and soon most of the women were applauding Mrs. Finley's words.

When the applause ended, someone spoke. "But I let my husband decide on such issues. I don't really want to vote about matters I know nothing about." A few women nodded, and Francesca tried to see who had spoken.

"Then my dear, I am very sorry." Mrs. Finley shook her head. "I realize that many of you might feel this way, and I have no ill will against you. I only ask that you think of the great advances we have made, and the benefits that we women have reaped from our husbands' efforts. But what about us? Are we lesser because we do not conduct business as they do?

"I assure you, every wife here who runs her household must oversee affairs similar to her husband's. We have responsibilities as well, and we should want to voice our choices like our men do."

Murmurs rose, competing with some applause. Clearly, Mrs. Finley had a divided crowd, and this made Francesca smile. The formidable woman probably thought most ladies believed as she did, and while Francesca had never thought much about suffrage, Mrs. Finley's ideas were thought-provoking.

The woman's ample cheeks flushed, and she dabbed at her forehead. "But I will not keep us any longer from our festivities. You can see the delicious clambake I have prepared for us, and the tables under the tent will be laid with all manner of delicious fare."

Two chefs appeared and began removing clams and oysters from where they had cooked in a pit along with roasted ears of corn.

"Utterly primitive," Francesca heard someone mutter. "An odder woman never lived."

She might be unconventional, but Francesca found her rather endearing. Mrs. Finley huffed and puffed as she scaled the beach path with the other women.

Francesca touched the older woman's elbow. "Mrs. Finley, are you feeling well?"

"A little dizzy." She wiped her forehead again. "I should have known better than to start this too early in the day. But Mrs. Smithson has her cotillion tonight, and since I wanted a lot of ladies to attend today, I could not have scheduled my clambake later."

"Everything smells wonderful." But then Francesca always loved *fruits de mer*. Her mouth watered at the sight of lobsters procured for the occasion.

"Sweet, sweet girl you are." Mrs. Finley patted her hand before darting to the nearest table. "Oh, Mrs. Astor, please do take this chair here. It will yet be in the shade for a while."

The other women took their seats, and Mrs. Finley situated herself next to Francesca. She ensured that everyone had a place setting and a tall glass of lemonade, and the servers began presenting the delicacies to the diners.

Francesca had eaten three clams when Mrs. Finley asked, "Where is your mother today?"

"She was not feeling well, and said she was going to stay home and lie down instead." Although Mother had seemed well enough at breakfast, and she had sent and received several messages throughout the course of the morning.

"I see." Mrs. Finley's lips sealed into a thin line. "I'm afraid, child, that my friendship with your mother was linked to our husbands. Dear Charles, I miss him so, had a good friend in your father. Our families have always been good allies."

"But then Alfred left."

"The stubborn boy with a hot head and a temper to match. I told him years ago to hold his head high. He wouldn't listen to his father, or to me, of course." She glanced at the rest of their tablemates, engaged in their own conversations. "Rumors die off if not given fuel."

"I know you are happy he's returned at last."

"To be sure. What a gift this last year has been. Seeing as I don't know how much longer my health will hold out." Mrs. Finley commenced fanning herself, and she stood. "Ladies, after the luncheon, I shall be glad to escort you through my home, and then we shall have tea."

But scarcely had the women finished their luncheon and talking than barely half a dozen remained. Mrs. Finley and Francesca were the only two who remained at their table, plus Victoria and three women at her table.

Mrs. Finley sighed. "I don't suppose you will stay for the tour and then tea. You've seen it already, Miss Wallingford."

"I don't mind, if Victoria would like to stay."

"Of course I'd like to stay. I haven't seen the house yet," said Victoria. "The tour will be a welcome relief from the heat of the day."

"Oh, we must get you inside, given your condition." Mrs. Finley stood. "It would not do for me to send you home ill because of the heat."

She bustled the remaining women into the house and whisked them on a whirlwind tour. The clock chimed four o'clock as they reentered the main entry hall of Tranquility.

The other four women apologized about not staying for tea, but they must return home to prepare for Mrs. Smithson's event. Victoria said she should really go back to Seaside and lie down.

"What about you?" Mrs. Finley looked at Francesca. "Are you going to desert me, too?"

"Francesca, don't leave on my account," Victoria said. "I can send the carriage back for you in an hour."

"All—all right."

"Don't sound so eager to stay, my dear." Mrs. Finley motioned to one of her maids nearby. "Mary, tea for Miss Wallingford and myself in the conservatory. There should be a good breeze, I daresay."

Within twenty minutes, Francesca found herself seated across from Mrs.

Finley. The woman poured tea for both of them then smiled.

"I suppose I should have ordered us lemonade. There's certainly something comforting about tea, though." Mrs. Finley held up the sugar bowl. "Sugar?"

"Yes, and cream as well." Francesca put sugar in her tea and stirred.

"I have to say I'm disappointed by the recent turn of events, both for you and for my son." The older woman frowned as she handed Francesca the cream. "Not many want to put up with a woman with strange ideas. Look at today, for example. Like rats leaving a sinking ship, and using the cotillion tonight for an excuse."

"I'm sure it's not as bad as you think, Mrs. Finley."

"If there were another dear, sweet, sensible girl like you out there for my Alfred, I would be inclined to agree with you."

Somewhere a gull cried as it likely soared on the breeze. "And if there were, Mrs. Finley, I would be both happy for Alfred to meet her and jealous of the young woman. You know the date of my upcoming wedding has changed."

"No. I had not heard. Sometimes the latest news escapes me. You poor thing. How are you dealing with that?"

"I'm resigned to it, I suppose. I keep praying for an answer, for something to change. But no answers have come. My faith is worn a bit thin, I'm afraid."

"I should tell you the whole story about Alfred, and maybe you will take heart."

"He already told me some of it."

Mrs. Finley continued. "Mr. Cromwell has been my friend since we were children. But we did not marry. Instead he went away to serve in the military, and I was home. There I met Alfred's father, Charles, and we built a good life. Succeeded, in fact, as you can see. But there was always Mr. Cromwell.

"Looking back, I see now that people were bound to talk. But I could not let him go, even as a friend. I could have loved him, before Mr. Finley. There were times he came as a houseguest. Mr. Finley was always home, you understand.

"Maybe it was a servant's whispers, I don't know who. But then I discovered I was with child, Alfred of course, and he was born exactly nine months after one of Mr. Cromwell's visits."

"But that should mean nothing."

"The similar hair color said plenty enough. But mind you, I was never unfaithful to Charles. Never. I held my head high and endured the unchangeable public opinion, but poor Alfred was the one who paid the price."

"Why are you telling me this?"

"Because you are strong like me, and you can endure whatever the future holds for you."

"Marriage to the count will be a rather permanent state to endure."

"One day, though, you must choose. You must hold your head high and choose to forget Alfred and step fully into the life with that count. Every day you delay this decision will make it all the more difficult for you."

"You *want* me to forget him?" Francesca's throat caught. She had been round and round the scenario a number of times, and the very idea set her into the doldrums.

"Sometimes in life, we must forsake what we want in favor of what we know must be done. Trust me, I know." Mrs. Finley sipped her tea. "I have never told anyone what I am about to tell you."

Francesca braced herself. "What is that?"

"At one time, when Alfie was small, I was sorely tempted to leave the life I had with Charles and join Mr. Cromwell. He never asked me to, but I could tell in his eyes sometimes." The older woman sighed. "I knew the cost to my family—and my faith—would be more than I wanted to pay. This is why the sooner you forget my son, the better off it will be for everyone."

The woman's words rubbed salt on Francesca's wounded heart. "I don't know how I can do that."

⚓

As soon as he entered the Newport Men's Club lounge, glances told Alfred something was wrong. Conversations ceased, and then whispers started. Surely his tie was straight, and his hair that was wont to stray was perfectly in place, just as any gentleman's hair should be. He checked to make sure that nothing had dropped on his tie at breakfast.

James was the first to rise from a cushioned leather chair and approach him. He clutched some papers in his hand. "You will not like this. We must speak privately at once."

"What is wrong?" Alfred remembered whispers about Mr. Cromwell and Mother.

"Outside. We can talk better there. Fewer ears."

They strode along the corridor, and Alfred snatched the papers from James. Telegrams from Western Union. From Colorado.

He read enough to tell him that his world was about to crumble. Mitchell Hamm was claiming Alfred Finley, styling himself as Alfred Wadsworth, was securing investments for a proposed Silver Light Mine while he lived in Colorado. Then, he left the state along with his partners' investments.

"This is preposterous." Alfred ground out the words. "I have dozens of friends and associates in Colorado who will vouch for me. Even Reverend Stone and his wife."

"But your foundation," James said as they continued along their way. "What will this nonsense do to it?"

Alfred burst through the front door of the club and took a deep breath. He'd been raised to be a gentleman, and the last bit of fighting he'd done was some boxing while at the university.

"Did anyone else receive this telegram?" Alfred glanced at the address again. "This one was addressed to you."

James nodded. "Worse, Father received one as well. As did Mr. Vanderbilt, who asked me about it this morning. Plus Octavius Millstone. I don't know who else so far."

"Mitchell Hamm is broke and bitter. He does not have the funds to send telegrams like this. Because I have a recent letter from the Stones, and they mention him specifically."

"Someone has gone to a lot of trouble and expense to attack your reputation."

"And I have a feeling I know who did. It must be someone who knew all of my contacts here in Newport. Mitchell has no way of knowing these people, nor would he have the wherewithal to find out this information without assistance." Alfred wheeled around and reentered the club. "Someone inside must know where Count de la Croix stays while he is in Newport."

"Do you think it's de la Croix?"

"Yes, because I know his secret."

"Secret?" James grabbed Alfred's arm. "What exactly are you privy to?"

"I should have said something as soon as I knew, but two things prevented me. First, I didn't want to make an assumption and be wrong. Second, even if I were right in my assumption, I did not think your parents would believe me. After all, I am the snubbed would-be suitor." Alfred ran one of his hands through his hair, not caring that it stood on end.

"I would not think that of you. But go on. Tell me what you know."

"While in New York, I passed by de la Croix's residence one morning. Lillian Chalmers was leaving. I see no reason why she would be leaving at that hour, and not arriving. I assumed, well. . ." The words tasted vile as they left his mouth.

James paced the landing at the top of the club steps. "This is not good. My parents should know this, although I'm afraid Mother would find a way to blame Francesca for whatever de la Croix has done."

"I thought of that, too. I do not wish to cause her more pain, but this knowledge troubles me." Alfred regretted not going to Mr. Wallingford right away. "This is why I think the count decided to discredit me to make sure I never talked about what I saw."

James stopped pacing. "But surely de la Croix is shrewd. I don't believe he would attack like this unless he felt threatened. You've said and done nothing until now?"

"You are the first I have told."

"Not even your mother?"

"Certainly not Mother." Alfred shuddered inwardly. "There is no telling what she would do if she knew, and might only make matters worse."

James looked thoughtful. "So de la Croix must think that if all this time has passed, and nothing has happened to him. . ."

"You're right. Of course this means if de la Croix has left well enough alone—as long as I have been silent, that is—only one other person could have done this."

"Mother." James slapped his forehead. "Francesca told me she'd threatened to make trouble."

"What she's done is nothing short of slander." Now it was Alfred's turn to pace. Between the two of them, they'd likely carve a rut at the top of the club steps. "It is common knowledge now that I'd been in Colorado. I suppose she could have hired an investigator quickly enough, with the right financial carrot dangling in front of the fellow's nose. And I imagine she paid Mitchell a pretty sum to draw up this ludicrous accusation."

"But it's enough to cripple our foundation before it begins."

Wise as a serpent, harmless as a dove came to Alfred's mind. "Either way, I need proof of who has done this to me, and I have an idea. You might not like it, though."

"What is that?"

"Would Victoria examine your mother's papers? Surely she's left record of something in her desk, especially if she believes no one suspects her."

"I don't know that she would."

As much as it hurt Alfred to say it, he did so anyway. "Maybe you could suggest to Francesca to start taking a deep interest in the wedding plans. She's a smart young woman. If we have proof, perhaps we can confront your mother about what she's done."

"That may work." James nodded. "In the meantime, you probably ought to return to New York and see what damage has been wrought there. I will try to quell the rumors here."

"I will give the matter much thought and prayer as well." Alfred now knew how his father had succeeded in business all those years. Rash actions did not always produce desired results. He wanted to rush to the Wallingfords' residence and confront them both and drag a confession from Mrs. Wallingford, but that would not work. However, a more subtle approach might. "I shall return to Tranquility and inform Mother I will be leaving sooner than I expected."

Chapter 13

Francesca stared at James and looked up from her sketchpad. "But I have let Mother choose everything for the wedding. Since she has been in a flurry lately, placing orders and sending telegrams, I have stayed out of her way. I am tired of battling, and she has left me alone at last."

They were sitting in the library as a summer shower pounded the windows. A fire in the fireplace helped drive some of the chill from the room.

"What did you just say? About telegrams?"

"She's been in and out, sending messages and such."

"Since when does Mother plan her fetes like that?"

"What do you know, James? What aren't you telling me?" Her brother wouldn't look at her, so she threw her drawing pencil at him.

James caught the pencil. "I have a good reason to believe Mother has been busy with more than wedding plans. Didn't you say she'd threatened to make trouble for Alfred?"

"Yes, she did." Francesca's cheeks burned at the memory of the way Mrs. McGovern had painted her interaction with Alfred in the garden.

"Well, I suggest you take more of an interest in these plans. Perhaps Mother has some records of these telegrams in her desk. Or, I don't know. Does she have her bank book here?"

"I don't know. I know she has a ledger that she keeps the household accounts on, for the parties and such." Mother had attempted to show her the ledger once, but Francesca was hopeless at sums.

"Perhaps she has withdrawn large amounts of cash from her account."

Francesca thought she was going to be sick. "What could Mother have done to Alfred?"

"Just look, and see if you find anything of importance. You'll know what it is when you see it."

"And if I learn something, what am I supposed to do with what I know?"

"Tell me what you find, and then I shall talk to Father. Perhaps he and I can confront Mother and get the entire story from her."

"All right. I will. Mother said something this morning about talking to a caterer. I shall ask to see her plans so far. Truthfully, I am curious." And anything to help Alfred.

James looked at his pocket watch and stood. "I must go now. I'm due to meet with someone to see if they can help Alfred."

"Please." Francesca rose from her chair as well. "Let me know what happens."

They entered the hall together, with James heading to the main entryway and Francesca heading toward Mother's sitting room. She had her desk there and kept every record of each transaction filed.

"James, I'm scared for Alfred."

"We must pray for him, and do what we can." He gave her a small smile before he left.

When Francesca entered the parlor, she found Mother at her desk, right where she expected to find her. Mother looked up, papers scattered before her.

"Yes?" Mother looked wary. Francesca hadn't approached Mother at her desk in days and, in fact, had avoided her.

"I understand you are securing a caterer, and I was wondering if I might see what your plans are." She hugged her sketchbook to her chest. At least her hands weren't shaking, and she thanked God for the calmness she felt.

"You weren't interested when I first mentioned my ideas. If I remember well enough, you said marrying Count de la Croix was 'unthinkable.' Why care now?"

"I. . .it will be easier, I realize."

"You care nothing for the count, and the wedding will be just like any other day to you. You said so yourself."

"I. . ." She could not find truthful words to speak.

"Very well." Mother pursed her lips together. "Here. I have several thank-you notes to write. You may compose them for me while I work on this."

Mother handed her a list, and her stationery. "You may sit at my desk. I must go fetch the fabric samples that the seamstress sent over."

Francesca's pulse pounded in her throat. "Thank you, Mother."

With a grand swish of skirts, Mother glided from the room and Francesca took two gulping breaths as she sat down at Mother's desk.

Now, James had mentioned two things. Telegrams and bank account information. If anything, Mother meticulously filed her records. Perhaps there was something about telegrams, or receipts, or. . .

Francesca found a stack of telegram receipts wrapped with a string. The first message made her freeze. *One thousand dollars to assist me. No one can know. Mrs. Andrew Wallingford.* The recipient was a Mitchell Hamm of Silver Springs, Colorado.

Mother reentered the sitting room, and Francesca stared at the pieces of fabric she carried. Her own fingers tightened around the telegram receipt she'd just read. The others lay scattered on Mother's desk.

"I'm sorry, I should have explained better about those thank-you notes." Mother glanced at Francesca's hand, then at the desk. "What are you doing?"

"Why did you send one thousand dollars to this man in Colorado? I can only guess why, but I wish to hear your explanation." Francesca held out the telegram receipt. When Mother tried to take it from her, she said, "No, I will hold it."

"Young lady, you are in no position to demand from me. I am your mother, and I deserve honor and respect."

"I have been trying to do those things in spite of what has happened to me. But this receipt shows me you have not been acting honorably." Francesca moved to go. "I am going to speak to Father about this. He must know."

"You will do nothing of the sort."

"Mother, all of Newport will know what you have done to Alfred. I don't know what you had this man in Colorado do for you, but even if you have done this secretly, you must know that people will discover the source of this attack against Alfred's character." Despite her mother's polished appearance, Francesca could only see bitterness, which radiated from her.

"He was warned. And I will have nothing ruin our plans."

"Mother, what *are* you talking about? Ever since I confessed to you my actions of that Sunday afternoon, I have done what I am supposed to do."

"Let us say that I saw fit to ensure he didn't think of interfering or overstepping his bounds again." Mother looked at her evenly. "But please, tell your father what I have done. He will support me in this decision, as always."

Francesca left the sitting room with the evidence in her hand. She had information for James, which he would undoubtedly give to Alfred. But his temper. What would he do when he saw concrete evidence of Mother's actions? Francesca knew there was only one thing left for her to do.

∞

Alfred didn't know what to do. He looked at the gentleman seated across from him in his New York office.

Octavius Millstone frowned. "Had I known of your questionable character, I would not have agreed to join the board of this foundation. While I tend to look the other way over men's indiscretions, I cannot ignore a man taking money under false pretenses."

"I assure you, Octavius, these allegations are simply untrue. There is no Silver Light Mine in Colorado, and I did not embezzle money from anyone and leave Colorado with it." Alfred had already sent O'Neal to start preparing statements to refute this falsehood. He feared that this fresh rumor would consume what was left of his good name.

Bearing the memory of seeing Francesca's fiancé with Lillian Chalmers had robbed him of sleep. Between that and the attack on his reputation engineered by Francesca's mother, he had ended up pummeling his pillow until dawn. No immediate answers had come.

"All the same, this is not good at all." Octavius rose. "I'm afraid I'll have to reconsider my agreement, or at least postpone it until this ruckus dies down. A man in my position can't afford a hint of controversy attached to him."

"I understand." Alfred stood and shook his hand. "I will have proof—soon, I hope—that this story is a falsehood. And I will also reveal the party responsible for this action."

"Smart man. Good luck to you, then." Octavius put on his hat and left the office.

Alfred returned to his seat. Nothing more could be done until he heard from James, and until O'Neal returned with his own news.

As for the matter about the count and Lillian Chalmers, Alfred wanted to head for the count's residence and not leave until he received an explanation. Either that or call a meeting with Mr. Wallingford. Neither would work. His head swam at the idea of Francesca's struggle to honor her parents' choice of a husband. The count would likely not remain faithful after marriage, when he obviously was not faithful during their engagement.

To be sure, Alfred had been tempted to elope with Francesca, but he had not given into that idea but cast it away. If only Francesca were engaged to a man whom she might one day grow to love. But a man who couldn't remain faithful even during betrothal? Alfred did not want to see Francesca destined to such a loveless marriage.

∽

Francesca paced her bedroom until Elizabeth answered her call. "Fetch my travel satchel, Elizabeth."

"Miss, are you going on a trip? What is going on?"

"Do not question me, but obey. I need to pack. Now." She would not, and could not, live another night under the same roof with the woman she called Mother. "I have some money, I believe enough to leave here with; and if not enough, I shall borrow some from a friend."

"Yes, miss." Elizabeth's shoulders slumped. "I shall get it immediately."

Francesca stopped her maid at the door. "Forgive me. I should not have been so sharp with you, when you have been a faithful servant. And even a friend. But if I do not divulge to you my plans, you shall be able to honestly say you know nothing of them later."

"Miss, leaving will solve nothing."

"I am tired of *doing* nothing." Francesca glared at the clothing she'd spread on the bed. She had no idea how she would fit a suitable wardrobe into one meager satchel. Perhaps she was more spoiled than she'd first thought.

"What has happened?"

"My mother has happened. She made good on her promise, and now people are looking at Alfred askance yet again. He didn't embezzle a cent." Francesca didn't want to believe her mother had actually spent money to get a man to lie against Alfred.

"Oh, dear."

"Please, get my satchel without further ado. If I hurry, I can take the last train to New York. Either that, or I shall sit up in the station all night and take the first train in the morning."

"Right away." Elizabeth bobbed her head and disappeared.

She would wait until the latter part of the afternoon and leave through the side door. If anyone saw her walking along the road, well, she'd figure that out when the time came. She could always go without a satchel and leave as if she were heading out the door for a stroll.

If only James were here. Not hours ago, barely after she'd bid him good-bye in the hallway that afternoon, he'd been called away to bring Victoria to New York. In her current physical state, she needed a doctor's care immediately, and they rushed from Seaside.

Francesca made herself pause for a moment. Larger problems in the world existed than her current state. What Victoria must be feeling. And here she'd been wrapped up in her own situation—unjust as it may be, she was not the only person going through a trial. She whispered a prayer for Victoria and her unborn child.

Perhaps she might meet James and Victoria in New York, and help care for Victoria at the family's residence until she could leave. Francesca went to find her shoes and realized she could likely only bring a spare pair. What was it that Alfred had said about knowing contentment? Being free with only two pairs of shoes would be better than life as she knew it with a dozen pairs.

A rattling of the door handle made her look up. "Elizabeth?"

"No. It is Mrs. McGovern." The woman's voice came through the door, but she did not open it and enter.

The sound of tumblers turning in a lock made Francesca leap to her feet and cross the room. She tried the door. Locked. "What are you doing?"

"Mrs. Wallingford's orders, miss."

"Please ask my mother to come here straightaway." Her voice squeaked, and her hands shook as she tried the door again. She would not lose her composure in front of this woman.

"Of course, miss."

"Where is Elizabeth?" Francesca clutched the doorknob.

"She is being dealt with."

Retreating footsteps on the marble hallway told her the conversation was over.

Locked in her room. Someone had seen Elizabeth with a satchel, probably Mrs. McGovern, or even worse, Mother. And of course, Elizabeth would have to tell them why she was carrying the bag.

Francesca sank onto the floor. Surely, this was a product of her imagination, and if she rose to her feet and tried the door, it would open. She reached for the knob again and pulled. The lock held.

She stood and paced the room. If she had a key to the room, she didn't know where it was.

"Francesca?" came Mother's voice.

"Mother, please tell me what is going on."

"I will not have you leave this house and disgrace our family. I have no idea what you have planned, but the fact you sent for your satchel says enough."

She would not scream, or plead, or cry. "Mother. . ." And neither would she lie and say she had not decided to leave.

"My mind will not change. I will not bend to this. Your father arrives tonight, and we shall address the matter further."

"Very well, then." Francesca set her jaw. She would speak to Father. Surely he would set everything right.

Mother left her, and Francesca went to her bed. Her prayers had done nothing. Her furnace still burned, and she would not be rescued like the men in the furnace.

"I want to trust You, heavenly Father." Francesca looked at the white paneled ceiling that might as well have covered a jail cell. "But everything seems to be getting worse."

Francesca looked at her bed, then looked at the doors that led to her small balcony. What if she were to tie the sheets together and lower herself to the roof of the first floor veranda, and then—

No, if she tried to dangle from the veranda roof and let herself to the ground, she'd break a bone or worse. And then where would she be?

Francesca went out to her balcony and gauged the distance. Yes, too far. She gazed out at a world that should have been open to her with possibilities, but a locked door and the shackles of her engagement made her look at it from a distance.

Chapter 14

Alfred looked out the window as the train traveled from New York to Newport. After the week's efforts, he looked forward to seeing Mother again and gaining a measure of peace from being by the ocean. He opened the latest telegram from Reverend Stone. True to his word, O'Neal had wired funds to the minister to assist the man in helping vouch for Alfred's innocence—on paper.

Attorney preparing papers. No such mine. No such dealings. Mitchell Hamm is wrong. Praying. He knew vindication was within his grasp, and the thought filled him with relief. He already knew he could do nothing about the rumors except present the evidence to those interested in his foundation and leave the rest to God.

Perhaps he'd have to wait for a time until he could launch the Finley Humanitarian Foundation, but the foundation would make a difference in young people's lives. If not right away, eventually. Patience and self-control were not easy lessons to learn, but he hoped Father would have been proud of him, had he known.

When the train trudged to a stop in Newport, Alfred saw Mother waiting for him on the platform. The heat had bothered her lately, and he wondered why she ventured out instead of sending the carriage to bring him to Tranquility.

"There you are," Mother said as he reached her. "I'm glad you have returned."

"This week, I have lived a nightmare."

"I know, I know. Which is why I decided to meet you at the station. We have much to discuss which cannot wait."

He held his leather satchel in one hand and offered Mother his free arm. "I know you have not been feeling well. You could have waited."

"I know, I know. But I am your mother, and I needed to do *something.*"

Minutes later, he had Mother comfortably situated in the carriage. "Do tell, Mother. What have you been up to?"

"Planning a dinner party for tomorrow night. Short notice, I know."

"I am not in the mood to entertain." He nodded at an acquaintance passing by in another carriage.

"This is exactly why we should entertain. I have taken the liberty, in your name, of inviting Mr. and Mrs. Andrew Wallingford, Mr. and Mrs. James Wallingford, Miss Francesca Wallingford, plus Mrs. Chalmers and her daughter Lillian for supper." Her eyes gleamed. "I understand the count has arrived from

New York also, and as he is the betrothed of Miss Wallingford, we shall include him as well."

"Why would any of them dine with me, besides James and Francesca?"

"Exclusivity. Mr. and Mrs. Vanderbilt will be present at supper, and the idea of a small affair including them likely proved irresistible to Mrs. Wallingford and Mrs. Chalmers."

"Just supper?"

"And a healthy helping of the truth." Mother patted his hand.

"What do you mean by that?"

"Yesterday morning, Miss Elizabeth McGovern, that sweet young woman who serves at Seaside, stole away to speak with me. Evidently Miss Wallingford had wanted to run away, and her mother locked her in her room."

"As if she were an animal." Alfred tightened his grip on his satchel, then forced himself to release it.

"I also had a very interesting luncheon with Mrs. Chalmers and her daughter. Evidently she has had her sights set on the count for some time."

"What do you hope to accomplish by this supper?"

Mother beamed. "As I said, everyone needs a healthy dose of the truth. Because 'ye shall know the truth, and the truth shall make you free.'"

∞

For two nights and one day, Francesca had been locked in her room. She ate in her room and only was permitted to leave to tend to her personal needs.

Father had not come to her room, and she wondered what kept him. Mother notified her that, despite her extreme reluctance, they would all be attending a private supper at Tranquility, and Francesca must prepare herself right away.

"The only reason is that Mr. and Mrs. Vanderbilt will be there. I can see no other reason why. My dear friend Catherine Finley has become too eccentric for my tastes." Mother went to Francesca's wardrobe. "You shall wear the gown you wore the night you and the count became engaged. He's in Newport, you know, and will accompany us tonight. It will not do for you to appear without him." Mother sounded as if she cared more for her appearance in front of Mrs. Vanderbilt.

"Of course, Mother, it would not." She only hoped Alfred wouldn't be at Tranquility. Mother had not mentioned him in days, so perhaps he remained in New York.

"Here is the dress. We leave at seven o'clock."

Promptly at five minutes until seven, the carriages lined up in front of Seaside, and Francesca inhaled deeply. Not that she hadn't been able to go onto her balcony during her confinement, but being free of her room made the air feel fresher.

Of course, she took the carriage with Philippe, who bowed low and kissed her hand before helping her onto the seat. She did not expect any proclamation of affection, especially not since the incident with the sewing needles.

"You look well tonight," was the first thing he said to her.

"Thank you." Francesca wondered if he knew about her enforced confinement. But she regarded him with an even gaze. He met her eyes briefly, then focused on the scenery passing by them.

She remained silent for the rest of the journey, and she found it curious that Philippe did as well.

Once Francesca endured the gauntlet of greetings at Tranquility—she could not bring herself to look at Alfred, who stood there as evidence of what she could never have—she docilely followed Philippe to the Finley dining room.

This was a grand room, but a room for a family to enjoy a meal, not the staged propriety played out in front of her. Mrs. Finley, though, greeted her like a long-lost friend.

"My dear, you and the count must sit near Alfred and myself." Once she organized everyone around the table, there were vacant seats.

"My guests, thank you for attending this evening. While it is a warm summer night, I trust that the cool refreshment accompanying the meal will stave off effects of the heat." She smiled at them in turn. "Mrs. Vanderbilt sends her regrets that she could not attend tonight, so I believe this is everyone."

Francesca couldn't give the atmosphere in the room a name. She ate a spoonful of the chilled asparagus soup and surveyed the group. Lillian looked particularly resplendent this evening, and kept darting glances toward where Philippe and Francesca sat. Philippe kept tugging at his collar and clearing his throat.

"Something to drink, Count de la Croix?" asked Mrs. Finley. "I apologize if the soup does not agree with you."

"I am fine, Madame Finley." He focused on his soup.

"Very well. The beef will be served shortly." Mrs. Finley nodded at him.

Other quiet conversations took place around the table, but Francesca kept her focus on her meal. She did not want her words to betray her, nor give her parents cause for alarm.

"Is this your last event of the season?" asked Mother from her place farther down the table.

"Yes, it is." Mrs. Finley dabbed at her forehead with her napkin. "I'm not planning to try to impress anyone again. My Alfred didn't care to have supper tonight—"

"Now, Mother," Alfred began, "I have had a very busy week—"

"My Alfred didn't care to have supper tonight, so it must be understood that he has nothing to do with this supper. I didn't tell him of supper until he returned from New York last evening."

Francesca wondered if he'd found any answers, or if James had been able to help him. So many questions, and with him nearby, without a way to ask. No one else said anything about Mrs. Finley's remarks about Alfred.

Philippe gave Francesca a stern look, and she stared right back at him.

"So, Miss Wallingford, how have your wedding plans come along?" asked Mrs. Finley.

"Mother has been planning and kept very busy. My dress will be finished at the end of September. We have selected the menu." And that was all she knew, after spending the last two and a half days in her room.

"What a wondrous life you shall have."

Truly, the woman was cruel to speak so in front of her own son and speculate on Francesca's life after marrying Philippe. "I'm sure it shall be quite grand. Count de la Croix, please tell me again how many homes we shall divide our time in."

"Paris, of course. And a home in the country. I have a flat in London when I must stay there, mostly for business. And New York as well." Philippe took the last sip of his soup. "But I have told my Francesca that I shall build her a home here in Newport if she so wishes."

Mrs. Finley smiled. "Miss Wallingford, how wonderful for you. And you shall have a chance to pursue your painting."

"I suppose I shall. Although supervising four different residences may take a great deal of time." Francesca set down her spoon.

A muffled noise from the other side of the table made Francesca look. Lillian had made a sort of strangled sound into her napkin. Her mother patted her shoulder.

"Miss Chalmers, are you all right?" asked Mrs. Finley.

Lillian nodded. "I'm fine."

"She has been in the sun too long today, I'm afraid," said Aunt Beatrice.

"Yes, the summer sun is quite draining," admitted Victoria. "James makes sure that I do not overdo things. In fact, we've been in New York at the doctor. Pardon me." At this, she blushed. "I should not speak of such things at the supper table, and as a guest."

"Nonsense." Mrs. Finley waved her soupspoon at Victoria. "We are all practically family here. I'm glad you are well. We shall pray for a healthy child."

"Thank you, Mrs. Finley." Victoria's color gradually returned to normal.

Francesca smiled, but the idea of bearing Philippe's children made her appetite flee, despite the tantalizing menu this evening.

"And one day, you shall have a family as well." Mrs. Finley touched Francesca's hand.

A sob made them all look in the direction of the sound. Lillian hiccupped. "I'm so sorry."

"What on earth is wrong?" asked Aunt Beatrice. "You've been looking forward to this supper all day long. This is most unladylike, Lillian."

"I don't care anymore!" Lillian flung her napkin onto the table and stood, knocking her chair backwards.

"Young lady, do tell us." Mrs. Finley glanced at Francesca, then back to Lillian.

"I, for one, no longer wish to live a lie." Lillian marched to the head of the table and stood near Philippe's chair. He looked ready to bolt.

"Miss Chalmers..." Philippe began.

"One thing I like about Mrs. Finley is that she tells the truth. No pretenses. Where is the endearing 'my Lily' that you call me? Philippe, I have had enough of hiding."

Francesca heard Mother gasp. "Beatrice, control your daughter, as I have controlled mine."

Francesca stood. "Mother, please. Let Lillian speak."

Fresh tears streamed down Lillian's face. "You cannot and must not marry Francesca."

Mother made a gurgling noise.

Now Philippe stood. "Miss Chalmers, it is, as you say, complicated. It is more beneficial for me to marry Miss Wallingford."

"Philippe, don't marry me out of a business obligation." Francesca loved voicing the words before everyone. Mother and Aunt Beatrice were exchanging words across the table. Father was trying to quiet Mother.

"You." Philippe pointed at Francesca. "Do not tell me what I should and should not do. I am so tired of you—you—acting as if you are my equal, or worse, more important than me. I am a count. I deserve respect. And Lillian always respected me."

"I will not bend to you merely because of your title." Francesca held onto the table edge. "The more you pushed me, the harder I resisted. And I am sorry if you thought I considered myself more important than you."

"Please, Philippe." Lillian tugged at his sleeve. "I don't have the financial means that my cousin possesses, but I love you. I adore you. I would do anything for you. Haven't I shown you that already?"

More uproar from the end of the table. In spite of the clamor, Francesca felt a peace steal over her. A sudden movement made her look to Mrs. Finley. The woman's face had taken on a gray pallor.

"Oh dear. Alfred—" Mrs. Finley grabbed a fistful of Alfred's sleeve. Then she slumped over onto her table setting.

"O'Neal!" Alfred stood and pulled his mother to a seated position. "Send for the doctor!"

The next few minutes were a blur to Francesca, with Lillian and Philippe begging their leave of the family; James running to Alfred's aid; Mother and Aunt

Beatrice murmuring about what might be wrong.

The last thing she recalled before Mother and Father whisked her from the dining room was Alfred taking one of her hands in his and saying, "Pray for Mother. And have faith." The strong squeeze he gave her made fresh hope bloom in her heart.

Chapter 15

Tranquility remained darkened for nearly two weeks. No word on Mrs. Finley, although Francesca had learned the woman had been hospitalized briefly. She knew Alfred's priority would be his mother, of course.

Mother had spent the time weeping, now that the wedding was off and scandal rippled through their society. One would think that she'd been the one preparing to wed the count. Now that Philippe and Lillian's secrets were out, Father had put his foot down and demanded Francesca's engagement and their business agreement be dissolved.

"But our Fran was to be a countess. . ." Mother had wailed.

"And you locked her in her *room*?" Father's voice thundered. "You may well run our households, but Seaside, nor any other of our residences, is a prison."

Then Father had disappeared back to New York after the weekend was over.

Francesca gladly gave up further French studies, but she kept the paints.

She was sitting in the parlor when Holmes appeared at the door. "A Count de la Croix to see you, miss."

"Thank you, Holmes. Please send him in." Francesca stood and went to the desk. Would she need a letter opener this time? No. But she touched the velvet box on the desk.

"Miss Wallingford," Philippe said as he entered the room. "You are looking well today."

"Why, *merci*, Count de la Croix." She held up the box containing the topaz and diamond necklace and bracelet. "Here. I cannot keep these. While this jewelry is beautiful in every way, I have a feeling it might be appreciated by someone else."

Philippe waved the box away. "I will not take them back, because I did give them to you with affection. Sell them and give the money to Mr. Finley for his foundation."

"Thank you very much. That is very generous of you. I'll do that." Francesca pulled Philippe's family ring from her pocket. "But you should keep this ring. I know it's important to your family."

"Oui." He took it from her, and as he did so, grasped one of her hands. "Would that things were different."

"No, Philippe." Francesca withdrew her hand. "You need someone who will adore you, as Lillian does. But do not break her heart. It is not often that we find

335

someone who loves us despite our wrongdoing."

He gave her a slight bow. "Mademoiselle Francesca, I was wrong the other evening. You do not have to act as if you are better than me. You *are* better, and I treated you most wrongly."

"Thank you. I. . .I wish you well, Philippe."

Philippe turned to leave, but paused in the doorway. "I hope Lillian grows to be as graceful as you."

And then he was gone.

Mother entered the sitting room, sniffling as she did so. "You could have been a countess. Now whatever shall we do?"

"I am going to wait for a young man to speak to Father, as should have happened a long time ago." Francesca hugged her mother. "And now that all of Newport knows what you have done to besmirch his reputation. . ."

"My own reputation is ruined." Mother sank onto a chair.

"Take heart, Mother." Francesca touched her shoulder. "One day it shall be someone else's turn to have stories fly around about them. You know how society works."

∞

Alfred thought the meeting had been most agreeable. He rose from the chair and shook the man's hand.

"You're certain of this?" he asked Alfred.

"I know it's quite soon after these recent events that have transpired, but I've prayed about it, and I know this is what I am to do. I only seek your approval and consent." Alfred thanked God, over and over, that this day had come at last. Even now, it seemed like a dream.

"Well then, Mr. Finley, if you and I and God agree," the gentleman appraised him as they faced each other in front of the library's fireplace, "I suppose there's one more person you ought to speak with."

"Do you know where. . ."

"Take the sea path." The man shrugged. "Where else would she be?"

∞

Francesca loved the sounds of the surf pounding the shore. Dusk was falling, and the sky flamed a crimson that faded into shades of purple and a deepening blue that would soon turn black. By that time, Francesca would be indoors, tucked into her room at Seaside and wondering yet again about Alfred.

Her paintbrush flew over the canvas as she attempted to capture the atmosphere just before night fell. Mother would say her use of color was "violent," but Francesca thought *vivid* more aptly described the colors. Poor Mother.

Mother wandered the halls like a shadow, almost as if she had been the one jilted. No, not jilted. Francesca still smiled at Philippe's words, that he believed she considered herself his equal. Not exactly the same, but then she'd recognized human nature was still human nature, no matter how prettily one dressed it up. She could hardly wait to tell Alfred about the jewelry Philippe had insisted she keep.

Elizabeth strolled along the shoreline, gathering shells. The young woman had a spring in her step. Evidently, a certain young man named O'Neal in Alfred's employ had spoken to Alfred, who in turn had spoken to her father, who had spoken to Elizabeth's parents. It would not surprise Francesca if another wedding would take place within the year, not on the grand scale that Francesca's might have been, but full of priceless love and laughter.

"Look, Miss Francesca." Elizabeth held up a shell as she trotted across the sand to where Francesca painted. "This is a large one."

"Beautiful. You should keep it and remember this night." Francesca wanted to ask her about O'Neal. "I. . .I shall miss you when you leave one day."

"Oh, I will still be here through the end of the year. After that"—and at this Elizabeth blushed—"we shall have a January wedding. Jonathan will have everything prepared then."

"I am truly happy for you." She really didn't need a maid. "You will enjoy being part of the Finley household, I am sure."

"I. . .I will miss you, too. And perhaps one day I shall borrow a dress and show up at one of the balls. You never know." They both smiled at the idea.

"Have you heard how Mrs. Finley is doing? Because I've heard nothing."

Elizabeth shook her head. "All I know is that Mr. Finley brought her to the hospital in New York, when the Newport physician could not help her."

"I will continue to pray for her, then, until I hear more." Francesca considered something for a moment. "She can be loud, but don't be afraid of her. She has a golden heart and will treat you well."

"Well, I'm sure having you as part of the Finley household will help as well."

Francesca couldn't believe her maid's words. Mother would have called it impertinent; Francesca preferred the term "bold." But she deserved as much after that spring's scheme in Paris.

"What are you talking about?"

Elizabeth gave an impish grin and looked past Francesca, toward the path that led to Seaside. "I think I will go look for more shells, miss."

Francesca turned and squinted at the shadows. A figure had just taken the last steps from the path and stepped onto the sand. The last rays of sunlight glinted dark red on his hair.

"Al?"

"Fran." His posture exuded a confidence she hadn't recalled seeing before. "I'm sorry I've been gone so long. Mother. . ."

"How is she?" Francesca closed the distance between them.

"She is recuperating." Up close, his eyes looked tired. "But I came to Newport when she threatened to drag me here herself. As she'll be confined to a wheelchair from now on, that's not likely, but I believed it unwise to take any chances."

"So, why have you come, and why did your mother threaten to drag you here?"

"I understand that your engagement to Philippe has been called off."

"And?"

"I have spoken to your father."

"And?"

"I am a man in want of a wife, but she must be most suitable."

"Oh, she must? What are the requirements one must meet?"

"She must be intelligent as well as beautiful, full of faith as well as laughter, compassionate as well as honest, impulsive as well as refined."

"That's quite a list."

"One more thing, too." Alfred took her hands in his. "She must always know her place."

"Which is?"

"With me, as you are right now." Alfred sank onto one knee on the sand. "My darling Francesca, there is nothing in my world that would make it more complete than if you would become my wife. No business transaction. Just you and me. Always."

"Of course, of course." She pulled him to his feet. "I would marry you whether you had millions or had nothing, no matter who your father is or what you own or where you live."

"So you agree?"

Francesca nodded. "It has been my prayer this long time, that this day would come."

"Then kiss me, and make our agreement complete."

And so she did.

Epilogue

D arling, I can't believe you wouldn't have a New York wedding." Mother fussed over the last details of Francesca's wedding gown. "And not even in a *church*. It's a miracle that the *Times* is covering the event at all."

"Don't fret, Mother." Francesca studied her reflection in her bedroom mirror. One last look at Miss Francesca Genevieve Wallingford before she became Mrs. Alfred Finley. "The reverend is more than happy to conduct the ceremony under heaven's roof on our lawn." She'd tried to talk Mother into agreeing to a seaside wedding, but Mother would not bend to that. Francesca figured the battle was not worth the struggle.

At least she and Alfred would be married within sight of the beloved ocean. Nearly two hundred guests waited on the lawn below for Francesca to appear— and that was the trimmed guest list.

The old whispers had died away after Mother's scheming had been revealed, and the society mavens decided to leave the couple in peace. After all, it was whispered, hadn't that sweet young Francesca Wallingford been through enough, barely escaping being wed to that philandering count?

He and Lillian were gallivanting through Europe now. At least that was the last report Mother had heard.

Sometimes during the wedding planning, Mother would sigh and remark that she could have had a count for a son-in-law. But it seemed that having a happy daughter made life much easier.

"I will go now, and let the guests know the service can commence." Mother scurried away, her hat looking like a swan had somehow alighted upon her head.

Francesca took up her bouquet. Time to meet Father and walk to meet Alfred at the edge of their sea cliff, where a small, covered altar had been built for the occasion.

When the rear doors to Seaside opened, and Francesca saw the expanse of lawn dotted with chairs, and beyond that, the sea, her heart quickened. Surely, God had delivered her out of the fire, unscathed, through His Providence.

The violins and instruments of the small orchestra swelled, and the sound drifted across the breeze.

"Ready, daughter?"

"Yes, Father. I'm ready."

She walked with him along the path, past their guests, and then Father released her to Alfred, whose eyes shone with love for her. All the worldly goods he could bestow on her meant nothing without that love. Perhaps the wealth would leave them one day, but so long as they had each other and the knowledge that true wealth could never be bought or sold, they would be the richest couple alive.

Alfred took her hand, and whispered, "I love you, Francesca Wallingford."

"Alfred Finley, I love you, too."

Note to Reader

While Marble House, the Breakers, Kingscote, and The Elms are actual "cottages" once used by the elite of Newport society at the end of the nineteenth century, Seaside and Tranquility exist only in the imagination. However, many of the Newport mansions disappeared over the years, and only a handful are left. I beg Alva and Consuelo Vanderbilt's indulgence as I use parts of their true story here, as well as make room for Tranquility and Seaside along Newport's famed Bellevue Avenue.

Also, Mrs. Oliver H.P. Belmont did not open the Newport County Suffrage League until the summer of 1912. However, who's to say that ladies didn't have the inclination to gather and discuss women's rights and suffrage in 1895? The ladies' suffrage movement had already taken hold in America by that time.

Lynette Sowell is an award-winning author with New England roots, but she makes her home in central Texas with her husband, two teenagers, and five cats. She has written four novellas and three cozy mystery novels for Barbour. This is her first historical romance novel. You can find out more about Lynette at www.lynettesowell.com.

A Letter to Our Readers

Dear Readers:

In order that we might better contribute to your reading enjoyment, we would appreciate you taking a few minutes to respond to the following questions. When completed, please return to the following: Fiction Editor, Barbour Publishing, Inc., P.O. Box 719, Uhrichsville, OH 44683.

1. Did you enjoy reading *Seaside Romance* by Darlene Franklin, Tamela Hancock Murray, and Lynette Sowell?
   - ❏ Very much. I would like to see more books like this.
   - ❏ Moderately—I would have enjoyed it more if _____

   _____

   _____

2. What influenced your decision to purchase this book?
   (Check those that apply.)
   - ❏ Cover
   - ❏ Back cover copy
   - ❏ Title
   - ❏ Price
   - ❏ Friends
   - ❏ Publicity
   - ❏ Other

3. Which story was your favorite?
   - ❏ *Beacon of Love*
   - ❏ *All that Glitters*
   - ❏ *The Master's Match*

4. Please check your age range:
   - ❏ Under 18
   - ❏ 18–24
   - ❏ 25–34
   - ❏ 35–45
   - ❏ 46–55
   - ❏ Over 55

5. How many hours per week do you read? _____

Name _____

Occupation _____

Address _____

City_____ State _____ Zip _____

E-mail _____

COLORADO LACE

THREE-IN-ONE-COLLECTION

What will it take for three strong
and determined women to see that
love is close to home? Enjoy three
romances from historic Colorado
by author Rachel Druten..

Historic, paperback, 352 pages, 5¾" x 8"